EMERALD ECSTASY

Emma Merritt

D1547795

ZEBRA BOOKS
KENSINGTON PUBLISHING CORP.

ZEBRA BOOKS

are published by

Kensington Publishing Corp.
475 Park Avenue South
New York, NY 10016

First printing: October 1986

Printed in the United States of America

To my collaborator, my friend, my helpmate, my love.
Without whom I could do all things
but with whom all things I do
are made more pleasurable and worthwhile.

This book is for you
PAUL LAVERNE MERRITT

Prologue

Susanna Reeves sat in the upholstered wing chair in front of the fireplace in the library. Her blond hair was pulled to the crown of her head in a chignon of curls, soft tendrils wisping around her face. Her sensuous lips lifted in a smile. Although she was a beautiful woman, her features were hard and sharp. Her face looked as if it had been sculpted from ice; her blue eyes were cool and glassy.

She looked through the opened door into the ball room. Closing her fan, she tapped the ivory and lace against her chin. Everything was so lovely, she thought, smiling. The Wedgwood Classical walls enhanced the beauty of her newly arrived Hepplewhite furniture. The French doors were open, and the cool evening breeze wafted through the room, bringing with it the clean aroma of the garden plants. Chandeliers with hundreds of candles glittered from the ceiling, and bowls of spring flowers colored the room, adding a sensual fragrance to the evening.

An invalid since her fall from her horse five years ago,

Susanna had established her own protocol, creating her own facsimile of the Parisian court. Not wanting anyone to see her being carried about, Susanna had the servants bring her into the ball room long before any of the guests began arriving. Sitting in her special chair at the head of the room, her husband standing behind, she greeted each guest as the butler escorted them in and announced them. Clearly her function was to be adored and worshipped.

This evening, however, Susanna had deviated from custom. Since she had invited Marguerite LeFleur to come early and join her and Jordan for a drink before the ball, she had the servants bring her into the library. Susanna hadn't been this excited about a ball in many years, not since her sixteenth birthday. Her breasts rose enticingly above the low decolletage of her dress as she drew in deep gulps of air in anticipation of the Magnolia Ball, as she thought about her confrontation with Marguerite LeFleur in particular.

Jordan Reeves, Susanna's husband of eight years, walked into the library. His dark, rugged handsomeness was complimented by the golden coat he wore with the ecru waistcoat and brown trousers. Lifting his hand, he unconsciously ran his fingers through thick, unruly black waves.

"Everything is lovely, sweetheart. As usual you've outdone yourself."

"Thank you, Jordan. I do enjoy balls. Although I can no longer dance, festive occasions uplift my spirits." When the muscle in Jordan's jaw twitched and he unconsciously winced, Susanna smiled, a calculated gleam in her eyes. Holding her hands out, she added softly, "But I don't blame you for the accident, darling. You had no way of knowing that the saddle wasn't cinched properly."

Jordan heard the accusation beneath the sweetness. His hand clenched into a fist, and his eyes narrowed, but he made no biting comeback. Not only did he have to live with his own guilt, but every day he was tortured by Susanna's unkind remarks and accusations. Leaning over, he kissed his wife on the forehead.

"Hmm. You smell wonderful, and you look beautiful." He caught her proffered hands in his and squeezed them tightly.

"Do I?" She dropped her head so Jordan couldn't see her eyes. "As beautiful as Blossom Hall's new mistress?"

Jordan gave no indication of his irritation. Five years of living with an invalid wife had conditioned him to accept, without any emotion, Susanna's ephemeral moods which vacillated from extreme highs to extreme lows.

"You're beautiful in your own way."

"And my way is sitting down because my legs are useless, isn't it, Jordan," she exclaimed, her voice verging on hysteria. "While Marguerite's way is riding over the countryside astride a horse like a man, wearing trousers and a shirt!"

"That's not what I meant and you know it," Jordan softly reprimanded. "You're quite the southern belle, gracious and ladylike. Marguerite, having lived in Philadelphia with her grandmother for the most part of her life, is rather a hoyden." Thinking about Marguerite's outspokenness and her outlandish riding gear of trousers, cambric shirt, and broad-brimmed hat, Jordan chuckled, his brown eyes dancing with amusement. His laughter gave his chiseled good looks a quality of softness. "To say the least," he added pensively, "Marguerite is unorthodox."

"To say the most, she's much more than beautiful," Susanna spat viciously. "I've never seen a woman who could be so appealing in such repulsive-looking clothes."

"Susanna," Jordan's voice pleaded, "don't start tonight. Let's enjoy the evening."

"That's easy for you to say," Susanna said petulantly. "You're up moving around, mingling with the guests—" Her voice lowered. "You can dance but I must sit in the corner by myself."

While that was hardly the truth, Jordan had no time to refute Susanna's statement. A knock on the door stopped further conversation. At Susanna's answer, the black butler entered the room.

"Miz Reed, Miz Marguerite from Blossom Hall is here to see you."

"Show her in, Reuben."

Marguerite LeFleur, a tall, statuesque woman, entered. Her hair was such a deep shade of brown it looked black. Parted in the middle, it was pulled into a braided chignon at the nape of her neck. Ringlets, softening the austerity of the hair style, wisped around her face. The low decolletage of her pink evening gown enhanced the creamy smoothness of her breasts, and the fitted bodice outlined the slender midriff.

A vision of loveliness, so different from the way she had been dressed when he saw her last, caused Jordan to catch his breath. Again he raked his hands through his hair and turned on his heel, moving to the table across the room. He lifted the crystal decanter and poured himself a glass of whiskey as Marguerite and Susanna exchanged greetings. Hearing the sounds but not really listening to the words, he quaffed his drink and poured another.

Patting the chair next to hers, Susanna cried gaily, "Come sit by me, Marguerite. I want you close enough that I can see your eyes as I talk." She smiled at her visitor. "One thing I've learned about you through the years is to watch your eyes when I talk to you. They're so expressive. I can tell exactly what you're thinking when I look at them."

Jordan was worried. He had seen the glazed excitement in Susanna's eyes, and he had felt the tension growing in her through the passing days. Susanna was becoming hysterical again, and when she was like this, no one, including Susanna, could guess what she'd do or say.

"Jordan," Susanna said, "pour Marguerite a drink, please."

"What do you want?" Jordan asked abruptly.

"Darling, after all these years," Susanna scoffed gently, "who better than you should know what she likes."

Innocently Marguerite said, "Of course, he does." Looking

10

over at Jordan, she laughed. "How long have you been fixing me drinks, Jordan?"

"Eight years." Susanna's voice twinkled. "You should know, you were my maid of honor."

Jordan brought Marguerite and Susanna their sherry. Taking hers, Marguerite murmured, "I didn't realize that you'd been married that long. It's amazing how fast time goes by."

"It used to fly for me," Susanna admitted, "but since the accident, time drags. Especially at night." Susanna set her glass on the table next to her. She shrugged and smiled, pushing her sad thoughts aside. "But through the years you and I have been friends, haven't we? Both born on adjacent plantations, me at Myles Rest, you at Blossom Hall, yet we're so different." Susanna plaited her fingers together and held them demurely in her lap. Studying them, she asked, "Do you ever regret that your mother and father traveled so much and left you in Philadelphia with your grandmother?"

"No," Marguerite replied.

"I could hardly wait for the times when you'd come stay at Blossom Hall, and I looked forward to my trips north to visit with you and your grandmother." Susanna raised her head, wisps of hair framing her face with a golden aura of innocence, and she laid her hand over Marguerite's. "Still we've always been the best of friends, haven't we?"

"Always." Marguerite smiled, glad to see Susanna so happy. Since the accident Susanna had changed so much. Many times when she came to visit, Susanna was depressed and sullen.

"We've shared everything, haven't we? Our joys, our sorrows."

Jordan's fingers tightened around his glass, and he closed his eyes. *Now he knew!*

"Yes," Marguerite replied, "we've shared everything."

Susanna removed her hand from Marguerite's and reached for her glass of sherry. She said, "Including my husband."

11

Marguerite's face jerked up; her eyes widened and her face paled. She drew back, so aghast at the suggestion she couldn't speak.

Jordan set his glass down and walked to his wife. Standing behind her, he dropped both hands to her shoulders and began to massage the bunched muscles. "Susanna—"

Susanna jerked out of his clutch. "Don't think for one minute that I'm not aware of what's going on behind my back, Jordan Reeves." Susanna's face, contorted in jealous rage, was ugly; it was sinister. "Ever since Marguerite arrived at Blossom Hall as the new mistress, you've been over there on the pretense of helping her. Well, I know what kind of help you've been giving her."

"No," Marguerite whispered, finally summoning her voice, shaking her head at the same time.

"It's not necessarily the plantation that you're interested in, is it, Jordan? It's Marguerite. Sure you want to add Blossom Hall to Myles Rest, but more than that you want Marguerite's body. A whole body."

"Susanna, for God's sake lower your voice. The guests will be coming in any moment and they'll hear you."

"I planned that they should," Susanna screamed. "I'll no longer be cuckolded by you and Marguerite. I'll no longer be an object of ridicule and pity."

"No one pities you but you," Jordan stormed, his brown eyes dark with anger and frustration.

"No," Marguerite cried, forgetting her drink, falling to her knees in front of Susanna, begging the invalid woman to believe her. "Jordan and I are not lovers. I'm your friend. I wouldn't do this to you."

"Wouldn't you?" Susanna's fingers suddenly closed over the strand of pearls that Marguerite wore. Marguerite squirmed, pulling back, but Susanna twisted them, choking her. She whispered, "Did you think you could fool me forever?" She laughed maniacally. "Well, you couldn't! I know Jordan gave you these." Her grip tightened, and she tugged on the necklace. Gasping, Marguerite lifted both hands, clawing at the pearls.

"Susanna," Jordan cried, running to Marguerite, "turn her loose. You're going to choke her."

"No," Susanna assured him as he worked to pry her fingers loose. "I'm not going to choke her, Jordan. I want Marguerite to live so she can suffer just like I've suffered for the past year since she's become the mistress of Blossom Hall."

Marguerite jerked her head so hard the necklace broke, the pearls rolling in all directions. Rubbing her throat, she scooted back from Susanna.

"You've always said they were your father's last gift to you, but I know better," Susanna continued. "Going through some of Jordan's old papers, I found the receipt for a strand of pearls. How well I remember that day two years ago when you and Amanda supposedly received your father's lost chest that had conveniently been stored at the dock. Remember, Marguerite! My twenty-third birthday. Amanda wore the antique gold chain, and you wore the pearls to my birthday party."

"No!" Jordan shouted.

"The receipt was dated that month and that year, Jordan," Susanna said. "Who were they for if not Marguerite?"

Jordan strode across the room, picking up the decanter, sloshing liquor all over the sideboard as he poured himself a glass. "You've been an invalid for five years, Susanna," he said, his voice strained.

"Who was she, Jordan?"

"No one of consequence," he said. "I—" He downed the drink in one swallow. "I'm not proud of myself, Susanna, but I had to—have—had—"

"It's not enough that you've had a lover," Susanna charged, "but you can't even be honest about it. You're protecting Marguerite. Always Marguerite, isn't it?"

"My God," Jordan bellowed, throwing the glass across the

13

room, finally giving vent to the anger that boiled inside him. "There would be no lovers if you'd be a wife to me. Because you can't walk doesn't mean that your body has stopped functioning. Just because you can't walk doesn't mean that I've stopped being a man with desires and needs."

Susanna's features were frozen. For a long time after his words had echoed into deathly silence, she stared at Jordan but she didn't see him. As if nothing had happened, she turned to Marguerite.

"You know, people around here don't like you and don't really consider you one of us. All this abolition talk you learned while you were living up North. But we tolerate you because you're a LeFleur." Susanna paused, the silence a dramatic ploy to build up the suspense. "By the time I get through with you, the community won't even tolerate you. You'll rue the day you came to live at Blossom Hall. You'll regret the day that you became Jordan's mistress."

"My God! Susanna," Jordan cried, "Marguerite is not and never has been my mistress. We've never—"

"No."

"You can't do this to her, Susanna."

"Just watch and see if I can't. I'll make sure the world knows what kind of woman Marguerite LeFleur is." She laughed, pushing her hand into her pocket, her fingers brushing against the letter she had received from Earl.

February, 1833
Sander Owen, Attorney at Law
New Orleans, Louisiana

Sander Owen pushed forward, the chair creaking as he moved. He dropped a sheaf of papers on the desk and rested his weight on both arms. "Your father and I were old friends," he said. "As you know, Edouard followed my advice and left a will which protects both you and your mother." Marguerite nodded. "As long as Amanda remained single she controlled the entire LeFleur estate until you reached twenty-five; even then she had the right to stay at the main house, drawing a handsome yearly income. As has been the custom of all the LeFleurs, your father made sure the plantation would stay in the family. If Amanda remarried, the control and ownership of the estate reverted back to the nearest LeFleur heir—in this case to you. As long as the estate is productive, your mother will still receive her yearly income."

Dressed in dark blue, Marguerite rose from the chair and walked to the window of Sander's office. Drawing her shawl closer about herself, warding off the chill, she watched the wind pelt the rain against the pane. "I'm sorry, Sander, I don't have the feelings about Blossom Hall that Papa did. For his sake I feel a moral obligation to keep it, but I'm afraid that I'm going to have to sell it."

"You can't!" Sander exclaimed, coming to his feet, his fist pounding the table. "My God, Marguerite, it's been in the family for over one hundred years! The LeFleurs were one of the founding families of New Orleans."

"I know all that, Sander, but I can't keep it! With the settlement from Grandmother's estate, I'm a wealthy woman, but I don't want to sink all my money into Blossom Hall. I have no guarantee that we can pull it out of bankruptcy." Marguerite lifted a hand, tracing a rivulet of rain with the tip of her finger. "I want you to search for the nearest LeFleur heir next to me."

For an obese man, Sander moved fluidly across the room and picked up one of the whiskey bottles, pouring himself a drink. "As much as I love your mother, Marguerite, right now I hate her. She never matured. At forty she's still a beautiful, spoiled child." Sander ran a hand through thinning gray hair. "Edouard never allowed her to grow up. Not only that,"

15

Sander grated, "until his dying day your father saw her only as the beautiful sixteen-year-old that he married and loved."

"That's true," Marguerite replied without rancor, "he didn't want her to grow up. Every trait that you don't like about Mother are the very traits that he loved, Sander. Through her he remained young, and he forgot that he was thirty years older." Marguerite smiled, her eyes far away. "You know something else, Sander? Mother didn't want to grow up."

"You aren't bitter?" Sander asked curiously, wondering how Marguerite felt about the unorthodox way she had been reared.

"No," Marguerite answered. "Staying in Philadelphia was my choice. Mother and Papa loved me. They wanted me to travel with them, but I didn't want to. I didn't enjoy the traveling."

"Considering how little you graced the plantation with your presence, it's evident that you didn't enjoy staying at Blossom Hall."

"Not by myself when they were gone," Marguerite said. "I preferred to be with Grandmother."

Lapsing into a pensive silence, Sander took several swallows of whiskey, draining the glass. He set it on the table. "After Edouard died, I tried my best to advise and guide Amanda, but she's a strong-headed, willful woman. If she could have, she would have dismissed me as she did the overseer when he pointed out her neglect of the plantation. All she wanted to do was to continue her travels around Europe, living like royalty and spending money as if it came from an endless source. Three years under her administration and I don't know if the plantation can be salvaged or not." He sighed, throwing his hands in the air in a gesture of defeat. "But I couldn't stop her spending! Thank God, Earl Taylor came along and married her when he did. If he hadn't—" His shrug ended the sentence.

"That's why I must sell it before it's too late," Marguerite

16

said. "Right now, I have plenty of money left which I want to keep. Also, Sander," Marguerite pointed out, "I want to visit Mother in Ireland."

Breathing deeply, Sander Owen sat down again, the chair creaking with the sudden burden. As he lifted his arms behind his head, the satin waistcoat pulled across his chest. "You don't have to go to Ireland, Marguerite."

"But I am," Marguerite averred with soft adamance. "Mother is quite homesick, Sander; she sounds depressed."

"Marguerite," he gritted, jerking his hands down, "can't I get through to you! Your mother has always used people, and now she's using you just like she did your father. She married Taylor thinking she would wrap him around her finger, but she didn't. Now she's pulling one of her tantrums which worked effectively with Edouard, but evidently Taylor won't give in, so she's calling for you."

Marguerite smiled. "That may be true, Sander, I don't know. Since I was settling Grandmother's estate when Mother and Earl began their whirlwind courtship and decided to marry, I didn't have the opportunity to meet him until the wedding. I can't say that I liked him, but Mother never asked my opinion nor my permission to marry him. Be that as it may, I'm going to her."

"So be it," Sander sighed. "May I make a suggestion?" After Marguerite nodded, he said, "Let me manage Blossom Hall for one year to see if I can get it on its feet financially. I'll lease the property for you, and at the end of that time you can make a decision as to what you want to do with it."

"In the meantime you will be searching for the nearest LeFleur heir next to me?" He nodded. Marguerite smiled. "One year then."

Sander held his hands out to Marguerite. "Make me a promise, Marguerite?" He paused, waiting for her affirmative nod. When none came, he said, "Before you make a decision to sell Blossom Hall, talk with me. Listen to whatever Earl Taylor

17

may advise you, but don't make a decision without first talking with me."

April, 1833
Port of New Orleans
New Orleans, Louisiana

His hat in his hands, the wind whipping his hair across his face, Jordan stood at the dock in New Orleans with Marguerite. "I had to see you one last time."

Tears in her eyes and throat, Marguerite only nodded. Jordan reached into his coat pocket and pulled out a handkerchief. Carefully he unfolded it, extending his hand, a long strand of pearls dangling from his gloved fingers. Marguerite gasped. She hadn't expected to see them again.

"I had these restrung for you," he said, placing his hat on his head, moving closer to her. "I'm sorry . . . sorry about everything."

"You couldn't help it," Marguerite murmured, reaching for the pearls, glad to have the last gift her father had given her.

Jordan shook his head. "No," he said, "let me." He lifted his arms, looping the necklace over her head. His fingers, slightly shaking, brushed against her skin as he straightened the pearls. "Every time you wear this, think of me. Remember the good times."

"I will," Marguerite whispered, lowering her head. Then she saw the large diamond pendent lying in the vee of her decolletage. Puzzled, she lifted her face to Jordan's.

"I had it put on for you. It's my way of telling you that I love you, and I don't want you ever to forget." Jordan's arms circled Marguerite's body, and he pulled her close to his tall, hard frame. He dropped his cheek to the crown of her head, his hat falling off. His tears dropped into the silky strands of hair. "Susanna is right, Marguerite, and she has every right to hate

18

me. I do love you, and there isn't a damn thing I can do about it. I can't leave her." Jordan's cry was ragged, bearing the agony of his soul. "She needs me, and there are the children to consider."

Marguerite pulled out of Jordan's arms. Intuitively she recognized the power that she wielded as a woman, as a woman whom Jordan loved, as a woman who could love him in return. Placing her hand over his mouth, responsible to the great love that she felt for him, she made the supreme sacrifice.

"You love me, Jordan, but not with a passionate love, not the kind of love that lovers must have." She smiled and nodded her head when Jordan murmured a protest. "Right now you think you do, but we love as friends." She clasped the diamond in her fist. "I'll never forget you. I promise that each time I look at the diamond I'll remember what a wonderful friend you are."

Standing on deck of the ship, her hand wrapped around the diamond, Marguerite waved at Jordan until he was nothing more than a dot on the horizon.

May 11, 1833
Ballygarrett
County Wexford, Ireland

Earl Randolph Taylor, Esq.

Sheridan Michael O'Roarke has always alluded you. He is an outlaw who walks around like a free man because you can't prove his guilt. His freedom constantly taunts you. But without evidence you can't lock him up; you can't try him; you can't judge him guilty and hang him. You have always wanted the evidence to prove that he is a traitor to the government. I can give you the evidence. The price is high, but I guarantee satisfactory results. If you're interested, bring ten thousand pounds and meet

19

me at 10 o'clock tonight at the Sullivan's old cottage.
Come alone. Do not bring any of your Red Coats.

In the darkened shadows of the spring night, the man was almost discernible as he slid out of the saddle and tethered his horse to the jagged remains of a picket fence. Pushing the haunting memories aside, he slowly treaded the weed-covered pathway to the deserted, cottage ruins. Unusually tense, his slightly shaking hand touched the oak door that hung ajar on a rusted hinge. Tentatively he shoved, the door creaking as he forced the opening wide enough for him to pass through. When he was inside the room, he peered through the darkness, seeing no one yet feeling an eerie presence.

Cautiously he moved to the pile of stones that marked the fireplace. Reaching up, he lifted his top hat and ran his hands through his thick, white hair. Hearing a noise, he plopped the hat on his head and jerked toward the sound, but he saw no one. Nervously he twined his gloved hands together and moved closer to the decaying outer wall.

Chills ran up his spine. He felt a movement; he heard the scratch of the match; he smelled the acrid aroma of burning sulphur; out of the corner of his eye he saw the sudden explosion of light. He spun around, but his foot struck a loose stone and he fell. By the time that he regained his balance and looked up, his only companion was a sputtering candle on the rickety table in the middle of the room. Again his eyes pierced the shadowed fringes of the room; again he saw nothing.

Long, tense, silent minutes passed, the breeze blowing through the room, causing the flame to flicker and ghostly shadows to dance over the cottage ruins. Nervous sweat popped out on the man's brow and in the palms of his hands. He heard the rustle of material from one of the corners.

"And good evening to you, Earl Randolph Taylor." The lilting voice, heavy with Gaelic brogue, was low and muffled. "As usual you're guided by your baser instinct which is greed.

I'm glad you didn't try to set a trap for me with your little red soldiers."

Earl laughed, apprehension thinning his voice. "But in the dark you can't see, can you? So you don't know but what they may be hidden around the cottage, waiting for my signal to capture you."

"Nay," the man confidently negated from another side of the room. "I was outside the library tonight, watching as you put the money into the bags." The man laughed again. "A full hour it took you, Earl Taylor, to decide against filling the bags with rocks. I also heard you give Lieutenant Clayborne his last minute instructions. He's to give you two hours before he and his Red Coats come to find you. I followed you here."

Fear replaced the apprehension. Earl hadn't known that another soul was within miles of him at the house or on the road. "Who are you?" Earl whispered, desperation giving the tone an unnatural, guttural sound. In contrast to the other man, his voice was older and deeper; it was distinctively British. His eyes darted around the circle of darkness, and he reached up, catching the hem of his waistcoat and jerking it down. "Where are you?"

A burst of laughter came from directly in front of Earl; then: "Right here, Earl." A figure, draped in a swirling black cape and hood, moved out of the darkness far enough that Earl could see his form but not so far that his features were illuminated in the candlelight.

"What—what information do you wish to sell me?"

"Do you recognize the cottage, Earl?"

"Yes," Earl mumbled.

"What's that, man? I didn't hear you. Speak up."

"I said yes," Earl repeated louder through clenched teeth.

"And whose was it, Earl? Or can you remember? Thirty-five years is a long time, and you were only twenty-two at the time, a young lieutenant in the army. Most of the folks who can remember the uprising say that Nelson Clayborne reminds them a lot of you when you were that age."

Earl's eyes moved over the ruin. His ears rang with the agonizing cries of dying women and children; their faces flashed through his memory. He closed his eyes, trying to shut out the haunting shrieks.

"Who was it that lived here, Taylor?" the man persisted.

"The Sullivans," Earl mumbled. He lifted his hand and wiped the perspiration from his brow. Again he tugged at the hem of his waistcoat, glad when the cool air touched his sweat-moistened body. "Now—" His voice broke, going from a squeak to a croaking bass. He cleared his throat. "Now tell me what information you have that is so important to me. Why this clandestine meeting in this godforsaken—" Earl's head jerked up, and his eyes, reflecting his fright, fastened on the man across the table.

"Aye, 'tis godforsaken." The cloaked figure quietly agreed. He moved from the darkness, his hand brushing against the crumbling stone wall. "But one time it was full of life, Earl. Can you remember when the Sullivans lived here?"

Earl lowered his head and fidgeted from one foot to the other.

"John and Ann Sullivan and their children. A mother, a father, three small children. The mother cooked the meals and tended the children; the father worked the fields; the children played around the house. Then one day the British soldiers came. They raped the mother in front of the children and father, forced the mother to watch as they killed the father and picketed the lads. The mother eventually went insane, Earl." He doubled his fist and hit the wall, stones tumbling to the ground. Earl jumped out of the way. "Just who caused it to be deserted and forsaken?"

"The past is over; it should be forgotten," Earl began, quaking at the anger of the man.

"Over, to be sure, but forgotten?" The harsh tones coldly interrupted Earl. "Remember, Earl Randolph Taylor, where there be Irishmen who speak Irish the atrocities of the English will never be forgotten."

"And do you speak Gaelic?" Earl asked curiously.

The man hesitated before he admitted, "I used to, Taylor. As fluently as the O'Roarke. But I've grown wiser through the years. I've learned that in Ireland, English and Protestantism are the keys to success and long life."

"Who are you?" Earl demanded, squinting his eyes.

"It's not time to give you my name," the figure said, moving to the center of the room, resting his black-gloved fingers on the tabletop. "But I'll give you a name by which you may call me from this moment forward." As he spoke his index finger glided over the dust-covered surface.

When he stepped back, Earl moved even closer to the table, looking down at the writing. "H-i-b-e-r-n-i-a," he spelled.

"Hibernia," the man explained. "Latin for Ireland."

Earl's eyes narrowed, and he looked across the flickering flame of the candle into the masked face that hid in the folds of the hood.

"Why have you come to me?" he asked. "I'm not Irish, and I'm not for Ireland. Neither are you."

Hibernia laughed. "To be sure, Earl Taylor, you're right. I'm not like Sheridan O'Roarke or Brice Stanton. I'm like you. I have no cause but my cause. And at the moment my cause and your cause is one and the same."

"Which is?" Earl murmured.

"Money. Power. Security. Position."

"All of these I have," Earl lied, thinking about his empty coffers, depleted through the years by his extravagance and mismanagement. "There's only one thing which I want."

Hibernia laughed. "One Wexford boy in particular who is a constant threat to all you've . . . shall we say . . . *worked* for these thirty-some-odd years."

Earl's eyes glistened with interest, and his voice vibrated with excitement. "O'Roarke."

"O'Roarke," Hibernia repeated softly. "With him dead the last thorn in your side would be removed, wouldn't it? No one to humiliate you; no leader for the rebellions; no one to champion the Irish cause in Wexford. No living O'Roarke heir to buy *his* property when it's auctioned for back taxes. Aye, Earl Taylor, I can understand your concern. O'Roarke needs to die soon."

Earl balled his hand into a fist, and his face contorted in anger. "The government gave me that property," he grated. "That was my reward for putting down the rebellion of '26."

Hibernia laughed, the sound hollow and void of humor. "Aye, we'll gladly admit to an uprising and rebellion in 1798 but hardly a rebellion in '26. On trumped-up evidence you had three men hanged, their only real guilt being their love of Ireland."

"Get to the point," Earl said. "You didn't invite me here to discuss the past."

"Nay," Hibernia replied, "I didn't." He moved out of the candlelight, his cape billowing behind him, giving him giantlike stature. "I came to offer you your heart's desire."

"Evidence to prove that O'Roarke is a traitor to England?"

"O'Roarke caught in the act; O'Roarke surrounded by concrete evidence of guilt," came the flat tones.

"This is hard for me to believe," Earl softly intoned. "Why are you willing to turn evidence on one of your own?"

"My reasons are my own."

"No," Earl quietly returned, his piqued interest obliterating his fear. "If I'm going to work with you, I must know the reason why you're selling O'Roarke out."

Hibernia turned, his face to the flame, the muted glow casting eerie shadows on the black satin triangle that hid his face in the folds of the hood. "I can never have the things I want out of life as long as I live here, Taylor. You'll not rest until I'm branded an outlaw and a political dissident. I want to leave and make a new life for myself, but I want to leave knowing that I can rebuild my life sumptuously in a new country. So I want money. The sum which I asked for in the message."

Although the amount had staggered Earl, he gave no

indication of his surprise. He lowered his head and wiped his hand across the table, erasing the letters Hibernia had written. "Indeed, you're asking for a great deal of money."

"Yes or no." Hibernia didn't equivocate.

Earl dusted his hands off, pretending interest in his gloves. "Agreed. I'll give you the money when you've delivered the O'Roarke into my hands."

Hibernia laughed. "Not quite, Mr. Taylor. To be sure, you're not playing me for the fool. I don't like or trust you. We're merely business acquaintances, striking up a bargain. You give me something; I give you something in return. You'll give me seven thousand five hundred pounds now, the rest when I hand the O'Roarke to you. Are you ready to strike a bargain?"

"I'm interested."

"Did you bring the money?"

"I brought half the amount that you specified in your message."

"Half?" Hibernia taunted caustically.

"That's all I have at the present," Earl explained.

"To be sure an' you do have more," Hibernia mocked. "I wouldn't have come to you with this offer if I hadn't known better. From the Irish you gained your title and your property, and you just acquired yourself an American widow in marriage, an heiress who brought you more than love." He laughed. "She brought you a fortune—her money and a large, productive plantation in New Orleans."

Earl laughed, the sound nothing more than a snort of disgust. "I married a fortune with a widow; all I received was a fortune-less widow."

"What do you mean?" Hibernia asked, for the first time doubt creeping into his voice.

"On our wedding night I learned the conditions of the will. Thinking I was marrying her for love, my beautiful wife had neglected to tell me that if she remarried, everything would revert to her daughter except a modest annual income." He spread his hands and waved through the air in disgust. "So my rich bride brought nothing into the marriage but herself and a piddling yearly income. Nothing has changed in my life since I married Amanda except my marital status. I'm still land rich, capital poor."

"And creditors pounding on your door." Hibernia laughed. "You live far above your means, and you've poured what little you have into schemes to frame O'Roarke and prove that he's a traitor. But he's always one step ahead of you. Because of him you're a discredit to your own government." The caped man laughed even louder, and he taunted, "Soon your land will be auctioned, Taylor, and O'Roarke has the money to buy it back, legally." Lifting his shoulders in a negligent shrug, he added, "As I see it then, we have nothing to discuss. No money. No deal."

"But I can get it," Earl called, anxiety tingeing his cry. "You'll have to give me some time." Thinking of Susanna Reeves's letters, thinking of the one that he'd received most recently, Earl's lips curved into a smug smile.

"I don't have time," Hibernia answered shortly. "I want my money immediately."

Afraid he'd lose the opportunity, Earl said, "It won't take long. I'm—I'm working on something right now." He lifted his hand to his face and plucked his bottom lip between his fingers. "Take what I've brought with me, and I'll give you the remainder when you turn O'Roarke over to me."

"I'll take the five thousand pounds, but I won't give you O'Roarke until you've given me another two thousand five hundred." He turned. "I'm not a patient man, Taylor, so don't make me wait too long."

"How do I know that I can trust you? You're Irish, and you're one of the boys of Wexford. How do I know you aren't setting me up?"

Hibernia walked closer to the table. "Go get the money, and I'll show you how you can trust me."

Bobbing his head vigorously, Earl rushed out of the ruins,

across the overgrown lawn to his horse. Reaching into the saddlebags, he extracted the bags of money. Racing back to the cottage, he threw them on the table. "Here." His hands shaking, he clumsily untied the strings. "You want to count it?"

"I do." Hibernia untied the bags and counted the coins. When he had finished, he scooped them back into the bags. Looking across the dimly lit table at Earl, he said, "You have everything to gain if I'm telling the truth and nothing to lose if I'm not. If I'm not telling the truth, I have everything to lose and nothing to gain." He lifted his hands. "All you have to do to test my sincerity is let O'Roarke know my true identity." Reaching into the hood, he untied the mask and lowered it. With both hands he pulled the hood back, revealing his face for the first time that evening.

Earl stepped closer, unable to believe his eyes. "You," he gasped. "My God, I would never have dreamed—"

"Aye! I'm the one," Hibernia replied. "But don't ever call me by name, Earl Taylor, or I swear you'll not get the O'Roarke. I'll kill you and suffer the consequences gladly. Do not let anyone know that I am giving you information or passing information from you to O'Roarke. Remember, from this moment on I am Hibernia to you."

"Why?" Earl beseeched nonplused, nodding his head all the while. "Why are you doing this? Do you hate O'Roarke so much?"

Hibernia retied his mask, picked up the moneybags, and moved away from the candlelight. His back to Earl, he said, "No man do I admire and respect more than Sheridan Michael O'Roarke. But, yes, Earl Taylor, I hate him. I hate him because he has a cause to which he's dedicated. I hate him because he can believe in something, and I can't. There's nothing he wouldn't do to break the yoke of English oppression, even to the sacrificing of his life. But as much as I admire and respect him, my hatred is greater. I'll be glad to see him swinging by the neck."

"He's done something to you," Earl remarked, intrigued with Hibernia's confession. "What?"

Tying the sacks together and slinging them over his shoulder, Hibernia nimbly leaped over the broken wall of the house. He laughed, the soft sound riding the wind. "That be for me to know and not you, Earl Taylor. You've learned as much about me as you shall: my purpose and my price. My reasons and my plans I keep to myself in order to keep my head."

The wind blew stronger, the gust blowing out the candle. The wick sputtered and spit. Darkness once again cloaked the cottage ruins. Earl Randolph Taylor stood, watching Hibernia gallop into the night, his black cape billowing behind.

Book I

Ireland

Chapter 1

June, 1833
Ballygarrett
County Wexford, Ireland

I met with Napper Tandy, and he took me by the hand,
Saying how is old Ireland? and how does she stand?
She's the most distressful country that ever yet was seen,
They are hanging men and women for the wearing of the green.

Waiting for the carriage to be repaired, Marguerite LeFleur stood beneath the shade of the huge, sprawling tree, enjoying the beautiful morning. The sun bathed the countryside with a golden warmth, and the brook, like a piece of blue ribbon, lazily twined the green rolling hills together, rushing over and around the large rocks in its bed. A soft wind, whipping Marguerite's skirt against her legs, rustled through the tall grass and the leaves.

Gazing into the distance, she lifted a hand to brush wisping tendrils of hair into the thick, brown coil at the nape of her neck. She modeled to perfection her pastel-gray riding dress, the latest in fashion for traveling. Wearing red gauntlet gloves,

31

she carried an expensive handcrafted riding crop and wore black boots. Perched at a saucy angle on her head was a silk top hat in matching gray, its diaphanous red veil flowing down her back, contrasting brightly with the soft color of the dress.

"Won't be long, ma'am, before we get this fixed," Paddy McLeary, the driver called. "Sorry I am that ye have to be a'waitin' so long. With yer mother and stepfather not being able to meet ye, this must be troublesome."

Looking first at the middle-aged black woman who lay asleep beneath the shade of the tree, then at the small man who labored so diligently to repair the open carriage, Marguerite smiled and answered, "That's all right, Mr. McLeary. Don't worry about it. You can't help the buggy's breaking."

"To be sure, ma'am," Paddy replied, adding, "if it had been possible, Mr. Taylor would have been here hisself to meet ye. Right upset he was that he couldn't miss that meeting in Bunclody today. Right important meeting it was."

Not interested in the reasons why her stepfather hadn't come, in fact relieved that he hadn't, Marguerite walked a little farther up the river. She called over her shoulder, "Who owns all this land?"

"That would be Mr. Taylor hisself," Paddy grunted, pushing a rock into the road.

"I knew Earl was wealthy when he married Mother," Marguerite reflected aloud, "but I had no idea that his holdings were this vast. He must indeed be a very wealthy man."

"Don't know about the money, but in property he's one of the richest here abouts." Panting, Paddy stood, taking off his cap and brushing his coat sleeve over his sweat-moistened brow. He pointed and waved the other hand. "All that belonged to the O'Roarkes at one time, but now Mr. Taylor hisself be owning it." He pointed a hand. "And that next to hissen be Mr. Stanton's."

"What possessed the O'Roarkes to sell their land?"

"Didn't sell," Paddy muttered. "It was the spoils of war for Mr. Taylor."

Marguerite's blue eyes swept across the rich, verdant landscape, carpeted with a thick growth of grass and cut into squares by low stone fences. Gentle hills and a splattering of trees here and there softened the craggy hardness of the land.

"Most people say my mother was fortunate to have met and married Mr. Taylor."

"Be some who would say she was fortunate," Paddy agreed noncommittally, evading a direct answer. He lowered his head, busying himself with the repairs, never letting Marguerite know he heard her doubts about Earl Taylor.

"Ireland is beautiful," Marguerite murmured, her thoughts straying to the last letters she'd received from Amanda. "When Mother gets over her homesickness, she'll love living here." Her voice was tentative as if she doubted the truth of her statement, as if she were waiting for reassurance.

"Aye," the old man answered, "to be sure, Ireland is indeed beautiful." As he pondered Marguerite's uncertainty, he rubbed his fingers over his beard-stubbled chin and surveyed the extent of damages on the buggy. "Yer mother do indeed seem to be happy." He hesitated before he said, "She's a little peaked today so Bridget, me niece, told me." His face to Marguerite's again, he grinned. "Bridget be one of the maids at the manor house. Mr. Taylor done said she'll be yers." His eyes darted to Jewel. "Don't rightly reckon ye'll be needing another one, ma'am, but if'n ye do a right smart'un Bridget be."

Marguerite smiled. "How old is Bridget?"

"She be about your age, ma'am." Then he added proudly, "Quite a lassie if I may say so meself. Ye'll be right happy with her, to be sure."

"Is she my mother's maid also?" Marguerite asked.

"Nay," Paddy called, dropping to his hands and knees so he could crawl under the carriage, "but she knows the black woman who yer mother brought with her from America. Likes her, Bridget does." Squinting at the axle, he grunted, "And how do ye feel about giving up yer plantation life and coming all the way from New Orleans over here to live?"

Paddy's question surprised Marguerite. She hesitated for a second before she slowly said, "I'm going to miss it, but now that I'm here, I'm quite excited about living in Ireland."

"'Twould be the trip in the ship that would get me," Paddy murmured, too caught up in his work to notice Marguerite's hesitancy. "I be a land-man meself. Four to six weeks on water would be too much for me."

Marguerite laughed and confessed, "I'm a land-woman myself." She paused, then added softly, "But circumstances can change the most adamant."

"To be sure! To be sure!" Squirming from beneath the buggy, he hopped to his feet and dusted his breeches. He said as he shuffled to a nearby clump of trees, "Not a bad break, ma'am. Shouldn't take me too long to fix it."

Nodding her acknowledgment, Marguerite said, "If you don't mind, I think I'll walk up here a ways."

"Not to worry, ma'am," Paddy returned. "Right pleasing it is to look at the Emerald Isle. Just stay close to the brook, so's I kin find ye when I finish here."

"If Jewel awakens before I return, tell her where I went."

"To be sure, ma'am."

Her eyes shining with excitement, Marguerite began to explore. Losing track of time and distance, she wandered the gentle hills and scampered over low stone fences. Eventually she stopped beneath the shade of a huge tree and leaned against the trunk. Warm from her excursion, she took her gloves off, untied her neckcloth, and unbuttoned her white ruched shirt a ways. She stood for a long time before her solitude was rudely interrupted by a man's cold and unfriendly shout.

"Do you make trespassing a habit, madam?"

Startled, Marguerite twirled about, facing the arrogant stranger. He stood, his legs slightly apart, his hands hooked on his hips, a whip dangling from the right one. The sun was to her face, its brilliance blinding her. Holding her hand across her forehead, she blocked some of the glare, but she couldn't see the man's facial features because his hat shaded his face. She did, however, notice his height and his width; she saw his lean muscularity, and she was aware of an aura of masculinity which surrounded him.

"I said, 'Do you make trespassing a habit, madam?'"

Unable to believe that he was addressing her in such an insolent manner, Marguerite asked, "Were you speaking to me?"

Making no attempt to hide his contempt, the man pointed his whip toward the work horses that grazed nearby. "Certainly, madam, you didn't think I was addressing the beasts of the field? I pray you have more intelligence than that. Now tell me what you're doing on my property."

"Your property!" Marguerite softly exclaimed, lifting a delicate brow. "If I'm not mistaken, sir, this land belongs to Earl Taylor."

The man quickly closed the distance between them, stopping inches in front of her. "Long before this land belonged to any Englishman, it belonged to the O'Roarkes," he drawled.

"Then, sir," Marguerite inquired haughtily, drawing to her full height, "why doesn't it still belong to the O'Roarkes?"

The man's eyes darkened, and his visage set in uncompromising lines. With deceptive calm he replied, although he didn't answer the question. "As long as I pay the rent it's my property. I think you'd better leave now. If you don't, you'll be totally responsible for what happens to you."

"Are you threatening me!"

"Nay," he countered, his voice whisper-soft and caressive, "such a happening would be too pleasurable to be considered a threat."

"How dare you!" Marguerite exclaimed, her carriage never changing, her facial expressions still set in a cold, condescending smile.

"Aye, madam." The man laughed. "I dare."

Marguerite's eyes were now a furnace of fury. "I don't believe you know who I am."

The words were a soft, sensual drawl, meant to incinerate

the hearer. Ordinarily Marguerite would never have stooped to such measures. She would never have used her social status to put someone in his place. But this man angered her as no one had ever angered her before.

"Oh, yes, Marguerite LeFleur, I know who you are all right," he said, sneering. "You've been all Earl Taylor can talk of. Said you'd be arriving in Ballygarrett about now." He paused, then said in thick Gaelic brogue, "I just be a'wonderin' *what* you be, Marguerite LeFleur!" His eyes fixed on the gentle curve of her breasts. His silence was eloquent; it was accusing and insinuating.

Inwardly Marguerite gasped at his insinuation. Outwardly her demeanor changed not a jot. "To an intelligent man who I am or what I am is no quandary," she returned cooly. "I am a woman, sir."

"To be sure," he murmured, his eyes once again savoring the statuesque beauty. "To be sure."

Ignoring him, wishing her body would do the same, Marguerite continued to speak. "I'm named Marguerite LeFleur, and I'm a stepdaughter to Earl Taylor."

"If that's the way you wish to describe yourself, madam, so be it. In Eire we call a woman like you a whore."

"A whore!" Marguerite was so outraged she trembled. She was meeting head-on with the same kind of rumors that she'd left in New Orleans. Was it possible for them to have traveled so far, so quickly? Still she retained her aplomb. "You don't know anything about me. Yet you have the audacity to point an accusing finger at me!"

A cold, cynical smile pulled Sheridan's lips. "I know quite a bit about you, madam," he retaliated. "For example, I know why you left New Orleans and came over here."

"Really!" Marguerite scoffed.

"Let's see now," he drawled. "What was her name?" He furrowed his brow as if he were in deep thought. "Your childhood friend, wasn't she?" He snapped his fingers and grinned. "Ahhh, yes, Susanna Reeves! I knew if you'd give me time I'd remember." Marguerite's eyes widened with disbelief; her face blanched. "What was her husband's name?" he taunted.

Marguerite's arm moved as anger surged through her body. Unconsciously she lifted her riding crop.

Watching her every move, her every expression, the man shook his head and softly said, "Don't you dare, Marguerite LeFleur. To be sure, I hold with the Old Testament code of a tooth for a tooth, an eye for an eye—" His gaze went to the riding crop. "A lash for a lash."

"Have you no idea what I can have Mr. Taylor do to you?"

In answer to her indignation the man threw his head back and laughed at her, deep, rolling billows of laughter. When he finally stopped, he slapped his whip lightly against the muscle-corded thighs that stretched the material of his breeches tight. He lifted his hand, yanked his hat off, and Marguerite saw that thick thatch of hair, burnished copper by the sun. She saw the bright, green eyes.

"I must say Earl Taylor has good taste in wenches, Marguerite LeFleur."

"First a whore, now a wench!" Marguerite blazed, angry because he dared taunt her, furious because he laughed away her threats, frightened because he knew her secret.

"Aye," he softly mocked, "and an audacious one, to be sure."

Unable to do more, she shouted her vexation. "You underestimate me, sir. Do you know exactly what I can do to you?"

"I know only too well." His mouth still quirked into that hateful smile. "And if you'll just lower your face, ma'am," he taunted, his eyes carefully assessing her body, "you'll see exactly what you're doing to me."

Marguerite's cheeks flamed. Without thinking she blurted, "No gentleman would treat a lady like this."

"Nay, pretty woman," he said, "to be sure a gentleman wouldn't. But I think it's safe to say that you're no lady, and

I'll certainly be the first to admit that I'm no gentleman."

Marguerite glowered at the swine! Jordan would never behave like this. He was a gentleman! And he treated her like a lady; whereas this man acted as if she were a common tavern wench! Yet her body had never reacted to Jordan's proximity the way it reacted to this man. She tingled all over, and her heart beat so fast she was almost breathless. Her body burned as those glittering eyes slowly, deliberately surveyed her from head to toe. The stranger completely undressed her, leaving her emotionally naked and vulnerable.

"I shall report your insolence to my stepfather," she finally retorted, turning away from him and his mocking laughter.

"Do that," he softly jeered, "and see where it will get you. It'll only upset your . . . ah . . . your stepfather, not me." He paused, a crooked smile curving his sensuous lips. "I don't guess you've been in County Wexford long enough to know that Earl Taylor can't handle Sheridan Michael O'Roarke. I've been told that I'm the thorn in his side." He added, "And by the way, this property happens to belong to Brice Stanton, not Earl Taylor, Daisy."

Marguerite stopped short; she spun around, her skirt twirling about her ankles. Incredulity was stamped on her face. *"Daisy!"*

"I'm by no means fluent in foreign languages, madam," he airily explained, "but I had a few lessons in French, and if I'm not mistaken Marguerite means daisy." He chuckled. "Daisy the flower."

Aghast Marguerite could only repeat limply, "Daisy the flower!"

Sheridan flipped his hat on his head, touched the brim in a cocky salute, and looked up at her, grinning. "Surely in all your years someone has called you that before, madam!"

"In—in—all my years," Marguerite sputtered indignantly.

Sheridan chuckled. "I would say, madam—" He narrowed his eyes and contemplated her. "That you are a spinster. About—"

"A spinster!"

"Can you not speak English well?" he asked. "Is it necessary for you to repeat everything I say?"

Marguerite stamped her foot. "In all my years I have allowed no one to call me Daisy. And I absolutely refuse to be called a spinster." She lowered her voice to an angry whisper. "Never call me that again. Do you hear me?"

Undaunted, he replied, "Aye, mistress, I hear you, but I shan't obey." His eyes twinkled with devilish delight. "I think I shall call you Daisy from this day forward."

"No, Mr. O'Roarke," Marguerite retaliated, "you will not call me that because we shall not be seeing each other again."

"Aye, Daisy," he softly taunted, "we shall. Providence has ordained it."

Too furious to retort, Marguerite turned and marched away from him. She hadn't taken many steps, however, before she stopped, spun on her heels a second time, and said, "Stay away from me."

Rich laughter rang across the clearing. "I stay away from you, Daisy." He was definitely amused. "Must I point out that you're trespassing on O'Roarke property?" He paused, again laughing at her transfixed expression and her shocked speechlessness. "Perhaps that is why you walked this way, madam?" He took a step, the end of the whip brushing against his leg as he moved. "Like I had heard about you, you had heard about the O'Roarke and were hoping to meet him! And now perhaps you're wondering what kind of lover he will be."

He stepped nearer Marguerite, his movement jarring her out of the stunned trance. Sheridan was entirely too near. Marguerite backed up, holding her hands out, warding him off. Though her movements spoke her wariness, her voice was loud and clear.

"Get away from me and stay away."

"I'll have no trouble staying away from you, Daisy," he intoned softly, moving ever closer, "but I have no doubt that you'll be hunting me up before long." He eyed her

39

speculatively, the green irises again lingering on the gentle swell of her breasts. "You'll soon grow tired of an old man fondling you. You'll be wanting a young man—his murmurs of love, his touches, his kisses—"

Marguerite was too angry to think or to care. Giving in to the rage that consumed her, she lifted her hand, and this time swung, thrashing Sheridan soundly across the cheek. The riding crop hit his face with an angry snap that echoed through the morning quietness.

Sheridan lifted his hand to the red line across his cheek. Marguerite's face blanched of color, and her heart drummed her fear. She wanted to run, but she refused to quell or give ground in front of this blackguard. O'Roarke reached out, caught her shoulders with both hands and jerked her against his chest.

"I warned you, Daisy LeFleur," he whispered, his lips unerringly moving toward hers.

Marguerite's sudden surge of resistance was nothing compared to Sheridan O'Roarke's determination. He banded his arms around her body, stopping her flailing, holding her prisoner. Her doubled arms, the balled-up hands, and the riding crop were pinned between them. Before she could scream for help, his lips captured hers in a hard, cruel kiss. When he finally let her go, Marguerite stumbled backward.

"You filthy swine," she swore with quiet vehemence, lifting her hand and rubbing it across her lips. "You'll rue the day you did this. I'll see that you're paid in kind."

Sheridan doffed his hat, a cynical grin quirking his lips, an enigmatic glitter in his eyes. "Consider the kiss repayment, madam. A taste of your lips is punishment enough." His eyes carelessly slid down her body. "Cold you are. A man would be a fool to want more." Sheridan laughed, the sinister sound cutting into Marguerite's sensibilities. "You're just the person for Earl Randolph Taylor. Ice for the fish."

Her eyes burning with tears, her hands curled into tight fists, Marguerite watched him turn and saunter away.

Swallowing her hurt, her anger, her mortification, she softly called, "Then add yourself to the list of fools, Mr. O'Roarke." If she had learned anything from men during her twenty-two years, she had learned that the more a woman resisted, the more a man wanted to conquer her. When Sheridan turned around, Marguerite added, "I know you want more."

Out of the shadows of the broad-brimmed hat, he stared at her. She was right. From the time that he had pilfered the big house library and read about her in the letters Earl received from a Susanna Reeves in New Orleans, Sheridan had been fascinated by Marguerite LeFleur; she intrigued him. And he did want more. Yet Sheridan contemplated lying because her conceit galled him, but her courage and defiance pleased him; her tall, slender beauty excited him.

Eventually he said, "Aye, 'tis a fact, lass, I want more." He waited a second, then added with a confidence that obliterated arrogance or conceit. "I shall have more, lass."

Subconsciously Marguerite recognized the truth of his assertion, but consciously she couldn't accept the prediction. She laughed scornfully. "No, Mr. O'Roarke, you shall get no more of me than the lash of my riding crop across your face. I shall see you dead before you touch me again."

Her dignity regained, her sense of justice appeased, Marguerite spun around, haughtily tilting her head in the air as she sauntered away. Soft laughter followed her.

"Ah, lass," Sheridan drawled, watching her move across the field, "you have spirit, and I like that. But you are young and foolish." His last words whispered across the meadow. "Never make a promise you cannot keep."

Chapter 2

A parasol shielding her from the sun, Marguerite looked at the passing countryside as the open carriage jostled down the path toward the town of Ballygarrett. Although this was her first time out since she'd arrived in Ireland two weeks ago, she couldn't concentrate on the beautiful scenery. Her mother's ill health was more than homesickness; it was more than a temper tantrum. Marguerite was glad that she hadn't allowed anyone to talk her out of coming. Rather than her mother's growing better, Amanda grew sicker with each passing day.

"Won't the horses go any faster?" Marguerite called impatiently.

"We be goin' as fast as we can," Paddy replied calmly, never raising his voice. "Don't be gettin' so worried, Mistress Marguerite. There be nothin' ye can do fer yer mother. So's ye might as well enjoy yer day out of the house."

"Uncle Paddy's right." Bridget McLeary's large eyes were soft with compassion.

Marguerite crushed the soft cambric handkerchief in her fist. "I just wish Mother hadn't insisted that I come to town for this fitting and for my new bonnet. It—it seems so silly. Her so sick and me—" She shrugged her shoulders, the low-cut pink satin bodice shimmering in the afternoon sunshine. "I need to be home nursing her, not gadding about the country being fitted for new frocks and bonnets." Thinking about her mother's last request, one made to please Earl, Marguerite looked at the young woman who sat across from her. "Certainly not attending dinner parties."

"But remember, Mistress Marguerite," Bridget gently pointed out, smiling, "yer mother is the one who insisted. Besides that medicine she takes makes her sleep most of the time, so she won't know if ye'r there. And it's not like ye left her alone. She has either of them two black maids."

Paddy nodded his agreement. "Aye, ma'am," he said, "and like yer stepfather said, it's high time ye got out of the house. Two weeks ye've been in County Wexford and most of the time has been spent in the darkened bedroom, sitting with yer mother." The words were hardly out of his mouth before he cried, "Whoa," and the carriage lurched to a halt.

"What's wrong?" Marguerite cried, jolted forward, her wide-brimmed pink bonnet knocked askew, the parasol jolted from her hand.

"To be sure, I don't know, ma'am," Paddy replied, reining the horses in. "But I'll be a'findin' out."

Brushing her bonnet out of her face and groping for her parasol at the same time, Marguerite said, "Can we go another direction, Paddy? I really want to get back to the house."

"No ma'am," Paddy murmured absently, "I don't think so."

His sparkling blue eyes quickly moved over the noisy crowd that blocked the street. His gaze finally centered on the two men who stood in the middle of the human circle. They tossed their hats aside and turned to face each other. Smiles curved their lips, and challenge gleamed in their eyes.

They raised their fists and deftly moved their feet as they danced around. Both were young men, tall and powerfully built. Both wore cambric shirts, gray-striped breeches, and black knee-high boots. Whereas one had a shock of copper-red hair that glistened in the sunlight, the other had black.

"No," Paddy firmly announced, resolve giving his voice a

44

stern finality, "we can't be a'movin'."

"We've got to," Marguerite insisted. "Do something."

"The horses can't be a'movin'," Paddy repeated a little stronger, "and I'm much too old to be a'pullin' the buggy meself."

Slacking the reins, Paddy grinned and pushed his cap back on his grizzled white hair; he settled down to watch. Nothing in life did he enjoy more than a pint of stout, a good tale, and a fight worth seeing. And sure as he was sitting here on Mr. Taylor's buggy seat this fight was one to behold!

"What's happening?" Marguerite asked. She craned her head to look around Paddy.

"A fight, ma'am," Paddy answered, a reverent hushness in his voice. "One of the best ye'll be seeing in these parts of the Emerald Isle."

Rising to her feet, Bridget asked, "And who would it be?"

When Paddy said, "I believe it's O'Roarke," Bridget caught her uncle by the shoulders, her head dodging from one side of his head to the other so she could see better.

"Aye, 'tis O'Roarke," Bridget murmured.

Marguerite stiffened, and her face blanched. Would she never escape the despicable man? she wondered. Desperately trying to eradicate the image of the man who had haunted all her wakening moments since she'd arrived in Ireland, Marguerite closed her eyes, but she found no respite. Sheridan O'Roarke's mocking face was indelibly imprinted on her mind. His hurtful accusations still rang in her ears.

"Do they be fighting with shillelagh, Paddy?"

"Nay, no clubs today that I be a'seein'," Paddy answered. "Looks like it's to be fisticuffs."

With agitated movements designed to take her thoughts off the O'Roarke, Marguerite concentrated on her parasol, twirling it around to see if any damage had been done when it fell to the carriage floor.

"Who's he fighting?" Bridget asked, her dark eyes glowing with excitement. "Oh—h—h—" At that moment her eyes landed on the contestants, and the exclamation thrummed into an awed silence. "Mickey Flynn."

"Haven't they anything better to be doing than . . ."

Marguerite's words faded into absolute silence as she lifted her head, her eyes fixing on Sheridan O'Roarke. Slowly she rose, laying the parasol aside, forgetting the reason why she'd come to town, forgetting everything but the O'Roarke. So caught up in Sheridan's masculinity, she forgot his mockery, his accusations. Though both men were about the same height and breadth—Sheridan dwarfed the other—he dwarfed all those around him.

"Nothin' so appreciated in all Ireland," Paddy explained patiently, "as an uncommonly good fight, ma'am. And this one promises to be an uncommonly good'un."

"What are they quarreling about?"

"Ah, lassie," Paddy droned. "In Ireland one doesn't have to have a quarrel to fight. We Irish just love a good, healthy brawl. But . . ." Paddy paused and ran the back of his hand over his beard-stubbled face. "'Tis far more than a quarrel between the likes of these—the one being the local magistrate in the pocket of Mr. Taylor and the other being the O'Roarke who's forever picking the pockets of Mr. Taylor."

"What is O'Roarke doing here?" Bridget asked, her eyes scanning the crowd as if she were searching for someone. "I thought he was going to get the tithe cattle—"

"And how should I know what the rascal is doing here?" Paddy snorted, interrupting his niece. Occupied with watching O'Roarke, Marguerite didn't notice the disapproving glare Paddy turned on Bridget. "I don't have time for the likes of him. Mr. Taylor would be more than a mite displeased for me to drink a pint and gossip with the likes of Sheridan O'Roarke."

Marguerite retorted dryly, "But it's all right if you watch O'Roarke fight. Mr. Taylor can't fault that!"

"To be a fact, ma'am." Paddy energetically nodded his head, in no wit perturbed by the accusation.

Marguerite laughed. Behind the unshaven face, the unkempt attire, and the jovial banter of an aging man, she sensed intelligence and alertness.

Paddy joined her laughter, continuing his defense with a conspiratorial wink. "Why, Mistress Marguerite, 'tis happening in front of me very own eyes, and there's not one thin' I can do about it. And to be considered, ma'am, none can give a better fight than O'Roarke. If he's a'fightin', I know I kin make me a little money on the side. I have no doubt a good wager has already been laid. Now, if'n ya don't mind, ma'am," he added, jumping from the buggy seat, "since we'll not be a'goin' any place any too soon, I'll be wagering a little money on the outcome of this, meself."

"I do mind," Marguerite sputtered, unaccustomed to treatment like this from servants. "I need to get down to Mrs. Fitzpatrick's—so I can get home—"

Ignoring Marguerite, Paddy tied the reins to a low-hanging limb on the nearest tree, and he shuffled to the pub, his voice joining the din as he waved his money in the air and laid his bet. Marguerite remained standing, her eyes never leaving the two men who laughed and boasted their prowess, taunting the other to disprove the claim.

"There's no need to worry," Bridget consoled her mistress in a soft, lilting voice. "Everyone will be watching the fight, Molly Fitzpatrick included. So ye won't be a'getting a fitting or yer bonnet until the fight is over." Bridget laughed. "This, Mistress Marguerite, promises to be a fight to be sure!"

"I suppose you'd like to lay a few bets yourself." Marguerite sighed her irritation.

"Now I don't suppose that I'd be laying any wagers, mistress. Paddy will do enough for the both of us. But I would like to get a closer look at the lads." Bridget turned beautiful blue eyes on Marguerite. "They say, mum, that none's so fair and brave in all Ireland as Sheridan O'Roarke. Perhaps ye ought to take more than a peek at him."

Marguerite couldn't stay mad at Bridget for long. Chuckling softly, she reached out and tucked an errant black curl inside

47

the bonnet. "And you, Bridget McLeary, what do you say? Is Sheridan O'Roarke truly the fairest and bravest in all Ireland?"

Color flushed Bridget's cheeks a beautiful rose. "Though all of Ireland thinks it be O'Roarke," she murmured. "For me, 'tis . . . 'tis . . ."

Before Bridget could say more, a deep resonant voice rose above the frenzied cries of the crowd around him. Sheridan wasn't shouting; his voice was the steely quietness of authority itself, hushing the crowd and commanding the full attention of all those around him.

"A fine day it'll be, Mickey Flynn, when ye can best me in a fight. Even in a drunken stupor I could lick the likes of ye." Sheridan's lips curved into a beautiful smile, and his eyes glittered his challenge.

"An' this is such a day, O'Roarke," Flynn returned. "The whole of County Wexford has turned out to see me in my glory." He nodded his head and waved his hand toward Marguerite's buggy. "Even Mr. Taylor's newly acquired daughter has come to cheer me on."

The fight momentarily forgotten, Sheridan O'Roarke shifted his gaze from Mickey Flynn's face, and he looked at Marguerite. When he saw her cheeks heighten with the embarrassment of remembrance, he smiled, and what began as a quick, curious sweep of the eyes turned into a long, leisurely inspection. Resenting the blatant stare, Marguerite pulled to her full height and glared defiantly back at Sheridan O'Roarke. Other than both hands tightly clutching the handle of her opened parasol, she betrayed none of her inner turmoil.

Masculine eyes moved over the close-fitting bodice of embroidered pink silk. They spanned the tiny waist, encircled by a wide ribbon sash tied at the front in a bow. Sheridan's gaze traveled the sleeves that billowed to the wrists where they fastened in a tight cuff, but his eyes lingered on the delicate, gloved hands, and on the long, slender fingers that twirled the parasol handle round and round.

48

The smile widening, O'Roarke's eyes lazily climbed up the midriff, tarrying on the low decolletage. He visually caressed the soft, creamy fullness of Marguerite's breasts that innocently peeked above the white lace and the pink satin. As if he had literally touched her, Marguerite's breasts tingled to life, and she drew in her breath. Sheridan's gaze lifted; their eyes collided; their gazes locked.

During the past two weeks, Marguerite had forgotten nothing about O'Roarke. His red hair gleamed like burnished copper in the sunlight, and his eyes were all the beautiful greens that Marguerite had seen since she'd arrived in Ireland. His crooked, rakish smile was devastating.

Suddenly with no warning, O'Roarke's expression changed. His smile faded into a sarcastic grin, and his green eyes flashed his hatred and contempt for the English, and although Marguerite was only Earl Randolph Taylor's daughter by marriage, to O'Roarke she was part of the hated English aristocracy. But neither his contempt nor his arrogance stopped Marguerite's perusal.

Living up to his preconceived idea of her reputation, she stared at him, seeing him anew. Her eyes crawled over every inch of the craggy, handsome face, down the broad neck, to the opened vee of his white cambric shirt. As he had overtly touched her breasts with the mocking green eyes, Marguerite as daringly let her gaze linger on the thick mat of copper curls that glistened on his chest.

Head and shoulders taller than many of the men hovering around, his broad shoulders stretched the soft material of his shirt tightly across his chest. Brawny, hair-covered forearms stretched from the cuffed white sleeves. Fisted hands rested on slim hips, and gray striped trousers hugged long and sleek muscle-corded legs. Black Wellington boots sheathed the legs from the knees to the feet.

"Since Taylor's stepdaughter is so newly arrived from America," Sheridan finally said, addressing Mickey, sultry lashes fanning over one cheek as he winked, "perhaps we ought to show her true Irish hospitality. Let's invite her in for a pint of stout and visit with her for awhile."

Though his tone was jovial and friendly, Marguerite knew an insult when she heard one.

"To be sure, Danny Boy," Mickey said, "we can't be a'doing that. You know as well as I do that a lady wouldn't be seen drinking a pint of stout in a pub."

"Aye," Sheridan drawled, his gaze on Marguerite, "a *lady* wouldn't." So caught up in Marguerite, Sheridan had forgotten his adversary.

But Mickey hadn't forgotten his. Taking advantage of Sheridan's preoccupation, Mickey's quick fist connected with Sheridan's jaw. The crack echoed through the streets of the small village, bringing a loud cheer from the crowd. Mickey laughed as Sheridan stumbled backward, both fists fanning the air.

"I've much better things to do today than be on me best behavior in front of a lady. Besides I'm sure her stepfather will be doing her the pleasure of showing her around, and for sure, Sheridan O'Roarke, he'd have ye in prison before he'd let ye near anything that belongs to him."

"'Tis so, to be sure," Sheridan grunted, dodging Mickey's well-aimed blows as he regained his balance. He gently dabbed the corner of his mouth, wiping away the dribble of blood. "That was a low blow, Mickey me darlin'."

He narrowed his eyes, angled his head and glowered at Mickey. The other man, his fists raised protectively in front of himself, reciprocated the scowl with deep, resonant laughter; the gusty sound ringing through the small town. His feet nimbly danced over the dusty street, and his gray eyes glistened. His black hair, brushed back from his face in deep waves, glistened.

"The beauty of the lady has driven ye daft, Sheridan Michael O'Roarke," Mickey Flynn responded. "That was a high blow, and a well-put one, if I may say so meself." He brought his right fist to his mouth and licked the tip of his thumb.

"Right ye are," Sheridan replied, oblivious of the huzzas of the crowd. All else forgotten for the moment, his eyes and thoughts centered on Mickey Flynn and the task at hand. "We have important things to do today." He hit Mickey in the chin, and he laughed as the constable reeled from the blow. "That's for gettin' my attention off the subject and taking advantage of me."

"And this," Mickey answered, his fist darting out, landing Sheridan a heavy blow, "is for—"

Before Mickey could get another word out, Sheridan hit him again. "'Tis past time for you to shut your mouth, Mickey Flynn, and fight."

Their fists flying, their bodies reeling, the men fought, the crowd moving with them. Mesmerized by the scene in front of her, Marguerite stood in the buggy and watched long after Bridget had disembarked and ran after the crowd. When the men moved on down the street out of sight, Marguerite stood the suspense as long as she could. She tossed her parasol on the seat and opened the buggy door. Lifting her full skirt and numerous stiffened petticoats, she jumped to the ground. Her slippered feet rushed over the road until she was running and yelling with the crowd.

She was hoarse from her screaming when she felt the tension that gripped the crowd. Whereas one minute they had been whooping and hollering, cheering the adversaries on, now they were silent—deathly silent. Not a word was spoken; before Marguerite knew what was happening, the crowd quietly dispersed.

A long cut above one eye, blood running down the side of his face, Mickey Flynn sat in the middle of the street too dazed to move. Paddy caught Marguerite's elbow with his hand, and he tugged her toward their carriage, Bridget running behind.

"Hurry up, ma'am," he whispered out of the corner of his mouth. "We must be gettin' out of the way. Soldiers are coming."

"They won't hurt us!" Marguerite cried in alarm.

"Probably not," Paddy returned, trying to shove her in the direction of the buggy. "But we Irish don't trust 'em. To them the only good Irishman is a dead one, and the English likes only good Irishmen." He added dryly, "If ye'll be looking at our cemeteries, ye'll find the community of good'un's growing steadily."

"Why are they here?" Marguerite asked, watching the villagers as they quietly disappeared into the buildings.

"They've come to seize and brand the tithe cattle."

"The what kind of cattle?" Marguerite exclaimed, her face jerking back to Paddy's.

"The cattle what belongs to the government church," Paddy grunted impatiently. Tired of trying to persuade Marguerite to move, he grabbed her hand and tugged.

Looking over her shoulder, Marguerite saw O'Roarke leisurely walking toward a horse that was tethered on the outskirts of town. "Why is he leaving?"

"'Cause he's got good sense which is more than I kin say fer us," Paddy grumbled under his breath; then he said louder for Marguerite to hear, "Word's out that O'Roarke knows something about a tithing rebellion in Bunclody two weeks ago, and the government fears he be a 'stealin' the tithing cattle here in Ballygarrett. Which he probably is. Now hush yer gabbing, lass. We'll have time to gossip later."

Unable to ask Paddy any more questions at the moment, Marguerite ran with him, her bonnet flying off her head, dangling down her back, her reticule bouncing from one side to the other. When she reached the buggy, she turned and looked over her shoulder at O'Roarke who stood complacently by his horse. She caught her breath; he was staring at her, too, a crooked, mocking grin on his face. Lifting a hand in an arrogant farewell, he brought it to his lips, then brushed her a kiss. As the soldiers rounded the bend, he donned the wide-brimmed hat, leaped on his horse and galloped away.

Marguerite stood for that moment longer, watching the lone

rider loose himself in a cloud of dust. With both hands she pulled the ribbons of her bonnet; then she recapped the shining sable-colored hair with the silk and frills. With Paddy's assistance she climbed into the buggy and picked up her parasol. After she sat down, she straightened her skirt about her. By the time Paddy sat across from her, the buggy was slowly moving down the main street.

Chapter 3

Paddy hadn't driven far when the soldiers drew up beside Marguerite's carriage. The lieutenant, his eyes on the distant horizon, barked, "Get this buggy out of the middle of the street, man. You're blocking our way."

"Sorry, sir," Paddy drawled, totally unrepentant.

"There's the constable, Lieutenant," one of the soldiers cried, pointing his finger at Mickey Flynn who staggered down the middle of the street toward them. "Something's wrong with him."

"Probably one pint too many," the lieutenant answered, not bothering to hide the contempt in his voice.

"No," Paddy mumbled under his breath, "that is not the case, sir. One O'Roarke too many." He chuckled, remembering the fight with relish. "Flynn has been in one fight too many. If it had been the pint," he sang in a rich baritone, making up the tune and the words as he went, "he would still be in the pub, spinning his tale, and drinking his ale, rather than sitting in the middle of the street on his tail." Truly delighted with himself, Paddy's chest swelled, and he cocked his head to the side with all the charm of a bird preening his feathers.

Marguerite couldn't contain her soft laughter. Not a dull minute was to be found when she was around Paddy McLeary.

He enjoyed life to the fullest and had a penchant for turning the most mundane event into an extraordinary occasion, a dull, dreary day into a holiday.

"What happened to you, Flynn?" the officer barked disgustedly.

"O'Roarke," Paddy muttered louder this time, pulling the reins, the horses blocking the soldiers' passage.

"O'Roarke!" the young officer cried, not even realizing that Paddy had answered rather than Mickey. "O'Roarke is here in Ballygarrett!"

"Aye," Paddy returned evenly, "we saw him not more than a minute ago, Mr. Clayborne."

"*Lieutenant Clayborne,*" the young officer barked. "To you, I'm Lieutenant Clayborne." The lieutenant nudged his horse forward, moving closer to the buggy. "Where did he go?"

Paddy shook his head. "That I don't be a'knowin', sir. He and Mickey Flynn were engaged in an excellent example of fisticuffs."

"You ineffective, boggling fool!" the officer shouted, jerking his head around, venting his ire on the man who limped down the street. "You know what O'Roarke is doing here in Ballygarrett! He's come to get the tithing cattle. Why didn't you send word to me instead of indulging in sports with him?" To Paddy the lieutenant shouted, "Get this buggy out of the way before I arrest you, man."

"An' watch who ye be a yellin' at." Paddy swiveled himself around, glaring indignantly at the lieutenant. "This be Mistress Marguerite, Mr. Taylor's stepdaughter, just come from the United States, and I was just a'driving her to Molly Fitzpatrick's shop to buy herself a new bonnet."

For the first time the officer saw Marguerite. Dumbfounded, he could only stare for a second. He, too, had heard Earl talk about his stepdaughter, but this was the first time that he had seen her. Slowly a smile curved the lieutenant's lips, replacing his frown. Quickly he dismounted and walked to the side of the buggy. Doffing his hat and bowing, he introduced himself.

"I'm Lt. Nelson Clayborne, ma'am." All the harshness had evaporated from his face and his voice.

Marguerite smiled and extended a gloved hand. "I'm Marguerite LeFleur."

He raised his head, his brown eyes sparkling with friendly interest. "I've heard about you, Mistress LeFleur. From the United States, I hear. New Orleans?"

Marguerite laughed. "I am."

Nelson closed his large hand around Marguerite's. He lifted it to his mouth, his lips softly brushing over the glove. "I'm so glad to make your acquaintance." The deep voice matched the velvet softness of the brown eyes. "New Orleans's loss is our gain."

Marguerite pulled her hand from his clasp, and her smile deepened. "Thank you, Lieutenant."

"Nelson, ma'am," he murmured. "Call me Nelson, please." He couldn't tear his gaze from Marguerite's face. Her eyes were beautiful. Outlined in midnight, they were the most vibrant blue he'd ever seen. He lifted a hand and ran it through tousled blond hair.

"Lieutenant, sir." Mickey turned his head and spit a mouthful of blood. Gingerly he rubbed the cut at the corner of his eye with one hand and laid the other on Nelson's forearm. "It's sorry I am, sir."

Nelson stared at the filthy hand that clutched his arm. His entire visage changed. Hatred swelled up in him in tidal-wave proportions. A good soldier, a man of duty, he loved and served his country, and only the love of country and devotion to duty could have persuaded him to come to this godforsaken, barbaric land. He despised and held in contempt the Irish and anyone who sympathized with their cause.

"Get your filthy hands off me," Nelson growled, snatching his arm away from Mickey's touch. "Your stupidity has probably cost us the tithe cattle." The officer's face twisted into disgust, and his lips thinned into hatred. "Before this is over, Flynn, I'm going to prove to Taylor that you're as

57

involved in this conspiracy as is O'Roarke."

Marguerite watched the episode with astonishment. She was amazed at the mercurial change in the lieutenant's actions and demeanor. Nelson's voice was now a venomous snarl, so different from the friendly tones he'd used when he spoke to her.

Mickey removed his hand, and he stepped back. His eyes, hooded with thick lashes, were cold and defiant. "No, Lieutenant," he softly drawled, "ye'll not be a'provin' anythin' of the likes. I'm not a part of any conspiracy." He laughed, the sound softly mocking; then he added, "If there be any conspiracy. But I have cause to hate you English. My mother was a Sullivan, and when I remember what the likes of you did to us Sullivans in '78 . . ."

The two men glared at each other, hatred gleaming in the depth of their eyes. The sudden shout of one of the soldiers broke the silence and the tension.

"Lieutenant, sir—" The man pointed in the direction Sheridan had ridden. "I see a rider on a horse the color of O'Roarke's." He pushed up and craned his neck, peering down the road. "Sir—" His voice shook with excitement. "It is O'Roarke. Other men are joining him, and they're getting away."

"After them," Nelson ordered. "Get those cattle before they do." Nelson clamped his hat on his head and shoved Mickey Flynn out of his way. Rushing to his horse, he mounted. "I'm sorry I can't stay and talk," he said to Marguerite, his tones once again friendly and warm. He placed a foot in the stirrup and gracefully swung into the saddle, "but I have business to attend." As he rode off, he asked, "Shall I see you tonight, Mistress LeFleur?"

"Tonight?" Marguerite murmured, momentarily nonplused. "I don't think so. We're dining out."

Nelson smiled. "So am I. Dinner at the Reverend Denby's." Understanding curved Marguerite's lips and she nodded. "I shall see you then, and we shall talk at our leisure." His words were lost in the thud of hooves and the creak of leather saddles.

"A fine day's work ye've done," Paddy muttered to Mickey as they watched the soldiers gallop away. "Ye've allowed yer vanity to lose ye a reward. Mr. Taylor will pay a handsome penny to get his hands on the O'Roarke and question him about Bunclody. And just be a'thinkin', ye stupid fool, what Mr. Taylor's gonna be a'doin' to ye if the O'Roarke's gets them tithe cattle."

Mickey spit again. "I know, Paddy. 'Tis me ownself I have to blame. I keep thinkin' I can lick the likes of O'Roarke."

"Perhaps ye can lick him," Paddy answered. "It's just that he outsmarts ye every time."

Mickey shook his head. "Aye, that'd be the truth, all right. I dunno which I hates the most, Paddy—the lieutenant or Sheridan O'Roarke. Both of them tries to make a fool of me."

"And both usually succeed," Paddy added unsympathetically, nodding his head. "An' I can see yer dilemma, Mickey, me darlin'. 'Tis a hard choice." He rubbed his hand over his cheeks. "Probably I'll have to settle on liking the O'Roarke the better of the two."

"Aye," Mickey answered.

"He's Catholic and he's Irish," Paddy pointed out.

"Aye," Mickey repeated. He pointed to the pub. "Tell ye what, Paddy, me darlin'. I've got to get me a pint to wash down the sorrow that I'm a'feelin', and the truth of the matter I could use some good company."

As Marguerite watched Mickey move out of sight, she looked at Bridget and spoke; however she addressed her question to neither of the McLearies in particular. "Why does Mr. Taylor want to question O'Roarke? What kind of conspiracy is he involved in?"

Neither Bridget nor Paddy was in a hurry to answer. Bridget darted her uncle a furtive glance. Paddy pulled his cap over his forehead and clucked the horses.

"That'd be a long story, ma'am, and me throat sure is dry— much too dry to talk for long." He grinned. "That's why, ma'am, that I do me best talking in the pub—good stout and a good audience."

Marguerite chuckled. "And no women! I'll tell you what," she suggested. "Bridget and I'll go into the millinery shop and look at material for my new hat. While I'm doing that you go into the Emerald Green Shamrock and have yourself a pint or two."

"Now that, ma'am," Paddy responded brightly, "is a right fine suggestion. A pint or two will loosen the tongue, and I can right finely answer yer question."

Marguerite and Bridget spent the better part of the afternoon in Molly Fitzpatrick's shop pouring through the pattern books first, then selecting frills. Sitting on the sofa in the small, cozy shop, Marguerite sipped her cup of tea and made her final selections.

"Decorate the crown of the bonnet with these flowers and these ribbons," she said, picking up the silk periwinkles and the blue ribbons from the table. She looked at the buxom woman who sat across from her. "Also, Mrs. Fitzpatrick, I should like to buy enough of this ribbon to trim the bottom of my skirt."

"Aye." Molly nodded, lifting a pudgy hand to push wisps of graying hair from her temples. "I have enough for that without ordering more."

The afternoon mail coach rumbled into town, the noise distracting the women. An admitted town gossip, Molly dropped her pencil on the table. Heaving her plump body out of the chair, she walked to the window, her taffeta skirt swishing as she moved. She pulled the curtain aside and curiously peered into the street.

"A stranger," she murmured as a man disembarked and waited for the driver to get his luggage from the boot. "An' it looks like he'll be staying for awhile. Has his valise with him, he does. A mighty big one at that."

Setting her cup down, Bridget ran to the window and peeked over Molly's shoulder. "Who is he?" she wondered aloud, not at all ashamed of her curiosity.

"From the United States, I'd be a'guessin'," Molly said, her eyes running from the top of his head to the bottom of his feet.

"The United States," Marguerite squealed, setting her cup down so quickly it teetered a moment on the saucer before it balanced on its bottom. She ran to the window, looking between Molly and Bridget. "How do you know he's from America?" Extremely homesick, Marguerite was unable to curb the excitement in her voice.

"The cut of his clothes," the woman responded. "Definitely American." Proud of her ability to assess people, Molly reflected aloud. "In his mid-forties, I'd guess."

Only Bridget heard Molly's last phrase. Marguerite was out of the shop, racing across the dusty street. Stopping in front of the man, she extended her hand. "Hello. I'm Marguerite LeFleur. Mrs. Fitzpatrick said you were American, and I am, too, so I—I—" Suddenly Marguerite stopped in mid-sentence. Embarrassed by her impetuosity, her cheeks flushed.

The man laughed, dropped his valise, swept his hat from his hand and bowed, all in one graceful motion. "Indeed your friend is right," he said, his eyes twinkling merrily. "I'm James Power, and I'm an American of sorts." He had the trace of an Irish lilt. He replaced his hat and lifted both hands, tugging his waistcoat over his stomach. "I was born near here, but twenty-some-odd years ago I emigrated to the United States—Philadelphia first, then New Orleans, finally settling in Saltillo, Mexico where I became a Mexican citizen."

Marguerite smiled apologetically. "I'm sorry that I seemed to be so impetuous. I'm not ordinarily so ill-mannered. I—I was lonesome for an American—and—"

"And that I can be understanding," James returned. "Where are you staying?"

"At the manor house," Marguerite replied, pointing in the direction of her stepfather's house.

Power looked first in the direction that she pointed; then he squared his gaze on her, his eyes narrowing. "And who might you be?"

Marguerite heard the slight, disapproving edge to his voice. However, before she could answer, Paddy quietly materialized. "She be Mistress Marguerite LeFleur." His voice was stern with censure as he placed his small body protectively between Power and Marguerite. "And who might ye be, stranger?"

The newcomer stared at Paddy for a few seconds. "I'm no stranger," he finally said. "I'm James Power, come home after twenty-odd-year or so."

By now a crowd had gathered, their curiosity clearly evident. "James Power," Paddy murmured, reaching up to scratch the back of his head, in the process tilting his cap forward on his head. Suddenly he chuckled. "Would ye happen to be the lad who lived—" He pointed a finger in one direction and measured the other about three feet from the ground.

"That I would," Power returned, his voice booming with laughter. "I'm here to visit with my sister."

"Aye," Paddy murmured, "an' no finer woman ever walked the face of the earth than yer sister. "Do ye remember me?" Paddy grinned.

Power nodded his head. "I rightly recollect the face, but I can't recall the name."

"Patrick—Paddy McLeary."

"Aye," Power exclaimed with a hearty nod of his head. "Of course, I remember Paddy McLeary. At the battle of Vinegar Hill you—"

"Come," Paddy said, clapping a hand on Power's shoulder, interrupting his reminiscences, "let's go into the pub and I'll treat ye to a drink. We'll talk in there."

Power smiled at Marguerite, crooked an arm for her and picked up the valise with the other hand. "I'll tell you what," he suggested. "Let's go to the inn so Mistress Marguerite can sit with us." His friendly eyes twinkled. "I'll settle into my room first. Then I'll come down and order my dinner. In the meantime I'll treat ye to a drink, and we can talk." As they walked across the street to the inn, Power asked, "Mistress LeFleur, what brings you all the way from America to Ballygarrett?"

"Her father," Paddy said, his words definitely the closing of the subject. "Earl Randolph Taylor."

Before Power could remark, Marguerite launched into the explanation that had become part of her name since she'd come to visit her mother. "Actually Earl Taylor is only my father by marriage, Mr. Power. My mother recently married him. Do you know Mr. Taylor?"

"Aye," Power returned slowly, his eyes clouding with memories, "I know him. There be no Irish in these parts who don't know Earl Taylor." He stood for a moment longer in the middle of the street, looking in the direction of the manor house. "I've never forgotten him." He paused. "Nor his exploits."

"Now, lad," Paddy said, ably steering the conversation into another vein, "for the moment let's forget Earl Taylor. Get me a pint of stout to slack me thirst, and we'll talk about ye fer a little while, Jamie, me boy. Such as what brings ye back to County Wexford after so many years of absence?"

"Him," James quietly stated, delving into his pocket for a handkerchief. He smiled grimly as he wiped the perspiration from his face. "I promised that I would be back, Paddy. So here I am."

"Aye," Paddy said. "Now tell me why ye came back—the very reason."

"What I propose will be changing the complexion of County Wexford greatly. 'Twill be one method of breaking the iron yoke of English oppression." His eyes twinkled. "One that will require no Irish bloodshed."

Paddy chuckled. "To be sure, this sounds right interesting, Jamie boy. But it sounds to me like being in Mexico has caused ye to forget what your countrymen be like. I'm sure the boys of

Wexford will be glad to know that we can break the iron yoke of English oppression, but surely ye know they do like a good fight."

"Paddy," Marguerite called as the buggy jostled down the narrow, stone-covered road toward the manor house, "don't you think James Power is an interesting man?"

"Now, ma'am," Paddy drawled, lifting a hand, his fingers rasping through his beard stubble, "I don't know that I'd say James Power was interesting." Before Marguerite could make a reply, he added, "However, I will allow that he had some mighty interesting things to say—about that property the Mexican government is wanting him to settle with Irish immigrants. What did he call the place, ma'am?"

"Texas," Marguerite repeated softly. "It sounded beautiful, Paddy. Grassy plains and rich farmland. Thousands of acres to be had almost for the asking."

"Ah, lass," Paddy said, shaking his head, "that'd be any Irishman talking after a pint or two. I wouldn't go putting much stock in it. It can't be much good or the government wouldn't be giving it away."

"He's telling the truth, Paddy," she said. "It's a wonderful frontier not far from my home. Americans have been going there for the last ten years." Marguerite glanced at Bridget who sat quietly in her corner. Laying a hand on her arm, Marguerite asked, "And why are you so quiet, Bridget?"

Bridget turned her head and smiled. "I was just thinking, mum, about—about my coming trip to County Clare."

"Don't worry," Marguerite reassured her, "everything will be all right. I've already explained to Mr. Taylor, and he quite understands your need to be with your sister." Marguerite reached out and caught Bridget's hand, intertwining their fingers. "And I know for a fact that neither Jewel or Annie will mind waiting on both Mother and me. I'm not that much trouble."

"Oh, no, mum," Bridget replied quickly. "I love being yer maid. Ye'r wonderful to work for." She looked at Paddy. "I was just—just wondering who would be taking and picking up the laundry and ironing. Ye know how particular Mr. Taylor is about his shirts and—"

Marguerite laughed Bridget's worry away. She couldn't imagine Earl's dour housekeeper not having every facet of housework under thumb. "I'm sure that Mrs. Simmons will have someone that she can send who will inspect the laundry as closely as you do."

"To be sure," Bridget replied, "but Paddy and I help Mary gather her turf. She is all by herself, and—"

"If it'll set your mind at ease, I'll do it myself," Marguerite interrupted with a promise. "I'll have Paddy drive me so he can gather the turf." Raising her voice, she said, "Will that be all right with you, Paddy?"

Paddy grinned and nodded his head. "Yes, ma'am, to be sure it will. I likes getting out meself."

Bridget laughed softly at her uncle. She teased, "It's not getting out that ye like, Paddy. Ye have a soft spot for Mary O'Roarke."

Marguerite tensed and whispered, "O'Roarke."

Paddy said on soft laughter, "Now, Bridget, how do you be a'knowin' that!"

Before Bridget could answer her uncle, Marguerite asked, "Is—is Mary O'Roarke any relation to Sheridan O'Roarke?"

"To be sure." Bridget grinned and replied quickly. "His mother." Then she said to Paddy, "Mary O'Roarke herself is the only person you dress up for, Patrick McLeary."

As Paddy and Bridget indulged in gentle banter, Marguerite withdrew from the conversation. When she had volunteered to pick up the laundry, she hadn't known that Sheridan's mother was the washwoman. Remembering Sheridan's prophetic remarks about her coming to look him up, Marguerite wanted to renege from her promise to Bridget, but a person of her word, she was now bound. Still she knew what would happen if

65

she chanced to meet Sheridan while she was at his mother's home. He would smirk his victory.

Glancing at Marguerite, Bridget saw the frown on her mistress's face. "What's wrong, mum? Did we say something that upset you?"

"No," Marguerite hastily replied, shaking her head, searching for a plausible excuse for her preoccupation. "I—I was—thinking about tonight. I wish Mr. Taylor hadn't insisted on my accompanying him to the Reverend Denby's."

· "Ah," Bridget droned, her interest perking, "but he and yer mother thought it would be for the best, mum."

Marguerite nodded her head absently, the lowing of cattle in the distance catching her complete attention. She lifted her hand and shielded her eyes so she could see the riders who herded the cows. Sitting upright, pointing in the distance, she exclaimed, "Why, that's Lieutenant Clayborne!"

Bridget turned to look. "To be sure," she said.

"Why are he and his soldiers driving those cows?"

"Those be the tithing cows I tole ye about, ma'am," Paddy returned, moving the buggy to one side of the road so the soldiers and the herd could pass. "Looks like he got to 'em before the O'Roarke did."

"How do you know?" Marguerite asked, turning her nose at the putrid smell of burning flesh.

Paddy pointed to the large, capital T on their rumps. "That be the established church brand, ma'am."

When Nelson was even with the buggy, he doffed his hat and smiled. "What a pleasant surprise! I'm certainly happy that I'm getting to see you again so soon, Mistress LeFleur."

"Hello, Lieutenant Clayborne," Marguerite replied, her eyes moving from the dust-covered uniform to the lowing animals with the new brand on their flanks.

The officer looked embarrassed. "Tithing cattle," he responded to the silent question. Marguerite lifted a blank face, her eyes leveling with his. "All farmers must pay a tenth of their produce to the established church."

"All farmers?" she questioned, "Even those who do not belong to the established church?"

Nelson had never had his actions questioned in such a direct manner before, certainly not by a woman. As much as he liked Marguerite LeFleur, she unnerved him. Didn't she know that women were not to talk about business and politics? He squirmed uncomfortably in the saddle.

"After all, ma'am," he said cooly, "the established church is the Church of England."

"Granted," Marguerite agreed. "I'm not quibbling over the definition or the institution. But I was under the impression we were in Ireland, Lieutenant, not England."

Nelson swallowed his irritation and kept his stiff lips curved into a pleasant smile. His reply, however, was rather edgy. "I know how you Americans feel about us Englishmen, Mistress LeFleur, but you'll do well to remember that Ireland is under English rule. And as long as she is ours she will be governed by our laws." Nelson flipped his hat on and waved his company onward. "Politics are meant for men, Mistress LeFleur. And in the future you should remember this. I'm sure that your father—"

"Stepfather," Marguerite corrected impatiently, tired of people bestowing paternity on Earl Taylor.

Nelson contemplated her a minute before he nodded his head and amended his statement. "Your stepfather will agree with me on this."

Marguerite chuckled. "Are you telling me that I'm speaking out of turn, Lieutenant Clayborne?"

Nelson flashed Marguerite his most winsome smile, and his eyes glowed. His horse danced and pranced in a circle, eager to be off. "Not at all, ma'am. I'm sure you're not apprised of the true situation. Once you are, you'll see that what we're doing is for the betterment of this barbaric country." Looking at his men who were down the road a ways, he nudged his horse forward. Waving at Marguerite, he called, "Until tonight."

Two riders on a sloping hill, hidden from view behind thick

foliage, watched the exchange between the soldier and Marguerite with interest.

"An' what are you thinking?" the one asked, reaching up to push a shock of black hair off his forehead.

"Shane, my friend," the other said, his lips curving into a mischievous smile, "I think it's high time—in fact, it's past time that we paid Mr. Taylor a visit. I think we should join him for dinner tonight."

"That I wouldn't mind," Shane replied, his blue eyes darkening with interest, "but I don't think Mr. Taylor is going to be home. Rumor has it that he's dining with the Reverend Denby."

"Then perhaps we should see if we can't get an invitation to the Reverend Denby's." Sheridan chuckled. "You know, I have a hankering for some English religion."

"Aye," Shane replied, his eyes on Bridget. "I have a hankering, too, Danny Boy, but it's not for the cold, formality of English religion."

"I think you should pay your Bridget a visit tonight, and while you're there, I have a few other chores I'd like you to perform."

Shane chuckled. "I might have known that ye weren't exactly thinking about my feelings for Bridget."

Sheridan reached over and knocked Shane's hat off, ruffing his friend's hair. "You're really besotted with our little Bridget, aren't you now?"

Shane pulled a face and playfully slapped at Sheridan's hand, but he laughed, too. "Aye, Danny Boy, and I'm not the only one with lovesick notions. Both Gavin and I saw how ye looked at Marguerite LeFleur today in town."

Sheridan stretched, picking up Shane's hat without getting off his horse. Throwing it at his companion, he said, "You're right, lad, from the first time that I laid my eyes on her I liked what I saw, and I do have notions. Marguerite LeFleur is one of the fairest ladies I've ever seen, her eyes being the color of the Irish sky. And she's a mighty feisty woman." He reached up and pulled the brim of his hat farther over his face, shading it from the glare. "I'll wager, Shane, that Earl Randolph Taylor finds Marguerite LeFleur more to his liking than her mother." He gently pulled the reins, turning his horse. "I understand that Mrs. Taylor grows weaker each day. Wonder what will happen in the manor house should her illness prove to be fatal?"

Shane stopped straightening his hat, and he looked at Sheridan. The two of them were closer than brothers. As children they had played together; as young men they had joined their fathers in the fight for Irish freedom; together they had watched their fathers die. Ever since, they had been active in the resistance, leading a gang the public had nicknamed the Wexford Boys. Shane could read Sheridan's expressions.

"What are ye planning?"

Lapsing into fluent Gaelic, Sheridan said, "Taylor has taken everything from us, Shane. Because of him we Irishmen are now peasants, unable until recently even to rent or own property. You, Gavin, and I live on the run like outlaws. My mother works as a wash woman, washing and ironing Earl Randolph Taylor's clothes. Your and Gavin's mothers are dead."

"Aye," Shane murmured, unconsciously replying in Gaelic.

"I have waited a long time, Shane, and still I'm in no hurry. I will repay him in kind. I shall take Taylor's most prized possession from him."

"And ye think it be Marguerite LeFleur herself?"

"Aye," the O'Roarke murmured, his eyes on the buggy that disappeared over the hill, "and her fortune. I shall take both from him. Before he has her, I shall take her. I shall use any means necessary to keep him from getting her fortune. If he still wants her when I'm through with her . . ." He shrugged, letting his words ride the soft, summer breeze.

Chapter 4

"There, now, it's done." Bridget carefully fastened the last shining curl into the cluster on top of Marguerite's head. Standing back to survey her masterpiece with no small amount of pride, she asked, "What do ye think, mum?" As she waited for Marguerite's reply, she laid the comb on the dresser and wiped her hands down the striped apron that covered her dress.

"Oh, Bridget," Marguerite exclaimed, gazing at her reflection in the mirror, "My hair—my face—I've never looked so beautiful in all my life."

"Beautiful ye are without me or my help," Bridget said softly, pleased with Marguerite's compliment.

Transfixed, Marguerite marveled at the miracle Bridget had produced. Her hair was drawn into a chignon of curls on the crown of her head. The severity of the style was broken by the soft ringlets that wisped around her cheeks. Makeup accented her classical beauty, adding soft color to her face and enhancing the sparkling blue eyes.

Marguerite jumped to her feet and scampered across the room. Her white batiste petticoats, frilled with ruffled lace and embroidery, swished softly as she moved.

"An even yer chemise and petticoats," Bridget said, "are so beautiful they would pass for a morning dress."

"Indeed!" Marguerite chuckled. "Molly Fitzpatrick has

71

really proven herself, hasn't she?"

"Aye," Bridget replied, adding dryly, "but she was paid well enough by Mr. Taylor."

Knowing the path Bridget's thoughts were traveling, Marguerite cast her young maid an amused glance. But she ignored the implication, saying, "Help me with my dress."

The blue-violet creation of satin, taffeta, and silk softly caressed the air as she held it up. Taking the dress from her mistress, Bridget eased the skirt over Marguerite's head and held the top as Marguerite slipped her arms in the sleeves. Moving behind Marguerite, Bridget caught the bodice in both hands and hooked it together. As she did so, Marguerite ran her fingers over her midriff.

"Be glad that ye'r as slender as ye are, mum," Bridget said. "Molly didna have to put near the bone in this that she does for Mrs. Denby."

Marguerite giggled softly as she pirouetted in front of the full-length mirror in the corner of the room. Her eyes glistened, reflecting the purplish hue of the material that swirled around her.

"Mrs. Fitzpatrick is truly a talented seamstress and milliner," Marguerite declared, running gentle, appreciative fingers down the skirt, "and you're a wonderful hairdresser."

Marguerite lifted her hand and touched one of the ringlets that framed her face. As she stood there, she admired the full, bell-shaped evening gown that was heavily festooned with deep purple silk flowers. Imported from France, they were the same color as the wide sash around her waist. The low-cut, off-the-shoulder bodice flattered her long, slender neck and smooth shoulders. Purple elbow-length gloves accented her arms and drew attention to the short, puffed sleeves.

"Now, if ye'll be seated," Bridget said, "I'll put yer hat on ye."

Complying with all the obedience of a child, Marguerite returned to the vanity and sat on the velvet upholstered stool. Holding her breath in anticipation, she watched as Bridget picked up the delicate piece of satin, created to be a perfect match for her dress. Looking at Marguerite's reflection in the mirror, Bridget set the evening hat in place on the very back of Marguerite's head with one hand and fluffed the huge bow and large feathers that topped the crown with the other.

"Almost ye'r ready," Bridget announced as she firmly anchored the hat with a long, pearl-headed hat pin. Opening the jewelry box on the vanity, Bridget picked up the strand of pearls. "These are indeed beautiful," she breathed, turning them over in her hands.

"Thank you," Marguerite said, her gaze moving until they came to the large diamond. Her eyes glistened with tears. "A—a gift of love," she murmured, thinking of both Edouard LeFleur and Jordan Reeves. "My—my father gave them to me for my eighteenth birthday. The last gift he gave me before he died."

"I'm sorry, mum," Bridget apologized, fastening the circlet of pearls around Marguerite's neck, "I didn't mean to arouse painful memories."

"You didn't," Marguerite assured her. "I've gotten over the dark period of—of Papa's death. Now I have a tendency to remember only those golden moments—like he would have wanted me to."

Marguerite lifted her hand and touched the necklace, adjusting it so the diamond laid above the decolletage, always a reminder to her of Jordan's love.

Sorry she had introduced such a sad subject, Bridget quickly asked, "Do ye miss yer huge plantation in New Orleans?"

Marguerite laughed softly. "I—" A knock on the door interrupted her.

"Mistress Marguerite—" The harsh, grating voice carried through the heavy wood.

"Yes, Mrs. Simmons."

Unconsciously Marguerite sighed her displeasure when she answered. Without opening the door, she had no difficulty conjuring up the image of the housekeeper who stood outside her room. Elvira Simmons's thin, gray hair was pulled straight back from her forehead and pinned into a small knot on the back of her head. Her eyes were beady, her nose, large and crooked. He gaunt facial features were set in a continual frown. When Elvira talked, her enlarged larynx bobbed up and down. Marguerite found the woman altogether obnoxious.

"Mr. Taylor would like to see you in the library, please."

"All right. Tell him that I'll be right down. I'm going to check on Mother first."

"Isn't one of your maids with her?" Mrs. Simmons asked sharply. Every day that passed she liked the two black servants less.

"Yes," Marguerite answered, barely restraining her irritation. "But I want to check on her myself. I'll visit with her while Jewel and Annie are changing duties."

"Mr. Taylor wants you immediately."

Marguerite balled her hands and clenched them at her sides. She had never liked the housekeeper from the first moment she had set foot in the house, and as time passed she liked Elvira Simmons even less.

"Well?" Mrs. Simmons's question grated through the door, breaking the silence.

"Thank you for delivering Mr. Taylor's message, Mrs. Simmons." Marguerite forced a calm in her voice that she was far from feeling. "Tell Mr. Taylor that I'll come as soon as I can." *And not one second sooner*, her tone implied.

"Suit yourself," Mrs. Simmons snorted. "I'll relay your message to Mr. Taylor." Then she added viciously, "Word for word like you said it, Mistress LeFleur."

"Thank you, Mrs. Simmons." Breathing deeply and composing herself, Marguerite turned to Bridget. "I must hurry. Later I'll tell you all about New Orleans."

Bridget nodded, her eyes anxiously scanning Marguerite's face. "Is there anything special ye want me to do tonight?" she asked. "Like sitting with yer mother so Jewel and Annie can rest? I know they must be tired. And I know ye must be, too.

The three of ye, sitting with her around the clock, mum."

Tears misted Marguerite's eyes. Bridget's concern really touched her. "No, thank you, Bridget. Annie will stay with her. Neither she nor Mother would have it any differently."

"Mistress—" Bridget called as Marguerite moved to the door. Her hand on the knob, Marguerite turned. Bridget rubbed her hands together nervously. "I know it's worried ye be about yer mother, mistress, and I . . . well . . . I . . ."

Seeing Bridget's uneasiness, Marguerite asked gently, "What's wrong?"

"Mistress Marguerite, Mr. Taylor wouldn't want me to be a'tellin' ye this because he considers it old wives' tales, but I know a woman who can save yer mother's life." The words tumbled from Bridget's mouth. "She—she has the gift, mum."

"The gift?" came the tentative question.

Bridget nodded. "The—the gift of healing, mum. She knows the herbs and medicines, and she has the faith in God."

"Who is this woman?" Marguerite asked.

"Mary O'Roarke."

O'Roarke. *O'Roarke!*

The word whirled through Marguerite's brain with such violence she wanted to run. Instead she dropped her head so Bridget couldn't see the emotions that blatantly defied control and paraded across her face. Would she never escape the man? she wondered. Would she never forget his scathing smile and mocking green eyes? Only two weeks ago she had first heard the name—had first seen the man—now it seemed that she, through her mother, was inextricably bound to him and to his family. Finally when she had stilled her fast-beating heart, she cleared her throat.

"Thank you for telling me about Mrs. O'Roarke, Bridget. I'll speak to her about Mother when I take the laundry in the morning."

"Don't—don't tell Mr. Taylor that I'm the one who told ye about Mary O'Roarke's gift, mum. He—he would be unhappy with me."

"Don't worry about Mr. Taylor's reaction, Bridget." Marguerite smiled reassuringly. "He's as interested in her recovery as I am."

Bridget doubted that, but she only said, "To be sure, mum, but he doesn't hold with Mary's gift."

Marguerite chuckled. "He's a man of science, Bridget, so it's hard for him to believe in faith."

Bridget moved to where Marguerite stood. Laying a hand on Marguerite's arm, she said, "Please, Mistress Marguerite, don't tell Mr. Taylor that I'm the one who told ye about Mary." The dark eyes pleaded. "Please."

"I won't." Marguerite placed her hand on Bridget's, sealing the promise. The two women looked at each other, and in that second each knew friendship had been bonded. "Why don't you take the evening off?" Marguerite suggested. "I won't need you until morning."

Bridget beamed. "Thank ye, Mistress LeFleur. Ye'r so thoughtful and kind."

Smiling, Marguerite closed the door and hurried down the hall to Amanda's room. Gently she tapped on the door, awaiting the maid's soft command.

"Come in."

The door silently glided open, and Marguerite slipped into the dim room. She stood for a moment, her eyes growing accustomed to the darknes. A single candle flickered on the table beside her mother's bed, and heavy drapes barred the windows.

"Hello, Jewel," she greeted the buxom black woman who shoved out of the chair next to Amanda's bed. "How are you feeling?"

"I'se jest fine," Jewel answered, her large brown eyes, frankly admiring her young mistress. "Is dat Irish maid treating you kindly, honey chile?" Jewel peered into Marguerite's face, searching for the truth.

"Wonderful. In fact, she's quite spoiling me."

Jewel patted Marguerite's shoulder fondly. "You could do

wid some of dat."

"How's Mother?"

Looking at the small, feeble woman on the bed, Jewel shook her head.

Awaking from her drugged after-sleep, Amanda overheard the question. The sick woman laughed weakly, the frail sound barely reaching Marguerite's ears. "You should ask me, dear, not Jewel."

Amanda Taylor, dressed in a pale yellow nightgown, was propped up on two large down pillows. Emaciated and ravaged by her illness, only traces of her former beauty remained. Her hair, at one time a rich and shining brown like her daughter's, was now dull and lifeless. Parted in the middle, a heavy braid lay across one shoulder.

Sitting on the side of the bed, Marguerite leaned over and placed a kiss on the pale cheek. "How are you feeling, darling?"

Amanda smiled tightly, her eyes cloudy with a mixture of pain and laudanum. "I think I'm getting better," she lied, pressing her hand against her stomach, praying the pains would let up and give her respite.

"I wish you could go with us tonight." Marguerite pushed tendrils of graying hair off Amanda's forehead.

"I do, too," Amanda whispered. She licked her dry, cracked lips and mustered another smile. "I—I always loved parties. I'll go with you next time. Promise." She drew in a deep, ragged breath. "You look beautiful, darling."

Marguerite looked down at her dress. "Thank you, Mumsey." Her voice shook as she lapsed into childhood dialect. Amanda touched one of the bows on the sleeve. "Mrs. Fitzpatrick made it for me."

"She did a wonderful job," Amanda murmured, her hands rubbing the cool, blue-violet satin. "It reminds me of one that I—" As a sudden pain gripped her, she convulsed and groaned.

"Mother," Marguerite cried, "what can I do for you?"

In fluid motion Jewel leaped from the chair and ran to the

night table. Dipping a cloth in the water, she wrung it out and moved to the bed where she wiped the perspiration from Amanda's brow.

"It's all right now," Amanda breathed, slowly straightening out. "It's gone."

"Do you want me to stay with you?" Marguerite asked, an anxious frown creasing her forehead.

"No," Amanda said, rolling her head from side to side. "Earl wants you to go with him tonight, and I want you to go, too. He would be so disappointed. He—he—" Amanda gasped her words between shafts of pain. "He's so proud of you, darling." Marguerite said nothing; she only smiled. "Annie will sit with me. I seem to rest better when she's here. When I wake up late at night, she reads to me."

Amanda lifted weak, trembling hands and cupped Marguerite's face. "I want you to have a good time, darling. Enjoy yourself." Amanda grimaced as another spasm of pain racked her body. When she had caught her breath, she said, "You don't have to go back to Blossom Hall, darling. You don't—you don't have to endure Susanna's insults and accusations. You don't have to worry about anything. Earl assured me that this is our home—your home. He wants you to stay here with us, darling."

Although Marguerite had her doubts about Earl Randolph Taylor's reason for wanting them in his home, she nodded. She knew her mother believed every word she was uttering, and Amanda was too ill for Marguerite to disagree with her. But every day that Marguerite was in Ireland she had more questions and doubts about the man whom her mother had recently married.

"The pain is stronger than usual." Amanda's words were almost incoherent so thickened they were with her pain. "If you'll give me some of the laudanum, I think I'll go to sleep, dear."

Marguerite stood and moved to the table. Carefully she measured the medicine and gave it to Amanda. Afterward she sat on the edge of the bed and washed her mother's face with a cool, damp cloth until Amanda fell asleep. Jewel sat in the chair, her chocolate brown eyes diligently on both mother and daughter.

When the soft knock on the door shattered the quietness, Marguerite said, "Yes?"

"Mistress LeFleur, Mr. Taylor is quite impatient for you to join him in the library." Mrs. Simmons's voice was heavy with disapproval. "He would have me remind you that he has been waiting for more than an hour."

"Tell Mr. Taylor that I will be down as soon as Annie gets here to sit with Mother. I'll not leave her alone."

"Humph," Mrs. Simmons snarled, angry because she was talking to a closed door, angry because a snip of an American girl continually defied her authority. "I'll go find that colored woman and bring her up here right now."

Marguerite slid off the bed and rushed to the door. She opened it with a violence as great as her rush of words. "You'll do no such of a thing. Annie is not one of the house staff, Mrs. Simmons. I bought her with my own money, and I have given her her freedom. She is my mother's personal maid. Not you nor anyone else will say one word to her." She glared her defiance into the birdlike face. "Tell Mr. Taylor that I will be down in fifteen minutes." With that Marguerite turned and slammed the door. As quickly she yanked it open again. "You might remind him that Mother is his wife, and he ought to be up here sitting with her."

Elvira pulled to her full height. "Mr. Taylor sat with your mother all afternoon while you were out." She spat the words. "Your mother is the one who begged him to leave so he could get some rest." Turning, the housekeeper marched down the hall, never looking back.

Her anger evaporating as quickly as it had come, Marguerite wilted. She closed the door and leaned against it.

"Honey chile," Jewel said, "you know I'se don't mind staying here wif your mama till Annie comes. You go on down there with Massa Taylor. I shore don't want no trouble."

"There won't be any trouble," Marguerite replied, retracing her steps to the bed. "Besides I want to be with Mother some, and you need your rest. You sit with her all day; Annie at night."

"But Massa Taylor, he be—"

"Don't worry about Mr. Taylor," Marguerite said, throwing her arms around Jewel. "You answer only to me."

The two stood together, locked in an embrace of love and friendship; finally Jewel pulled away, patting Marguerite on the shoulder.

"I'll go get some rest, honey, and I'll send Annie up here, but you come get me if you need me."

"I will," Marguerite answered.

Before the old servant moved out of the room, she patted Marguerite on the shoulder again. Marguerite sat down in the chair, watching her mother's even breathing as she slept. She was still sitting there when the door opened, and Annie walked into the room, several books tucked under her arm.

"I'm sorry I'm so late, Miz Marguerite," the white-haired woman apologized. "I didn't know I was so tired until I tried to get up."

Marguerite smiled. "Don't worry about it. We'll work out a schedule so that we rotate days and nights. We'll take turns sitting up with her." Marguerite stood. She lifted the cover and tucked it under her mother's chin. "She likes for one of us to sit with her at night, so we can read to her."

Annie nodded, setting the books on the night table as she came to stand beside Marguerite. She looked at Amanda's face, relaxed and smiling in sleep. "She's always loved to read, Miz Marguerite. She taught me how when she was a little girl, and I was already a grown woman." The black woman's eyes misted with tears. "She began by reading to me; now I read to her." Marguerite put an arm around the woman and hugged her. Sniffing, Annie added, "She used to sit over there by the window and embroider while I read."

80

Unconsciously the two women looked at the forgotten frame in front of one window, everything exactly like Amanda had left it the last time she worked on her tablecloth.

"I don't want to go, but Mother insisted."

"That's right. You go on and try to enjoy yourself. I'll take care of your mama." The servant stepped back. "You look beautiful, Miz Marguerite. You remind me of your mama when she was a young girl." She smiled. "You'll turn plenty of heads tonight."

Marguerite laughed. "The evening doesn't sound as if it's going to be too thrilling."

She was interrupted by a knock on the door that was accompanied by a sharp reprimand. "Mistress LeFleur—"

Knowing she could postpone the inevitable no longer, Marguerite ran to the door and opened it. The quickness of her action stopped the staccato rapping. Never had Mrs. Simmons looked more like a biddy waiting for feeding. Her beaked mouth opened and shut several times in succession, the small beady eyes rounded, and she blinked rapidly in surprise.

"Thank you, Mrs. Simmons," Marguerite announced, sailing past her. "I'm on my way down now."

Recovering quickly, Mrs. Simmons spun on her heels. "I shouldn't be at all surprised but what Mr. Taylor isn't angry," she taunted, her larynx bobbing up and down as she spoke. Clumping down the hall, she brushed past Marguerite, arrogantly descended the stairs, and opened the library door. She heralded the young woman's entrance. "Mr. Taylor—"

Dressed in a black double-breasted tailcoat, a top waistcoat in bottle blue, and gray tight-fitting trousers, Earl Randolph Taylor stood in front of the opened French doors, a glass of whiskey in his hand. He turned at the sound of Mrs. Simmons's voice, his eyes quickly sliding over the dour woman who hovered in the opened door and lingered appreciatively on the lovely young woman who swept past the housekeeper into the library. He caught his breath. Marguerite was more beautiful than he had ever dreamed.

Although he was cold and austere, Earl Taylor was a strikingly handsome man. Looking at him, one would never guess he was in his late fifties. His silver hair was brushed in deep waves from his face, and his gray eyes were vibrant and alive. He was tall and lean, with trim waist and hips and unusually broad, muscular shoulders. Because of his youthful physique, he wore his clothes well, all of them custom made and the latest in fashion, imported from the continent. Walking to his reading table, he set the glass down.

A smile curling his full lips, he moved across the room, holding his hands out. "My dear," he softly intoned, his voice deep and resonant, "the wait was well worth it. You're a vision of loveliness." His hands captured hers, and he held them, longer than manners dictated. "I shall be the envy of every man at dinner tonight."

Irritated because he was infatuated with Marguerite and didn't upbraid the girl for her tardiness, Mrs. Simmons cleared her throat. "Is there—"

"No." Earl dismissed the housekeeper sharply, never taking his gray eyes off Marguerite's face. "There's nothing else tonight, Elvira. I'll see you in the morning."

When the door closed, Earl asked, "May I pour you a glass of sherry, Marguerite?"

"Please," she murmured, glad to put some space between them.

As he moved to the crystal decanters, Marguerite couldn't help but admire him; still she couldn't help but be wary of him, too. His attention—not parental in the least—was becoming more and more apparent. She walked to the opened door, breathing in the cool, spring air. When Earl walked up behind her, she turned quickly and took the glass. Skirting the intimacy which the sofa offered, she moved to the leather chair, one of a matched pair that sat in front of the fireplace.

"I'm worried about Mother," she said quietly, sitting down. "She's getting worse." She lifted the glass to her lips and sipped her drink. "When I was in town today, some of the

82

women who came into the shop were telling me that Mrs. O'Roarke has the ability to—"

"I've heard about Mrs. O'Roarke's gift," Earl interrupted smoothly, sitting down in the chair beside Marguerite, "but I don't put too much stock in local tales, Marguerite, and neither should you." He smiled, dismissing Mary O'Roarke from the conversation. "I'll be the first to admit that I've been remiss concerning your mother's health."

He leaned back, crossing his legs. "I tried to persuade Amanda to see a physician, but she refused. And I didn't argue with her." His hands moved in a beseeching gesture. "To be perfectly honest, my dear, I thought your mother was suffering from an acute case of homesickness." He smiled. "And you were the remedy, I thought."

"I'm afraid not," Marguerite sighed.

"No," Earl exclaimed, shaking his head in self-frustration and regret. "Since you've been here, I've been so caught up in affairs of state." He paused, and when he spoke again his voice was throbbing with recrimination. "I shouldn't have listened to her, Marguerite. I realize that now, and after visiting with her all afternoon, I took matters into my own hands. I sent word to my personal physician, Dr. Cable. He'll be here tomorrow to examine her."

Pushing her misgivings aside, Marguerite laid her hand on Earl's. "Thank you," she whispered, tears misting her eyes. "Thank you for caring so much for Mother. She's—she's all I have. Both Papa and Grandmother are dead . . ." Marguerite paused, regaining her composure.

Earl looked at the beautiful hand that splayed creamy white over the black coat sleeve. He lifted his other hand and placed it over hers, pressing her soft, warm flesh between his. "And you, my dear," he added softly, lifting his face to gaze into her eyes, "must remember, I care for you."

The warmth of his voice and the intimacy suggested by his gaze startled Marguerite. When he leaned forward to press his lips on her forehead, she jerked her head back and blinked in surprise. Seeing her sudden fright and withdrawal, Earl smiled, the gesture totally disarming and paternal. He patted her hand and laid it back on her lap.

"Now, my dear, at your mother's request, I bought you a gift."

"Another gift?" Marguerite exclaimed, a hint of exasperation in her voice. "But you shouldn't have, Mr. Taylor. You've already bought me so much."

"Not Mr. Taylor," he gently chided. "Call me Earl." When Marguerite didn't immediately repeat his name, Earl said, "Amanda and I discussed this, Marguerite, and we agreed that it would be impossible for me to try to replace your father." Inwardly Earl shivered; he abhorred the thought of Marguerite considering him in such a light. "And neither do I want our relationship to be so formal that you call me Mr. Taylor all the time." He smiled. "So Amanda and I agreed that you should call me Earl." Marguerite nodded, forcing herself to say his name.

Delighted to get his way, Earl turned. Smiling to himself, he walked across the room to a door behind his desk. Opening it, moving into the small room, he unlocked his strongbox, taking something out. When he again stood in front of Marguerite, he held out a beautiful necklace.

"I had the dress made to match these stones," he said, holding the vibrant jewels next to her satiny skin.

"I can't," Marguerite gasped. "I—I just can't."

"Of course you can." With dictatorial curtness, Earl sloughed her arguments aside, and as was becoming his favorite tool of persuasion, he used Amanda. "Your mother and I discussed it. Here," he said, his hands going to her neck, "let me unfasten these pearls, so you can wear my jewels."

But this time Marguerite was not to be persuaded, no matter what her mother wanted. "No." She jerked her head away from his touch and jumped to her feet so fast she dropped her half-filled glass of sherry. Her hand flew to her pearls, her fingers curling protectively around the diamond. "I won't."

Her cry turned to an apologetic whisper. "My father gave me these, Mr. . . . ." Seeing the reprimand in his eyes, Marguerite groped for the unfamiliar name and finished lamely. "Earl." She implored him to understand. "I appreciate all you've done for me—taking me in with no questions asked after all that Susanna's accused me of, the clothes—" She waved her hand toward the necklace that hung from Earl's fingers. "The gifts, but—I can't accept your jewels."

The smile never left Earl's lips, but his eyes turned glassy and cold. He disliked being thwarted. He wanted no one, absolutely no one—not even Marguerite's dead father or mother—to come between him and her. Ever since he had first seen Marguerite in New Orleans, he had wanted her, but at the time he was already engaged to Amanda. Besides he hadn't thought she fit into the scheme of things. On his honeymoon he had learned how wrong he had been. At Amanda's remarriage the plantation reverted to the most direct LeFleur heir, which was Marguerite. The moment Earl learned of Marguerite's inheritance he had begun to plan and to scheme anew.

Once he and Amanda were settled in Ireland, he convinced Amanda to write Marguerite, asking her to join them. When that hadn't proved fruitful, Earl had underhandedly joined in the persuasion. Intercepting all Amanda's mail and reading it first, he had particularly enjoyed the letters which Susanna Reeves, the invalid mistress of the adjoining plantation, had written. Without Amanda's knowledge, Earl had taken advantage of Susanna's bitterness and jealousy. He had written to her, subtly watering and feeding the seeds of doubt in her suspicious mind about a growing love affair between Jordan and Marguerite.

Not knowing Marguerite, Earl wrongly figured that she would never again show her face in New Orleans after the way Susanna had defamed her. He thought she would flee in shame, but he'd learned that Marguerite was a fighter. She didn't run from rumors and gossip. Then he had switched tactics. Only when he began to intimate Amanda's illness did he gain Marguerite's attention and response. Now that she was here, that ultimate possession was within his grasp, Earl didn't intend to lose her.

"I'll return the jewels to the strongbox, my dear, for right now, but we'll discuss your acceptance of them another time," he eventually averred, breaking the long, tense silence. Lowering his lashes, he dipped his head curtly as he returned to the desk. The click of the jewelry case resounded through the otherwise silent room.

Marguerite stood, rushing across the library. She laid her hands on his arm. In no way could she anger Earl. At the moment her future, and her mother's as well, was in his hands. Until Marguerite decided what she was going to do with her life and until Amanda was well again and could be moved, they had to have Earl Taylor's friendship.

"Please, Earl," she beseeched, her eyes wide. "Please understand. I'm not ungrateful."

Earl smiled. He captured her tiny hands in his, and he squeezed reassuringly. "I quite understand, my dear." He leaned forward, this time pressing dry, cold lips on her forehead. "Forgive me for moving too fast with you." His hand began to shake with the intensity of his emotions. "I—I have never felt about another individual as I do you."

Marguerite inwardly recoiled from his touch, but she didn't act rashly. Slowly she pulled away, looking at him with illuminated, rounded eyes. She smiled. "It'll—it'll take me a little while to accept you as my—as my father."

Earl momentarily stiffened, but eventually he laughed. "What a sweet child you are," he murmured. "So full of innocent delights. I have never met anyone like you before, Marguerite."

"Nor I you," Marguerite returned, lowering her lashes so he couldn't read the disgust in her eyes.

She gently tugged her hands loose and stepped back. Although she didn't let him know it, Marguerite knew that parental affection was not Earl Taylor's declaration or intention. Having married Amanda wasn't enough. He wanted her, too—he wanted her as a man wants a woman. His mistress? Her question unanswered and plaguing her, she moved away from him. Her gaze swept to the circular stain and the empty crystal goblet.

"I'm sorry I spilled the sherry," she apologized.

"Don't worry about it," Earl said dismissively. "I'll tell Mrs. Simmons about it on our way out." Hearing a noise at the window, Marguerite abruptly turned. "What's wrong?" Earl asked.

Never taking her eyes from the softly billowing curtains, Marguerite shook her head. "I thought I heard something."

Surprise flashed across Earl's face. He rushed to the door, opened it and stepped into the garden. After he looked around, he returned to the library. He needed Hibernia's help in apprehending the O'Roarke, but it frightened him to think the man was always lurking about, his presence never seen, only felt. A scowl distorting Earl's face, he turned, retracing his steps. Before Marguerite could see his irritation, he smiled.

"Nothing that I can see. Probably just a cat." He closed and locked the door; then he moved to the desk and picked up his gloves and top hat. "Shall we go, my dear? We don't want to keep the Denbys waiting, do we?"

Chapter 5

The lanterns glowed brightly, illuminating the elegant interior of the carriage as the huge vehicle bounced over the rocky road to the reverend's home. Irritated with himself because he had moved too quickly with Marguerite, Earl kept the conversation light and desultory. A wonderful host, he whiled away the miles, entertaining Marguerite with humorous stories that kept her chuckling during the ride.

Her misgivings once again pushed to the back of her mind, Marguerite enjoyed Earl's company and his conversation. When they arrived at Reverend Denby's home, she was awed by the elegance. The Georgian-styled mansion glowed with imported chandeliers and colorful flowers. Unlike the manor house which was comfortable and functional with a beauty and graciousness that reflected the land and the people itself, the Denby's home was definitely continental with exquisite ceilings, delicate furniture, rich hangings and treasures from all over Europe.

"Good evening, Earl." Like a vulture, Luella Denby swooped down upon them. "I'm so glad you could make it." She turned to Marguerite, her watery eyes critical and disapproving. "And you, my dear, we're so happy to have you. We've heard so much about you."

"Thank you for including me in your invitation, Mrs.

Denby," Marguerite softly intoned. "I'm happy to be able to come in my mother's stead."

"Of course, my dear," Luella simpered dismissively, turning to Earl. "How is Amanda?"

"She seems to be getting worse," he replied. "I've sent word to Cable. He's to come examine her tomorrow."

Because etiquette demanded, Earl stood conversing with his hostess, but as quickly as he could, he excused himself and Marguerite so they could mingle with the other guests. Proud of Marguerite and acting as if she were a prized possession on display rather than a person in her own right, Earl kept her by his side as he introduced her. Although she was irritated with Earl's proprietary manners, Marguerite went through the motions of civility: She exchanged greetings and polite conversation with a smile.

As they approached Nelson Clayborne, resplendent in his dashing uniform, Earl said, "Nelson, I'd like for you to meet Amanda's daughter, Marguerite LeFleur."

Nelson smiled into Marguerite's eyes. "Ah, Mistress LeFleur." He caught Marguerite's extended hand in his, and he bowed low, his lips touching, lingering on the soft material. "So we meet again. What a pleasant surprise."

Earl's face swung accusingly to Marguerite. His tone was harsh. "You've met Lieutenant Clayborne?"

"This afternoon, as a matter of fact," Nelson said, straightening up. "I had the pleasure of meeting your stepdaughter in Ballygarrett."

"Ah, yes," Earl murmured, his finger pressed against pursed lips. "When you went to Mrs. Fitzpatrick's to see about the bonnet to match your new dress, my dear."

Again as soon as etiquette deemed proper, Earl propelled Marguerite to the other side of the room, keeping distance between her and Nelson. Both Marguerite and Nelson smiled. Earl's jealousy was causing him to behave badly and conspicuously.

Standing next to a middle-aged man of medium height, Earl

said, "Marguerite, I'd like for you to meet Brice and Martha Stanton. Brice is the owner on the property next to mine."

Breaking her gaze with Nelson, Marguerite turned to the couple, whom she immediately liked. Brice's face was wreathed in a smile, and his eyes twinkled mischievously. In an unconscious gesture, he ran his hand over his balding head. Martha was a small, slender woman who dressed in the latest fashion. Her ecru satin gown and hat complemented the black hair that was pulled into a chignon of curls on the nape of her neck.

In a deep voice that was unusually soft and friendly, Brice said, "Martha and I are so glad to see two beautiful women gracing Taylor's home after so many years."

"And you must come see me, my dear," Martha warmly added. "I would love to sit and visit with you."

After a succulent meal—no less than seven courses—turbot, patridges, chicken, veal, mutton, and lobster all in one sitting—the small group retired to the drawing room. Congregated at one end, the men discussed business in low tones; the women at the other end pretended to talk about the latest fashions.

But the women's conversation crept to the political activities in the community, and Marguerite soon learned these inevitably centered on Sheridan O'Roarke. The youngest woman present and the newest one to Ireland, Marguerite leaned back in her chair, listening more than joining the discussion. Allowing her thoughts to roam outside the cramped social circle of the Denbys, she looked around the room.

She saw the butler swing open the doors and head directly for Wilbur Denby. The servant's face was creased with frustration, and his movements were agitated and nervous. He whispered in the reverend's ears. Denby jumped up from his chair, his entire body twitching in agitation. He looked from Earl to Brice and back again.

"What's wrong?" Brice asked.

Denby pointed a shaking finger at the door. "The—the O'Roarke is . . ." His squeaky voice shook as much as his finger. "The O'Roarke is here. He wants to see you and Brice."

Brice smiled and shrugged. "If Earl doesn't mind, I have no objection."

Earl slowly rose and moved to stand behind his chair, his hands resting on the back. Brice left him no alternative. He nodded, saying curtly, "Send him in."

The butler had hardly moved through the door before the tall, broad-shouldered giant swept past him, arrogantly sauntering into the salon, his polished knee-high boots clicking against the wooden floor, alerting everyone to his presence.

"Good evening, Reverend Denby. Please pardon the intrusion, but I needed to see Taylor on important business."

Sheridan O'Roarke's baritone voice, stripped of its country vernacular, was now polished and sophisticated. He smiled, looking first at Brice, then at Earl. The green eyes flickered to Nelson who stood between Earl and Denby.

"Good evening, Lieutenant Nelson."

"Good evening."

Nelson's eyes narrowed; his lips thinned, but he behaved with military decorum. Nothing would he enjoy more than arresting O'Roarke and seeing him grovel for mercy instead of arrogantly swaggering around, defying legal authority. One of these days he would, Nelson promised himself, have the evidence to prove what he suspected: that Sheridan was a traitor.

Unable to resist the taunt, Nelson said, "I guess you heard how we handled the rebellion at Bunclody."

"Rebellion?" Sheridan returned laconically, his gaze slowly shifting around the room. "Hardly a rebellion. A few men wanting to get their milch cows back. But to answer your question, Lieutenant, I did hear about it. You know how news like that gets around in the pubs."

Marguerite was unable to take her eyes off Sheridan. He was devastatingly handsome. His hair was brushed back from his face in deep, subdued waves. He wore tan buckskin breeches that fit like a second skin and black Wellington boots. His jacket was made of emerald green velvet, his waistcoat buff-colored satin, both accenting his chest and shoulders. His white shirt had a high collar coming up to cheek level, and the cravats were low, making a double band around the neck.

"My men were attacked by that—that mob of peasants—" Nelson gritted, angry at the way Sheridan manipulated people by the force of his presence.

"That wasn't the way I heard the story," Sheridan interrupted smoothly, shifting his gaze to Nelson. "I heard tell that your soldiers killed seventeen unarmed men who were trying to get their milch cows back." He shrugged. "Of course, I heard the tale in the pub."

Losing interest in Clayborne and the story, Sheridan's eyes moved, and before Marguerite knew what was happening, before she could avert her gaze, Sheridan had locked his to hers. Although she saw the mockery in the depth of those eyes, she refused to break the stare; she refused to quell before the man. She would never give him the pleasure of knowing how much he affected her.

Unable to endure the silence that had settled on the room, Denby pointed a long, skinny finger at Sheridan and shrilled, "Those cows belong to the government, O'Roarke."

"Do they now?" Sheridan softly intoned, never taking his eyes off Marguerite.

"Of course, they do!"

Not listening to Denby, Sheridan's eyes slowly, caressively slid down the length of Marguerite's body, lingering on the tiny point of the slipper that peeped from beneath the hem of her gown. As slowly as it had come down, the gaze moved upward to the highest feather of her evening hat. When O'Roarke finally looked into her face again, he lowered an eyelid in an audacious wink.

"Can't you see what he's doing?" Earl barked, his gaze traveling the fiery path from Sheridan's face to Marguerite's.

He gripped the back of the chair so hard his knuckles whitened. Blood rushed to his face. "He's baiting us, playing on our emotions. He came here to start an uproar."

"Nay, Earl Randolph Taylor," Sheridan softly drawled, his eyes moving to the large diamond that rested so evocatively in the vee of Marguerite's decolletage. "I didn't come to create an uproar. I came to take care of business. I went to your house, but your housekeeper told me that you were dining with the reverend, so I came over here."

"Out with it, O'Roarke," Earl snarled. He despised the way Sheridan O'Roarke was publicly leering at Marguerite. He despised the way O'Roarke was toying with him. "What did you wish to see me about?"

"The tithing cattle which your men collected today." Sheridan paused before he added, "Two days early, wasn't it, Earl?"

Earl shifted his weight uneasily. "We—we heard a rumor that the cows were in danger of being stolen."

Sheridan hiked a brow and shook his head. "You can't be too careful in these troublesome times, now, can you? But, of course, you did realize that the cattle belonged to the tenants till the day after tomorrow."

Despising O'Roarke for calling him to task in front of so many witnesses, Earl said, "I was protecting government property, and—" He paused, collecting his thoughts and his wits. "And I was protecting my tenants. If the cattle had been stolen, the tenants wouldn't have been able to pay their taxes."

"No matter how good your intentions, Taylor," Sheridan softly reminded him, "the milch cows shouldn't be government property until day after tomorrow."

Aware of the tension between O'Roarke and Marguerite, Earl snarled, "I can't prove it, but I know that you're behind this tithing rebellion in County Wexford, Sheridan O'Roarke." Earl barely controlled his temper. His face was red, and his eyes smoldering. "One of these days I'll get the evidence I need to prove you an outlaw, to prove you a traitor to the crown, and when I do, mark my words, you're going to hang."

"Don't be making promises that you can't keep, Earl," Sheridan chided as though he were speaking to a child. "You haven't been able to prove anythin' on me yet."

With fluid grace he walked across the room. Taking a small leather bag from his coat pocket, he pulled the strings. The bag open, he held it upside down, letting coins of all denominations splatter against the tabletop, some rolling onto the floor.

"I have come to make you an honest offer for some of your cattle to replace those which you're so kindly protecting for your tenants." Sheridan paused, his gaze moving from Earl to Denby to Clayborne. "English money in return."

"Some of my cows!" Earl exclaimed.

"Aye," Sheridan calmly replied. "I can't very well be buying back the ones you took today. Your efficient Lieutenant Clayborne has already placed the church's mark on them." He chuckled. "And every Irishman in the world knows they're holy property now, Earl. With that huge T on their flanks we can do nothing with them." His face a mask of innocence, he added, "That holy T makes them unfit for barbaric infidels like us Irish peasants."

Brice Stanton laughed loudly. He looked from Earl, to Denby, to Sheridan. When it was evident that Earl was not going to answer, he said with relish, loving to iterate Earl's impulsive stupidity, "The man has come to you with an honest offer. In fact, with the only solution to the situation which now exists. O'Roarke's paid you the taxes in specie, so you must return the peasant's milch cows. But you can't return the same cows because they boast the church's brand." Again Brice chuckled, thoroughly enjoying Earl's discomfort. "Next time don't be so impulsive and anticipate your renters."

Sheridan's smile softened. He liked Brice Stanton. Although an Englishman, Stanton was honest. He was kind and generous to his tenants, and all through the years when the Roman Catholic church had been sorely oppressed, he had built a small building on the back of his manor and allowed his tenants to worship.

Still Earl didn't respond. Frowning and rubbing his hand over his head, Brice asked, "What more do you want, Earl?"

"Aye," Sheridan mocked, "what more do ye want, Earl?" Knowing he had lost the battle to the O'Roarke, Earl shrugged. "Come to the house tomorrow—"

"I'd like for us to sign an agreement of purpose tonight," Sheridan interjected. "That's why I interrupted your dinner. I wanted witnesses to the transaction. That way none of us can back out of the deal. I'll give the money to Brice, and he can come with the tenants tomorrow to select the cows, and you'll give each one of them a bill of sale."

"I'll select the cows," Earl thundered.

"Nay," Sheridan answered. "The tenants will make their own selection, and Brice will be sure that you charge a fair market price." O'Roarke turned to Brice. "What are they getting in England for beef?"

"You have no right," Earl hissed, his eyes venomous.

"Nay, Earl, you're the one who made the mistake," Sheridan reminded him. "You acted too hastily on this one."

"You're the one who started the rumor to make me think that the cattle were going to be stolen," Earl snarled.

Sheridan chuckled. "You shouldn't be so quick to listen to rumors, Earl."

"Come," Brice said, leading the way out of the salon. "Let's go into the library where we can discuss the details in private."

As soon as the men had disappeared through the doors, gossip buzzed through the women's lips in sandpaper undertones. Marguerite knew nothing, so she was permitted to listen in peace. But listen, she didn't. Her turbulent thoughts were centered on the fiery-headed giant who had so arrogantly disrupted the evening.

Thirty minutes later Earl returned to the salon. "Come, dear," he briskly addressed Marguerite. "We must go."

"Have you finished?" Marguerite asked, peering around

him for a sign of O'Roarke's return.

"As far as I'm concerned, I'm finished. I have an important meeting to attend tomorrow at Wexford, so I'm leaving early."

"Is the—" Marguerite paused. She almost said O'Roarke's name, and with Earl in his present state of mind she knew that would be a dire mistake on her part. "Is the man going to come pick his cattle up in the morning?" she asked nonchalantly.

"No," Earl said, again conceding defeat. "Brice and the tenants will pick them up."

The good-byes said, Earl and Marguerite climbed into the carriage and headed home. Although she was bubbling with curiosity about O'Roarke, Marguerite harnessed her inquisitiveness. Sitting across from Earl, she watched the light of the swaying lantern as it played across his face. For a moment she pitied him. He looked like a spent, old man.

Sighing deeply, he lifted his head and looked across the coach at her. "I'm sure you're wondering, my dear, about the man who disrupted our lovely evening."

Marguerite smiled, thinking that it was more Earl's lovely evening that had been disrupted than hers. With O'Roarke's arrival, her evening had livened up.

"He's a militant Irishman," Earl murmured, "determined to overthrow the government. He hates me in particular, and he goes out of his way to thwart me and to harass me in public." Earl's fingers curled around the edge of the seat as he thought of his humiliation at the hands of the O'Roarke.

"Why does he hate you?" Marguerite asked.

"Because—" Earl felt the speed of the carriage slacken. Scooting over, he pulled the curtain aside, shoved his head through the window and called to Paddy, "Why are you slowing down?" By the time he completed his question, the coach came to a jarring halt, and masked riders approached from all sides.

"Because, Earl Randolph Taylor, we have need of yer services." A black, hooded cape swallowing him, one of the riders opened the carriage door and pointed a pistol in Taylor's face. "I think it would be in yer best interests, Mr. Taylor, to disembark."

Frightened of the sinister-looking bandits, Marguerite cringed into the upholstery.

"Of all the gall!" Earl snapped.

"More than you possess," the highwayman mocked, the cold, gray barrel resting on Earl's cheek. "We Wexford boys are a braver lot than you, Earl Taylor! Now out of the carriage."

Quietly Earl set foot on the ground. Without moving, Marguerite stared through her window at the two riders who sat on their horses, their guns pointed at her.

"Now," the voice said to Earl, "give me all yer money."

Earl thrust his hand into his coat pocket. "I don't have much with me," he began, extracting a handful of bills.

"I know exactly how much ye have," the man said, "so it'll pay ye, Earl Taylor, to be honest with me."

"Be sensible," Earl spewed. "I wouldn't be carrying a large sum of money on me to a dinner party."

Marguerite's attention was diverted from Earl when she heard the soft click of her carriage door opening. She turned her head, fright written on her ashen face.

"Sorry, ma'am," another masked highwayman apologized softly as he lightly settled his large frame next to hers. A smile in his deep, throaty voice, his brogue heavy, he added in a voice that was strangely familiar, "I have a desperate need of money. Ye see, my kind of business requires it." He chuckled softly at his own witticism.

"Don't you dare touch her," Earl shouted, lunging for the door.

The first highwayman caught Earl by the shoulder and hauled him back. The man inside the coach moved closer to Marguerite, lazily sinking into the thick, luxuriant upholstery. "Search him, lad. See what he has concealed in all those clothes. He may be lying to us."

"I'm telling the truth," Earl shouted.

The outlaw's gun barrel lowered to the waistcoat, tapping the top button.

"I don't have any more money on me," Earl repeated, his voice shrill, almost hysterical. "Take me to my house, and I'll open my strongbox to you if it's money you're after."

"No need," the man in the carriage answered. "We've already been there. I found some beautiful jewels, and—" As he began to describe the contents of Earl's strongbox item by item, Earl groaned and angrily lunged toward the carriage a second time and was as easily hauled back. Unperturbed, the man ordered, "Now, Taylor, let me see if you have a money belt tied around your waist."

His face burning with anger and humiliation, Earl slowly stripped off his jacket, dropping it to the ground. He unbuttoned his top waistcoat, then the under vest. Trembling hands unfastened the white bow-tie neckcloth.

"Please," Earl begged, holding his hands out in a supplicating gesture.

Marguerite cringed as she heard Earl's begging. Not only were the highwaymen stripping him of his clothes, they were divesting him of his integrity. She wouldn't stand idly by and allow them to do this. Forgetting her own plight and fears, she shoved forward.

"Leave him alone," she shouted.

The man in the carriage caught her by the shoulder and gently pulled her back. "To be sure, boys, she has spirit. That's more than Taylor has." Although the bandit laughed at Marguerite, the gravelly tones, muffled by the mask, lauded her courage. He shoved her against the plush padding of the seat; then he whispered in her ear, his warm breath splaying against her ear. "In truth, lass, if we don't search him, my boys will insist that we search you. With him we're searching for money. With you—" He shrugged and paused for a moment before his hand went to her neckline, gently tracing the path of the lace ruffle over her breasts. "Now me I don't mind."

Trembling her rage, Marguerite slapped his hand away.

"You're despicable."

"Utterly," the highwayman answered.

The bandit outside the coach tapped Earl's shirt buttons. "Let's see what's under this embroidered linen shirt, Mr. Taylor."

Gritting his teeth, his lips pressed firmly together, Earl unbuttoned his shirt. When he didn't immediately slip out of it, the man poked his pistol barrel under one side and picked it up. "What's this?" he muttered.

"It's not a money belt," Earl growled, slapping the man's hands away.

"Now if ye would look, me darlin's!" Gusty laughter sounded through the quiet, spring night. The outlaw slipped his gun into the waistband of his trousers. Taking both hands, he slid Earl's shirt off his shoulders. Letting the material fall to the ground, he pushed Earl closer to the lantern so that he was fully illuminated in the night. "Look, boys," the bandit shouted, pointing to the basque that hung over Earl's shoulders with quilted chest and shoulder pads.

"Is that his money belt?" another called curiously.

"Nay," the masked rider returned, his eyes lowering as he peered closer at the boned cotton around Earl's midriff. "Blessed Mother of God!" he cried, stepping back, his voice lifting with incredulity. "'Tis a corset, lads. A corset such as me dear wife wears." He couldn't believe his eyes. He iterated for the third time. "The man is wearing two corsets! One to make his waist smaller; another to make his chest and shoulders bigger and broader. Why, boys, his chest and shoulders are the kind you take off at night and put on in the morning. Holy Mother of God," he exclaimed, "I never have seen such a sight in all me born days!"

The man's surprise was so genuine that Marguerite couldn't keep a smile from touching her lips. When she heard the strange sound coming from the top of the carriage, she knew that Paddy was laughing. Consumed with hatred for the O'Roarke, Earl was no longer aware of the sounds and people

100

around him. The flame of revenge burned hotter and brighter.

"No wonder he presents such a fine figure; all padding and no brawn," another mocking voice added. "Like his carriage, I suppose his muscle was all imported from the Continent."

"I guess you were right, Taylor," the bandit in the carriage drawled boredly. "You don't have a money belt on." He dismissed Earl with a casual wave of his hand. "Take him away," he ordered, his hands moving to Marguerite's waist. Although she twisted, she couldn't pry herself loose from his grip. "Far enough that he can't see, but not so far he can't hear all that's being said and imagine what's being done." The highwayman laughed softly, the sound full of delightful anticipation.

"How dare you!" Marguerite hissed.

"I dare." He grinned beneath the mask, and although Marguerite couldn't see the gesture, she could feel his amusement. "And you like."

"You don't know what I like," Marguerite declared.

"Aye," he murmured, "I know what you like."

"If—if I had a weapon," Marguerite warned him, sounding far braver than she felt, "you wouldn't take advantage of me like this. I would—"

Her heart pounded so loudly she knew he could hear it. She knew the man behind the mask; she recognized him—the strength, the audacity, the magnetism between them. She understood his cunning, and she knew they were playing a dangerous game.

"And do you know how to use a weapon?" The bandit queried, his words thickly laced with laughter.

"Quite well, my lord highwayman," Marguerite announced proudly. "I have a well-rounded education. I can ride a horse and shoot a gun with the best of men."

Through the thick folds of the material, Marguerite saw the man shake his head. After a while she heard him say, "I'm not interested in what you can do with the best of men, lass. I'd like to know if you can do anything with the best of women."

Anger blinded Marguerite to fear or reason. She lunged toward him, lifting her hands to claw him, but the bandit caught both her wrists. "Given the chance," Marguerite grunted, "I would kill you."

Holding her writhing body close to his, he laughed, and Marguerite wilted against him. "Nay."

"Please," Marguerite begged, unnerved by his presence and his touch, "get out and leave us alone. Can't you see that we don't have any money on us?"

"No specie perhaps," the bandit corrected, his voice still low and muffled but lacking in Irish dialect. "But perhaps you have something I could take in trade."

His grip slackened, and Marguerite pulled away from him. Reaching out a gloved finger, he traced the necklace that hung around her neck, lightly touching the creamy span of skin that pillowed the jewels. Unobtrusively he moved closer to her, pushing her farther into the corner of the carriage. Marguerite, mesmerized by those shaded eyes, by that resonant voice, didn't recoil from his touch. Her breath caught in her chest, and her lungs hurt; they felt as if they would burst any second.

"What—what do you mean? Something I could give you in trade?" Her voice was breathy with fear.

"Innocence or pretense," the bandit murmured. "I haven't figured out which yet, but I shall find out . . . soon."

He didn't unfasten the necklace; rather his finger, outlining each of the perfectly shaped pearls, finally reached the diamond that nestled in the vee of her decolletage.

"Until I find out, ma'am," he quietly vowed, the words sensually drugging Marguerite, "I will explain so that there is no doubt whatsoever of my intentions."

He leaned even closer, lifting the bottom edge of his mask. Before Marguerite fully realized that he was putting his words into action, the bandit softly pressed his lips on hers. Quickly galvanizing into motion, Marguerite insinuated both arms between them, pushing her fists against his chest. The man was as quick; again he caught both her wrists in one hand and moved her hands; then both his arms banded her body, locking her arms to her side, pulling her against the broad width of his chest, blatantly introducing her to the needs and desires that raged through him.

Refusing to give in to the man and his demands, Marguerite clamped her teeth together, closed her lips, and twisted her head from side to side. Her protests were rendered nothing more than muffled moans, and her resistance bruised her lips.

"Nay, lass," the man finally murmured, lifting his mouth, "this will never do." Relaxing his hold, he turned slightly, bringing Marguerite's body into even closer contact. He caught her around the waist, his hands slowly moving up until they cupped the fullness of her breasts. "A kiss I have need of, and a kiss I must have—I will have."

Tears of frustration burned Marguerite's eyes. Fighting the traitorous emotions that surged through her body, she used every ounce of her strength to push against the bandit, her hand sliding down his chest.

"And if you won't give me one willingly," he murmured, easily overpowering her, "then I'll take it."

Marguerite twisted her head from side to side, evading his touch, but the man's fingers wadded in the hair at the nape of her neck, and he stilled her movements. As his firm lips settled on hers, the outlaw pressured Marguerite into the seat, his body stretching beside hers. The one hand held her prisoner, the other hand roamed at will over her midriff, stopping to cup her breast.

When his fingers touched the sensitive tip that throbbed against the confines of the material, Marguerite gasped, unwittingly opening her mouth to a deeper invasion of his lips and tongue. Her fighting futile, Marguerite retreated to passivity, but even that tactic proved ineffective. Her body warmed and glowed to his gentle touches; her lips softened and pouted, her breasts swelled beneath his tutelage. As the heat of his passion and the fire of his determination melted her flagging resistance, Marguerite's arms slowly circled his

103

shoulders, and her hands dug into the material of the thick jacket.

When he eventually lifted his face, he chuckled lowly. "And it seems, ma'am, that you have desperate needs also. You've been away from your lover in New Orleans too long, it seems." His lips lowered again, softly feathering across the satin contours of her breasts, sending a tremor of passion through her body. "Perhaps I can make up for it. You and I should get to *know* one another. You know, getting to *know* one another in the true Biblical sense."

The continued mockery, the sarcasm, jolted Marguerite back to the present, making her remember Earl, who stood outside the carriage hearing all that was going on. She jerked out of the highwayman's arms.

"I don't want to know you," she hissed between clenched teeth, "and I want you to get out of this carriage right now."

"You don't want to know me," he mocked softly. "You mean, Mistress Marguerite, that you don't want to know the touch of my fingers stroking your hair like this." He lowered his head. "You don't want to know the feel of my lips on your neck like this."

Gasping for breath and swallowing the tremor that welled in her chest, Marguerite jerked away from him. She reached up, her hand closing over the diamond, and she yanked her beloved necklace loose. "No," she said, "I don't want to know you." Throwing the pearls at him, she spat, "Here, take them! And get out! Leave me alone."

He looked at the necklace for a second before he dropped it into his coat pocket. Then the masked face looked into hers again. He spoke, and oddly his voice was gentle. "I'm sorry that I must take this, but it's absolutely necessary. I'll repay you someday. I promise."

Again Marguerite was caught in the sensual web that this man so easily wove around her; again her heart beat to the cadence of his words and his touch. "Empty promises," she scathed, hiding the trembling of her body and soul behind

104

anger and outrage.

He pulled the glove from his right hand, and he slid a small yellow-gold ring off his little finger. Tenderly he lifted Marguerite's hand in his and slipped the ring over her fourth finger. "The earnest of my promise." So little said, yet so much promised.

"O'Roarke?" she asked softly. "Are you O'Roarke?"

Opening the carriage door and lithely springing down, he turned to look up at her, his face an extension of the dark, shadowed hood.

When he didn't answer, she spoke again, urgency in her tones. "Who are you?"

"Surely ye be a'knowin' that, me lady." Marguerite nodded and opened her mouth to speak. Before the words came out, he laid a finger across the parted lips. He smiled. "In England I would be called Rob in the Hood."

"Rob in the Hood," Marguerite repeated softly, her lips moving against his fingers.

"Aye." The highwayman levered up on the boarding step. Leaning forward, he placed warm lips over hers in a slow, good-bye kiss. His wine-scented breath splayed against her skin. "Good night and sweet dreams, Marguerite LeFleur. May they all be about me."

Chapter 6

Immediately on arriving home, Paddy, singing a catchy tune, went to the coach house. Earl headed for the library, and Marguerite followed, remaining in the door, surveying the open strongbox and the papers strewn on the floor and desk.

"One thing about O'Roarke; he's thorough," Earl said, slowly walking through the clutter, kicking a portfolio aside with the toe of his shoe.

"Is there anything I can do to help?" Marguerite asked.

"No," Earl returned calmly, turning to face her. Rather than his being disturbed and angry as Marguerite had thought he would be, he seemed pleased. "I'll need to go through to see which papers he's had access to." He retraced his steps and took her hands in his. "Good night. I'll see both you and Paddy in the morning, and we'll decide how we're going to handle this." He smiled, curling his fingers into a fist of triumph. "I have O'Roarke right where I want him."

"But, Earl—" Marguerite began.

"Hush," he softly commanded. "Go on to bed, and we'll discuss this further in the morning."

Too tired to argue, Marguerite went upstairs to check on her mother and to get Annie to help her undress. Finding both Amanda and Annie asleep, Marguerite tiptoed out of the room. After she locked herself in her bedroom, she leaned against the door and smiled. She totally disliked O'Roarke, but she couldn't help chuckling every time she remembered him, arrogantly sauntering into the Denby's drawing room.

Then she thought of Earl's strange behavior since they'd arrived home. She recalled his last comment. Although she knew Sheridan O'Roarke was the highwayman as well as did Earl and Paddy, she was loathe to admit it verbally. Though Paddy might despise O'Roarke, Marguerite wondered if the coachman would betray a fellow countryman to the hated English landlord.

As she walked across the room she unpinned her hat and tossed it into a nearby chair. Knowing she would have to tackle the hooks and eyes on the back of her bodice by herself, she saved that task for last. Sitting on the edge of the bed, she unlaced the ribbons and pulled off her slippers. She unrolled her stockings and shed her petticoats, leaving them bunched on the floor where they dropped. Her hands behind her, her fingers groped for the bodice fasteners.

When the breeze wafted through the room, gently billowing the lace curtain, softly touching Marguerite's flushed skin and wisping ringlets against her cheeks, she ceased her movements. Vaguely she knew something was different; something was wrong. Slowly she turned and looked at the window that had been closed when she left earlier in the evening.

Her dress partially unhooked, her hands dropped. She didn't move. Someone was in the room with her. She felt the presence; she heard the soft breathing. Her first impulse was to call for help, but she stifled the scream. Even if someone could hear her, he couldn't get to her quick enough to help.

Perspiration beaded in the palms of her hands; her heartbeat accelerated, and her breathing quickened. She looked at the door; she looked at the window. Both beckoned, but neither offered escape. She had only one other alternative. Slowly, so as not to arouse the intruder's suspicion, she inched toward her night table beside the bed. Taking off her earrings, she pulled the drawer.

As she dropped the jewelry into a small box, Marguerite stepped between the table and the bed. She opened a leather case and eased the flintlock revolver out of its bed. Her hand curved around the butt, one finger touching the trigger. When she heard the quiet swish of material, she turned, but she could see nothing except the dark shadows.

"I know you're in here," she said, injecting bravado into her voice. "I want you to know that I have a gun, and I won't hesitate to shoot."

The silence lengthened. Marguerite's hands were so wet and she trembled so, she could hardly hold the gun steady. Suddenly a warm, callused hand covered hers. "Guns are dangerous, lass. Let me take this."

The familiar, husky tones roughly rubbed over Marguerite's exposed and raw nerve endings, allaying her fears, at the same time raising her dander.

"You," she hissed, twisting from the highwayman's grip.

"I'm afraid so," he said quietly, unloading the chambers, blending into the shadows because he was clothed in black.

"How did you get in?" Marguerite whispered.

He laid the gun on the night table and moved to the opened window, tossing the bullets out. "Here," he replied, standing in the swath of moonlight that poured through the opening.

"Why did you come?" She searched through the blackness of the hood to find a face, to find an identity, to know for sure that Robin Hood was indeed Sheridan O'Roarke.

"I wanted to see you again," he admitted, the measured tones indicating his sincerity.

"Why?" Mesmerized, she moved across the room to stand in front of him, both of them gilded silver by the same band of light.

"Surely you know the answer to that, madam." His voice smiled. "But like all women your vanity demands an answer, so I'll answer. You're an enchantress, madam, and you've captured my heart."

"I don't think so," Marguerite murmured. "You wouldn't

have endangered yourself by coming here just to see me."

Soft laughter teased her. "Wouldn't I, lass?"

"Don't—don't you know what Earl will do if he finds you here?"

"You saw how ineffectual Earl Taylor is against me." Gusty laughter burgeoned, a deep, melodious sound filling the room. "But I'll set your mind at ease, colleen. He'll not find me unless I wish to be found." His hands cupped her face, his fingers splaying through the curls that wisped against her cheeks.

"He'll—he'll hear you," Marguerite murmured, her voice tremulous. "His—his bedroom is—is—"

"Nay," he countered, unperturbedly, "Earl Taylor won't be hearing me. He's in the library preoccupied with other matters at the moment. Besides this house was well built, and it was built to afford privacy. No one can hear what's going on in this bedroom."

The tips of his fingers trailed paths of fire down her cheeks, up again to her brows. "Your eyes are the most lovely shade of blue that I've ever seen," he murmured. "They remind me of the sky above Eire."

"How do you know my eyes are blue?" The soft words caressed his ears.

"They could be no other color." He softly chuckled. "Besides I saw them in the lantern light in the carriage."

"Who—who are you?" she whispered.

"A man who desires you very much."

"Even though you think I'm sleeping with Earl."

"Nay, lass, I don't think you're sleeping with him."

Guiding her face closer, his lips touched each eye, the hem of the mask gently wisping over her face. Marguerite's eyes closed beneath the love stroke, and she caught her breath. Her heart was pounding so furiously, her blood rushing through her body so fast, she thought she would faint. Feelings—wonderful feelings—she had never known she possessed coursed through her being.

"O'Roarke?"

"If you want me to be," he replied dismissively.

"I—I just want you to be yourself," Marguerite murmured. "No masks. No disguises. I want to know who you are, and I want you to know who I—"

"Let me love you, lass," he murmured, disregarding her words.

Marguerite shook her head, and she lifted her hands to push him away. "No," she cried. "I can't . . . despite what you think, I—"

She never finished her confession; the man's lips covered hers and his whispered "yes," melded into a slow, languorous kiss. When he lifted his mouth from hers, he turned her around, his fingers deftly moving down her spine, setting her on fire. Then they wisped across her shoulders as he pushed the material over her arms. Marguerite trembled as his hands touched virgin flesh. To keep her gown from falling below her breasts, she clutched it to her chest.

"No," she whispered. "I—we can't."

"But we can," he said, easily sweeping her argument aside. "Let me show you how wonderful it can be."

His hands caught the bunched dress material from her fists and dropped it. Marguerite felt the cool, evening air stroke her flushed, naked skin as her dress slid down her body, pooling around her feet. His hand teased her shoulder with butterfly-soft touches; his fingers crooked under the straps of her chemise; he tugged. The thin cotton material fell down, touching off brushfires of passion in her lower stomach as it grazed her throbbing breasts. Slowly his hands moved, never breaking the mesmeric bonding between them. His palms cupped her breasts, and Marguerite gasped. She tingled to life beneath his tender touches; the muscles in her stomach shuddered.

Of their own volition her hands lifted, slipping into the folds of the hood. Reaching behind his head, she untied the dark triangle and dropped it to the floor at their feet. When she

111

touched the warm flesh of his face, she swayed toward him. He breathed deeply, raggedly, and his hands slid around her body. Inebriated with the feel of him, Marguerite's fingers read every detail of his face. She memorized the craggy, masculine terrain.

Then her hands cupped his chin, and she guided his face to hers. Although she couldn't see in the darkness, her lips unerringly reached for his. Softly with a childlike innocence but with a woman's desires, she explored his lips, his cheeks, his eyes. Tormented by her tentative love touches, the hooded man could no longer passively receive. With a moan of acquiescence he became the aggressor.

He angled his face, his mouth settling on hers in a soft kiss that quickly deepened as passion in all its beautiful savagery raged through both of them. He lifted his hand, touched the corner of her lips with a finger, and coaxed her to open her mouth for the fullness of his kiss. As his tongue gently greeted her lips, slipping into the velvety warmth of her mouth, Marguerite moaned, and she pressed herself into the hard, rugged frame. Her arms rounded his body; her fingers clutched his shoulders.

When Marguerite thought she could stand no more, Sheridan broke the kiss, but he didn't break the mesmeric spell he had woven around her. Moving without seeming to move, he placed both hands in the small of her back, and he lowered his head, insinuating it between their bodies. Her breasts brushed against the soft fabric of his coat, her hips against the throbbing growth of manhood.

His mouth spread fire from her collarbone to the gentle slope of her breasts; his hips, gently pressing against hers, fed the fire in her loins. Trembling in his arms, her legs too weak to hold up the weight of her body, Marguerite reached into the hood, tangling her hands in the thick mass of red hair. His lips circled the aching tip, and he adoringly sucked her breast.

Gasping aloud, breathing deeply, her stomach convulsing with a hunger she'd never known before, Marguerite tenderly cradled the head against her bosom. She held him; she whispered to him; she loved him. He moved, not much—just enough to envelope both of them in his cape.

"Love me," she whispered, unconsciously giving voice to the desires of her heart.

Hidden from reality, transported to another world, Marguerite thought of nothing but his touch and her needs that fully surfaced, burning away all inhibition. Her fingers touched the buttons on his shirt, feverishly, clumsily slipping them through the opening. Jealous of the fabric that kept her from fully touching him, she brushed her hand over the hair-roughened chest and pushed the cambric aside. Then she pressed herself against him, flesh searing flesh.

As he picked her up in his arms and moved across the room, she said, "Show me how wonderful it is between a man and a woman."

Something about her whispered plea stopped Sheridan, jarred to memory the words she had muttered a few minutes earlier. He paused a moment before he gently deposited her on the bed. His ardor dampened, his conscience guilty, he sat beside her, the mattress sagging beneath his weight. As he opened his mouth to say something, a blood-curdling roar pierced the silent house.

"Damn Sheridan O'Roarke to the lowest and hottest pit of hell! I'll kill him myself to make sure he goes there."

Sheridan O'Roarke began to chuckle, softly at first then louder. He gently pushed Marguerite to one side and pulled the cover down. When he had resettled her, covered and tucked her, he kissed her lightly; then he rolled off the bed.

"I'd better go," he whispered, moving across the room. "To be sure Earl Randolph Taylor is about to have a fit, and the whole household will be awakened."

Sitting up, clutching the cover beneath her chin, Marguerite cried, "Will I see you again?"

One leg out the window, Sheridan looked across the room at her. "To be sure, love."

Without another word he was gone. Clad in nothing but her pantalettes, Marguerite flung the covers aside and raced across the room, stooping on the way to pick up her chemise. But with it came a black satin handkerchief: Sheridan's mask.

With one hand she held her chemise over her breasts as she peeked into the garden. In the other she crumpled the mask. She saw the black silhouette, standing proudly for that one minute, his cape billowing in the wind. He had been waiting for her; he had known that she would look out the window after him. He waved, and she could have sworn that he blew her a kiss.

Then Marguerite heard Paddy—someone—whistling that familiar refrain.

Golden sunshine spilled into the library through the opened windows, but the early morning brightness did nothing to dispel the heavy, tense atmosphere. Marguerite, wearing a bottle-blue riding skirt with a white bodice, sat in one of the chairs in front of the fireplace. The only evidence of her irritation was the tippy-tap of her boot on the floor. Clutching his cap in both hands, holding it to his chest, Paddy stood in front of Earl's desk.

Shaking his head, he said, "It's sorry that I be, Mr. Taylor, but it was dark and those highwaymen were wearing hoods and capes. I just can't swear that it was O'Roarke, sir, and I didna see no one leaving the house."

"Dammit," Earl shouted, doubling his fist and pounding on the desk, the movement pulling the bronzed green velvet of his coat taut across his padded undershirt. "You know as well as I do that it was them, man." His eyes contemptuously raked over the scared man. "Is it because you're Irish, Paddy, and you want to protect O'Roarke?"

Marguerite could take no more of Earl's shouting and his accusing. For over an hour he had been grilling the servant, but to no avail. Dropping her hand, pulling her eyes from the small gold band that rounded her fourth finger, she stood and moved away from the fireplace.

"Please, Earl," she said quietly, before Paddy could answer. "This isn't getting you anywhere."

She moved to the table, lifted one of the decanters and poured two glasses of whiskey. One she handed to Earl, the other to the coachman. "Paddy is telling the truth. There's no way any of us can make positive identification that the highwaymen were O'Roarke and his men. None of us can prove that O'Roarke robbed you."

Even as she uttered the words, Marguerite knew they were a lie. The man who had held her in his arms the evening before was O'Roarke. She had known it in the carriage; she had known it in the bedroom. Modesty forced her to hide behind the fantasy he had created with Rob in the Hood, but love demanded truth; passion reinforced it. Her fingers had recognized Sheridan O'Roarke's face; her body had recognized his touch.

"Always he has an alibi," Earl muttered, quaffing his drink in one swallow. "Yesterday O'Roarke's men were all over the north of County Wexford passing out handbills announcing a secret meeting. Where were we? Out chasing six or seven straggly milch cows. Cows that I had to keep because I had Clayborne brand them. In their place I had to give O'Roarke some of the fattest in my herd." He slammed his empty glass on the table. "I must—I *must* apprehend him! And soon." His voice lowered, and he muttered to himself, "I must—I must get the money."

"No one can make a positive identification," Marguerite repeated, worried about Earl's condition.

"No, sir," Paddy interjected, "it were dark. Too dark," he repeated solemnly, holding the glass and cap behind him with one hand, crossing his fingers with the other hand and raising his eyes to heaven. "Why, sir, to be sure, as close as ye were to me, I couldn't even see ye. Why, sir," he added, "I couldn't even hear what the rogues said about ye."

Earl's face flamed red, and one hand, of its own volition, went to his chest, the other to his stomach. Marguerite, unable to keep a straight face when she looked from Paddy to Earl, lowered her head. When Paddy dropped his head, burying his face in his hat, and made strange, choking sounds, she rushed to the rescue.

"Here, Paddy!" She took the glass from him. "Let me get you some more whiskey. You've developed a bad cough. I noticed it last night."

"To . . . be . . . sure, ma'am." He hacked between each word, gratefully taking the brimming glassful of amber liquid. After he had drank it, he lifted a hand and wiped his mouth. "I surely do be a'thankin' ye, ma'am," he said. "The only thin' that tastes any better to me than good whiskey is a pint of stout." He pounded his chest with his free hand. "Me chest and me cough have worsened since those rascals held us up." He wrinkled his forehead and pursed his lips. "Musta been keeping us out in the chilly night air, ma'am."

Valiantly managing to keep a straight face, Marguerite asked, "Are you all right now, Paddy?"

"In truth," he drawled, rubbing his chest. "I think, ma'am, that another drink might be a'helpin' me chest." After Marguerite refilled the glass, she walked to the French doors, unlatched and threw them open.

"I wasn't sure how many of those masked bandits surrounded me," Earl muttered, his entire body burning with humiliation, his shattered ego demanding revenge. "There wasn't a damned thing I could do about it."

"No, sir," Paddy said, a pious innocence on his bland face. "We were surrounded by them thieves, and nothing we could do about it, sir. Why, sir, ye were brave. Ye got out of the carriage and challenged them thieves. As fer meself, I was shaking, sir." He nodded his head vigorously. "Yes, sir, I was shaking all over."

"Dammit to hell," Earl raved. "The audacity of that man." He clasped his hands together behind his back and paced up

116

and down in front of the fireplace. "Came right into my house, robbed my strongbox, rode over to Denby's and bought *my cattle* with *my money*. And that's not enough for him," Earl continued, seeking to exorcise O'Roarke's ghost through confession. "He—he—"

Earl couldn't bring himself to say more. He walked across the room, refilling his glass. Anything to take away the memory, but drink hadn't helped last night, and it wasn't helping today. He'd never forget what O'Roarke had done to him. Earl took a gulp of the fiery liquid and shut his eyes. The remembering was as humiliating as the happening. He would never forget the scarecrow that sat in his chair beside his bed, dressed in his undergarments, waistcoats, and shirt. The sheet of paper with his name in bold, black letters. The message:

I know what you're up to, Earl Randolph Taylor. After last night I know what you want—of what you sorely need. Your treasure chest doth indeed seem to be empty. What a shame if I get the treasure instead of you! Like you, I'm looking for a fortune to wed. May the best man have the manor house!

"Earl," Marguerite said, gently jarring him from the painful memories, "forget about last night. No matter how right you may be. Not one of us saw O'Roarke. All we saw were masked outlaws."

"I'll get him yet," Earl vowed, his eyes flaming with hatred. "I promise the O'Roarke will swing from the gallows."

"Why is there such hatred between you and O'Roarke, Earl?" Marguerite asked.

Earl finished his drink and set the glass on the edge of the desk. "It's a long story, my dear, that began many years ago." Earl dismissed Paddy with a nod and lifted his hands to straighten his cravats. "From the very beginning the O'Roarkes have been rebellious."

Shuffling to the door, Paddy turned, his hand on the knob.

"Devin O'Roarke, Sheridan's father—" Earl looked up and saw Paddy loitering at the door. "You may go," he snapped curtly .

Paddy nodded. "If I may, sir . . ."

Exasperated, Earl snapped again, "What is it, Paddy?"

"It's to Mistress Marguerite, that I'd be a speaking, sir."

"Go ahead," Earl sighed.

"What time will ye be planning to—to leave?"

Earl turned questioning eyes on Marguerite and spoke before she could answer. "Where were you planning on going, my dear?"

"To pick up the ironing."

Earl's brow furrowed with displeasure. "Surely you understand, Marguerite." His voice was sharp and rebuking. "I have servants to perform menial tasks. There is no reason for you to have to drive to a peasant's house to pick up the laundry. You're not a washwoman."

"I know that," Marguerite said soothingly, "and I can understand your feelings. At the same time, Earl, my doing these tasks is not demeaning. No shame is to be found in honest labor." Her voice was firm with conviction.

Paddy's brows lifted, and his eyes glowed with admiration. Marguerite LeFleur was made of strong stuff, nothing like Earl Taylor. Quietly the coachman stood by the door watching the two, listening to their exchange. He appreciated Marguerite's ability to manipulate Taylor.

Earl walked to the liquor cabinet, silently castigating himself. Because Marguerite was a strong-willed person, nothing like her timid mother, he constantly underestimated her. But mold her he would; bring her under thumb he would, even though it would take time.

"Forgive me, Marguerite," he said quietly. "I'm still not quite myself." He smiled, the gesture hollow, never reaching his eyes. "I'm not criticizing you, my dear. I understand that you Americans have a different philosophy from us." He moved closer to her. "I'm simply pointing out that I have a

118

certain position and status in the community that must be maintained. One not so different from yours as mistress of a large plantation. And the Irish are much like your slaves. No matter how much it may hurt you, you sometimes have to whip them into submission. At all costs you make them respect you." His voice hardened as his thoughts turned to Sheridan. "I will have their respect," he averred. "I demand that from them."

"My father never beat his slaves," Marguerite returned calmly. "He always told them that one could never beat respect into anyone; nor could he demand it; he must earn it." She smiled. "I'm sure, however, that as wise as you are, you're doing everything in your power to earn the people's respect." Without giving Earl an opportunity to retort, Marguerite moved back to the topic of their conversation. "If you're so adamant about my not going to get the ironing, I'll defer to your judgment. But you'll need to speak to Mrs. Simmons about sending someone."

"Speak to Mrs. Simmons," he murmured, clearly unprepared to tackle the housekeeper.

Acting as if her picking up the laundry mattered little, Marguerite nodded. Deep inside, however, she desperately wanted to go. She wanted to meet Mary O'Roarke. She wanted to talk with her about Amanda's illness; she wanted to see Sheridan's home. More, she wanted to meet his mother. Even to herself Marguerite couldn't admit that she wanted to know more about the man who had so captivated her thoughts and her passions.

"I'll let you handle Mrs. Simmons," Earl said. "As mistress of—"

Softly, firmly came Marguerite's answer. "I'm not the mistress of this house, Earl. My mother is."

Irritated because of his slip, Earl hastily said, "I only meant, dear, that during her illness you should consider yourself mistress."

Mollified somewhat, Marguerite replied, "Since you've

119

phrased it like that, I shall." She smiled at him tentatively. "I'm just not sure how Mrs. Simmons will adjust to my taking over. Quite rightly, she's likely to resent taking orders from an outsider, like me."

Proud of Marguerite's tactics, Paddy punched his fist through the air, silently cheering her on. Marguerite, seeing both the gesture and the amusement that crinkled the old man's face, almost smiled.

Earl, engrossed in his own thoughts, had forgotten all about Paddy's presence. Accepting the logic of Marguerite's argument, he raised his hand and caught his lips between his fingers. "You're right. Absolutely right. I simply wasn't thinking. Last night's events have really shaken me. We certainly don't want to get Mrs. Simmons in a dander." He smiled. "Go pick up the ironing for Bridget."

Then he added, "But, please, my dear, make other arrangements for next week. I'm worried about you. You spend so much of your time nursing your mother, and now you're engaging in menial tasks." Moving closer to her, he sighed and shook his head. "It's just too much for you." He added placatingly, "Besides I wanted you to go to Wexford with me this afternoon."

Mrs. Simmons pushed past Paddy and walked into the study. Her austere face was creased in irritation. "Mr. Taylor, there's a James Power to see you."

Turning toward the housekeeper, Earl said, "Do I know him?"

Mrs. Simmons shook her head. "I told him that you were busy this morning, but he insisted on talking with you. He's quite upset, sir. Said something about passing out handbills and having meetings across the country."

"Oh, him," Earl exclaimed, his face screwing up in disgust. "Just what I need. A new breed of dissidents."

Remembering the jovial Mexican impresario, Marguerite immediately came to Power's defense. "He's not a dissident, Earl. He arrived yesterday from Mexico to recruit settlers for land grants in Texas."

"And how do you know so much about him?" Earl inquired dryly.

"Paddy and I talked with him at length about his colony in America," Marguerite answered.

"You talked with him!"

Inwardly Marguerite recoiled at Earl's possessive anger, but she said nothing. She only nodded. "He arrived yesterday while I was in town getting my bonnet."

"You're going to have to control your impetuosity," Earl scolded sharply. "You're not in America any longer. You're far too friendly and forward for a woman. Behavior like that can get you into all kinds of trouble."

Elvira Simmons's lips curled into a smile. It was about time that Earl exercised discipline with the girl. When Earl spun around, however, the housekeeper wisely voided her expressions and presented a bland face.

"Inform Mr. Power that I'm leaving for Wexford shortly and will be unable to see him today." Earl snapped the orders as he returned to his desk. He flipped through the pages of his appointment calendar, finally stopping. He thumped an index finger on the sheet. "Tell him that I'll see him next Tuesday. Ten o'clock in the morning."

Waving Paddy through the door, Marguerite ran past Mrs. Simmons, calling over her shoulder, "I'm leaving, Earl. I'll be back later."

Before Earl could change his mind, Marguerite raced up the stairs to her bedroom. A smile on her face, happiness surging through her body, she closed and locked her door. Dropping the key into her pocket, she walked to the dresser. Sitting in front of the mirror, she angled the top hat over her forehead and reached up to straighten the dark-blue gauze veil. Then she slipped into her tightly fitted navy-blue jacket and picked up her gauntlet gloves and riding crop. As she passed the mirror, she flashed herself a jaunty smile of self-satisfaction.

Chapter 7

Before leaving, Marguerite moved down the hall to Amanda's bedroom. She wanted to check on her mother and to tell Annie she was going to Mary O'Roarke's to pick up the ironing. As she walked, her black boots snapped briskly on the highly polished wooden floor. Opening the door, she eased into the curtain-darkened room, the stale odors of smelling salts and medicines causing her to cough.

"How is she?" Marguerite whispered when she neared the bed.

"Not good." The aged servant slowly pushed out of the shadowed chair and moved to the bed. "She sleeps most of the time now, Miz Marguerite. When she's awake she's in so much pain, she can hardly stand it."

Marguerite walked to the night table beside the bed and looked at the bowl of cold broth. Picking up the spoon, she swirled it through the liquid. "Has she eaten anything today?"

Annie nodded. "Several spoons of the soup. I try to get as much down her as I can." Her voice broke. "God knows I'm a'trying."

Marguerite put her arms around the frail woman. "I know," she assured Annie. "You're doing the best you can. We all are." Silently the two stared at Amanda until Marguerite said, "I've got to carry the laundry to Mrs. O'Roarke's, but I'll be back to sit with her this afternoon and tonight."

"I can't sleep, Miz Marguerite." Tears ran down Annie's cheeks. "I don't want my little girl to die. She's never been strong, but—Lordy, why did she have to come to this strange country to get sick and die?"

"She's going to be all right, Annie. I promise you she's going to get well." Marguerite held the black woman until she was spent from crying. Trying to reassure Annie, trying to reassure herself, Marguerite said, "Mr. Taylor's physician is going to examine her this afternoon. If he can't help her, I know someone who can. According to Bridget, Mrs. O'Roarke can nurse people back to health."

Annie looked up and smiled, a gleam of hope in the depth of her eyes. "Do you really think she can help us, Miz Marguerite?"

Marguerite wasn't sure, but she nodded her head. "Now let me get Jewel to sit with her until I come back," she suggested.

Pushing out of Marguerite's arms, Annie wiped the tears from her eyes and sniffed. "No, ma'am!" she declared. "You'll do no such a thing. I'll sit here with her until you come back."

With a heavy heart, concerned about her mother and the faithful old servant, Marguerite descended the stairs and walked out of the house into the backyard. She looked around until she spied Paddy at the door of the coach house. She waited while the horse clopped across the cobblestone.

As Paddy assisted her into the wagon, Earl leaned out the study window and waved. "I'll see you at lunch," he called, the words more a command then a reminder.

"If I can," Marguerite returned, swishing her parasol open, holding it in front of her face, blocking out Earl's image.

Paddy climbed into the driver's seat and grabbed the reins, lacing them through his fingers. "Here we go, ma'am."

Breathing deeply of the clean brisk air, Marguerite leaned back to enjoy her ride down the picturesque river road. Although the morning mist kissed the earth, the sun was shining brightly, and the land was draped in the most beautiful shades of green that Marguerite had ever seen. Sequestered fields, dipping and rising over the gentle hills, were separated into neat rectangles by stone walls.

Pulling his cap over his eyes, Paddy whistled, his tune blending with the rush of the river.

"That's catchy, Paddy," Marguerite remarked. "I heard you singing it last night." She smiled at the memory. "You have a beautiful voice."

"Do I now, ma'am?" Paddy murmured. "And what do ye be thinkin' about Ireland?" he added, turning off the main road onto a narrow lane.

"I think it's beautiful," Marguerite said, breathing deeply. She lifted her head, enjoying the warm rays of sunshine. "Just who is O'Roarke, Paddy, and why do he and Earl hate each other so much?"

"Well, ma'am," Paddy hedged, "I can't be a'saying for sure."

"Yesterday you promised to tell me about O'Roarke," Marguerite reminded him.

"Aye, ma'am," Paddy murmured, "so I did. To be sure I did." He clucked the horses; then he said, "'Tis a bloody story, ma'am. Certainly not a pretty one for the O'Roarkes." As was his habit, Paddy paused before he began his tale. "In 1798 the Irish united to overthrow the government. Before this, the O'Roarkes owned the manor house and all the surrounding land. During this battle, the Briton yeomen murdered Sheridan's grandparents and his two older brothers—both wee babes at the time. Sir Devin and Lady Mary, Sheridan's parents, weren't broken or defeated." Paddy chuckled. "'Twasn't long before there was another O'Roarke. But the English were after Sir Devin. And a right they had to be. He was still working to bring about Irish freedom. About ten years ago him and two of his best friends, Colin Dempsey and Neal Kenyon, were hanged as traitors after a hasty court-martial based on lies and flimsy evidence. Mrs. Dempsey were a sick woman and died soon afterward, most says from grief. Mrs.

Kenyon were killed in a queer accident. Only Mary O'Roarke and the three boys survived. Sheridan, Shane Dempsey, and Gavin Kenyon. The three of them's become closer than brothers." Paddy didn't speak again until he stopped the wagon in front of a gate. "And that's about it, ma'am."

"The property was given to Earl."

"Aye, ma'am," Paddy called, jumping down to open the gate, "the government gave the property to Mr. Taylor."

"In what kind of conspiracy is Sheridan involved?"

"All Irishmen are working for their freedom from the British," Paddy replied, leading the horse through the gate. "Some one way; some another." He dropped the reins and walked back to close the gate. "And I reckon that it might as well be me a'tellin' ye as anyone else: Mr. Taylor is the one what led the attack on the O'Roarkes during the uprising. He killed Sheridan's folks, and him it was who gave the false testimony against Sir Devin, Colin, and Neal. A right the O'Roarke, Shane and Gavin have to hate the man, mistress—a right all of us has to hate Taylor."

Her stomach churning, her heart hurting for Sheridan, Marguerite asked no more questions. Riding in silence the rest of the way to Mary O'Roarke's, Marguerite was lost in thought. Last night even though she had found the highwayman's reactions to Earl's undergarments amusing, she had resented their humiliating and taunting him. Now she understood O'Roarke's driving force, his relentless desire for revenge.

"Here we be," Paddy announced.

Marguerite stared at Sheridan O'Roarke's home, a whitewashed three-room cottage with a thatched roof. Though humble, it was one of the most beautiful homes she had ever seen. Cloistered by a covey of trees, it nestled between a gentle sloping hill and a brook. Three chimneys, two at each end of the cottage and one in the kitchen, jutted through the roof. On one side of the door sat a chair and a large table; several large washtubs lined the other.

"Now, Mistress Marguerite," Paddy said, climbing down

and assisting her out of the wagon, "you go on inside. I'll unload the wagon."

"Top o' the morning to ye, Paddy McLeary," a beautiful lilting voice rang from the doorway.

"And the same to ye, Mary O'Roarke," Paddy called. "I've brought someone to see ye."

Mary dried her hands on her apron and walked into the yard. "Of course, ye did. Ye've been bringin' her every Saturday for the past few years." Around the wagon now, Mary saw Marguerite for the first time. Surprised, Mary lifted her hand and pushed back the loose wisps of gray hair that fanned across her forehead.

"This be Mistress Marguerite LeFleur," Paddy said. "Mr. Taylor's stepdaughter."

Mary smiled slowly, the gesture so similar to Sheridan's that Marguerite's heart lurched. When she spoke, however, her voice and tone were guarded. "To be sure I'm pleased to meet ye, Marguerite LeFleur. What brings ye out here?"

"Bridget has gone to County Clare this very day to care for her sister who's having another babe," Paddy said, moving to the back of the wagon, dropping the flap.

"An' would that be Isabella?" Mary asked.

"The same," Paddy answered, heaving one of the baskets over his shoulder. "So's Mistress Marguerite's come to pick up the laundry and the ironing."

"I'm sorry," Mary apologized, "but I haven't quite finished it." She walked toward the house, following Paddy. "I've been nursing Mrs. Kelley."

"An how is she?" Paddy asked, ready to tackle another load.

"For ninety-five she's doing just well." Mary laughed, leading Marguerite into the house. "If ye don't mind waiting, Mistress Marguerite," she said, pointing to the ironing board that lay across four chairs, two at each end, back to back, "it won't take me long to finish."

Marguerite smiled at the older woman. "I don't mind."

Moving to the fireplace, Mary knelt down, putting more turf

on the fire. Marguerite, holding her gloves and her riding crop, looked at the interior of the cottage. Spotlessly clean and shining, it truly reflected Mary O'Roarke. Sitting on the mantel were beautiful china figurines, a few possessions from earlier and happier years, Marguerite thought. In the center was a lacquered jewelry box. On a high shelf to the right of the fireplace was a large clock, the chimes softly striking the hour.

Mary looked up in time to see Marguerite running lovely fingers over the box. "That be my mother's," she said. "All I have left of her now." She chuckled quietly. "The jewelry's been gone a long time."

"A music box?"

"Aye," Mary replied.

Marguerite smiled. "My grandmother gave my mother one similar to this. May I listen?"

"Aye."

Marguerite lifted the lid, letting the soft, plaintive melody fill the small room. "That's the song that Paddy whistles all the time," she exclaimed.

"Most Irish do be singing that," Mary explained. "It's 'The Wearing of the Green.'"

"Do ye need me to get ye another load of turf?" Paddy asked, interrupting the conversation as he walked into the room with the last basket of soiled clothes.

"Aye," Mary grunted, pushing to her feet, "I would certainly be thankin' ye for that. With Sheridan gone I have need of a man." She moved the irons closer to the fire. "Do ye want to use the donkey cart or yer wagon?" she asked.

"I'll take the wagon," Paddy replied, shuffling out the door, slinging his cap on his head. "That way I can get ye enough for many a load of washing and ironing."

"Mrs. O'Roarke," Marguerite began, watching Mary select potatoes from a small wooden box and place them in a bowl. "Bridget told me that you . . . that you had . . . a . . . gift?"

Mary held the potato in her hand for a long time before she said, "Aye, I have a way with nursing sick people back to health." She picked up another potato, rolling it around in her hand, picking the eyes out with her thumbnail. "Why do ye want to be a'knowing?"

"My mother has been ill ever since I joined her. Each day she gets weaker and weaker."

"What be the symptoms?"

"She has terrible stomach cramps, and she eats very little. She's so weak she can't get out of bed."

"What has the physician said?"

"She's refused to see one. Yesterday Earl, my—my stepfather, decided to take matters into his own hands. He's insisting that she see one, so he's sent for his personal physician."

"What kinds of food has she been eating?" Mary asked, moving to the table.

"Only broth now."

Mary set the bowl down and walked to the door where she gazed at the distant horizon. God had given her the gift of healing, and she knew she couldn't discriminate in her use of it. But she hadn't been back to the manor house since the government had evicted her and Sheridan, immediately after Devin's hanging. She had prayed for years before she got over her bitterness and forgave Taylor. But returning to the home that had once been hers, treating the woman who had become the mistress in her stead—Was this more than she could bear? Mary wondered. Surely God in his infinite mercy wouldn't ask this of her!

"Mrs. O'Roarke," Marguerite softly spoke, "I know what a sacrifice I'm asking you to make, but my mother's dying. She's a sweet and wonderful woman. She'd never knowingly hurt anyone. And she knows nothing about your past." When Mary didn't answer, Marguerite closed the distance between them. Reaching out, she laid her hand on the older woman's arm. "Please."

Mary turned, her eyes landing on the beautiful hand, soft and uncallused. She looked at the small gold band that circled the fourth finger. Her eyes widened, and she lowered her head even more.

"That's—that's a pretty ring ye have on," she said. "Where would ye be a'gettin' it?" A work-roughened finger touched the decliate design of leaves and roses.

Marguerite looked at the ring; she gazed at the washwoman's stubby fingernail. "A—a highwayman gave it to me the other night," she stammered.

"A highwayman," Mary mocked gently.

Marguerite nodded her head and whispered, "Sheridan. He gave it to me in exchange for my pearl necklace."

"His grandfather gave it to his grandmother when they were wed," Mary said softly, tears in her voice.

Slowly Marguerite uncurled her fingers, removing her hand from Mary's arm. "Would you like to have it back?" she asked.

Mary shook her head, blinked her eyes and swallowed her tears. "Nay," she said. "It doesn't belong to me; it's Sheridan's. His father gave it to him just before he died, so he has a right to do with it as he sees fit."

"Mrs. O'Roarke," Marguerite began, "I wouldn't want to keep something that was as precious as this ring is."

In a gesture that surprised both women, Mary reached out and caught Marguerite's hand. "Ye keep the ring. It will be best not to anger O'Roarke."

"I'll—I'll take care of it," Marguerite promised.

Mary nodded, and her eyes pierced Marguerite's. "Aye," she drawled. "I believe ye." The older woman turned again, the movement dismissing Marguerite. Mary's eyes slowly traveled the horizon. Eventually she asked, "What does Taylor think about yer asking me to tend yer mother?"

"It wouldn't matter to me how he felt. I will do anything to save her life."

Mary nodded. She admired Marguerite's courage and loyalty. She approved of her love for her mother. "Let me think about it. I'll give ye my answer before ye return to the house." Mary moved to the table and picked up the bowl of potatoes and a small knife. Sitting on a long wooden bench next to the wall, she began to peel the potatoes. "While I'm waiting for the irons to heat, I'll give it some thought."

"That's a lot of food for one person." Marguerite eyed the mound of potatoes as she moved about the room.

"Aye," Mary quietly returned, "but old habits die hard." Her eyes took on a faraway look. "I've always been accustomed to cooking for hearty boys—Devin and Sheridan." Her voice grew reminiscent. "Shane Dempsey and Gavin Kenyon after their parents died."

Mary sat the bowl aside and walked to the door. "Have ye ever seen the likes before?" she asked, abruptly changing the subject. "Eire is a country of gentle, rolling beauty." She looked at the meadows, seeing their graceful beauty anew. "Because of the vivid greens we often call it the Emerald Isle."

Moving so that she stood behind Mary, Marguerite looked at the mist that muted the glaring heat of the sun, rendering a soft velvet touch to the emerald terrain. "No," she murmured, "I've never seen anything so pretty." Thinking perhaps Mary would like to be alone with her memories, Marguerite said, "If you don't mind, I think I'll go for a walk. The day is much too beautiful to waste. The sun is shining, and spring is everywhere."

"Go ahead," Mary replied, in a calm, soothing voice. "When ye get back the ironing will be done, and I'll have fresh bread cooked and some tea brewed. We'll talk some more."

Marguerite slipped out of the cottage, walking beside the brook, listening to the soft rush of the water. Unconsciously she softly hummed the song that Paddy had been whistling earlier. She stopped at a large clump of shrubs and sat on the low, stone fence, watching the large farm horses as they munched the grass. Then she saw the figure, moving toward her. At first it was no more than a small dot on the horizon, but slowly it grew in stature, into Sheridan O'Roarke who suddenly loomed in front of her. His booted feet were straddled, braced to the ground, and his fisted hands rested on his hips, his whip swinging lazily against his thigh.

"Hello, Mistress Marguerite," he said, taking another step, his movement jarring Marguerite out of the stunned trance. "Are you sitting out here by yourself in hopes of meeting the masked highwayman?"

"No," she denied, her hand flying to her face, brushing tendrils from her cheeks and eyes.

"A shame," he murmured, his gaze hypnotic, his smile dazzling. "I thought like him you were hungry for more than mere kisses shared in a carriage." Another step closer. "Or interrupted kisses."

Scooting back until the stone fence bored into her back, Marguerite held her hands up, warding him away. Last night she could deal with him; he had been an extension of her romantic fantasy. Today he loomed larger than life, menacing and ominous.

"Please, don't come any nearer."

Sheridan knelt beside her, so close that his warm, ale-scented breath splayed across her flushed cheeks. His voice was soft and caressive. "When you make me feel the way I do and when I can make you feel the same things, why should I stay away?" he asked. The smile softened into beguilement. "Besides you're the one who's taken the trouble to come see me."

His hand was on her face, his fingers tapping her chin, the whip lightly grazing Marguerite's throbbing breasts through the layers of material. "Somehow I don't think you're hunting the mythical Rob in the Hood," he whispered, his head lowering, blocking the sun out altogether. "I think you're searching for reality, for more than passion and desire; I think you're looking for fulfillment, Daisy LeFleur."

Marguerite could feel nothing but O'Roarke; she could smell nothing but the herbal fragrance of his perfume. She tried to wiggle away from him, but again the stone fence reminded her that she had no chance of retreating.

"Don't—don't call me that. I told you when we first met

that I didn't like to be called Daisy."

"Why not?" he asked as softly. "Daisy is more gentle and more lovable, the kind of woman that appeals to me."

"Maybe I don't want to appeal to you."

"To be sure, you do," Sheridan countered, laughter swirling in the green irises, amusement crinkling the corners of her eyes. "Just as I want to appeal to you."

In one abrupt but smooth movement, he broke the intimacy of the moment. He tossed his hat aside and sat down next to her, propping himself against the fence. Disappointed with his show of disinterest in her, Marguerite watched him pull a blade of grass.

"So," he said, breaking the silence, "if you didn't come to see me, why did you come, Daisy LeFleur?"

"To get the ironing."

"Already pandering to Earl's desires," he said, his voice devoid of emotion.

"No," Marguerite returned, refusing to rise to his bait. "Earl didn't want me to come."

Sheridan quietly laughed, remembering the note he'd pinned to Earl's pillow. "Earl knows O'Roarke, and he has a right not to want you to come, lass." Turning his head, he gazed at her. "Surely it was more than ironing that caused you to defy him!"

Refusing to give Sheridan the satisfaction of an answer, Marguerite let the words hang in silence between them. When she spoke again, she said, "Paddy told me about—about you and Earl."

Immediately an invisible hood fell over Sheridan's face, hiding all his expressions. "Did he now," he said, his voice guarded but casual. He slid into the grass on his back, crossing his arms behind his head, using them as a pillow. He turned toward her and smiled. Completely ignoring Marguerite's comment, he said, "Surely your life is more interesting than mine, Daisy LeFleur. Tell me something about yourself."

Irritated, Marguerite shrugged and shook her head.

"What's your middle name?" Sheridan asked curiously.

Marguerite clasped a hand on the nape of her neck, pushing errant curls into her chignon. "Belle."

"Marguerite Belle LeFleur," he repeated. "Let's see now."

In spite of herself Marguerite chuckled. "Another lesson in French?"

Sheridan grinned. "If I remember my French lessons, Daisy, your name translates to beautiful daisy the flower."

"Loosely."

"So now I shall call you Daisy Belle."

"What does your name mean?"

"Wild man."

"Which you are?"

"Aye." He spoke so softly his voice was part of the wind. "Tell me about your life before you came to live with Earl, Daisy Belle."

Recalling the hurtful accusations he had hurled at her the first time they had met, Marguerite calmly replied, "When I first met you, you seemed to know all about my life in New Orleans."

"I was repeating things I had read in letters Earl had received from a Mistress Susanna Reeves."

"How did you come to be reading Earl's mail?" Marguerite demanded.

Sheridan grinned. "Earl and I share his library and reading material. I had occasion to be in his office one night, looking for some information, and a stack of letters from a certain Susanna Reeves happened to be lying on top of his desk." He shrugged a shoulder. "It was late, and Earl was out, so I had plenty of time to read. Curiosity got the best of me, and—" His grin turned into a chuckle. "You can guess the rest."

"Do you always invade people's privacy?"

"If they have something I need or want." His eyes caught and held hers in a timeless bonding. "Now tell me about you and Jordan Reeves. I've heard only Susanna's side of the story."

"I don't know what Susanna wrote Earl," Marguerite said, "but I can imagine. She's a sick woman—emotionally more than physically."

"She believed you were her husband's mistress."

Marguerite nodded, gazing into the distance. "She should have known better. I wouldn't have betrayed our friendship like that. I think too much of her and Jordan." Marguerite's voice softened when she spoke Jordan's name. Sheridan's eye slit, but Marguerite wasn't looking at him, so she didn't see the change in his expression.

"What about your and Jordan's child?"

Marguerite looked at Sheridan, raising a brow. "Evidently Susanna left nothing out of her letters." Not answering immediately, she pulled her legs up, wrapped her arms around them, and rested her chin on her knees. "There is no child; that's just a figment of Susanna's imagination."

"Was there any basis for her suppositions?"

Marguerite shrugged. "Yes, to be honest, there was."

"She told Earl that Jordan spent most of his time at The Oaks."

"He did," Marguerite replied flatly. "Mother wasn't a good business woman, and she let the plantation fall into disrepair after Father died. As a friend and a fellow planter, Jordan was helping me."

"Exactly what kind of *friend?* That's the question, Marguerite LeFleur," Sheridan said, irritated with himself because he was jealous of Marguerite and Jordan. "Exactly what kind of help was he giving you?"

"Not the kind you're implying," Marguerite snapped. She struggled to her feet. "Why must everyone think I was Jordan's mistress? That I carried his illegitimate child?" she cried. "Susanna. Now you."

Bounding to his feet at the same time, Sheridan stood beside Marguerite. He looked into her blazing eyes. Surprising himself, he said, "I don't know if you were his mistress, Daisy, and for some reason I don't care if I ever know. This I would like to know. Do you love him?"

Unable to answer the question, not really certain of the answer herself anymore, tears welled in Marguerite's eyes. When she left New Orleans, she hadn't known what to think. At times she had thought herself to be in love with Jordan. But lately since she'd met O'Roarke, she realized that with the death of her grandmother and the remarriage of her mother, she was lonely. Jordan had provided the friendship and companionship that she so desperately needed.

Marguerite suddenly smiled. That was it! She had mistaken Jordan's friendship and kindness for love. Seeing the softness replace the anger in Marguerite's eyes at the mention of Jordan's name, Sheridan took her silence to be an admission of her love for Jordan Reeves. Believing this, Sheridan still couldn't tear his gaze from the large, dilated eyes, his face the only reflection he could see. He couldn't understand his reaction. Why should he care that she was in love with another man? Why should he care that she may have been this man's mistress? He wasn't asking for love or fidelity. She was a pawn to be used against Earl Taylor. *Nothing more.*

True, Sheridan desired Marguerite and wanted the pleasure of her body, but he didn't want to get close to her. He didn't want to care about her. Yet she looked so helpless, so vulnerable that he wanted to wrap his arms around her, to draw her to his chest, and to reassure her. A man filled with contradicting emotions, he gave in to his feelings. He reached for Marguerite, but she spun on her heels. With a sense of acute loss, he watched her run across the meadow.

Chapter 8

That others had believed Susanna's lies hadn't bothered Marguerite nearly as much as Sheridan's believing them. Her hurt was so deep Marguerite couldn't contain the tears that scalded her cheeks. When she finally reached the white stucco building, she dropped to the bench, her hat toppling into her lap. When her sobs stopped and she regained her composure, she stood and walked into the house, moving straight across the kitchen to the mirror.

"To be sure," Mary said, not looking up as she folded the last shirt and placed it in the basket at the foot of the ironing chair, "ye'r back right on time." She walked to the fire, draped her hand with a heavy dishcloth, and lifted the kettle. Seeing only Marguerite's back, Mary said, "I'm finished with the ironing meself, and I'm ready for a cup of tea." As soon as she set the kettle on the table, she walked to the door and gazed into the horizon. A smile on her lips and in her voice, she said, "Aye, for sure, there's Paddy's come with a wagonload of turf. I know he'll be ready for a cup of hot tea."

"It smells delicious," Marguerite said, looking at her reflection. "It smells like more than tea."

"Aye," Mary replied, wisely ignoring the teary sniff in Marguerite's voice. "Soda bread cooked over a peat fire, homemade butter, and a good stew. What I raised my family on." Mary chuckled softly, and her voice grew dreamy. "My Sheridan, though he's eaten the best, prefers my bread and stew."

Thinking about her last encounter with Sheridan, Marguerite lifted trembling hands and uncoiled her hair. She repinned and swept it into a swirling braid.

Quietly Mary returned to the table where she poured the tea and sliced the bread. Afterward she set the kettle in the ashes at the edge of the fire, picked up a long-handled spoon, and stirred the cauldron, adding a few herbs. Both women lapsed into an introspective silence as the wagon slowly lumbered to a halt in front of the cottage.

"And what do I smell," Paddy cried, bounding into the house, clapping his hands together in anticipation, "but my favorite brew, cooked by my favorite cook."

"And it sounds like ye've been to County Cork and kissed the Blarney Stone yerself," Mary scoffed gently.

"Aye," Paddy admitted, yanking his cap off and stuffing it into one of his coat pockets, "I've been to County Cork, even to Blarney Castle, but 'tis not blarney that I be a'speakin' to ye this day, Mary O'Roarke."

In the mirror Marguerite watched Paddy and Mary as they looked at one another. Knowing that she was intruding on a most intimate exchange, Marguerite remained where she was, saying nothing, doing nothing. She saw the smile on Mary's lips and face; she saw the glow in those beautiful eyes so like O'Roarke's. Marguerite caught her breath at the radiance that transformed Mary into a beautiful woman, and she wondered if she would ever find that kind of love herself.

"I've not unloaded the turf yet," Paddy said. "I'll do that after a cup of tea." He grinned. "'Twill be enough to do ye till next Saturday."

"And I'll be a'thankin' ye, Patrick McLeary. So will my boy for yer takin' such good care of me."

"It's not gratitude that I be a'wantin', Mary," Paddy replied, oblivious to Marguerite's presence. "An' it's not because of yer boy that I be a'doin' it."

The thudding of hooves interrupted the spellbinding moment. Paddy raced to the window, but Mary remained by the table, her knuckles turning white as she dug her fingers into the back of the chair.

"'Tis the Red Coats," he muttered, running his hand over his chin. "Now what can they be a'doin' here, Mary?"

Aware of the tension that permeated the room, Marguerite nervously settled her hat atop her head and anchored it with a hat pin. She was fluffing the gauze veil when she heard the knock on the door. At the same moment that the bangs sounded in the room, Nelson Clayborne stuck his head through the open door. Because Marguerite was at the other end of the kitchen, Nelson didn't immediately see her.

"Where's Shane Dempsey?" he demanded harshly, entering without an invitation, shoving past Mary, almost knocking her down. "I know he's here. Where have you hidden him?" The question wasn't out of his mouth before he stamped across the floor, threw his shoulder against the door and plunged into Mary's bedroom.

"Why should ye think Shane be here?" Mary asked, her quiet words following the lieutenant into the other room.

Stunned by Nelson's outrageous behavior, Marguerite spun around. She glared at the soldiers; the two who hovered at the entrance, the ones who emptied the baskets of clothes and others who unceremoniously dumped the peat over the yard. Marguerite marveled at Mary's and Paddy's aplomb. As if nothing out of the ordinary were happening, Paddy leaned against the windowsill and softly whistled, and Mary, oblivious to the banging of doors and the thud of furniture being dragged across the floor in the adjacent room, walked to the dresser. She picked up three plates and bowls and returned to the table.

"Where is he?" Nelson demanded irritably, crossing the kitchen in three long strides. He grabbed Mary's upper arm and jerked her around, causing her to drop the dishes on the table with a clatter. "I know you're hiding him here."

"Lieutenant Clayborne!" Marguerite's reprimand boomed through the room.

As if Marguerite had ordered him to do so, Nelson unhanded Mary, and he turned around, surprised eyes leveling on Marguerite.

"Mistress LeFleur," he finally sputtered, his voice limp with shock and chagrin, "what a surprise!"

"Not nearly as surprising as your visit and ill manners, Lieutenant!"

Forgetting Mary, Nelson moved toward Marguerite. "As I've already told you, Mistress LeFleur," he said, his smile and tone testy, "this is a situation which you, being newly arrived from the United States, do not understand. And it would be in your best interest if you—"

"The situation as I see it," Marguerite quietly interrupted, "is this. Uninvited, you charged into Mrs. O'Roarke's cottage and were roughing her up. You have strewn Earl's clothing all over the yard, not to mention dumping the peat that Paddy so laboriously gathered this morning."

Nelson's eyes narrowed, and his nostrils flared. He barely controlled his temper. "You do not understand, madam—"

"I understand courtesy, Lieutenant Clayborne." Marguerite's boots clicked against the wooden floor as she moved across the room, the tapping of her soles as ominous as the tone of her voice. "And I understand the law. Is martial law in effect, Lieutenant?" Before Nelson could answer, she asked, "Do you not have to produce a search warrant before you charge into a house searching for someone who doesn't live here?"

"Mary O'Roarke is suspect of receiving contraband," Nelson said, his eyes swinging to the table which Mary had set. "Weapons, Mistress LeFleur, which will be used by these barbaric savages to rebel against the legal, civilized government of this island."

"Ye'll have to be finding weapons around here before ye can do more than accuse me," Mary returned unperturbedly, slicing the bread.

"We have evidence to prove that Shane Dempsey is guilty, and if Shane Dempsey is guilty, so is O'Roarke and Gavin Kenyon. And you," the lieutenant said, pointing a long, slender finger in her face, "Mary O'Roarke, are probably an accomplice with this band of outlaws."

"An accomplice ye'll come nearer to proving that I am, Mr. Clayborne." Mary walked to the dresser and picked up a butter crock which she set on the table. She lifted the domed lid. "The truth be, if Shane came to my house asking for shelter, he'd receive it, and if any one of the three lads you mentioned brought me contraband to hide from the English, I would."

"See there," Nelson shouted, throwing his hands in the air in frustration. "Openly admitting that you'd harbor a fugitive from justice."

"Nay," Mary countered, "I didn't say I would harbor a fugitive from justice. I said I would harbor an innocent victim from the revenge of Earl Taylor."

Moving from the windowsill, Paddy chuckled. "To be sure, Mr. Clayborne, Mary's more than an accomplice. She be like Shane Dempsey's and Gavin Kenyon's mother, and she be Sheridan's mother for sure."

When the soldier in the door laughed with Paddy, Nelson scowled him to silence. Turning, the lieutenant walked into the second bedroom, returning shortly. "I know Dempsey's around here, Mary O'Roarke, and I'll find him." Nelson moved to the table, stopping in front of the older woman. "And I know he's hidden the contraband around here, and when we find it . . . which we will . . . Mr. Taylor will see you in prison along with your son. Do yourself a favor, woman. Tell me where Dempsey and the contraband are hidden."

"Even if I knew," Mary replied, her face expressionless, her voice bland, "nothing would make me tell you." She added, her voice ringing with conviction, "Earl Taylor has taken everything I have away from me, Nelson Clayborne, but he'll not get Sheridan as long as I live." She shrugged, the

141

animation dying from her tone, giving way to a dull resignation. "As far as the contraband, I dunno what ye'r talking about."

"So be it," Nelson snapped at the same time that he clicked the heels of his boots together. He turned to Marguerite. "May I escort you home, Mistress LeFleur?"

"No, Lieutenant, you may not. I'm here to pick up the ironing, and I shan't be leaving without it. Paddy drove me over, and he'll bring me home. Furthermore," she added, looking at the three cups of tepid tea and the plates on the table, "Paddy and I are dining with Mrs. O'Roarke." Casually she lifted her hand, unpinned her hat and took it off.

"As you wish," Nelson hissed, watching her walk across the room. "What shall I tell Mr. Taylor?"

"Since what I do is none of your business, I suggest you tell him nothing. But I have a feeling that you will make it your business, so tell him what you will. When I return to the house, if anything needs explaining, I will explain."

At the door Nelson turned and stared at her, contempt and disgust written all over him. "Believe me, Mistress LeFleur, you will have much to explain when you arrive at the manor house." Outside the door, he called, "And you have much to learn about living in Ireland."

"If ye'll be sitting yerself down," Mary said before Nelson was out of hearing distance, "we'll be a'eatin'."

Paddy, a smile on his face, shuffled to the fireplace. Marguerite took off her hat and laid it on the small table beside the fireplace. Then she removed her gloves, laying them on top of the hat. She watched as Paddy propped the ironing board against the wall and dragged the chairs to the table. As she sat down in one, she heard the bedroom door open. She looked up to find Sheridan O'Roarke lounging indolently in the jamb. Her surprise was so great, she gasped his name.

"None other." He doffed his hat and twirled it across the room, clapping when he ringed the rack on the wall.

"You were hidden here all the time!"

"'That I was." He turned laughing green eyes on Marguerite first, then his mother. Across the kitchen in two strides, he took the small form in his arms.

"Danny Boy," Mary scolded fondly, "have all of ye gone daft? Shane being chased like an outlaw by the Red Coats, accused of hiding weapons! What next? You."

"Don't worry, Mother," Sheridan soothed on a soft chuckle. "Everything is all right."

Mary pulled out of his arms and walked to the dresser. "Why did ye come?" she asked, picking up the fourth plate.

Sheridan opened his mouth as if he were going to speak; then he closed it. He moved to the table and lifted the ladle, brimming with potatoes and meat. "This, Mary O'Roarke. This is why I came home. I missed your cooking." He picked up a slice of bread and spread the butter on thickly. He looked at the tepid tea. "Is this anything to be serving the prodigal son returning home?"

Mary laughed. "I'll be a'boilin' more water, Danny Boy. Lieutenant Clayborne interrupted our cup of tea."

Sheridan looked at Marguerite, a lid lazily covering one of the sparkling green eyes in a blatant wink. "And top of the morning to you, Mistress LeFleur. I'm rightly pleased to see you here."

"Where were you hiding?" Marguerite asked, consumed with curiosity. "The lieutenant searched every nook in that room."

"Not every nook," Sheridan returned, dismissing the subject. He laid the buttered bread beside her plate. Lifting the ladle, he gave her a large helping of the potatoes and meat. "Eat hearty," he instructed her. "This is some of the best cooking in all Eire."

The savory odor was inducement enough for Marguerite to eat. She dipped her fork into the food and lifted it to her mouth. As she did so, Sheridan's gaze fastened to her hand—to the gold band on her fourth finger. Stopped in motion, Marguerite's eyes followed the path blazed by his. When his

143

attention moved from the ring to her face, she dropped the fork on the plate with a clatter. Unnerved by the events of the morning, unnerved by his nearness, Marguerite laid her hands in her lap and laced them together.

Both Paddy and Mary saw the exchange between the two. Paddy pretended to be preoccupied with eating. Mary, the kettle in hand, paused in front of the fireplace. Not sure what Sheridan was planning, she frowned her anxiety and concern. In a world of Sheridan's making, Marguerite was aware of nothing that was going on around her. Her only thought was Sheridan. As if it were the most natural thing in the world for him, as if he and Marguerite were lovers, he reached into her lap and captured the ringed hand. He lifted it.

"'Tis a beautiful ring, Mistress LeFleur."

"Thank you, Mr. O'Roarke," she returned, her eyes fixed on the handsome face.

"And it looks beautiful on your hand."

Again she whispered, "Thank you."

"Where did you get it?" he asked.

"A—a highwayman gave it to me."

"An' now, why would he do that?"

Lost in the gentle swell of crystal-green pools, Marguerite said, "I don't know."

"Don't you now?" His hand squeezed hers; the tender expression in his eyes squeezed her heart. At that moment Marguerite knew she was falling in love with O'Roarke.

Mary picked up the pot of freshly brewed tea, filling Sheridan's cup before she set it on the table. Breaking the mesmeric bond between the two, she said gruffly, "Here's yer tea. And now, Danny, tell me how are ye faring?"

Marguerite pulled her hand from Sheridan's clasp, thankfully reaching for her cup. Cradling it in both hands, she lifted it to her lips and took a large swallow, the newly poured liquid scalding her as it flowed down her throat. Covertly she watched Sheridan as he ate and talked with his mother and Paddy. She couldn't take her eyes off the strong, callused hands or the russet-haired forearms.

When the meal was over, Sheridan rose and moved across the room to the hat rack. "Let's go outside, Paddy, and I'll give you a hand with stacking the turf."

"A hand I'll appreciate," Paddy quipped, "but the job calls for more than a hand, methinks."

Sheridan donned his hat at the same time that Paddy pulled his cap from his pocket. The two men, laughing and talking, walked outdoors.

Although Marguerite was a little embarrassed and apprehensive after the way Sheridan had behaved in front of his mother, she stayed in the kitchen with Mary.

When she began to stack the dishes, Mary said, "Nay, lass. Ye don't come to visit Mary O'Roarke and clean up her house. Ye be the guest."

"Mrs. O'Roarke," Marguerite began, "I—I—"

"You don't owe me an explanation." Mary walked to the dresser and picked up a large bowl. She quickly filled it with water from the wooden bucket that hung on the wall. Her back to Marguerite, she said, "What ye and Sheridan do is yer business."

She replaced the dipper and lifted the kettle, pouring hot water into the bowl. She submerged the dishcloth in the water and laid the bar of soap next to the bowl. "An' as much as I love my son, I must warn ye, Marguerite LeFleur, that he is filled with bitterness and hatred. He'll be a'usin' anyone that he has to. Ye included." Taking a knife, she scraped bits of soap into the dish water. "Memories are long where people speak Irish, and Sheridan speaks Irish fluently."

Not understanding Mary's warning completely, Marguerite remained silent. She scraped the plate and carried the dishes to the older woman. Mary took the stack from her and lowered them in the bowl of water. She lifted her face and gazed pensively at Marguerite.

"I'm not tending to your business, lass, but be careful."

Marguerite returned to the table and gathered the cutlery

and the cups. "Why are you warning me? Surely you're as bitter as Sheridan. You have a right to be. Surely you hate Earl Taylor as much."

Mary washed the plates and laid them in another bowl full of warm rinsing water. She waited awhile before she answered. "Nay, lass, no one has a right to be bitter, but I was. I did hate Earl Taylor. Now I only hate what the English have done to us. I had to push these feelings aside if I were going to help my people, and they needed me." She paused, reaching for the drying clothing. "Hate and bitterness were separating me from God. I was allowing Earl Taylor to stand in the way of my faith and my gift." Mary dried the dishes and set them in the groove at the back of the dresser.

"Mistress Marguerite," Paddy called from the doorway, "I be a'thinkin' that we should be on our way. The turf's stacked, the ironing's loaded, and Mr. Taylor's going to be unhappy that we're not there to see him off to Wexford."

Mary dried her hands on her apron and walked to the door. Marguerite moved to the mirror. She lifted her hat and pinned it in place. Just as her fingers touched the filmy veil, she saw Sheridan's reflection in the doorjamb. He leaned against one side of the frame, his hand braced against the other. The two of them stood for the longest time, staring at each other through the mirror. Finally Marguerite lowered her head and pulled her gloves on. Picking up her riding crop, she walked to the door. Sheridan remained where he was standing, not allowing her to pass.

"Are you going to Wexford with Taylor?"

Marguerite smiled. She heard the thin line of jealousy beneath the curiosity of the question. Wanting to punish Sheridan for having hurt her earlier, she said, "Maybe. He wants me to."

Sheridan laughed. "Nay, Marguerite LeFleur, you're not going with him." He moved, his hand rising, his fingers cupping her chin. "You'll be staying home, waiting in your moonlit room, hoping the masked highwayman will come to fulfill your dreams and to fill your bed."

Shaking her head, Marguerite slowly pulled her face from his light clasp. "I may not go with Earl, Mr. O'Roarke, but it won't be because I'm waiting for you." Her tone was even and firm. "I'll be home tending to my mother."

Sheridan's eyes sobered, and sincere concern clouded them. "Aye, lass," he said. "I've been hearing about her illness. And I be wishing her good health."

They looked at each other that one second longer that stretched into time immeasurable. Then Marguerite, walking straight toward the buggy, swept past Sheridan through the door into the brightness of the afternoon. However, before she could climb in, Sheridan was by her side. His hands circled her waist as he lifted her, easily depositing her in the leather seat. His hands lingered a little longer than was necessary, and his eyes, looking into hers, made a silent promise. Tearing away from the gaze, Marguerite heard Mary speak to Paddy.

"An' I be a'thankin' ye for all ye've done for me, Patrick."

Paddy climbed into the buggy and took the reins in his hands, intertwining them between his fingers.

"I'll see ye again next Saturday?"

"Aye."

Mary looked at Marguerite. "And ye, Mistress LeFleur, come back and see me again."

Releasing Marguerite, Sheridan stepped away.

"I will," Marguerite promised, and she leaned forward. "Mrs. O'Roarke—"

Mary lifted a hand to her forehead, shielding her eyes from the glare. She stared pensively at Marguerite, knowing the question, although Marguerite didn't voice it. Finally she nodded her head and slowly said, "I'll tend to yer mother."

"Thank you, Mrs. O'Roarke," Marguerite breathed, tears brimming in her eyes. "When can you come?"

"Later this afternoon."

Marguerite nodded. "Shall I send a buggy for you?"

"No, I'm accustomed to seeing after myself. I'll come in

my cart."

Mary and Sheridan stood, watching the buggy as it drove out of sight. When Mary turned and entered the house, Sheridan followed. "What kind of game are ye playing, Sheridan?" she asked when she stood in front of the dishpan.

Standing in the doorway, his back to his mother, Sheridan continued to scan the horizon, watching the buggy until it disappeared from sight. "What do you mean?"

"Marguerite LeFleur."

"I find her attractive."

"Rumor has it that Earl Taylor also finds her attractive." Mary hung the cups from the hooks on the shelf. "Could that be yer attraction?"

Sheridan walked to his mother and caught her to his chest in a hug. "Mother, don't go worryin' yourself about nothing."

"If it were nothing," Mary retorted, "I wouldn't be worried. Why did ye give her yer grandmother's wedding ring?" Unable to answer that question himself, Sheridan shrugged. "She's an innocent lass, Danny—"

"Nay, Mother," Sheridan interrupted, "she's not so innocent."

Mary said, "Leave her alone. Don't let yer bitterness and hatred spill over on her."

"You like her?"

"She's different from Taylor," Mary said evasively. "She's American not English, so she doesn't think like Taylor."

"You're going to go see her mother?"

"Aye," Mary replied. "She's been sick for several weeks, getting worse each day, Marguerite says. I promised that I'd see what I could do for her. Her ailments are strangely like those Eliza suffered from."

Sheridan lapsed into a pensive silence. Eventually he said, "Shane was wounded last night. I've hidden him over at Stanton's."

"How?"

"Somehow Clayborne found out that we were moving the

148

goods from Wexford here. Shane acted as the decoy, leading the Red Coats on a wild-goose chase while Gavin and I moved the goods."

"Is Shane hurt bad?"

Sheridan shook his head. "Brice cleaned the wound and dug the slug out, and we've hidden him in one of his barns. I'll keep him there until he regains his strength and can travel."

"Do any of the lads know that Brice is working with you?"

"No, there's been too many coincidences lately. Clayborne showing up in the most unexpected places at the right times." He sighed. "I don't know who to trust anymore."

"Have ye ever thought that maybe you can't trust Brice?"

"Aye." Sheridan's answer was an extended sigh. "I've thought of that."

Mary waited a moment before she said, "Taylor's house was robbed last night."

"Aye," Sheridan replied.

"Do ye know who did it?"

"Aye."

"Who?"

Sheridan lifted the lid off the bread box and cut himself a slice of bread. Liberally spreading the butter, he said, "When Shane saw Bridget the other night, she told him that she had overheard Taylor telling Clayborne that a shipment of weapons were on their way. New and better weapons from England for the soldiers in County Wexford."

"Why more weapons?" Mary sighed. "The English seem to be creating enough havoc with their old ones."

"After the incident over the tithing cattle in Bunclody, the government decided the English needed to be better armed in order to quell rebellions by conscious-less men like us," Sheridan said. "To keep us from stealing the weapons, Taylor is keeping the arrival time and place secret. I was looking for the letter. We need to intercept them."

"Did you find it?"

He nodded. "Too easily. I have a funny feeling about it. I

149

feel like I'm being led into a trap." He dropped the lid on the butter crock.

"Why?"

Taking a bite of bread, he said, "Everything is falling into place without any rough edges; there's no missing pieces." Pulling a chair from the table, he sat down. When Mary poured him another cup of tea, he absently thanked her. "Earl's making a pretense of looking for Shane and the contraband, but—" He leaned back. "Something's wrong, Mother. I can feel it."

Mary sat on the bench against the wall, combing her hair. "Maybe Taylor's running scared, Danny. He doesn't dare let the Wexford boys get hold of news like this." Mary chuckled. "Without weapons look at what ye've done to him. Think what it would be like if ye were equally armed."

Her hair combed, Mary moved to the fireplace, lifting the kettle of boiling water. She carried it into the bedroom, filling her tub. After adding two kettles of cold water, she undressed and bathed. She was drying off when she heard the horses galloping into the yard. Clutching the towel around herself, she ran to the window and peeped through the shutters.

"Put your hands up." Nelson Clayborne's shout rang through the house. "I've got you covered, Shane Dempsey."

Sheridan's gusty laugh filled the building. "You've got me covered, Clayborne, but you haven't got Shane Dempsey and you haven't gotten the stolen goods. He'd be a fool to be anywhere near Ballygarrett."

"Where do you have him?" Clayborne demanded. "I know he's around here. He's wounded, and I followed him to the house."

"Search the house," Sheridan invited. "However, you'll need to wait until my mother has dressed." He pointed to the bedroom. "She's bathing now, so's she can go to the manor house and look at Mrs. Taylor."

Nelson's brows knit in surprise. "Does Mr. Taylor know

that she's coming?"

Sheridan shrugged. "As I see it, Lieutenant, that's meddling. To be sure, it's none of your business." He grinned. "Anyhow you'd have to ask Taylor that question. Only he can answer it."

"Where's Mistress LeFleur?"

"I'm sure you saw her and Paddy drive away," Sheridan answered. "You've had the house under surveillance."

"You're taking your mother to Shane Taggart," Clayborne accused venomously, "so she can tend his wounds."

Mary, fully dressed, opened the door and walked into the kitchen. In one hand she carried a black satchel. "Back so soon, Lieutenant?" Nelson inclined his head, but he didn't speak. To Sheridan she asked, "Will ye empty the tub for me, please. I'm going to look for some herbs before I go."

"Neither of you is fooling me," Clayborne charged. "I know where you're going."

"You're welcome to ride with us or follow behind," Sheridan said disinterestedly, moving into the bedroom and returning with the tub of water. Moving outside the cottage, he emptied the tub and slanted it against the wall. "To make your following easier, I'll tell you this. We're going to Brice's first to check on the cattle which I bought last night. Then we're going to the manor house."

Clayborne's eyes slit. "*You're* going to the manor house?"

"Aye." Without another word, Sheridan turned and walked to the rear of the cottage, hitching the donkey to the cart. When he rounded the house, only Mary was in sight.

"Do you think they've gone?" she asked as she climbed on the cart.

Sheridan reached up and pulled the hat brim over his forehead. He chuckled softly and shrugged. "Our going to the manor house has addled Clayborne. He's not sure what to think or to do."

As Mary tied the ribbons of her bonnet under her chin, a smile tugged her lips. She settled the satchel on the seat

151

between them. "To tell the truth," she admitted, "our going to the manor house has addled me, too." She sighed. "'Twas one of the hardest decisions I've ever had to make, Danny."

Sheridan reached over and laid one of his hands over his mother's. Squeezing gently, he said, "You don't have to go."

"That I do," she returned softly.

Chapter 9

As Marguerite's hand closed on the knob, the library door swung open. Elvira Simmons, dressed in black, with a white-lace coif perched on the back of her head, seemed to swell from nowhere and blinked accusingly at the young woman. Dropping her heavy key ring into her pocket, the housekeeper clasped her hands together.

"It took you a long time to collect the ironing, Mistress LeFleur."

Ignoring the barbed remark, Marguerite asked, "Is Earl in?"

"No!" Reprimand was heavy in Elvira's tone. "He left for Wexford immediately after lunch. He waited for you as long as he could before he had to leave."

Again Marguerite ignored the accusations. "Thank you." As she walked to the staircase, she heard Elvira close and lock the library door.

Marguerite was almost to the landing on the second floor when Elvira said, "We expected you back for lunch."

Her hand on the banister, Marguerite halted. Slowly she turned around, her skirt swirling around her feet. She smiled cooly, again deliberately ignoring the housekeeper. "Has the doctor been to see Mother yet?"

"No."

Disappointment swelled within Marguerite, but she only

said, "We'll have a guest for afternoon tea. You may serve us in Mother's room."

Elvira glared at Marguerite. "A guest?" she repeated, gulping her words more than saying them.

"Mrs. O'Roarke." Marguerite announced the name with flourish.

"Mary O'Roarke!" Elvira swallowed convulsively, and her larynx bobbed up and down. "Have you gone mad!" she exclaimed, visibly recoiling as if she had been struck. "How dare you invite any of the O'Roarkes to this house! Have you any idea what they've done to Mr. Taylor?"

Marguerite walked down the stairs and stood in front of Elvira. "Don't ever speak to me in that tone again, and don't ever question my right or authority." Marguerite's eyes were flinty with resolve. "I shall invite whomever I choose to this house, and I will answer to Earl and my mother only. Is that clear?"

Elvira quelled beneath Marguerite's gaze. Shrinking away, she moved toward the kitchen, muttering under her breath, "You'll rue the day you did this to me, Marguerite LeFleur."

"Mrs. Simmons." The curt tone was a command. When Elvira turned around, Marguerite said, "I expect you to treat my guest with civility and to bring her directly to my mother's room. If Mrs. O'Roarke has occasion to make a complaint about your treatment of her, I shall have Mr. Taylor reprimand you."

Hatred smoldered in Elvira's eyes, but she managed a brusque, "As you wish."

"I wish."

Elvira added spitefully, "I shall treat her civilly, but not because I'm afraid of you or your threats." She moved closer and lowered her voice. "Mark my words, girl: Earl Taylor will never reprimand me over the O'Roarkes. He hates them, Marguerite LeFleur. He hates them." The old woman stared at Marguerite defiantly for a long time before she huffed in disgust, turned and walked away.

154

Marguerite wasted no time with second thoughts. Quickly dismissing Elvira and her words from mind, she raced up the stairs to her mother's room.

"How is Mother?" she asked Annie, closing the door.

Her eyes red and swollen from crying, Annie rose and moved toward Marguerite. "No better," she sniffed. "Lawdy, Lawdy, Miz Marguerite, I don't want her to die, but I'd rather she be dead than living like this."

"Me, too," Marguerite said, holding the old woman in her arms, looking down at the sallow form on the bed. She feared the worst for both of them. "Mrs. O'Roarke is going to come examine her this afternoon."

Annie pulled out of Marguerite's arms and walked to the night table. She swirled a washcloth in the water and wrung it out, replacing the one that was on Amanda's forehead. She sat down in the chair that she had so recently vacated and resumed her vigil. Marguerite walked to the dresser on the far side of the room. Looking at her reflection in the shadowed mirror, she reached up, unpinned her hat and took it off.

"Let me change clothes," she said softly, "and I'll come back to sit with Mother, so you can sleep some."

"I don't think I can sleep, chile. I'm just too worried."

Marguerite smiled. "We'll both sit with her then." She unbuttoned her jacket and slipped out of it. Kneeling in front of Annie, she said, "If you'll unhook me, I'll change clothes." Her dress unfastened, Marguerite scurried to her room and rang for the maid to prepare her bath. Afterward she put on a simple white cotton dress, trimmed with blue ribbon. Unplaiting her hair, she recombed it, pulling it back at the nape of her neck in a shining coil twist, soft fluffy curls wisping around her face. She pinned a blue silk rose to the side of the chignon. Picking up a bottle, she liberally dabbed her favorite fragrance behind her ears and on her wrists.

When she returned to the bedroom, she moved to the bed and stood over her mother. The only evidence of life in the frail body was Amanda's shallow breathing. Annie, exhausted from her vigil and her worry, dozed in the chair. Worried about the old servant, Marguerite caught her shoulders and gently tugged Annie to her feet.

"Come," she whispered, "and lie down on the day bed. When Mrs. O'Roarke arrives, I'll wake you."

Although Annie protested, she was asleep soon after she lay down. Marguerite tucked a blanket over her; then she returned to the bedside. Looking at the bowl of uneaten broth on the night table, she sat down, not stirring until the doorbell chimed through the house. She heard the low drone of voices and the footfalls on the steps down the corridor. She was at the door when she heard the soft knock.

Mrs. Simmons threw open the door. *"Your guest!"* she announced, civility barely disguising her contempt. Moving to the night table, the housekeeper picked up the empty water pitcher and set it on the tray of uneaten food. "I'll refill this for you and send it up later. Shall I empty the water?"

"Not now."

Marguerite answered Elvira, but her gaze was on Mary O'Roarke who stood inside the door, clutching her satchel. The older woman waited for her eyes to adjust to the darkness before she walked to the night table, setting her bag down. Then she moved to the bedside and gazed at the sleeping figure.

Not expecting anyone else to be with Mary, Marguerite was startled when she heard O'Roarke's voice. "Anyone would be ill in this place!"

Marguerite jerked around. Sheridan stood in the door, his shirt tautly stretched across his shoulders, his sleeves still cuffed several times. Astonished at his coming with Mary, Marguerite stared at him. She stood so dumbfounded that Elvira had to push her aside to pass with the tray and pitcher.

Mary's eyes swept around the room. She motioned toward the drapes. "To be sure, we could do with some fresh air and sunshine, not to say a little light."

Hastening to obey, Marguerite ran to the window, quickly pulling the drapes aside and tying them. She raised the glass

156

and flung open the shutters. When she turned around, haloed by the golden sunshine, she found Sheridan staring pensively at her. He hadn't moved; he still lounged in the door in that familiar indolent pose, one shoulder on one side of the frame, a hand braced against the other. His eyes locked on hers, excluding all others.

"How long has your mother been asleep?" Mary asked.

"Since early morning," Marguerite replied absently, her gaze still locked on Sheridan. "Annie gave her a dose of laudanum before breakfast."

Mary leaned over Amanda, looking at the sallow, sunken cheeks and the dark-ringed eyes. "Who suggested that you give her laudanum?"

"Earl did when Mother was in so much pain," Marguerite replied.

"I don't want you to give her any more," Mary said. "No matter how much she might beg for it." She looked at the medicine bottles that lined the stand, encompassing them with a wave of her hand. "Throw all of these away."

The unfamiliar voices and activity aroused Annie. She sat up and looked around. When she saw Marguerite and the strange woman hovering over Amanda, she quickly jumped to her feet.

"What are you doing?" she cried.

Mary O'Roarke turned her head and looked at the old woman whose face was creased in worry, her eyes clouded with fear. "I'm going to save her life if I can," Mary replied. "But I'll need your help."

"Yes, ma'am," Annie quickly answered.

"She needs constant care."

"We've been doing that," Marguerite defended.

"I don't mean sitting beside the bed with her day and night," Mary explained. "I mean care. The proper medicines and herbs. The right foods and drinks at the appropriate times." Mary looked at Marguerite; she sighed, catching the younger woman's hands in hers. "To be sure, I wish I could say that your mother is going to live, but I don't be a'knowin'." Mary's gaze lifted, shifting from Marguerite to Sheridan who had walked closer to the bed. "I'll do my best, but she be in the hands of the Almighty now, child."

"Do what you have to." Marguerite's words were an agonized whisper.

"I would like to move her to my cottage."

"Move her?" Annie exclaimed, galvanizing into action.

Mary nodded. "I can give her constant care only if she's with me."

"I don't know," Marguerite murmured, nervously lifting her hand to her face, running her fingertips over her temple. She knew Earl was going to be angry at her for having allowed the O'Roarkes into his home. He would be furious if she allowed them to take her mother home with them. Yet, as if compelled by the force of a lodestone, Marguerite looked at Sheridan.

"She wouldn't be asking to take your mother," he said, "if she didn't think she could save her, and if she didn't think it was important."

Marguerite nodded. "I understand, but I need to think about it. I have to think about Earl."

"That I be a'understandin'," Mary replied.

"Here's your tea." A tray in her hands, Mrs. Simmons stood in the doorway, her starchy arrival stopping the conversation. Immediately behind her was a maid with a pitcher of fresh water. "Put it on the night table," the housekeeper instructed.

Mrs. Simmons stopped in the middle of the room and turned around, taking in all the changes. Her face screwed into a frown as she looked at the opened drapes and window. Lifting her face in the air, not bothering to hide her snort of disdain, she moved to the table. Without a word, she set the tray down and motioned the maid out, following closely behind.

Marguerite crossed to the table and picked up the teapot. "Mrs. O'Roarke, would you and Sheridan care for a cup of tea and some cucumber sandwiches?"

"Hungry I'm not," Mary answered, "but I will have a cup of tea."

As Mary and Sheridan moved to the chairs that circled the table, Marguerite poured Annie a cup of tea and stirred in the cream and sugar. Walking to the bed, she handed the black woman a sandwich and the drink. "Eat something before you dry up and blow away. Then I want you to go lie down and take a nap."

Annie nodded. "Yes ma'am, I reckon I do need to sleep a mite." She took her food and sat in the chair closest to Amanda. "But I don't think I will. I think I'll jest sit here with your mama. And," she added quietly, "if you let your mama go with them, I want to go, too."

"It's all right with me," Marguerite answered, a smile on her face. "We'll have to check with Mrs. O'Roarke." Marguerite's heart swelled with love for the faithful servant.

His eyes on Marguerite, Sheridan sat down beside his mother. Taking his hat off, he laid it on the floor beside his chair. Without thinking, he raised his hand and casually swept his fingers through the thick waves. He observed the smile that played across Marguerite's face, touching her lips, lingering in her eyes. He saw the softening of her countenance as she looked at the black woman.

Unable to tear his gaze away, he watched her as she returned to the table. The sun filtered through the gossamer, hinting at the fleshy beauty beneath. The gauzy white material of her dress, unobstructed by layers of starched petticoats, clung to her as she moved, accenting long, slender legs, making Sheridan acutely conscious of her body.

Caught up in her own thoughts, Marguerite was unaware of Sheridan's scrutiny. She sat down opposite Mary and picked up the teapot. Having filled the cups, Marguerite set the pot down and looked at Mary. "If Mother goes with you, Annie wants to accompany her. She's been Mother's maid ever since Mother was a baby."

Mary understood Marguerite's concern; she heard the

unspoken question. "I don't mind her staying with me." If anything, the older woman understood the bond of love. "To be sure, I'll enjoy the company."

In silence they drank their first cup of tea. On the second cup, Marguerite asked, "What do you think is wrong with Mother?"

Mary set her empty cup down. "I don't know. What did Mr. Taylor's physician say?"

"He hasn't arrived yet."

Sheridan's eyes narrowed, and he looked from Marguerite to Amanda. "When was he called?"

"Yesterday," Marguerite replied in a small voice.

"Yesterday!" Sheridan's exclaimed. "Why did Earl wait so long?"

Compelled to defend her stepfather for her mother's sake, Marguerite said, "Mother didn't want him to."

Sheridan opened his mouth to say more, but Mary laid her hand on his arm, silencing him. Standing, she said, "Thank ye for the tea, Mistress LeFleur. I'll be a'goin' now. What have ye decided?"

Rising with the older woman, Marguerite's head swiveled in the direction of the bed. "Take my mother with you."

"Are ye sure?"

"Yes," Marguerite replied firmly, "I'm sure."

Mary nodded. "We'll need Paddy to hitch the wagon, and we'll be needing some blankets and pillows for a pallet." At the night table she snapped her satchel shut and picked it up. "I'll drive the cart home, Sheridan." She moved to the door. "You come with Paddy and Mrs. Taylor."

Following Mary O'Roarke, Marguerite hurried out of the room into the backyard, calling orders to Paddy. As quickly she returned to the house, going through the linen closet for blankets and pillows. By the time she had a pallet made in the back of the wagon, Sheridan was easily carrying Amanda down the stairs.

"What do you think you're doing?" Earl's voice thundered

160

through the house.

"I know what I'm doing." Sheridan softly returned as he descended the last stair. "And I know what you're doing, Earl."

Earl laid his hat and gloves on an entry table. He said, "My actions are not yours to be questioned." Calmly he reached up and smoothed his hair. "Take Amanda back to her bed."

Marguerite, having entered the hallway in time to hear her stepfather, rushed forward. "But Earl," she pleaded, her hands on his arm, "the physician hasn't come—"

Earl looked at Marguerite, his eyes softening. He patted her hand. "I know, dear, that's why I didn't go to Wexford. On the way I met the messenger whom Cable had sent." He reassured her. "Cable has been detained by an emergency." His eyes twinkled. "A birthing, but he'll be over directly." He reached into his pocket and withdrew the crumpled sheet of paper. "You may read his note."

Marguerite shook her head. "Mrs. O'Roarke thinks she can cure Mother, Earl."

"Marguerite," Earl spoke firmly, his hand tightly gripping hers, "I know it appears to you that I'm callous, but believe me I have your mother's health and best interests at heart. I'm not going to let her go with the O'Roarkes." His gaze moved from Marguerite to Sheridan, and his voice was flint hard. "Not under any circumstances. Mrs. O'Roarke is a superstitious Irish woman, not a physician. I will not trust Amanda's life to her care."

"But—"

"That's final, Marguerite! I'm your mother's husband, and I will make the decision." He looked at her pleadingly. "Please believe me, I know what I'm doing."

"Aye," Sheridan droned sarcastically, "you know what you're doing, Earl Taylor. When it comes to a matter of choosing between life and death for someone else, you're good at choosing death."

"As if you're so innocent," Earl gritted, his eyes narrowing,

161

his mouth thinning into a line of hatred. "Go put Amanda back in her bed, and get out of my house before I have you arrested for kidnapping."

"You can't have him arrested for kidnapping," Marguerite said quietly, moving past Sheridan. "I asked them to take her." To Sheridan she instructed, "Put her back on the bed."

Earl stood at the bottom landing. "You won't regret this, Marguerite."

Marguerite never stopped climbing the steps. "When Mother awakens, Earl," she said, her voice growing fainter as she moved higher, "I'll ask her what she wants to do. If she chooses to go to Mrs. O'Roarke's, I shall take her there myself."

"All right," Earl acquiesced easily, not wanting to alienate Marguerite totally. "If Amanda chooses to go there, both of us will take her."

He started up the stairs behind her and Sheridan, but Paddy shuffled into the hall, calling to him. "Mr. Taylor! Mr. Taylor! To be sure, I need to speak to ye for a minute."

"Can't it wait, Paddy?"

"No, that it can't." Paddy took off his hat and clutched it with both hands against his chest. He looked around to make sure no one could see or hear him. He lowered his voice, keeping his eyes on the stairs. As soon as Sheridan and Marguerite were out of hearing range, he said, "I need to be a'tellin' ye what I saw today when I was taking Mistress Marguerite to get the ironing."

Earl looked at Sheridan's disappearing form; he looked at the small man who waited at the bottom of the stairs. He didn't want to leave Marguerite and Sheridan alone in the bedroom, but he also wanted to hear what Paddy had to say. Finally he sighed and walked down the stairs.

As he opened the door to the library, he said, "This had better be good, Paddy."

"I think ye'll find what I heard and saw interesting." Paddy grinned. "And when ye see what I found and brought back to ye, ye'll really be happy."

In the room Sheridan gently deposited Amanda on the bed and stood back while Marguerite adjusted the covers. "What am I going to do?" she whispered. "Mother's all I have left."

The heartfelt cry touched Sheridan. He reached for Marguerite, pulling her into his arms. He held her close, giving to her of his strength, reassuring her. He didn't say anything; he simply laid his cheek on the top of her head. He'd had plenty of experience with dying, and he knew there was no comfort in words, no matter how well meant they might be. The only solace to death was the living.

"I'll stay with you, lass," he said.

Marguerite shook her head against his chest. "No." Her words were muffled against the soft material of his shirt. "I would like it, but your presence here would create so much trouble."

"None that I can't handle," Sheridan returned.

Marguerite pushed her head back and smiled wearily. "I don't think I'm up to handling it."

Sheridan cupped Marguerite's face in his hands. "If you need me, day or night, send Paddy for me."

"Can you trust him?"

Sheridan shrugged. "As much as I trust anyone."

"Where your mama?" Annie cried from the door.

Turning to her, Marguerite said, "Earl doesn't want her to go to Mrs. O'Roarke's yet. I've agreed to wait until she awakes and let her make the decision."

Sheridan moved toward the door where he stopped. "I'll explain to Mother. And remember what I said. Anytime." Then he disappeared down the hall, the closed door muffling his footsteps.

"Miz Marguerite," Annie said, "you just go rest a little while. I'm gonna stay with your mama."

"I'll tell you what," Marguerite suggested. "We'll both sit with her. Since those other chairs are too uncomfortable, you lie down and I'll sit."

163

When Annie opened her mouth to protest, Marguerite shook her head. She led Annie to the small bed on the other side of the room and eased her down. Afterward she covered her with a light quilt and said, "If Mother awakens, I'll get you up."

Accepting Marguerite's promise, Annie turned on her side, closed her eyes and went to sleep. Not wanting to sit yet, Marguerite went about straightening the room. She stacked the dishes on the tray and tugged the bellpull for the maid; then she folded the quilt at the foot of her mother's bed.

"You rang, ma'am?" A round-faced young girl poked her head through the cracked door.

"I'd like for you to take these dishes to the kitchen."

"Yes, ma'am."

After the maid had gone, Marguerite sat in the chair beside her mother's bed, idly flipping through the books from which Annie had been reading. Tiring of this she walked to the window and stared at the front gardens. She basked in the late afternoon sunshine that poured into the room, bathing it with a comforting warmth. She was still standing here when Amanda stirred and quietly groaned.

Rushing to her mother's side, Marguerite dipped a cloth in the washbasin and wrung it out. Kneeling beside the bed, she twisted the linen, letting small drops fall on Amanda's dry lips. Then she folded the cloth and laid it across Amanda's brow.

"Marguerite." Amanda's voice was so raspy and thick she could hardly be heard. "Marguerite." Her voice rose in panic. "I can't see you."

"Here I am, Mumsey," Marguerite said, leaning closer, her hands gently touching Amanda's face. "I'm right here with you."

"Marguerite, I'm—I'm dying." No fear; just a calm statement."

"No," Marguerite countered forcibly, barely able to keep the tears back. "You're not dying, Mumsey."

Weakly Amanda lifted a hand and touched Marguerite's

cheeks. She tried to smile, but her lips were too dry and cracked. "You—you look so much like your father." She gasped as pain racked her body. "He—he was as handsome as you are beautiful, my darling."

Wiping the damp cloth over Amanda's face, Marguerite said, "Mrs. O'Roarke, the lady who does the ironing—she's—she's very good at nursing people back to health, and she thinks she can help you, Mumsey. But she wants you to stay at her house."

"Mrs. O'Roarke," Amanda whispered, her mind so cloudy with drugs that her thinking was slowed down. Then she remembered. "No!" she cried, her voice hardly above a rough whisper.

"Yes," Marguerite insisted. "Bridget says she's very good at healing sick people."

Amanda ran her tongue over her fevered lips. "That woman was taking care of Eliza—of Earl's first wife—when she died."

Not knowing much about Earl's past life and certainly knowing nothing about his first wife, Marguerite said, "I trust Mrs. O'Roarke, Mother, and I don't think it was her nursing that killed Eliza."

With dull, listless eyes Amanda stared at Marguerite for a long time before she nodded. "Have you—" Amanda winced with pain. "Have you talked with Earl about it?"

Marguerite nodded and prevaricated somewhat. "He said the decision was up to you."

Amanda closed her eyes and breathed deeply. "He—he said he was going to get his physician."

"He hasn't gotten here yet," Marguerite said. "He's on his way now."

"I—I think we'd better wait for the physician before we make a decision," Amanda whispered weakly. "I—I don't want to do anything that would anger Earl, darling. He's been so good to both of us. The final decision should be his."

"Thank you, my darling wife," Earl said from the door, his words and his presence startling Marguerite. She hadn't heard

165

him enter the room. Quietly he approached the bed. When Marguerite stood and moved to the night table, he sat beside Amanda, taking her hand in his. "I'm so sorry that you're suffering. I wish it were me rather than you." His expression was tender. "Although you can understand how I feel about Mrs. O'Roarke's nursing you, I haven't ruled her out." Reducing Marguerite to a recalcitrant child, he said, "I merely asked Marguerite to wait until Cable has seen you before she lets Mrs. O'Roarke nurse you."

Amanda nodded, her drugged lids slowly drooping over her eyes.

"If Marguerite isn't pleased with Cable's diagnosis, I'll take you to Mary O'Roarke's cottage myself."

Too sleepy to do more, Amanda smiled, and she slightly moved her head. Earl lightly brushed his fingers through the hair at her temples until her breathing told him she was asleep again.

Looking toward Marguerite, he said, "Because you don't know about my first wife's death, you can't understand my behavior this afternoon. I'm sure you think I'm callous." His soft tone begged for understanding. Marguerite squeezed the water from the washcloth. "Taking Amanda to Mrs. O'Roarke's won't anger me. It would hurt and disappoint me, but I understand your anxiety." He paused. "May I tell you about Eliza?"

"If you wish," Marguerite returned listlessly.

Earl was irritated with Marguerite's disinterest, but he was determined to tell her the truth about O'Roarke and to shatter her fantasies about the man. He'd lost one woman—and the fortune he stood to gain at her parent's death—to the blackguard, but he wouldn't lose another.

"Because I was a devoted soldier, caught up in my career, I didn't realize that the years had passed, and I had no family, no son or daughter to inherit my estate."

"In England or here?" Marguerite asked.

"In England or here?" Earl repeated, clearly puzzled by

the question.

"What estate are you talking about?" she clarified.

"This one," Earl replied, despising Marguerite for demeaning him and making him justify his acquisitions.

"The O'Roarke's property."

Earl didn't approve of Marguerite's judgmental statement, but he knew he must move cautiously or all his plans would be to no avail; they would be destroyed before they had begun.

"It belonged to the O'Roarkes one time, but when Devin O'Roarke was exposed as a traitor and his conspiracy revealed in 1826, the property became government property."

"And it was given to you for services rendered the crown," Marguerite finished.

"As a matter of fact, it was," Earl returned, hesitating only a second before he added, "I returned to England later that year and met Eliza Watkins with whom I immediately fell in love, although she was thirty years my junior. A year later we were married, and I brought my bride to Ireland to be mistress of the manor house. We hadn't been married a year before my beautiful wife died." Earl's pause was a dramatic prelude to his next statement. Wanting to see Marguerite's reaction, he looked at her. "Mary O'Roarke killed Eliza and the baby she carried."

Marguerite sucked in her breath, but she averted her face from Earl's searching gaze. She turned, hanging the damp cloth over the brass rail at the end of the night table. The movement put the sun to her back, and the golden light filtered through her petticoats, outlining her slim figure. Earl's eyes slowly moved down—the breasts, the tiny waist, the rounded hips, the slender legs. So like Eliza, he thought. He forgot his reason for looking at her; he forgot his train of thought as his body involuntarily responded to her beauty.

Aware of his burning, greedy eyes on her, Marguerite moved out of the sunlight and walked to Amanda's sewing frame. Sitting down behind the hoop, she picked up the needle and began to embroider. Not because she wanted to know but because she wanted to stop Earl's staring, she asked, "How did Mrs. O'Roarke kill Eliza and why?"

Ousted from his fantasies, Earl blinked vacant eyes at her. "Oh—yes—Eliza—" he mumbled, dropping his face so Marguerite couldn't see the effusion of embarrassed color.

Never had he desired a woman as much as he desired Marguerite—not even Eliza. At first he had been interested only in Marguerite's money, but the more he was around her, the more he wanted her. And he would have her! She *would* give him the child he wanted.

Finally he said, "I loved unwisely, Marguerite. I forgot that Eliza was a mere child, not a woman. An extremely spoiled child at that, given to tantrums if she didn't get her way."

Talking about Eliza resurrected painful, humiliating memories for Earl, memories that couldn't be laid to rest until he had avenged himself at Sheridan O'Roarke's expense.

"I lavished money on her; I adored her, but that wasn't enough. She wanted to live in Dublin where she could go to the balls, the theater, the concerts. But I couldn't take her as frequently as she wanted to go. I had my duties. She began going to Dublin by herself."

He stopped speaking, stood and walked to the window, his back to Marguerite. He gazed pensively out the window.

"Although I couldn't prove it, I knew she'd met a man and had a lover." The tone of Earl's voice changed. "When I discovered she was with child, I knew it wasn't mine. When I confronted her, she admitted that she had a lover and that she was carrying his child. She—she laughed at me," he confessed, his speech ragged. "She told me that she'd never loved me. Her family forced her to marry me. She loved—she loved a damned Irishman."

Earl closed his eyes and moved his hands, clenching them into tight fists. Slowly he sank into the past, unable to give voice to the events. He would never forget the night he had confronted Eliza. Wearing a dressing gown, she sat in front of her dresser, brushing her hair. Hearing him enter the room, she had looked at him through the mirror.

He felt the same anger raging through him that he'd felt six years ago when Eliza had dropped the brush on the dresser, stood, and turned. Instead of being repentant and ashamed, she had laughed at him. Her laughter still rang in his ears, taunting.

"Who is it?" he had demanded, running across the room, his hands clasping Eliza's shoulders. Shaking her, her hair flying in all directions, he screamed, "Tell me who the bastard is? I'll kill him. I'll kill him with my own bare hands."

"Kill him!" Eliza gasped between gales of laughter, her head rolling from front to back. "You're not even man enough to make love to me. How do you expect to kill a man?"

Earl shook her more forcibly. "Who is your lover, Eliza."

Wild laughter filled the room. Earl's hands slid to her throat, his fingers curling around it. He began to squeeze. "Who is your lover, Eliza?"

Eliza twisted and writhed in Earl's clutches; she frantically fought for air; her eyes bulged, and her fingers curled over Earls as she tried to loosen his grip.

Tighter he squeezed. "Tell me, Eliza, or I shall kill you."

"Sh—" The letters were no more than a rasping hiss, a struggle for life.

"Sheridan!" Earl exclaimed. "Your lover is Sheridan O'Roarke?"

Falling to the floor, her hands rubbing her neck, Eliza rasped, "You hanged his father for a traitor, Earl. You took all his land, you forced his mother to become a washwoman." She swallowed, closing her hand around her sore throat. "But you haven't been able to touch O'Roarke, have you? He's a thorn in your side, constantly pricking you. And what are you going to do about me?" She paused, then smiled. "I'm married to you, so legally my child is yours. O'Roarke's child, not yours, will inherit all that now belongs to you but rightfully belongs

169

to O'Roarke."

O'Roarke's child, not yours, will inherit all that now belongs to you but rightfully belongs to O'Roarke!

"That's why you hate O'Roarke?" Marguerite's question jarred Earl from his ruminations.

He turned, watching Marguerite as she skillfully pushed and pulled the needle and thread through the material. "Just another of the reasons."

Earl walked to the night table and picked up the washcloth. Sitting on the edge of the bed, he gently washed Amanda's face. "Not long after that Eliza ran away. By the time Brice and I found her, she was at Mary O'Roarke's cottage, barely alive. She was too weak to move, so I immediately sent for the doctor. He did all he could, but he was unable to save her. She and the baby died."

"You think Mary O'Roarke did it?"

Earl lifted the washcloth and held it suspended in the air. "I have no evidence, but I know Mary O'Roarke did it. Whether it was intentional or not, I don't know. In her ignorance she could have given Eliza the wrong kind of herbs, something poisonous, or . . ."

Marguerite knotted the thread and clipped it. "Or?" she asked curiously.

"Or she could have despised the English so much that she didn't want her grandchild to be part English. Perhaps she didn't want her son to love an Englishman. The Irish aren't above murder, you know."

Marguerite weaved the needle through the material, a stream of colorful thread flowing through the air. "Nor any other race."

"That's the story," Earl said smoothly. "I thought you'd be interested." He stood, draped the washcloth over the brass rod and moved to the chair. Sitting down, he bridged his hands together. "Whatever you and Amanda wish to do," he concluded, "is my wish. I wanted you acquainted with all the facts before you made a decision."

"Thank you," Marguerite said dryly.

An hour passed in complete silence between Marguerite and Earl before Amanda stirred and opened her eyes again.

Marguerite dropped the needle, jumped up, and ran across the room. Leaning over the bed, she asked, "Are you hungry? Would you like to have some soup?"

Amanda shook her head. For the longest time, she looked at Marguerite, her eyes slowly moving over the features of her daughter's face as if she were memorizing each one. Finally her lids grew so heavy, she couldn't keep them up. Once again Marguerite moved back to the embroidery. More silent hours passed, and Marguerite and Earl continued to sit. As the evening shadows lengthened, Marguerite rose and lit the lamps. Soft, golden light illuminated the room.

When the door bell chimed through the house, Earl bounded up and smiled. "That's Cable."

In a few minutes, Mrs. Simmons knocked on the door. "Mr. Taylor, Mickey Flynn is here to see you."

Earl truly looked dumbfounded. "I thought surely that was Cable." He looked at the clock on the mantelpiece. "I thought he would be here by now." To the housekeeper he said, "Show Mickey into the library, Mrs. Simmons, and tell him that I'll be right down." As he walked out of the room, Marguerite heard him say, "Send some food up for Marguerite. She's exhausted."

When next the door opened, Jewel walked into the room. Seeing Marguerite standing at the foot of the bed, looking at her mother, the servant whispered, "Miz Marguerite, is everything all right?"

Marguerite nodded. "It's fine, Jewel."

"Does you want me to sit wif her tonight?"

"No, I'll sit with her until the doctor comes." Marguerite turned to the servant. "Get some more rest while you can."

"Honey chile, I don't be getting any rest. I sleep because my

171

bones gets so weary and my eyes gets so heavy, but I don't rest." Jewel walked to the small bed and looked at the sleeping Annie. "She be wore out, too."

"That's why I'm letting her sleep," Marguerite answered. "If she doesn't get some rest, she's going to be sick, too."

Jewel smiled. "Tell you what, honey chile. I'm gonna go down to thet kitchen and fix you something to eat." She ran a hand down Marguerite's cheeks. "Fill these out and put some color back in yore face. You need some of Jewel's good ole home cooking. How about dat?"

Marguerite gave her a ghost of a smile. "I'd like that."

When Jewel was gone, Marguerite returned to her vigil. Changing the washcloth on her mother's forehead every ten or fifteen minutes, she marked time as she waited for the doctor to come. Amanda wakened, opened her eyes, and smiled at Marguerite. She caught Marguerite's hands in hers.

"I . . . I . . ." She licked her dry lips and swallowed. Marguerite moved to the night table and poured her a glass of water. Holding her mother's head up, Marguerite touched the glass to Amanda's lips. After she swallowed, Amanda laid back down. "I love you," she whispered.

"I love you, Mumsey."

"Is Annie asleep?"

Marguerite didn't answer Amanda's question. Rather she said, "I'll get her."

Quickly Marguerite moved across the room, and the second her hand touched the black woman's shoulder, Annie was on her feet. She hobbled across the room, sitting on the edge of the bed. Her work-rough hands tenderly cradled Amanda's.

She smiled. "Hello, baby. How are you feeling?"

"Better." Amanda's eyes sought Annie's as she said, "You've been like a mother to me, Annie."

Annie nodded. "You've been my little girl."

"If . . . if something should happen to me, take care of Marguerite."

"I will, honey chile. I sure will."

172

Peace seemed to erase the pain and suffering from Amanda's face. "Thank you." She looked beyond the wrinkled black face to Marguerite's. "Take care of Jewel and Annie, darling."

"I will," Marguerite promised.

Amanda smiled and closed her eyes, dozing again. Annie sat on the edge of the bed, and Marguerite sat in the chair. Both watched Amanda. By the time Earl entered the room, Jewel had returned with the food that sat untouched on the table in front of the window. The two black women and Marguerite stood at the foot of the bed. Amanda was resting peacefully.

"Cable won't be coming," Earl said, moving across the room. "In his rush to get over here, his buggy overturned, and he's been injured. That's why Mickey came. He's the one who found him." When Marguerite didn't reply, he added, "I promised you that I'd let Mary O'Roarke nurse your mother."

Still no answer.

"I'll tell Paddy to hitch the wagon, and we'll take Amanda to the O'Roarkes."

"It's too late now."

The words seemed to come from far away as if they were spoken from outside her body.

Chapter 10

The funeral was over, and the people were walking away, but Marguerite remained at her mother's grave, the morning breeze gently swirling the black veil around her face. On either side of her stood Annie and Jewel, also garbed in black, their tearstained faces hidden by the mourner's veil. Since Amanda's death two days ago, they had stayed with Marguerite day and night, refusing to let anyone come near her, refusing to give ground to anyone—including Earl.

Despite Earl's insistence, Marguerite wasn't ready to leave the grave side. To do so was the final separation from her mother. Yet Marguerite didn't cry; she had no tears. Without anyone's being aware of her scrutiny, she studied the small group as they moved toward their carriages. Acquaintances of Earl's, Marguerite thought, listening to their chitter-chatter and trills of laughter. All of them had come because of Earl. None of them knew her or Amanda; few of them mourned her mother's death. Perhaps the Stantons—they were the only ones who seemed to be genuinely grieved.

Despite the warmth of the morning sun, Marguerite shivered, suddenly realizing how alone she was. But as quickly as she felt the chill, she was warmed. She felt the gentle touch of someone's eyes, and she gazed beyond the immediate cluster of people to Earl who stood next to his open carriage; she gazed at Paddy who stood beside Earl. He didn't look like himself, Marguerite thought. Today he was a formal coachman, dressed in Earl's livery colors. Upward her gaze went to the hill, the hill that was colored green with trees and thick grass and was splashed golden with sunshine; the hill that gave life—that promised life—in spite of death.

She stared for the longest time before she saw a movement. Then her breath caught in her chest. Sheridan Michael O'Roarke, dressed in his finest, stood on the hill, looking down at her. His suit was somber in grays and blacks, his waistcoat in creamy brocade. His top hat, so incongruous with his usual wide-brimmed hat, was in his hand. The sun touched his auburn hair, burnishing it to copper. He hadn't forgotten, Marguerite thought, her eyes locking on the craggy countenance. And he'd come to her because he cared. He understood how she felt. For the first time since Amanda had died, Marguerite felt the sweet sting of tears, the blessed release of her sorrow.

Unmindful of the crowd, Marguerite suddenly moved, bounding through the cemetery, racing across the field, up the gentle slope of the hill, and Sheridan, before anyone could see him, moved into the cover of the trees. Surprised, Earl turned and watched Marguerite, wondering where she was going. He quickly scanned the countryside, but he saw no one. When he started as if to pursue Marguerite, Paddy laid a restraining hand on his forearm.

"I wouldn't be a'doin' that, sir. She be a'grievin' right now and wants to be by herself." He removed his hand and clamped his stiff cap on his head. "Private time, sir."

"Someone needs to be with her," Earl argued.

Approaching the carriage, Jewel and Annie heard Earl. Annie said, "I think someone is with her, sir."

Paddy's eyes widened. Had Annie seen O'Roarke? Would she tell Taylor? Before the maid could speak, he said, "To be sure, sir, I think someone of greater importance right now than ye or me is with her."

Earl wheeled around, searching the distance. "Who?" he demanded indignantly.

Annie lifted the veil from her face and flipped it over the hat. Her face was void of any expression, her eyes red and swollen from crying.

Again Paddy spoke, stammering as he sought for a plausible answer. "She be . . . with . . . with God, sir." Paddy smiled at his ingenuity. "That's right, sir. She be alone so she can talk with God about her dear mother's death."

Annie smiled at Paddy and nodded her head. "Leave her be, Mr. Taylor."

"Are you suggesting that we wait for her here?" Earl demanded incredulously, clearly irritated over Marguerite's actions. "Doesn't she realize that the Reverend and Mrs. Denby have graciously prepared lunch for us?"

"No, sir," Jewel softly returned, "Miz Marguerite don't realize nothing but her mother's dead. She ain't thinkin' 'bout no socializing or no meal. She's thinkin' about the hurt in her heart, the emptiness in her life." The veil hid Jewel's face, but it did nothing to disguise the intensity of her gaze. "It ain't so far that we can't walk home. Ya'll go ahead to the house. I'll wait here for her, and we'll come directly."

"To be a'mindin' yer business ain't my intention," Paddy said, "but, sir, the woman be a'tellin' the truth. She can stay and wait for the girl and walk her home. Ye can go on back and entertain your guests until Mistress Marguerite arrives."

Too caught up in her own little world to know what was happening, Luella Denby cried, "Are you ready, Earl?"

"Yes. Yes, I'm ready," he called out.

Nearing the carriage, Luella's eyes rushed over the diminishing crowd in search. "Where's Marguerite?"

"She wanted to be alone with her grief for a little while," he explained. Uncertain what to do next, Earl looked around, first at Luella, then at the others who had boarded their carriages; he looked at Marguerite's receding figure. Waving Luella back to her carriage, he smiled. "We'll be on our way shortly."

177

Under his breath he swore to Paddy. "My God! What could have possessed Marguerite? I do have a position to maintain in the community! I don't want her walking home like a cotter," he snapped irritably. His gaze swept over Annie and Jewel, and he sighed. "The three of us will ride with the Denbys. You stay here and wait for Marguerite." Clamping his jaws together, he moved toward the Denbys' carriage, calling over his shoulder to Paddy. "Get her home as quickly as you can."

Paddy nodded. "That I'll be a'doin', sir, to be sure."

Marguerite ran into O'Roarke's outstretched arms. Her arms circled his body, and she burrowed her face in his brocade waistcoat. Tears scalded her cheeks, and sobs racked her body as she cried for her dead: her father four years ago; her beloved grandmother less than a year ago; now her mother. Dropping his hat unheeded to the ground, Sheridan held her close, murmuring softly and soothingly to her.

"I'm sorry," she gulped.

"Don't apologize," he crooned. "Don't be ashamed of your tears, lassie. They be good for you. My mother says they cleanse the soul of grief."

Gently he eased to the ground, bringing Marguerite with him. He unpinned her hat and carelessly tossed it aside; then he cradled her against himself, rocking her back and forth, softly singing to her. When her crying was spent, he cupped her face in both hands and lifted it to his.

"An' now, Daisy Belle LeFleur," he whispered, his mouth moving closer to hers, "'tis time you tasted life again, time that you learned in the midst of death life is to be found."

His lips covered hers in a warm, gentle kiss, one that consoled her battered spirit; one that soothed her bruised, aching soul; one that asked nothing, only gave. Then he held her securely in the circle of his arms. She was starved for the life he promised, that he extended to her. She was desperate for his solace. Her arms circled his body, and she clung to him.

"Why?" she sobbed. "Why did Mama have to die, Sheridan? She was so young and beautiful."

Having no answers, Sheridan could do nothing but hold her as she emptied the cistern of her sorrow through the shedding of tears. Finally she wilted against him, the sobs slowing to occasional hiccups. When he heard no more sniffs, Sheridan eased away, looking down at her.

"Ahh, lass," he said, his green eyes twinkling, "in these clothes I feel like the bird that's been trussed for dinner." He stripped out of his coat and waistcoat, dropping them beside him. "I can stand this binding but for a short time."

Reaching for her, he again folded her into his arms. Sharing her sorrow and pain, he began to talk softly, telling her of the Irish legends and heroes. Marguerite didn't hear the words. Instead she listened to the lilting beauty of his voice; she listened to the message of love his heart communicated to her. But even then Marguerite's loneliness, looming like a monster, compelled her to snuggle. Her breasts pressed through the thin fabric of Sheridan's shirt, brushing against his skin.

Sheridan stammered over his words and finally stopped, drawing a deep breath. His body, with a mind of its own, responded to Marguerite's inadvertent caresses. But he knew this was not the time or the place. Marguerite's loneliness would make her a victim rather than a lover. If he made love to her now, he would be raping her body and her soul. Struggling with his errant emotions, Sheridan gently scooted back, stretching out.

Propping on an elbow, he said, "I have always wanted to see your hair hanging, lass, the sun shining through it."

One by one he pulled the pins out, dropping them into the crown of her bonnet so she wouldn't lose them. He uncoiled the thick, shining chignon, running his fingers through the silky strands. When it hung in riotous abandon, swirling around her face and over her shoulders, Sheridan could only stare.

"Do . . . do you like it?" she asked tentatively.

"Aye. It is more beautiful than I had imagined."

"Have ye been kissing the Blarney Stone, Danny, me boy?" Marguerite gently mimicked.

"Nay," Sheridan returned, sitting up, an enigmatic expression glowing in his eyes. He teased in return, "An' I'll not have ye calling me Danny Boy, Mistress LeFleur. Never in all me life have I allowed anyone but me own family to call me Danny."

"Danny Boy," Marguerite murmured, liking the sound and the taste of his name. .

The whispered words died into silence as he stared at Marguerite. Mesmerized by the virile handsomeness, overwhelmed by the emotions which surged through her body, so innocent she didn't understand where loneliness merged into desire, Marguerite gazed at Sheridan. She was his for the taking, but Sheridan couldn't.

Compelled to confess, she whispered, "Sheridan, about Jordan and me—"

"It doesn't matter," he softly replied, reaching up, cupping her face in his hands. He guided her head to his chest. He pulled her closer, silently holding her until they heard Paddy's whistle. Sheridan shifted, again moving her. Marguerite looked up, blinking in surprise.

"Paddy's coming," he said softly. "You need to be getting to the house." Amusement softened the craggy visage. "The Reverend Denby and his wife have prepared your funeral luncheon, so I overheard. They'll be expecting you."

Bemused, Marguerite stared at him. Food was the furthermost thing from her mind.

"Mistress Marguerite," Paddy called from a distance. "'Tis time we were getting along. Mr. Taylor be a'waitin' lunch fer ye."

"She'll be along, Paddy," Sheridan answered.

"You didn't come to me," she whispered, thinking of the last two nights. "I sent Paddy after you, but you didn't come to me."

"I did come." Marguerite flung her head over her shoulder,

180

her hair swishing in Sheridan's face. "And guarding you each night was one of your black servants."

"Why didn't you let me know?"

He chuckled. "You were sleeping too peaceably to disturb, sweet. Both you and your black angel."

Marguerite lifted her arms, coiling and repinning her hair. By the time she perched her bonnet on her head, Sheridan was on his feet. He held out his hand and helped Marguerite up. They walked to the edge of the clearing.

"Have you decided what you're going to do?" Sheridan asked.

Marguerite watched two burros, one dark brown, the other a creamy white, as they ambled up the dirt road, stopping to munch on the grass along the way. "Because I have no one, Mother wanted me to stay with Earl." Her eyes moved to the beautiful yellow flowers that dotted the hillsides. "So does he. He said this is my home for as long as I wish it to be."

"Do you wish it to be?"

Marguerite shrugged, averting her face from his gaze. Sheridan caught both her shoulders in his hands, and he wheeled her around. Silently he demanded an answer.

"I—I don't know."

"Where will you go if you don't stay here?" His voice hardened. "Back to New Orleans?" *Back to Jordan*, he almost said.

"Perhaps." Without breaking the gaze, Marguerite said, "Earl told me about Eliza."

Stooping, Sheridan picked a blade of grass, sticking it in the corner of his mouth. Chewing on it, he leaned against the trunk of a tree. He looked at Marguerite, thick sultry lashes hooding his eyes. He crossed his arms over his chest.

"Did he now?" His tone was guarded, his expression wary. "And what did he tell you, lass?"

"That she . . . that she loved you."

Sheridan laughed, the sound devoid of humor. "I'm sure Earl told you more, Marguerite LeFleur. He wouldn't have wasted his time or yours just to pass around idle gossip. He's as adept at killing people with his words as the Red Coats are with their swords and guns. So out with it."

"She was with your . . . with child when she died under mysterious circumstances."

"And he was partially right," Sheridan concurred, Marguerite's heart sinking with the admission. "She did die under mysterious circumstances, but none of them was my making, lass." Marguerite could tell by his tone of voice and his set expression that he had explained as much as he intended to. "When will you know what you're going to do?" he asked.

Disappointed, Marguerite listlessly said, "I don't know."

"You're not really thinking about staying with Earl, are you?"

"I—I don't know what I'm going to do," Marguerite repeated, irritated because Sheridan was quizzing her, pushing her into explanations that she wasn't ready to give, irritated because he asked for what he wasn't willing to give her. "I—I don't have any place to go."

"What about your plantation?"

"I can't. There's Jordan to consider."

Without thinking of her emotional exhaustion, Sheridan thundered, "Jordan!" His hands clamped on her shoulders, spinning her around in one quick move. "Will you never get over your married lover?"

Tears filled her eyes, and she struggled out of his grip. "He isn't my lover, Sheridan. He's the lease-holder on my plantation."

"The leaseholder on your plantation!" The words escaped through Sheridan's lips like the quiet but stinging crack of a whip. "You had no consideration for his wife at all, did you?" His voice thundered across the clearing; he was angry with Marguerite for having turned to Jordan, angry at himself for caring that she did. "Was this another ploy of yours to hang on to Jordan? Have you thought about the mental anguish his wife must be going through? But you don't care, do you? You don't think of anyone's feelings but your own."

"Yes, I care," Marguerite cried, tears streaming down her face.

Fate was so cruel. In one vicious stroke after another, Marguerite's world tumbled in on her; her heart crushed beneath the load. First her family, one by one. Now Sheridan.

"I just wish someone loved me enough to be concerned about my feelings like everyone is Susanna's. And not because it's any of your business, I didn't lease the plantation to Jordan. I gave my attorney my power of attorney, and unknown to me he leased it."

In clear view Paddy, both hands in his uniform pockets, his cap pulled low over his eyes, walked up the road, whistling loudly. When he saw Marguerite and Sheridan, the whistling stopped and he smiled.

"Top o' the mornin' to ye, Sheridan O'Roarke. Right surprised I am to be seeing ye here." He grinned as he watched Sheridan stoop and pick up his top hat and waistcoat. "An' all dressed up." Paddy turned to Marguerite. He saw her swollen eyes, the recent tears. Gently he said, "I don't mean to be a'tellin' ye what to do, ma'am, but—"

Marguerite managed a weak smile and nodded her head. She was glad that Paddy had interrupted them. She knew that Sheridan didn't love her; he just wanted her. Simple lust. He still believed that she'd been Jordan's mistress. His coming to her today had been a part of his plan to make love to her.

"It's time to be going," she sniffed, adding, "I shouldn't want to disappoint the Denbys."

In a surprising gesture, Sheridan reached out, catching her chin in his hand. His touch—his voice—both were gentle; they were like a soft cloth smoothing the ragged edges of her despair. "I worry about you, lass, and I care."

Like a volcano, Marguerite was a boiling cauldron of emotion, ready to erupt at the least provocation: his anger, his indifference, his caring. She jerked her chin from his grasp. "Do you?" She forced back her tears, ashamed because her

183

heart clung to his sweetness, because she wanted it so much. "Well, don't. I can take care of myself."

"I wonder," Sheridan mused aloud, seeking the answer in the depth of lush blue eyes. "I wish I knew." He stared at her for an extremely long time before he said to Paddy, "Take care of her, Paddy McLeary, and let me know if she needs me."

"That I will, to be sure."

Sheridan, hooking his coat and waistcoat over his shoulder with one hand, strode through the small thicket of trees to his horse. Easily and gracefully swinging into the saddle, he smiled and waved.

"I'll be seeing you again, Daisy Belle."

She shook her head. "No."

He nodded. "I must, lass, and I will. Both of us know that." With a sweep of the top hat through the air, he was gone. Marguerite heard him whistling as the horse galloped down the road.

"That's the same song that you sing and whistle," she said, listening to the familiar melody. "Mary called it the 'Wearing of the Green.'"

"Aye," Paddy returned offhandedly, "though the British don't like it, lass, we Irishmen are fond of wearing the green, and till the day we wear it permanently we sing about it."

Chapter 11

Paddy and Marguerite lapsed into silence as they walked toward the carriage. Mulling what Earl had told her about Eliza and remembering O'Roarke's casual dismissal of the subject, Marguerite said, "Earl told me about Sheridan and Eliza."

Lifting his arm, Paddy took off his cap and wiped his sleeve across his forehead. "You don't say, ma'am."

Irritated, Marguerite said, "Don't you be doing it too, Paddy McLeary."

"Doin' what, ma'am?" he questioned innocently.

"Hiding behind jargon," she retaliated. "I think perhaps Queen Elizabeth was quite right to get so exasperated with Lord Blarney, and I think all you Irishmen are related to him. All of you are alike. Think you can constantly hide behind a glib tongue."

Paddy opened the carriage door. "A glib tongue is all that's been left the Irishman, ma'am. It's become his weapon; with it we lash back at the enemy. It's become our fortress; through our songs and laughter we hide from oppression and despair."

Settled in the carriage, Marguerite asked, "What about Eliza and Sheridan, Paddy?"

He closed the door. "That's not my story to tell, ma'am. When O'Roarke is ready to tell you, he will."

"I gave him the opportunity today," she said pouting, "and

185

he didn't."

"'Twasn't the proper time."

"Do you think he'll tell me, Paddy?"

"To be sure, lass, if he thinks it's any of your business." He stepped closer to the carriage and tilted his face so that he was looking directly at Marguerite. "But, lass, I would wait for him to be a'tellin' me. Don't be a'pushin' the man too quick toward painful memories."

When Marguerite arrived at the manor house, she disembarked from the coach and entered through the back door. Not alerting anyone to her arrival, she slipped up the servants' stairs to the second floor. As she walked she yanked her gloves and hat off. Opening the door, she tossed them on the bed. She turned to lock the door when a shout stopped her.

"Miz Marguerite!" Annie called. "I was worried about you, chile."

Marguerite smiled warmly at the old woman. Holding her hands out, she clasped both of Annie's. "I just wanted some time to myself."

"Yes, ma'am," Annie said, her eyes twinkling. "I know just who you wanted to be by yourself with." Both of them laughed together. "Do you want me to help you undress?"

Marguerite shook her head. "No, you go rest. I'll do it." She sighed. "I'm in no hurry to spend the rest of the day with Luella Denby, listening to her incessant chatter." In afterthought, she added, "By the way, have they eaten lunch yet?"

Annie shook her head. "No, ma'am. The guests are in the parlor, but Mr. Taylor's been in the library since we got back from—" Annie sniffed back her tears. "Since we got back. That lieutenant was waiting for him on important business."

"Good!" Marguerite breathed a sigh of relief. "I'll comb my hair and go to the parlor."

So preoccupied with repairing her toilette, Marguerite forgot to lock the door after Annie left. As she moved toward the dresser she shook her head, letting her hair gently wave around her shoulders. Her hand closed around the brush handle at the same time that she heard the knock on the door and Earl's call.

"Marguerite, is that you?"

"I'll be out in a moment, Earl," she replied, as the knob turned and the door opened.

Aghast that Earl would come into her room uninvited, Marguerite whirled around facing her stepfather, her back to the dresser. Earl couldn't take his eyes off Marguerite. She was more lovely than ever. Her hair was hanging in wild disarray around her face; her cheeks were heightened with color, and her lips were full and red. Desire stirred through his body, heavily settling in his groin.

"I wasn't aware that I invited you into my bedroom," Marguerite quietly admonished.

"I'm sorry," Earl said, his eyes never leaving her face. "I—I was worried about you, my dear. And when I heard the carriage and saw Paddy, but not you, I—" He smiled appealingly. "I just couldn't help myself." He walked farther into the room, closing the door.

"I'm sorry I'm late," Marguerite explained cooly, her eyes moving to the foot of the bed. "I messed up my chignon when I took my hat off. If you'll give me a few minutes, I'll comb my hair and I'll be down for lunch."

"We'll be waiting for you in the parlor," he said, making no effort to leave the room. "Please give me just a minute, Marguerite. I didn't know when the Denbys would leave," he continued, "and something unexpected has just arisen. I . . . I need to talk with you . . . alone."

"You could have suggested that I meet you in the library," Marguerite pointed out. "By coming to my bedroom, you're compromising me."

Earl rubbed his hands together, his brows furrowing. In his haste to talk privately with her, he hadn't thought about her reputation. "I'm sorry, my dear." He spread his hands in a supplicating gesture. "Your mother's illness, her death, your health—these have been uppermost in my mind. I'm afraid I haven't been thinking very straight for the past two or three weeks." He waved toward the chair. "May I please sit down and talk with you while you comb your hair?"

About that time the door opened, and Jewel swept into the room. She drew to her full height, and her bosom heaved as she drew in several deep breaths. Her brown eyes centered disapprovingly on Earl, but she spoke to Marguerite.

"As soon as Annie told me that you wuz in, honey chile, I came running." She took the brush from Marguerite and pushed her into the dressing chair. "I'll do this for you."

"Can't you let Marguerite do it, Jewel?" Earl asked, obviously displeased with the servant's intrusion. "I'm talking with her at the moment."

"Dat's all right wif me," Jewel returned, running the brush through Marguerite's hair. "I don't mind you talking wif her." Jewel smiled into the mirror, looking at Earl through the reflection. "Jes' play like I can't hear, Massa Taylor, 'cause I ain't gonna repeat nothing I hear you say to my little girl. And I ain't gonna leave her. I promised her mama that I'd take care of her, and protecting her reputation is part of dat responsibility."

Earl sighed his irritation, and Marguerite smiled. "I don't want you to make a decision about your future yet, Marguerite," he said. "I want you to know that you're welcome to stay here at the manor house with me as long as you like."

"Thank you, Earl, but you've already told me that," Marguerite returned. "Annie, Jewel, and I appreciate your kindness. I'll let you know my decision as soon as I receive an answer from Owen. What I do depends on his answer."

"Ah, yes," Earl said, lowering his face as he brushed lint from his trousers. "The letter you posted to your attorney." He lifted a hand out of habit and absently straightened his cravats. "I shall be leaving tomorrow to tend to some very important business."

Marguerite looked at him in surprise. "This is sudden, isn't it?"

Earl nodded. "That's why I barged into your room. I just learned about it when I returned home. I shall be gone several weeks. I—I—" he stammered. "I don't suppose that you'd like to come with me?"

"No," Marguerite returned quickly, not giving the invitation a thought. "I don't think so."

Earl nodded. "That's what I thought you'd say." He hesitated, watching Jewel deftly plait Marguerite's hair and coil it into a chignon. "I'd like for you to promise me that you won't leave until after I return then."

"I won't."

Jewel tucked the last pin into the chignon. Then she worked with the ringlets that framed Marguerite's face. Picking up the hand mirror, Marguerite turned on the stool so she could survey her hair. She reached up and twirled one of the curls.

"Where are you going?" she asked.

Before Earl could answer, Jewel lightly tapped Marguerite's hand and scolded, "Leave dem curls alone, Miz Marguerite. I don't have no time to fuss with 'em no more before lunch." She lamented, "I do declare, you all the time got to have yore hand in the pie, whuther it's yore pie or not."

Her question to Earl forgotten, Marguerite grinned at Jewel. Glancing over her shoulder, she directed her question to Earl. "Should I change dresses?" She lay the mirror down and stood.

Earl rose with her and held his arm out. "No, you look beautiful as you are, my dear." His gray eyes perused Marguerite's face, the heightened color, the twinkle in her eyes. "You're so much like your mother—only stronger and more vibrant."

Marguerite's expression changed drastically. Immediately Earl regretted having so thoughtlessly uttered the words. He reached for her hand and tucked it under his arm. Patting it, he led her out of the bedroom and closed the door behind them.

"I'm sorry, Marguerite. I didn't mean it the way it sounds."

"I know."

In the hallway, Earl stopped walking and turned to Marguerite, so close his breath, reeking of his favorite liquor, assailed her nostrils. Unconsciously she pulled back, trying to escape the revolting odor.

Lowering his voice, Earl said, "Thank you for agreeing to remain at the manor house until I return. I promise you won't regret your decision."

"Oh, yes," Marguerite said, smiling, adroitly tugging his arm and guiding him down the hall so she could escape the intimacy which he was initiating, "you never did say where you were going."

Earl hesitated only momentarily before he said, "Dublin."

Marguerite lifted her delicately shaped brows. "To Dublin town," she said softly. "Your business must indeed be important."

Again Earl stopped walking, and his voice livened up. "Indeed, Marguerite, it is most important."

Without thinking of the consequences, Marguerite said, "I've always wanted to visit Dublin."

Again Earl hesitated; then he said, "I would love to have you go with me. I'll show you the sights." Immediately Marguerite started shaking her head. "A trip would be good for you, my dear," he said. "Get you out of the house and away while I'm having the master bedrooms redecorated." Earl smiled when Marguerite's head jerked up in surprise. "A small gift for you, my dear. While you're deciding what you want to do, I didn't want you constantly reminded of your mother's death—so soon after your beloved grandmother's."

Earl's face was so kind, his words so gentle, his intentions so benevolent that Marguerite instantly warmed to him. Tentatively she smiled. "I don't know how to thank you," she began.

"Come to Dublin with me," he enticed. "Let me show you how wonderful Ireland can be. My business will be finished in a couple of days. After that I'll devote my entire time to your entertainment. We'll go to balls, to the theatre, to the concert." His smile pleaded with her. "You deserve it, my dear, and it would give me such joy to show you some pleasure after so much sorrow in your life. Susanna's false accusations; your family's death."

Marguerite's eyes glowed at the thought, and she was caught up in Earl's fantasies and promises. Seeing that she was about to capitulate, Earl said, "I'll have new clothes designed for you in Dublin. You'll be the toast of the town."

The dreamy look evaporated from Marguerite's eyes, and she opened her mouth to protest, but Earl laid a silencing finger over her lips.

"It's not what you're thinking. This is your mother's money." He smiled, nodding his head. "I refused to take any of her money." Quite the schemer, intelligent and crafty, he added, "Now tell me which maid you wish to take with you, Marguerite, Bridget or Jewel, or do you wish to take both?"

Again surprise hiked Marguerite's brows. Before she could say a word, Earl spoke. "I think we should leave Annie so she can recuperate. She's old, and tending your mother has taken its toll on her." He pressed for an immediate answer. "Will you go with me?"

Marguerite again moved toward the stairwell. "This is so sudden. I need more time to think about it. I'll give you my answer in the morning."

"Would that give you enough time to pack?" Earl asked, the two of them descending the stairs.

Marguerite smiled. "If not, Jewel and I can join you later. By the time we arrive your business will be out of the way."

"Yes," Earl exclaimed, his face brightening up. "Yes, my dear, that's the answer." He looked at her, his excitement growing, and Marguerite couldn't help but chuckle at his exuberance. Earl threw back his head and laughed, enjoying life as he hadn't in many years. "Marguerite, you're so wonderful for me."

"Thank you, Earl." Grandly she swept into the parlor on his

arm, looking up into his face.

"Hello, my dear." Luella Denby heaved herself out of the chair and moved across the room, her corset creaking as she walked. "How are you feeling now?"

"Quite well, thank you," Marguerite graciously returned, hearing the soft chimes of the door bell in the background. Her eyes swept the crowd for Martha Stanton's friendly face. On finding it, Marguerite excused herself and moved toward the woman. Before she reached Martha, however, an uproar disturbed the small gathering.

"I don't give a damn what the man's doing. Lieutenant Clayborne has said I can't hold meetings and pass out brochures about my land grant in Mexico without clearing it with Taylor. I have an appointment, and I demand to see him right now. My business is as important as his, and I don't have time to be fighting with the government the short time that I'm here."

Recognizing James Power's voice raised in anger, Marguerite didn't stop to think. Acting impulsively, she rushed into the entrance hall. "Mr. Power," she said, extending her hand in greeting, "how nice to see you. Can I do something for you?"

"Mistress LeFleur," James said, his face red from his outburst, "to be sure, it's nice to see you again. But it's your stepfather whom I need to see."

Irritated with Marguerite's lack of social demeanor, Earl frowned, but she left him no choice. He must follow. "Mr. Power," he said silkily, moving past Marguerite and leading the way into the library, "I'm Earl Taylor. I'm sorry I was unable to meet with you this morning, but my wife recently died and we were conducting the funeral."

"It is sorry that I be," James returned contritely, looking at Marguerite.

She smiled, sitting in one of the chairs in front of the fireplace as Earl waved James to one in front of his desk.

"Now, Mr. Power, what can I do for you?"

"I would like to know, Mr. Taylor, why after you said I could pass out handbills, you rescinded the permit."

"Surely, Mr. Power," Earl returned sharply, "you can understand my position. We English have dealt with one insurrection after another in this bloody country, and I will not knowingly sanction another bloodbath."

"Holy Mother of God!" James swore softly. "I've told your men time again I'm not trying to start a rebellion. I'm an impresario," he said proudly, waving his hand eloquently as he talked. "I'm trying to gather immigrants to settle in Mexico." He raised his voice, curled his hand into a fist and leaned forward, hitting Earl's desk. "To be sure, man, I'm trying to alleviate some of the suffering that leads Irishmen to rebel. I'm mustering up as many of the peasants and cotters as I can to take back to Texas with me."

Unconvinced by James's words, Earl said, "So you say, Mr. Power, but we have cause to believe that you're dealing in contraband." Earl opened the drawer on his desk and extracted a sheet of paper. Unfolding it, he said, "Here is a list of people whom Lieutenant Clayborne tells me you've visited—not once but several times."

As Earl began to recite the list of names, James interrupted him. "To be sure, I've visited those people," he said. "They be my relatives as well as peasants and tenants, who barely make a living in this land under you English landlords—the majority of whom are absent, living in England. I'm offering them a new world, a new opportunity."

Laying the list on the table, Earl thumped his finger on the paper. "These people, Mr. Power, are the ones who are under suspicion of being involved in a smuggling ring and in a conspiracy against the established government."

James stood, reached across the desk and picked up the sheet of paper. Crumpling it in his hand, he tossed it down. "Mr. Taylor, please weigh my words carefully. I am not involved with these people's politics, and most assuredly I am not a smuggler. I didn't come all the way from Mexico to get

193

involved in an uprising."

"You were involved with the uprising of 1798."

Marguerite saw James's hand ball into a fist. "I was a lad of ten years, Mr. Taylor." His voice hardened. "But I'll tell you this: Had I been older I would have been involved with it, and I would have seen the likes of you dead."

"And so—" Taylor laughed nastily. "How do I not know that you've come home with revenge on your mind."

James opened the small portfolio which he carried and pulled out several sheets of paper, handing them to Earl. "Here, you may read my advertisement yourself. See what I'm doing."

Earl took the sheets, scanning them. Satisfied, he laid them on his desk. "Your only interest is to take people back to Mexico with you?" Power nodded. "I'm sorry that we've disserviced you," Earl said smoothly, "but surely you can understand our position."

"No disrespect meant, Mr. Taylor," James Power said, closing his portfolio, "but I don't give a damn about you or your position. I'm interested in giving these people a new life and a new chance. Now if you don't mind, sir, please leave me alone. Tell your feisty lieutenant what I'm doing and that I have your approval so I can do my job."

"I believe Lieutenant Clayborne requested that you give him a list of towns and villages which you plan to visit each week," Earl said.

"He did," James returned curtly, again delving into the portfolio. He handed Earl another sheet of paper.

Taking it, Earl read it silently. Laying the paper down, he said, "A good many port cities, Mr. Power—some of the best for receiving and sending smuggled goods to the American frontier." He looked at Marguerite. "Will you pour Mr. Power and me a drink, Marguerite?" Then he said to Power. "I've done quite a bit of research during the past week, Mr. Power, and I've learned that the part of Mexico from which you come ..." He paused, as if thinking, then said, "Texas, I

194

believe, has many Americans settling within its boundaries."

James accepted the glass. "That's right," he acknowledged. "That's why the Mexican government has given me the tract of land. Mexico wants to build a buffer between the interior and the United States, a buffer with people who have a cultural and religious similarity to the Mexicans."

Earl took his glass from Marguerite, quietly thanking her. "I also learned, Mr. Power . . ." He heightened the suspense by stopping to take a swallow of his drink. "That the frontier people of Texas, like you Irish, are a lawless breed themselves, despising the Mexican government and her economic policies," he continued.

"That may be true," James begrudgingly acknowledged.

"What better circumstances for smuggling. The Irish resent the government's economic policies as much as the Texans resent Mexico's. Each of these malcontents would benefit from an illegal association with the other, would she not? Each would bypass the . . . ah . . . shall we say, the cumbersome clogs of economic machinery in the mother countries?"

James set his glass down with a thud, the liquor splashing over the sides, spilling on Earl's desk. "I see that the established government has changed little since I left." He raised his voice and stoutly defended himself. "I am not over here, establishing a smuggling ring or route. I have told you my purpose, and that's that. Either you believe me or not." He stood, his portfolio in hand. "Now, sir, I'll bid you good day. With or without your help, Taylor, I shall pass out handbills, and I shall have meetings in order to gather my people to return to Texas." He walked to the door. His hand on the knob, he turned to look at Earl. "I shall go directly to the head of government, sir. Surely all the established officials can't be as narrow-minded as you are."

"You may do just that," Earl returned unperturbed, "but until you have a written release from someone with more authority than I, you will keep me apprised of your activities. In particular, Mr. Power, I want to know when you're leaving for Mexico—the exact date and time. I want to know what coach you're taking and what ship."

"An' my answer to you, Mr. Taylor, is what you want and what you get are two different things."

The slamming of the door reverberated through the room long after James Power had departed. Marguerite moved to the desk and picked up one of the handbills which he'd given Earl. "You were rather hard on him," she said quietly.

Earl ran nervous fingers through his hair. "I suppose I was. I don't know," he said, quaffing his drink in several large swallows. He set his glass down and looked at Marguerite, smiling sheepishly. "I've got so much on my mind, Marguerite, problems and concerns you wouldn't begin to understand." He paced back and forth in front of the fireplace. "I must break the smuggling ring, and I'm not convinced that James Power isn't part of it. I know O'Roarke is, and I shall soon have evidence. For all I know Power is their connection. I just can't take a chance."

Inwardly Marguerite started, but outwardly she maintained her aplomb. She read the brochures. "I don't think Power is. He's not involved with your Anglo-Irish problem. I believe him."

Earl chuckled. "The innocence of the young."

While Earl cleaned off his desk, Marguerite folded the brochures and eased them into her pocket. She picked up the two glasses and carried them to the tray. As she walked in front of the opened french door, she thought she saw a movement, a shadow, but she couldn't be sure. She stopped, and she looked again. Setting the glasses down, she walked into the garden and looked around, but she saw nothing.

"There now," Earl said, locking his desk. He looked at Marguerite who was staring at the floor. "Is anything wrong, dear?"

"No, just peculiar. Someone's strewn picked clover all over the pathway."

Earl walked across the room and looked at the shamrocks

that swirled around her feet. His eyes sparkled with excitement, and a smile of triumph curved his face. A sign from Hibernia! His plans were coming to a head beautifully. Soon Marguerite and her fortune would be his, and O'Roarke would be dead. Without giving expression to his pleasure, Earl said, "Right now, let's join our guests, my dear. I'll talk to Paddy about this later."

"Yes," Marguerite murmured. She cast one last glance over her shoulder, but she saw no one. However, in the quiet stillness she heard the whistling in the courtyard. She saw Paddy standing beneath the window, looking up. She recognized the tune. She felt a chill as clouds amassed, momentarily hiding the sun.

Chapter 12

After Marguerite closed the last trunk, she pushed to her feet and stood gazing around the room—so empty now that her mother was gone. Slowly she moved through the maze of boxes and crates until she stood in front of the dresser. She picked up her mother's jewelry box. As she opened the lid, soft music spilled into the room, taking Marguerite back to happier times. Listening to the melody, she looked at her mother's assortment of jewelry, in particular the gold chain that glimmered against the black velvet—her father's last gift to Amanda. The pearls he'd given to Marguerite, the long gold chain to her mother. Unbidden tears came to Marguerite's eyes.

"Anythin' I can do to help you, mum?" Bridget's voice softly touched Marguerite's ears.

"No," she replied, reaching up to flick the tears off her cheeks. She closed the lid and turned around, holding the music box under her arm. "I'd like for you to distribute my mother's clothes to the needy."

"To be sure," Bridget replied, a smile on her face. "The people will be a'thankin' ye, mum. Ye'r so kind."

"Just practical," she answered. "You're the one who is kind, and I'm glad to have you back."

"And I'm glad to be back, Mistress Marguerite," Bridget confessed. "Much as I love me sister and her wee babes, they did get on me nerves. I think it's much better to start out with one at a time."

"I agree," Marguerite said, and the two laughed. Treading her way across the room to the door, Marguerite added, "While I go tell Mrs. Simmons that I've cleared the room of all Mother's belongings, you find Paddy. After lunch we'll load the wagon, and—"

"Ye'r forgettin', mum," Bridget reminded her, "Paddy is on his way to Dublin with Mr. Taylor." Marguerite grimaced. "But not to worry. I'll get Kennie, the stable boy, to help me. He's a right bright young lad." A twinkle in her eyes, she added as she slipped out of the room, "More, he's right strong. Why, we'll even deliver these before the day is over."

"Bridget," Marguerite called before the young girl disappeared down the hallway. "I'll be gone for a while this afternoon. Will you check on Annie for me?"

Bridget smiled, and her face burst into warm sunshine. "To be sure, Mistress Marguerite. I'll take care of her. Don't ye be a'worrin' none." At the door, Bridget turned. "By the way, mum, do ye mind if I take the evening off?"

"Not at all." Marguerite smiled.

After Bridget left, Marguerite stood for a moment longer, reluctant to leave the last memory of her mother. Her hand closed over the brass knob, and she pulled the door after her as she stepped into the hall.

"Jest ain't right," Jewel muttered, coming to meet Marguerite. "It jest ain't right, Miz Marguerite."

"What isn't right?" Marguerite asked, twining her arm through the black woman's.

"You going to meet Massa Taylor, and your mama barely in the grave. Ain't respectable," she declared.

"It isn't respectable or you just don't want me to go meet Earl?" Marguerite questioned, moving to the heart of the matter.

Jewel chuckled, her white teeth sparkling. "I don't like dat man, honey chile. He sends shivers down my back sometimes

200

the way he looks at people, almost as if he wanted to kill them."
She paused, adding pensively, "As if he had the power to kill
'em at will."

Marguerite laughed. "Your imagination is running wild,"
she chided lovingly. "Earl may be a harsh man, and certainly I
don't agree on his political philosophy in regards to the Irish,
but I don't think he's evil."

Jewel stopped walking, and she turned, facing Marguerite.
The sober, dark eyes penetrated the blue ones. Emphatic came
the words: "Yes ma'am, Miz Marguerite, you kin mark my
words. Dat man is evil. Beware of him."

Marguerite was spared an answer. Elvira Simmons appeared
on the landing. Less hostile since Amanda's death, she said,
"Lunch will be served in half an hour, Mistress LeFleur. And
as soon as you're through with your mother's room, I'll have
the maids start the cleaning."

"I'm finished with the packing," Marguerite replied. "I've
asked Bridget and Kennie to move the trunks out this
afternoon, so we should be finished today."

Elvira's head bobbed approvingly. "Good. I'll start the
maids on the room in the morning." She reached into her
apron pocket and pulled out the brass key ring. "I'm going to
take this evening off if it's all right with you," she said more
than asked. "A friend of mine is ill and because of the funeral
I—"

Marguerite smiled. "That's fine with me, Mrs. Simmons.
You've been so generous with your time, why don't you take
several days off if you wish. I'll be here to supervise the
household, and there's no urgency on cleaning Mother's
room."

Elvira's glassy eyes sparked with life, but as suddenly they
dulled. "What about your trip to Dublin? Mr. Taylor said
you'd be joining him."

"Uh . . . yes, I'll be going to Dublin," Marguerite replied,
carefully selecting her words, "but we won't be leaving for
three days, and I'll spend those packing my clothes. By taking

off this afternoon that would give you two and a half days' rest before you started cleaning." Wanting to be by herself, Marguerite hoped she could persuade Elvira to take the time off. "When you return, we'll be ready to leave, and you can start the cleaning with no one underfoot."

"All right," Elvira replied quickly, liking the idea. "Follow me into the library, and I'll give you the keys, telling you what each belongs to." She walked briskly ahead of Marguerite. "I've already taken care of the meals. The cook has the menu for the rest of the week. So you just need to see that the servants don't slough off." When she reached the library, she laid the jangling brass ring on Earl's desk, and she continued to talk, her monotonous drone going on and on as she explained each key.

Instructions echoing in her ears, Marguerite was glad when Elvira finally walked out of the library. "And if you need me," the older woman called over her shoulder, "you know where I'll be and how to contact me. It's not more than a two hour ride."

"If I need you, I'll send for you," Marguerite promised. "But don't worry. I can take care of the house for a few days. Enjoy your holiday." Finally Elvira closed the door, and Marguerite breathed a sigh of relief.

After lunch Marguerite helped Bridget and Kennie pack the wagon and saw them off. Then she went into the kitchen and prepared lunch for Annie. Carrying a tray, she moved into the servant's wing.

"Annie," she said, softly knocking on the door. "I've brought you something to eat."

"I'm not hungry, Miz Marguerite." The tones were lethargic and disinterested.

"But you've got to eat."

Balancing the tray in one hand, Marguerite opened the door with the other. Her back to the entrance, Annie sat in a rocking chair in front of the opened window, the sun shining across her frail form. Draped over her shoulder was a shawl, and resting on her lap was an opened Bible.

Marguerite walked to the reading table beside the old woman and set the tray down. As she removed the lids from the dishes, the savory odor filled the small room. "Doesn't this smell good. The cook said to tell you—"

"She was too young to die, Miz Marguerite."

"I know," Marguerite whispered, not far from tears herself. She knelt in front of the old woman and laid her head against Annie's knees. "But all the grieving in the world isn't going to bring her back, Annie."

"No, ma'am, it ain't," Annie answered, her gnarled hand lightly brushing through Marguerite's hair. "But I can't help grieving. I miss my little girl so much."

"She's better off where . . . she . . . is," Marguerite said, sniffing back her tears.

"I know that, but knowing it still don't help the pain none. My head knows, but my heart don't seem to understand." After a long period of silence, she said, "Part of me's gone, Miz Marguerite. A big part of me."

"Annie," Marguerite asked, "how would you like to go home?"

"Back to Blossom Hall." Annie gently rocked back in the chair, and her eyes closed. "I'd like that, Miz Marguerite, but I'm gonna stay wherever you stay." She lightly finger-combed the hair at Marguerite's temples. "Are you going to stay here with Massa Taylor?"

"No," Marguerite whispered fervently, "I'm going home, too."

"What about O'Roarke?" Annie asked, her eyes on the opened window, her gaze wandering the verdant green meadows that stretched endlessly around the manor house. When Marguerite didn't answer, Annie lowered her face. "He seems to be smitten with you, and you seem to feel the same way about him."

"Just smitten," Marguerite mumbled, wishing Sheridan felt differently about her. "Nothing more binding." Lifting her head, she pushed away from Annie. "We can't return to Blossom Hall, Annie, but I have an idea." She reached into her pocket and pulled out the crumpled brochures that James Power had given her. Hand-pressing the wrinkles out, she laid them on Annie's lap.

"I'm going to visit with Mr. Power this afternoon," she said. "The other day he told me and Paddy about acres and acres of land that the Mexican government is willing to sell, so I'm going to buy us some land in Mexico." She tapped her finger on the map. "Right here. We're going to build a new life for ourselves, Annie—a life without Earl Taylor and Sheridan O'Roarke."

Annie smiled gently. She heard everything Marguerite did and didn't say. "That sounds right fine for you, honey, but I'm too old to begin over again. I wouldn't be much help to you."

"Yes, you would," Marguerite insisted. "Just listen, Annie."

Marguerite sat with Annie for several hours, talking with her about Texas as the old woman ate. When Annie was through, Marguerite stood and gathered the empty dishes. "Is there anything else you want me to get you before I leave?" Annie shook her head and lowered it, again taking solace in her Bible reading. "I'll be down later to check on you." Marguerite stepped out of the room and closed the door.

She hurried to her bedroom and with Jewel's help changed clothes, putting on her gray riding habit. Then she had one of the grooms saddle her a horse. Soon she was galloping across the fields toward Ballygarrett, her heart lighter than it had been for several days. It was even lighter when she returned to the manor house several hours later.

Going directly into the kitchen, she said to the cook, "Mrs. O'Grady, since no one is home but me, we're not going to bother with setting the table tonight. I'd like to have dinner served in my room later. If you'd like to take the day off tomorrow, you may leave as soon as the kitchen is cleaned up. Jewel and I are accustomed to looking after ourselves."

Mrs. O'Grady's lips curved into a bright smile, and she bobbed her head, wisps of pearly white hair brushing her temples. "I would be a'likin' that to be sure, mistress. When do ye be a'wantin' me to return?"

"Day after tomorrow," Marguerite called over her shoulder, walking out of the kitchen.

Going directly to her room, Marguerite took her hat off and laid it, her gloves, and her riding crop on the dresser. Then she reached into her skirt pocket and extracted the crisp sheet of paper, moving to the window to open it. She smiled as she read the receipt. By the time she reached Dublin, James Power would have booked in his name passage for three to New Orleans. Refolding the piece of paper, she turned and walked to the large, opened trunk that sat in the middle of the room. Kneeling, she placed the document in one of the side compartments for safekeeping. Then she began her packing. As dusk softly settled in the room, Marguerite heard a knock on the door.

"Miz Marguerite?"

"Yes." Marguerite folded a petticoat and laid it on the trunk.

Jewel opened the door and poked her head around the frame. "Are you ready for supper?"

Flexing her shoulders, Marguerite said, "I am, but I'd like to take a bath first."

Jewel grinned and pushed through the door, the large copper tub in hand. "I figured dat, so I brought the tub, and I got two kettles of water boiling."

Marguerite stood, turning her back to Jewel. "Unfasten my dress, please."

After Jewel unhooked the dress, Jewel left, and Marguerite slowly shed her clothes, carefully laying them across the foot of the bed. Unable to take off her boots without help, she lay back on the bed, clad in nothing but her chemise and pantalettes. Weary from her busy day, she closed her eyes and rested for a minute.

When she heard the door open, she said, "Jewel, before you

pour the water, will you help me with my boots?"

"Yes ma'am," Jewel replied, setting the kettles on the floor beside the tub. She dropped her thick dish clothes and walked to the bed. "Lawsy me," Jewel grunted as she bent over and helped Marguerite take her boots off, "I don't know why you wear these things so tight, chile. They can't be comfortable."

Marguerite laughed. "They're the latest fashion."

"Lawsy me," Jewel mumbled, shaking her head, "give me comfort any day to fashion, Miz Marguerite."

Her boots off, lying on the floor beside the bed, Marguerite walked to the dresser and picked up her mother's jewelry box. Winding it, she returned to the bed, lay back down and lifted the lid. Closing her eyes, she listened to her mother's favorite melody. She heard Jewel humming the song as she poured the water into the tub.

"When do you want your supper, Miz Marguerite?"

"I don't know," Marguerite returned, her voice drowsy with sleep. "I'll come get you when I want it."

"Your bath is ready," Jewel announced, moving toward the door.

"Thank you."

"You betta get in dat water before it gits cold."

Marguerite heard the door close, but she didn't stir from her cocoon of peacefulness. Then she heard the door reopen, and she mumbled, "Don't fuss, Jewel. I'm getting up."

"Personally I think you're fine right where you are." O'Roarke's voice boomed through the bedroom, awakening Marguerite.

Bolting up, she opened her eyes, blinking in surprise. Sheridan leaned against the door, his arms folded over his chest, his face shadowed from the brim of his hat.

"What are you doing here?" she gasped, edging off the bed, her feet hitting the floor.

"Surely, lass, you knew that I would come." Sheridan stripped the hat from his head and tossed it on the table closest to him. His eyes shining with anticipation, hair curling in glorious disarray around his face, he moved toward Marguerite.

"I told you not to," she said, her eyes never leaving Sheridan's face as she groped frantically for her dress.

Sheridan sat on the bed between her and the dress, the mattress sagging beneath his weight. His hand caught hers, and he stopped her searching. "Nay, lass," he softly chided. "It's too late for that. You know it as well as I do."

His hands moved to her shoulders, and he guided her backward. Using his weight, he pressed her body into the softness of the mattress. He made no pretense about his intentions; he left Marguerite with no doubts. His lips met hers, and though the touch was light, passion shuddered through Marguerite's body. Her response changed the gentle introduction into a fiery kiss, deep and demanding.

With a moan Marguerite's hands slid across his chest around his shoulders, her fingers gripping through the cambric material to burn into his skin. Under his guidance she opened her lips to the fullness of his caress, her body quivering when his tongue touched the sensitive, virginal hollows within her mouth.

Sheridan began to stroke her with slow, sensuous deliberation, easing his hands over her body, telling her by his touch that he was as aware of her nakedness beneath the thin chemise as she was. Finally his hand closed over her breast. He held it, savoring its fullness, its beauty; then through the white material he coaxed the delicate mounds to an aching arousal. His thumb teased the nipples with light, feathery strokes that made them stiffen with yearning, that made them swell enticingly against the gauzy undergarment. When Marguerite thought she could stand the erotic torment no longer, Sheridan moved his hands, lifted his face and pressed ardent little kisses along her chin, down her neck, to her breasts, nipping at her flesh as he went.

Moving slightly, his mouth on the tip of her breast, he blew, his hot breath oozing over her skin like thick, warm honey.

Again and again, moving from one breast to the other, he breathed the life of desire into her until Marguerite felt passion, primitive and rugged, ignite within her body, bursting into a million erotic brushfires.

Easing away from her, he ran his hand down her midriff, across her stomach. He slipped his fingers into the open crotch of her pantalettes, and he touched her maidenhood. Never having been so intimately caressed before, Marguerite gasped with shock at first, but soon her gasping was sheer pleasure. Her body surging with desire, she arched, her body intuitively begging for more than fleeting touches. As his fingers touched the sensitive pleasure point, teasing and tormenting her, Marguerite writhed, pressing closer to him, seeking the impassioned touch once again.

With a soft chuckle, Sheridan drew away from her, his lips brushing against her cheeks as he moved his mouth to her ears. "See, lass, you can't deny my touch. Your body is hungry for a man's possession."

Her face burning with shame, Marguerite tried to twist out of his arms, but Sheridan held her fast.

Unable to understand Marguerite, Sheridan instantly regretted his words. "'Tis nothing to be ashamed of, lass," he said, looking into the color-heightened face and the large round eyes. "We want each other." His hand lightly trailed down her arm. As she involuntarily shivered, he added, "We can give each other great pleasure."

"Sheridan," Marguerite implored, her luminous eyes begging for a hearing, "please listen to me. Let me explain."

"Nay, lass," he said, laying a silencing finger across her mouth. "There's no need for explanations."

"But I'm not what you think. I wasn't Jordan's—"

Sheridan's hand covered Marguerite's mouth as he kissed a fiery path to her hairline, and he nuzzled his face in the sweet scent of her hair. "Hush, lass. I spoke the truth the other day. What you were or what you did isn't important. I only know that you have created a wanting in me so great that it must be

208

slaked. I know that only you can alleviate this hunger." Pulling his head back slightly, he looked into her face. "I hope you feel the same way."

When Marguerite licked her dry lips and nodded her head, he turned her over, unhooking her chemise, his fingers gliding over the creamy smoothness of her back as he separated the material. Enjoying each moment of discovery, he pushed the cotton aside and stared at her creamy white skin for a long time. Then he leaned over her, his lips touching her fevered skin. Marguerite whimpered small cries of ecstasy, and her body trembled uncontrollably beneath the expertise of Sheridan's touch. Her cry turned into a moan of pure pleasure as his lips moved down her spine and brushed back and forth across the small of her back at the waistband of her pantalettes.

Lifting her, he pulled the sleeves of the chemise down her arms, and he discarded the garment, tossing it across the room. He turned her over and stared at her naked beauty. When Marguerite gazed into his face, she sucked in her breath. She had seen his eyes angry, arrogant, even conceited. She had seen them icy and warm, but she had never seem them as an impassioned emerald green—fevered by desire to untold beauty.

His thumbs traced languid circles on the upper swell of her breasts, Marguerite squirming her delight. Then with a reverent softness he cupped both her breasts and kneaded them together, slowly pushing his palms across the fullness until they rested on the throbbing peaks. Finally, after an eternity of exquisite torment, his lips closed over one of the nipples, his tongue playing around it with tantalizing skill. Marguerite gasped her pleasure. Her hands lifted, and her fingers tangled in the thick, silky red hair. She gasped again when he transferred his attentions to the other taut peak.

Marguerite fisted her hands in his hair, lifted his head and guided it to hers, claiming his lips in an infinitely long, satisfying kiss. Then Sheridan brushed his mouth down her face and her neck, his lips kissing first the soft, scented curve of neck and shoulder on one side, then on the other. Again and again his lips and hands moved over her body, spreading the fevered desire of his wants all over her.

"Marguerite, I'm going to make love to you."

"No," she whispered, sanity making one last, ineffective effort, her body making no protest at all.

"Yes," he said, his voice as soft as hers.

"Not until you understand—"

Not knowing if this was a game she was playing, not caring at the moment, too consumed with the passion that raged through his body, Sheridan murmured, "Let's not waste time with words, Daisy Belle."

His lips moved up the line of her neck, finding the throbbing pulse point in the tiny hollow by her ear. He nipped the lobe, and when he spoke, his hot breath sent exquisite shivers through her body.

"I understand all I need or want to."

Knowing that arguments and discussion were futile now, Marguerite pushed her doubts and inhibitions aside. She suddenly smiled, her face blooming with happiness. She lifted her hands and, reaching for the top button of Sheridan's shirt, she undid it. She opened the second one and looked into Sheridan's face, but he said nothing. His breathing was shallow and ragged. Marguerite's hands trembled slightly as she touched the third button and slid it through the opening.

Scooting up, she pulled the material aside, her lips touching the hair-roughened triangle that she had revealed. "Yes," she murmured, her lips moving provocatively against his skin. "Yes, Sheridan, please make love to me."

Sheridan gathered her close, and Marguerite closed her eyes, giving herself up to the slow, hungry kiss. Their lips met, fused, then, in unison, moved again. She opened her mouth for the delving search of his tongue, and she moved her hands over his bare chest, feeling the slick sheen of perspiration that covered his body. She felt the acceleration of his heartbeat; she heard the change of his breathing as he responded to her touch.

"I've wanted you ever since I first saw you, lass," he confessed, his voice gruff with passion. "Even though I knew you were Jordan's mistress, I wanted you. Even though I knew Earl was grooming you for himself, I wanted you."

This time Marguerite made no attempt to refute his accusations. This time they didn't bother her. She smiled, twining her fingers together and looping them at the nape of his neck. Soon he would understand.

"And I've wanted you, my Irish dissident, ever since I first saw you."

Sheridan's hands lifted, and he gently untwined Marguerite's. Moving slightly, he shrugged out of his shirt. As he tossed it aside, he slipped to the edge of the bed. Before he knew what was happening, Marguerite was kneeling on the floor in front of him, helping him pull his boots off. He could hardly keep his hands off her. Her hair hung about her face and shoulders in tangled beauty; her breasts were sheened with desire; her pantalettes opened at the crotch to reveal her most intimate secret.

Marguerite, watching the expressions that crossed his face, enjoying the passion that smoldered in his eyes, tipped her tongue and rounded her lips. She smiled when Sheridan drew a deep, ragged breath.

"Ah, lass," he cautioned, "much more of this, and I will take you without delightful foreplay."

"Ah, lad," Marguerite mimicked, inebriated on her prowess as a woman, as a lover, "before you can do anything you'll have to get these clothes off." Her hot eyes rested on the bulge in the crotch of his pants.

Desire as hot as molten lava oozed through Sheridan's body, completely covering him with a suffocating awareness of the woman in front of him. Inwardly quaking with anticipation, he smiled at her and held a foot out.

"First my boot, madam."

His boots cast aside, Marguerite peeled his socks off and

leaned back, balancing on the heel of both hands, her breasts peaking through long, shining strands of hair. She watched him shed his clothes.

When he was naked, he stood, his legs straddled, his hands on his hips, making no effort to hide the sure sign of his arousal. Although Marguerite hadn't lit a candle or a lamp and the room was soft with dusky shadows, she could see Sheridan well. At first she was slightly embarrassed. She had never seen a naked man before, but the rush of desire soon obliterated her moral restraints.

She visually caressed his virile body; she savored his sleek, work-muscled body. Unashamed, she let her eyes rove over his nudity, moving from his feet upward. She delighted in his long, powerful legs, the hair-roughened expanse of muscular chest, the powerful arms, and the perfectly sculpted shoulders.

For moments on end he stared into the desire-softened blue eyes. His body trembled from the intensity of her gaze; he felt her caress as if she had touched him physically. Then, in a graceful movement so out of keeping with his large, powerful frame, Sheridan knelt in front of her.

His hands moved to the waistband of her pantalettes, and he unbuttoned them, the two pieces of material falling open to reveal the curly sable brown triangle. Slipping his hand in the opening, he cupped her buttocks, lifting her body, so he could pull her pantalettes off. Marguerite arched her body and twisted, helping him with the task.

Turning her on her stomach, he ran his finger down the indentation of her spine; then he leaned over, letting his mouth follow the same path. When he reached the small of her back, he lingered, his tongue tracing hot, fiery designs. Farther down he went, kissing the firm, round buttocks. As his fingers slid between her legs to touch the soft femininity, Marguerite groaned, and her body shuddered with convulsive desire.

He kissed down the back of her legs, his fingers brushing lightly against the bottom of her feet up her calves, his lips and fingers meeting at the dimple behind her knees. Emitting soft whimpering sounds, Marguerite couldn't control the quaking in her body. Throbbing and aching, she turned over. She begged for release from the erotic torment.

But Sheridan wasn't feeling merciful. On his knees now, he leaned back to look at her, the first time that he'd seen her completely naked. His eyes moved from the pale oval face and luminous blue eyes to the slender neck, down to her breasts.

His hands glided up her arms and over her smooth, naked shoulders before they gently encircled the slim column of her throat. His thumbs stroked lightly at the hollow above the joining of her collarbone. Then his hands slid over her breasts, over the midriff, finally circling the small waist. He pulled her to her knees and then closer to his body.

"I promise," he murmured, his lips coming toward hers, "I will make this your most pleasurable time. I will push all memory of Jordan Reeves from your mind; I'll make you forget his touch."

"Yes. Yes," Marguerite murmured as she gave herself to the pleasure of his kiss. As the kiss deepened and became more urgent, Marguerite moaned her acquiescence and moved so that her body molded perfectly to his, soft against his hardness.

When Sheridan finally broke the kiss, his lips nipped down the cord of her neck, stopping in the soft curve where neck met shoulder. His hand slid down her stomach, his fingers moving farther down. Levering above her, he put his knee between her legs, and his hand brushed against the point of highest sensitivity, stroking, preparing her.

Marguerite tensed. "Sheridan . . ." she began, a trace of apprehension in her voice.

"Don't be afraid of me," he murmured, wondering why she was so skittish, hating Jordan for having instilled such a fear in her. "I won't do anything to hurt you." His lips at her ears, he promised, "I'm going to give you greater pleasure than you've ever experienced in your life, lassie."

"I'm not afraid," she admitted, slowly sliding her hands up his back, her fingers tracing the indentation of his spine. His

213

skin was warm and smooth. She could feel his muscles moving, responding to her touch.

Sheridan scooped her into his arms and carried her across the room. He laid her on the bed and stood for that one minute, looking down at her. In the evening shadows that played softly through the room, Marguerite could see his rugged features. She smiled and lifted her hands, beckoning him to her.

Placing one knee on the bed, Sheridan obeyed, his expression intent, his sensual mouth set in a controlled line. He caught his breath. Desire, hot and unashamed, flamed in the darkening depths of his emerald-green eyes. Aware of the passion that pulsated through Sheridan's body, Marguerite felt an answering fire spark to life within her. For the first time in her twenty-two years she wanted the fulfillment of a man's possession; she must have *this man's* complete possession.

Sheridan lowered his head, his mouth unerringly finding hers. Again he possessed it deeply, demandingly, his control almost broken. Hungry for total consummation herself, Marguerite met his urgency with a sudden yearning of her own. This time when he spread her legs apart, she followed his command. When his hand prepared her, she moved with him, arching up and against him. When he levered over her, she opened her body to the virile thrust of his need.

But when he touched her, she tensed and closed her lips. "Sheridan," she whispered, drawing up as his throbbing hardness touched her. "I . . . can't. Don't."

"You can't," he gritted. "You won't." He pulled back to glower at her. "You've led me this far, and now you say you can't."

Tears of frustration sparkled in Marguerite's eyes. "You don't understand."

Sheridan bit back his retort. He smothered his sigh. He didn't understand her hesitance. Was she soothing her ego and her conscience? Yes, he decided. She wanted him to force her. Smiling to himself, Sheridan reversed the tactic. He'd never taken one unwilling maiden in his life.

"No," he said, pressing small kisses over her face, her neck, and her shoulders, "I don't understand. But if you want me to, I'll stop." He lifted his head.

Marguerite's eyes, wild and luminous, stared into his. Too innocent, she didn't recognize Sheridan's ploy.

"Do you want me to stop, Daisy Belle?"

"No," she whispered. If she had no more when she returned to America, she would have this moment, this memory forever. No one could wrest it from her.

Slowly Sheridan moved his hand over the sensitive inner arch of her femininity. When Marguerite's breathing was shallow and rapid, he gently placed his manhood inside of her. When she tensed and gasped, when he felt the small obstruction, he knew.

Dear God. He knew. He understood. But he'd gone too far to retreat now. He couldn't have—he wouldn't have stopped now. His twinge of conscience was lost in the surge of joy that flowed through his body and soul.

Alternately whispering endearments in her ears and kissing her, Sheridan didn't move for a few seconds. His hands explored her body, rebuilding the fire of desire, spreading the flames all over her body. When Marguerite lifted her arms and locked her hands behind Sheridan's head, and when she began to move her hips around his hardness, he slowly moved within her, gently at first, then more urgently as their desire mounted, carrying her to the realm of womanhood, him to the realm of ultimate fulfillment. His lovemaking was gentle and unselfish. His thoughts were for her first, him second.

For the first time in many years he was making love, not lust. For the first time in her life Marguerite was in love and was making love.

Chapter 13

Soft lamplight flickered through the room, shading Marguerite and Sheridan in a rosy glow. Naked, both stood in the bathtub. Sheridan poured water over Marguerite's shoulders, watching as it sluiced down her slender length, rinsing the suds from her body.

Abruptly he dropped the washcloth into the water, his hands cupping her shining, water-slicked shoulders. He pulled her close. "Dear God, Marguerite, if only I'd known that you were a virgin. If only I'd listened to you, instead of believing those letters that Susanna had written to Earl."

The anguished cry came from the depth of his soul, but mere words couldn't express his feelings. He was a mass of chaotic and contradicting emotions. He was elated; he was filled with remorse. He was glad that he had made love to Marguerite; he was glad that he'd been the first one. At the same time he was sad that he'd taken so much from her and had no intention of giving to her in return. He was condemned because he was using an innocent as a pawn in this deadly game of revenge. He was ashamed that he'd misjudged her so. He was angry that he'd placed himself in such a compromising position. So many times Marguerite had told him; she had tried to convince him. His mother had warned him. But he had listened to neither of them. He'd been too wrapped up in revenge.

The green eyes pierced her with their throbbing intensity. "Marguerite, I . . . I . . ."

Marguerite smiled, and this time she was the one to lay a silencing finger over his mouth. "I'm not sorry," she told him, stepping out of the tub, bending for the towel, her buttocks brushing against his thigh. "I wanted you," she said, her love-softened voice muffled as she blotted her hair.

Unable to look into her eyes, Sheridan took the cloth from her, toweling her with gentleness. As he crouched in the tub, he ran his towel-covered hands down her legs. Lowering a hand, Marguerite touched the crown of his hair, twirling russet curls around her fingers.

"I love you, Sheridan O'Roarke, and I wouldn't have it any other way."

Sheridan's hands momentarily tightened around her calf, and he pressed his forehead against her thigh. He sighed, unable to lift his face to hers. The full consequences of his action hit him, and he bowed beneath the weight. Like Earl, he was cruelly using Marguerite; cruelly using her in a personal war about which she knew nothing. He couldn't let her know that he didn't share the same emotions with her. He couldn't let her know the real reason for his making love to her.

And even now—after—he didn't love her. He cared, but caring wasn't loving. Besides, he reasoned in an effort to vindicate himself, he had nothing to offer her. Soon—very soon, he was riding to Wexford Harbor to intercept the weapons that were being sent from England. He could only hope for the best. If he escaped this time, he might not the next. Earl was slowly but surely closing in on him. He was an outlaw on the run. An outlaw, dangling on the end of a rope.

Drawing in a deep gulp of air, he straightened up and lightly swatted Marguerite's buttocks. "You're dry now. Go put some clothes on before—"

Marguerite giggled, the trill of laughter a beautiful melody. "That sounds more promising than threatening."

Sheridan playfully scowled at her; then, using her towel, he

218

dried off. As Marguerite scampered across the room toward the wardrobe, he unknowingly sighed his dilemma. The door open, her hand on her dressing gown, Marguerite turned to look at him.

"What's wrong, darling?"

"Nothing," he lied, unwilling to hurt her or to burden her with his thoughtlessness. "I was just thinking about . . . the real world outside this beautiful room."

Relieved, Marguerite yanked the gown from the shelf and grinned. "Together, my love, we shall make the real world as beautiful to live in as this room is."

Walking to the washstand across the room, Sheridan hung the towel over the bar; then he moved to the bedside. "I wish we could," he breathed. "I really wish we could." But even as he said the words, he wondered whether such a wish was possible now.

"Miz Marguerite." Jewel's knock and call echoed through the room. Dumbfounded, looking at Sheridan, Marguerite couldn't answer. Again Jewel called. This time her voice was louder, more concerned. "Miz Marguerite, is you all right?"

"Answer her," Sheridan rasped, jerking his breeches up.

"Y—yes," Marguerite stammered.

"Is you sure?" Jewel asked, jiggling the doorknob, trying to open the door. Clearly she didn't think so.

"I'm fine," Marguerite replied, her hands frantically jabbing through the air as she searched for her sleeves.

"Is you ready for your dinner?"

Running to the bed, Marguerite fumbled through the pockets of her riding habit for her key; then she moved to the door. As the lock clicked, Jewel shoved open the door with such force that Marguerite stumbled backward. With all the fury of a storm, Jewel rushed into the room. First she took in Marguerite's disheveled appearance: the hair, loosely piled on the top of her head, damp tendrils wisping around her cheeks; the fingers that nervously played with the dressing gown sash; the eyes that couldn't quite meet hers. Next the black woman

219

glared into every corner, her disapproving gaze moving from the bathtub in the center of the room to the messed-up bed. Her scowl finally landed on Sheridan, who was buttoning his shirt.

Jewel's hands fisted, and she rested them on her ample hips. Her bosom heaved. "How'd you git in here wifout anybody knowing it?" she demanded, not bothering to hide her anger.

Sheridan smiled, and he gently said, "Through the back door."

"Don't you know you ain't supposed to be in here wif Miz Marguerite? What's decent folks gonna be thinking?" The large eyes moved to her mistress's face, and Jewel could tell by the color that mantled Marguerite's cheeks that her worst fears had been realized.

"Jewel . . ." Marguerite said, clearing her throat, injecting authority in her tone. Her fingers twiddling with the sash of her dressing gown spoke her embarrassment and her chagrin; they betrayed her innocence of clandestine assignations. "I'd like for you to serve dinner for two in here tonight."

"Miz Marguerite—"

"Send Kennie to remove the bathtub," Marguerite continued, ignoring the servant's imploring. "Also I'd like a bottle of wine to accompany the dinner. I think we'd like to have . . ."

Marguerite continued to give orders, desperately trying to ignore the hurt and the warning in the large brown eyes. Turning, she moved across the room, tying the sash of her dressing gown more tightly around her waist.

When Marguerite had finished, Jewel said, "I'll bring your dinner, Miz Marguerite, but I want you to know, dis ain't—"

"Jewel," Marguerite said quietly, having too much respect for the woman who had been her companion since childhood to speak otherwise, "I know what I'm doing."

"No, honey chile," Jewel contradicted with all the vehemence of love, "I mean to tell you, you don't know what you're doing." The black servant said no more. She walked out of the room, closing the door.

"Do you want me to leave?" Sheridan asked.

Looking at Sheridan, swallowing her hurt, Marguerite said, "No, I want you to stay."

Her eyes were so large, so filled with confusion that Sheridan couldn't remain where he was. In two long strides he was across the room, drawing her into the protective circle of his arms. Welcoming his warmth and his strength, Marguerite wrapped her arms around him and nuzzled her head against his chest.

He scooped her into his arms and retraced his steps, settling her on the bed and sliding in beside her. Shoving pillows behind his back, he leaned against the headboard, pulling Marguerite in his arms. Listening to the rhythmic beat of his heart, she ran her finger around the buttons on his shirt.

"I wish it could be like this always," she said.

"So do I, lass," Sheridan said, his murmur a heartfelt cry.

Marguerite was hurt that Sheridan never admitted to loving her, but she pushed her feelings aside. She'd gone into this with her eyes open, and she had known the possibility existed that Sheridan only wanted her, that he would never love her. And now she couldn't—she wouldn't push him into a marriage of necessity. She would settle for no less than love.

"When do you have to go?"

"I must leave tomorrow evening," he said, his breath fanning across her forehead and cheeks.

"Where are you going?" Marguerite forced the words through her trembling lips.

"I can't say, lass." Sheridan closed his eyes, his hands tracing quiet designs on Marguerite's upper arm. Unable to tell her about the shipment of weapons he was going to intercept, and unable to dispel the heaviness that lay on him in regard to the outcome of the mission, he said, "I don't know what the future holds. I may not get to see you again."

Marguerite started, her eyes flying open. She jerked out of his arms. Lifting tear-filled eyes, she forgot her pride; she forgot her resolve; she begged. "Take me with you, Danny. Please take me with you."

"I can't," Sheridan returned, his voice thick and husky with tears. "Living with an outlaw is no life for you."

"I love you." The blue eyes, shimmering and bright, defied him to ignore her declaration.

Sheridan cupped her face with both hands. "Just days ago, Daisy LeFleur, you thought yourself to be in love with Jordan Reeves. Now today you fancy yourself in love with me."

Two tears sparkled down her cheeks as she shook her head. "I never said I was in love with Jordan," she managed, her voice trembling as much as her lips. "You're the one who came to that conclusion. You're the one who wanted to believe that. I—I think—I've loved you since the first day I saw you, Sheridan O'Roarke." The confession of love hung between them, like a delicate string, only to be snapped asunder by a knock on the door. Moving out of Sheridan's arms and sliding off the bed, Marguerite called, "Come in."

The door opened, and Kennie came into the room, his eyes darting from Marguerite to Sheridan. "You wanted me to take the bathtub out, ma'am?"

"Yes," Marguerite replied, turning her back to the young man.

Uncomfortable silence filled the room as Kennie dragged the tub across the floor. Before he was out, Jewel appeared in the hall, wheeling a serving cart. She breezed through the opened door, not stopping until she reached the table in front of the window.

"Here's your dinner, Miz Marguerite."

Jewel spoke as a servant, her gaze purposefully averted from Sheridan who still sprawled lazily on the bed. She set the table first, then lifted the lids from the serving dishes. Next she opened and poured the wine.

Walking back to the door, she asked in the same stilted voice, "Is there anything else, Miz Marguerite?"

"No," Marguerite replied, her heart breaking to see her

trusted friend reacting like this.

"Shall I come back later for the dishes?" Jewel asked.

"No, you can get them in the morning."

Unable to help herself, Jewel looked into Marguerite's face, and she shook her head. She opened her mouth to speak, but she closed it without saying a word. Gently she shut the door behind her retreating figure.

Pulling on the drawer of the serving cart, Marguerite took out two candles and the crystal holders. Walking to the lamp, she removed the globe and the chimney and she lit the candlewicks. She blew the lamp out and returned to the window, setting the candles in the center of the table. She turned and held her arms out to Sheridan.

"Are you hungry?"

His eyes on the swell of her breasts that were revealed in the opening of the dressing gown, he nodded his head. "I've eaten not long ago, lass, but I'm starved." Marguerite's head lowered, and she knew what he was talking about. Soft color fused her cheeks, and excitement colored her eyes. "What do you prefer?" she asked.

Sheridan was off the bed and across the room before her words had died into silence. "I prefer you, lass, but we'll have some physical nourishment now. We'll save the sweets and delicacies for later."

Across the table from each other, they ate their meal, drank the wine, and indulged in desultory conversation. When they were through eating, Sheridan refilled their wineglasses. Carrying both of them, he moved to one of the chairs that set in front of the fireplace. As he sat down, he handed Marguerite her glass and motioned her into the chair beside him.

"What have you decided to do?" he asked.

"Earl's asked me to accompany him to Dublin," Marguerite answered. "He's going to have the house redecorated."

"You're not going!" Sheridan barked his disapproval, setting his glass on the floor with a thud.

With trembling hands Marguerite lifted her glass and sipped

the wine. "Earl hasn't said it, Sheridan, but I'm sure he wants to marry me."

"Of course, he does," Sheridan exclaimed, jumping to his feet, angrily pacing the floor, walking back and forth in front of Marguerite. "You're not daft. Surely you can see what he's been scheming for so long. You're young, beautiful, and wealthy. Don't you know that's the reason why he—"

Sheridan stopped himself shoft just before he accused Earl of murdering Amanda. He wasn't prepared to prove the accusation, and Marguerite was too grieved for him to throw idle words at her. He knelt in front of Marguerite's chair and laid his hands on her legs.

"Marguerite, don't stay here with Earl. For God's sake, don't marry him. He's a cruel man; he's evil."

Marguerite still didn't tell Sheridan that she was leaving Ireland for good in two days. She ran a finger around the top of her glass. "You don't want me, and you don't want Earl to have me. What do you want for me, Sheridan?"

Stunned and speechless, Sheridan could only stare at her. Picking up his glass, he sprinted to his feet. He swallowed the remainder of the wine. "Is there no one you could stay with in New Orleans for the time being?"

"There is, and I have friends in Philadelphia with whom I could stay, but I don't wish to return to either place. I don't wish to stay with friends."

"What are you going to do, Marguerite?"

Too hurt to reply, forcing back the tears, Marguerite sipped her wine. Although she had known from the beginning that Sheridan didn't respect her, she had hoped that once he knew the truth, thing would be different. She took another swallow of her wine.

"Don't worry about it, Sheridan. I told you once before that I can take care of myself. Tell me about Eliza."

"To hell with my past," Sheridan thundered. "I'm talking to you about your future. What are you going to do?"

Pulling her legs up in the chair and locking one arm around

them, she rested her wineglass on her knees and looked above the rim of the crystal goblet. "Like your future, Sheridan, mine is for me to decide, and I don't owe you any explanation or any reasons for whatever choice I make." She smiled, her eyes distant and removed. "By virtue of our having made love, of your knowing all about my past, and by our lives having crossed, your past is of interest to me. It—it will be all that I have of you." She smiled sadly. "I'm asking so little."

Sheridan sighed, his conscience weighing heavy. Marguerite was right. She was asking little. He didn't fear the past; that he had plenty of. His future was the uncertainty in his life. Finally he said, "Eliza was a spoiled child who loved to manipulate people. Although she married Earl, she didn't love him. It was an arranged marriage for the convenience of her parents and Earl." He paused, twirling the empty glass around in his hands. As if defending Eliza's actions his voice softened. "She was only sixteen when they married. He was forty-six, thirty years her senior."

"She loved you."

Lost in memory, Sheridan continued in the same quiet voice: "The first time I saw her she was on horseback. Her hat had fallen off, and her hair was streaming down her back. When she saw me, she stopped, and we just stared at one another. She was beautiful. I fell in love with her at sight. We began to meet. She loved me . . . that is, I thought she loved me, but I'm not sure if Eliza loved anyone but herself. In the end, however, she outschemed even herself."

Again he paused, but Marguerite said nothing; she waited for him to continue.

"Eliza wanted both of us: Earl's wealth and his position, my love and virility. She used both of us." He stood and moved to the table, refilling his glass. "But soon country towns and hamlets and country boys lost their excitement and appeal; they weren't good enough for Eliza, so Earl took her on several trips to Dublin. After that Eliza began to make the trips whether Earl could go with her or not. She and Bridget made the trip many a time."

Sheridan lifted the glass and took several swallows of wine. Instead of returning to the chair, he restlessly moved around the room.

"Bridget McLeary?"

"Aye, the same. She was Eliza's personal maid, too," Sheridan answered. "The trips to Dublin stopped, and we learned through Bridget soon afterward that Eliza was with child. But Bridget was worried. Eliza was having a hard time carrying the child. She was quite ill."

"Was it your child?"

Sheridan shrugged. "No, lass. It wasn't my child. I hadn't touched her for months. But Earl always thought it was mine. He believed she was meeting me in Dublin." Sheridan's lips twisted into a cynical smile. "I carry the blame for many crimes and sins that I didn't commit, lass."

"Earl said it wasn't his."

"Probably not." Wishing the wine were stronger to wipe out the memories, Sheridan quaffed the remainder of his drink in several large gulps.

Remembering Earl's accusations, Marguerite asked, "How did she die?"

"Not by my hand as Earl claims," Sheridan declared. "Knowing that she was dying, Eliza came to me." He strode across the room and poured the last of the wine into his glass.

"She loved you."

"I like to think so. She was so weak she fell off the horse in front of the cottage." Sheridan's voice was thick with tears. "I carried her into the house and put her to bed. Mother and I tended her day and night, but . . . she died. The babe died with her. To keep his name clear and untarnished, Earl let it be known far and wide that Eliza died under my mother's hands."

Marguerite set her empty glass on the floor beside the chair, and she pushed to her feet. Moving to Sheridan's back, she looped her arms around him, her hands clutching his shoulders. She laid her cheek against his back. She felt his anger-tensed muscles and his loss and anguish. She could understand his hatred and his bitterness. The English—first Earl, then Eliza—had stripped him of everything he loved.

"Don't think about it," she whispered, letting her love spill over on him.

Dropping his glass to the floor, Sheridan turned, catching her in the close circle of his arms. "Why must there be so much between us?" he murmured. "Why could I have not met you so many years ago, Daisy Belle, when there was a chance for me to love? A chance for us to love?"

Marguerite said nothing; she had already offered him her love; he must accept it. All she could offer him now was the solace of her body.

Marguerite lifted her face at the same moment that he lowered his. Their lips met, communicating a reciprocal need. Sheridan began to pull her dressing gown off with the same urgency that she unbuttoned his shirt and his breeches. Clumsy in their hurry, each pulled away and quickly divested himself of clothes. When they were naked, they came together, sinking on to the rug, ummindful of the hard floor underneath.

Their coming together was primitive and earth shattering. It was a gentleness at the edge of violence; it was rough, devoid of prolonged foreplay, yet it was an expression of utmost tenderness. Sheridan's moist, pliant lips settled on Marguerite's mouth and moved against hers. As he stretched out, half over her, Marguerite's mouth slackened invitingly beneath his, and she responded with uninhibited warmth. His body, pressing her into the floor, was weightless. His giving and his loving was the warmth of life itself.

A deep driving hunger melded them together. Her arms circled his body, and her fingers dug into his shoulders. They carried each other away from worries and concerns to another world free from the apprehensive unknown.

They had tonight, and it would have to last a lifetime.

Chapter 14

"At this time of night!" Marguerite exclaimed, pushing up on her elbows, peering at Sheridan who was dressing across the room.

"At this time of night," Sheridan answered, tucking his shirt into his trousers. "And do be quiet. We don't want the entire household to wake up and accompany us." His booted feet silently moved over the floor toward the door.

"Where are you going?" Marguerite whispered, bolting upright, forgetting about the sheet.

His hand on the knob, Sheridan turned and looked at her, his eyes slowly touching the riotous mass of hair that framed her face, the vivid eyes, the pouting lips, the slender neck, the creamy breasts. As his gaze lingered, Marguerite's body responded to the visual caress, and her nipples hardened; her stomach tensed. She opened her mouth and traced her lips with the tip of her tongue. Unashamed, she beckoned Sheridan to return to bed, and he obeyed.

Sitting beside her, placing both hands palm down on the mattress on either side of her, he leaned over, kissing the sensitive tip of each breast. Marguerite's head rolled back, her upper body arching. Sheridan's hands moved to her waist, slowly easing up over the midriff to cup the underside of her breasts, pushing the nipple fully into his mouth. Gently his tongue swirled, sending excruciating pleasure through Marguerite's body. Sighing her delight, she closed her eyes and twined her hands together at the back of Sheridan's head.

"I can't get enough of your body," Sheridan murmured, his lips moving over the creamy fullness of her breasts. "And you've become quite the temptress in a matter of hours, lass. Already you would change my plans, and I had my heart set on our having a picnic."

Inebriated on love, Marguerite laughed, the musical sound filling Sheridan's heart with happiness. "Let's have our picnic here, my darling," she suggested, "hidden in our world. No one would think of your being here with me. We're quite safe."

Sheridan turned his face, his cheek resting on her breast and collarbone. "I wish we could stay, lass, but we can't." As he talked, his warm breath splayed across her skin, his life's vapor becoming a caress. "And I must be gone before daybreak. I don't want to compromise you."

Marguerite giggled softly. "As if you haven't already compromised me, Sheridan O'Roarke."

"The only ones who know that I'm here are Jewel and Kennie, and they won't tell Taylor," he said.

"I know Jewel won't," Marguerite said. "How can you be so sure about Kennie? And what about Bridget?"

"Kennie and Bridget are part of us." Sheridan pushed to his feet and grabbed Marguerite by the hand, pulling her to the edge of the bed. "Hurry and get ready, Daisy Belle. Tonight and tomorrow are ours, so let's make the best of them." His voice lowered. "The night's almost gone."

Tonight and tomorrow, and the night's almost gone.

The words reverberated in Marguerite's mind, causing her heart to ache. Tonight and tomorrow may be all she'd ever have with Sheridan.

"I want to show you something beautiful," he pleaded, misreading her hesitancy.

Marguerite smiled and nodded her head. For this man she would willingly flout social inhibitions and morals.

"I'm going to take you to a place that I've never shared with anyone before."

Still at the edge of the bed on her knees, Marguerite swayed against Sheridan, her breasts pressing into the soft material of his shirt. She looped her arms around his neck and laid her face against his chest.

"Not even Eliza?" she asked.

"No," Sheridan answered, "not even Eliza." His arms rounded her body, and his hands slipped down to cup her buttocks. "We're going on horseback." He pulled back, smiling into her face. "I'm going to see just how good a horseman you are, Daisy Belle LeFleur." Leaning, he kissed the top of her nose. "Now, get dressed, you wanton woman, while I get the horses."

Smiling, stretching sinuously, Marguerite watched him move across the room. When his hand closed over the knob, she called, "Wanton I've proved myself to be, Mr. O'Roarke. A lady? Definitely not. So no sidesaddle."

Sheridan turned, a grin on his face. "Are you sure, Mistress LeFleur?"

"Never surer of anything in my life."

"Anything to please a—"

"A woman," she supplied. "A woman in love."

Sheridan cast her a tender smile. "Aye, lass, a woman in love."

As soon as Sheridan left, Marguerite slipped off the bed and raced to the wardrobe, her face glowing with the night's aftermath. Grinning, she knelt and rummaged through a small chest, squealing her delight when she found her shirt and trousers. Because Jewel hated them, Marguerite hadn't been sure that the servants had packed them. Dragging them out, Marguerite chuckled. Although Jewel had been the one to sew the trousers and shirt, she would be shocked to know that her charge was wearing them tonight.

Quickly Marguerite dressed and combed her hair, pulling it back at the nape of her neck with a blue ribbon. On her way out of the room, she stopped at the wardrobe and got her long cloak. Throwing it over her shoulders, she slipped out of the room into the corridor.

She heard the library door close. Puzzled that anyone would be in there this time of the night, her steps slowed. Sheridan or the staff? she wondered. Quietly she descended the stairs. When she reached the room, she opened the door and peered through the darkness, but she didn't see or hear anyone.

Being extra cautious, she felt her way to Earl's desk and pulled on the top drawer. Extracting the tin of matches, she struck one. Holding it in one hand, she removed the globe and the chimney from the lamp and lit the wick. In the brilliant flare of initial light, she blew the match out and searched through the shadows for any telltale signs that someone had been here. As she set the globe on the desk, she struck something.

Her head lowered, and she saw the keys where she had left them when Mrs. Simmons had left. *Oh, no!* she thought, clutching them in her hand, looking around the room. With these anyone would have access to the entire house, especially to Earl's private possessions and papers.

"Here you are," Sheridan whispered, opening the door and walking into the room. "I couldn't find you."

Marguerite turned her head, a thin thread of suspicion on her words when she asked, "Where have you been?"

"First, I had to change saddles on your horse. Then I stopped by the cellar for this." Holding up several bottles of wine, he grinned. "I got us something to drink. I didn't think Earl would miss this."

"He might not, but Elvira will." She shrugged. "But who cares?" She laughed with Sheridan and held the keys up. "I don't know what I'm going to do with these. In order to get Mrs. Simmons out of the house, I had to become the guardian of the keys. I don't want to take them, but I don't dare leave them."

"Why don't you take them to Jewel? I have a feeling that

your champion is awake, love. Let her know you're going with me. I'll be waiting for you in here," Sheridan said. "We'll slip out through the garden."

"You've got the wine," Marguerite said, "but what about the food?"

"Everything's ready," he replied, folding his hand over the top of the chimney and blowing the lamp out.

"You couldn't have done all that so quickly."

Soft, husky laughter caressed Marguerite's soul as Sheridan enfolded her in his arms and pulled her tightly against his chest. "I didn't, love. I had planned to take you there to make love to you, but when I found you lying in such a beautiful state of undress I was momentarily sidetracked."

Pretending outrage, Marguerite pulled away and looked into the shadowed visage. "You were so sure that I'd go with you."

"No," he confessed, their lips touching, his breath mingling with hers, their life essence becoming one, "but I hoped and I prayed that you would."

Marguerite's arms slipped out of the cloak and circled Sheridan's body as she gave herself to his kiss. When he lifted his mouth, he said, "Take Jewel the keys before I make love to you right here."

Pulling out of his arms, Marguerite laughed and danced away. When she returned, Sheridan was standing in the garden, waiting for her. Happier than she'd ever been in her life, Marguerite ran to meet him. Hand in hand they scampered through the garden to the horses that were hitched to nearby trees.

"And let's see how you're going to do this, mistress," Sheridan whispered, moving close to Marguerite's horse to give her a hand in mounting. "You're going to look a sight with all your petticoats bunched up at your waist."

"Stand back, knave," Marguerite commanded in a whisper-soft voice. With a flourish she threw her cloak over one shoulder, lifted her foot to the stirrup and gracefully swung into the saddle.

Delighted with his woman, Sheridan chuckled quietly. "Ah, lass, how unladylike. But I must admit that even in the moonlight I can see that trousers are most becoming on you." Standing beside her, his hand resting on her thigh, he looked up. "Also I must admit that I like the unladylike qualities in you." He moved to his horse, quickly mounting, and the two of them galloped away, enveloped by the night, their capes billowing behind.

"You ride as if you were born to the saddle, Daisy Belle."

"I feel as if I were," Marguerite replied. "I don't remember my grandfather. He died when I was three, but Grandmother told me that he had me riding a horse before I could walk." Her hair flying behind her, the wind gently whipping her face, Marguerite smiled as she recalled her childhood. "Since I was the only grandchild, they doted on me."

"Your grandparents lived with you?"

"No," Marguerite replied, "I lived with them. Mother and Papa traveled all the time, so I stayed in Philadelphia."

Although Sheridan was surprised by her answer, he only said, "I thought you'd been reared on the plantation in New Orleans."

He asked her no more questions. Respecting people's privacy, he didn't intrude. If Marguerite wanted to tell him, she would without any coaxing from him.

"After Grandfather died, there was only Grandmother and me. On holidays and special occasions Mother and Papa would come home, and Grandmother and I would travel to Blossom Hall so we could all be together. As she grew older and unable to travel, Mother and Papa came to Philadelphia to see us, and I saw Blossom Hall less."

Sheridan moved closer, caught her hand and squeezed gently. He sensed her reticence to discuss her past. "Don't talk about it if you don't want to."

"I don't mind," she replied quietly. "I had a wonderful childhood, even though many people considered it strange and unorthodox. Everyone loved and doted on me: my father, my

234

mother, and my grandparents."

"Yet you're not spoiled, nor are you one of the idle rich, Daisy."

Marguerite chuckled. "And just who or what do you think I am now?"

"I'm not sure," he answered thoughtfully. "After reading through Earl's letters from Susanna, I thought I knew all about you, but now, after tonight, I find that I don't know anything about you at all." He paused. "Yet I know that you're not the same kind of person that Earl is."

"Thank you," Marguerite said.

"Why did you lease Blossom Hall?" Sheridan asked.

"Being reared in Philadelphia by my grandmother," Marguerite replied, "I have a different set of values from my father—economically, socially, and politically." She sighed. "As long as Mother remained single, the hall was hers. After she remarried, I inherited it along with a huge, outstanding debt that Mother had incurred as a result of her extravagant living and poor management, but I inherited none of Father's affection for the place, none of his drive and determination that would give me incentive to invest all my money in it. I should feel guilty, but I don't."

She turned her head, tendrils of hair whipping across her face. "I've instructed my attorney to locate the nearest LeFleur heirs. At the end of the year when Jordan's lease is up, I'm going to put the hall up for sale. The LeFleurs will have the first chance at purchase. If none of them want it, then—" She shrugged.

When Sheridan said nothing, she ventured, "My attorney thinks I'm crazy for not wanting to keep it. Do you?"

Sheridan smiled lazily. "Nay, lass, I think you're beautiful." His eyes touched her lips. "Kissable. Lovable. But not crazy." His finger gently brushed against the center of her palm, sending shivers of delight cascading down her spine.

"I . . . I thought since the manor house was once yours . . ." Her voice was breathy; his touch was creating such a maelstrom of emotions, she found thinking difficult. Sheridan smiled. "Do you ever wish you had the manor house back?" she finally sputtered.

Sheridan was silent for a moment. He had successfully pushed thoughts of Earl, the manor house, and revenge out of his mind. Now Marguerite had innocently resurrected them, calling them to the forefront. He stopped stroking her hand as he thought about all Taylor had taken from him.

"Aye, lass," he finally said, "it's a recurring dream of mine."

"Is that why you're fighting Earl?"

"Nay. My cause is more than the house and property now. I want freedom for all the Irish. That's why I fight people like Earl Randolph Taylor."

"Why not through the political structure?" Marguerite asked. "Legally and honestly?"

"Maybe there was a time when I could have done it that way, lass. I dunno. But not now. I'm an outlaw, and if I'm caught I would be prosecuted and hanged." He grinned, trying to lift some of the heaviness that descended on both of them. "Legislation is only words on paper, love. Somehow it takes years, if ever, before its spirit begins to trickle down to the peasants. Someone has to be out here with them in order to protect them, and who better than Sheridan O'Roarke."

Marguerite twisted in the saddle and looked imploringly at him. "Sheridan, I'm a wealthy woman. Let's you and I—"

Sheridan squeezed her hand, but he didn't smile. To be sure, he had Marguerite where he wanted her, exactly where he had guided her, but he felt none too good about it. His victory was turning sour.

"Earl Taylor may marry women for their fortunes, lass, not I."

But wasn't it the same difference? he wondered. He was going to marry her to keep Earl Taylor from getting her fortune.

"You have no future here, Sheridan. It's a matter of time

before you're apprehended. You and I can leave. We get away from your past and start anew in America."

Sheridan chuckled, a sad quality to the laughter. "Somehow, Daisy Belle, we Irish have no future. We just have a past that keeps happening over and over."

"Sheridan, we can have a future," Marguerite insisted. "I know we—"

Suddenly not wanting to talk about marriage anymore, and wishing he could spit out the bitter taste of what he was doing to Marguerite, Sheridan eased up in the saddle and pointed. "Look."

Marguerite didn't follow the direction of his hand; rather she continued to look at him. "Sheridan," she cried, "listen to me."

Sheridan looked at her and smiled, that devastating slow smile that sent her into rapture. "I've listened, lass, and I promise I'll think about it." The smile deepened. His words weren't intended as a game strategy. At the moment he wanted to forget Earl and revenge. "Push your sad thoughts aside and share the glory of my world with me."

Disappointed, Marguerite dropped her head and blinked back the tears. "All right," she mumbled.

Sheridan tucked his hand under her chin and lifted her face. "Don't ruin our evening with your pouting, little one." With his other hand he pushed wisps of hair from her face. "I promised I would think about your proposal, and I shall." Leaning over, his lips brushed against hers, breathy and teasing. His kiss wasn't one of passion but one of promise. "Right now, indulge me."

Marguerite smiled and nodded. Following the sweeping motion of his hand, she looked around herself. The hush of the evening descended, bringing a serenity and reverence to the beauty of the river that majestically gushed from its protected covering of verdant forest. Moonlight spilled over, painting everything silver. Carefully Sheridan guided his horse across a shallow ford, and Marguerite followed. On the other side they moved single file down a narrow path following the river.

Finally they reached a clearing, and Sheridan stopped. Quickly he dismounted and waited for Marguerite. Together they walked to the small, one room cottage that was nestled into the side of the mountain. He opened the door and led her inside. Moving across the room, he fumbled on the table until he found the tin of matches.

When the candle was lit and its glow illuminated the room, Sheridan turned to her, held out his hands, and smiled. "Welcome to my secret home, my darling."

Marguerite ran across the room, throwing herself against Sheridan and wrapping her arms around him, laying her cheek on his chest. "There's so much about you that I don't know, and so little time for us to be together."

Sheridan held her longer, saying nothing. Then he slid his hands up her arms, and his fingers gently gripped her shoulders. Setting her away, he smiled into her face. "Let me get the fire started, lass. Else we'll freeze to death."

Soon a fire blazed in the fireplace, and a warm coziness filled the room. "Fill the kettle with water," Sheridan instructed, "and I'll get our things."

In a few minutes Sheridan reappeared in the cottage, setting a large basket on the table. Lifting the lid, he extracted several bottles of wine. Two he set on the table, the third one he held, reading the label. Grinning, he said, "Wonder if Earl will miss this."

Marguerite chuckled. "If not Earl, Elvira Simmons will."

Setting the bottle down beside the others, Sheridan continued to unpack the basket. "Are you hungry, lass?"

"Yes."

The intensity of her answer caused Sheridan to look up. He held a loaf of bread suspended in the air. Slowly he laid it on the table, never taking his eyes off Marguerite. He moved across the room, enfolding her in his arms. Marguerite lifted her face; he lowered his, their lips meeting in a desperate, urgent kiss— in more kisses—but no more than kisses.

238

Their needs and wants transcended sexual fulfillment at the moment. They needed to cuddle and to hold; they needed to learn as much about the other as possible; they wanted to savor their last moments together. Lying on a pallet in front of the fireplace, propped on pillows, the two of them sipped their wine and talked about everything but their future; at the moment neither one of them had one, and certainly not one together.

Finally, Marguerite's eyes grew so heavy she couldn't keep them open any longer. Snuggling up to Sheridan, she burrowed into the warmth of his chest, sighing contentedly when he wrapped his cape over them. Cradled in his arms, she slept.

Sheridan watched the flames as they leaped into the air, delicate and graceful spires that disappeared into the night, never to be seen again, and so quickly replaced with another that telling one from the other was impossible—that missing one was impossible.

Was Marguerite right? he wondered. Had he been fighting his cause the wrong way? Perhaps politics was the way. He could marry her and use the LeFleur fortune for a good cause. Why not? With money he could— Yes, he thought, laying his head on the pillow, he'd go to Dublin; he'd join league with Dan O'Connell. Getting the weapons would be his last job outside the law.

Mumbling in her sleep, Marguerite turned over and rolled into a tight ball. Sheridan smiled and curled his frame around hers. Maybe he and Marguerite did have a future together after all. She loved him, and he cared for her. She need never know the reason why he was marrying her. Closing his eyes, his face softened by his thoughts, Sheridan dropped into a peaceful sleep. When he finally awakened, the aroma of tea and food filled the room.

Slowly he opened his eyes, sleepily watching Marguerite's booted feet as they silently moved around the table and back and forth across the room. When she knelt in front of the fireplace to fill the teapot with water, his gaze drifted higher up. The tight-fitting trousers stretched tautly against her body, clearly outlining the beauty of her long, slender legs, the round buttocks, the small waist. The white cambric shirt, tucked into her pants, pulled against the gentle swell of her breasts.

Although her back was to him, Marguerite felt the warmth of his gaze. "Tea or me?"

Sheridan chuckled deeply. "Can't I have both, lass?"

She turned, her eyes twinkling mischievously. "In which order?"

"Ah, Daisy Belle LeFleur, I knew you'd be a hard woman."

Marguerite laughed, tossing her hair over her shoulder as she turned to face him. "Not nearly as hard as you." Her gaze boldly moved down his body. "And not in the same places."

Scowling, Sheridan pretended seriousness. "Perhaps I wasn't far wrong in my first opinion of you. You are an audacious wench, Marguerite LeFleur. Quite audacious."

Marguerite set the teapot on the floor and squirmed beside Sheridan, her hands sliding up his chest. "But you like."

He cupped her face in his hands, drawing her nearer. "Um-hum, I like," he murmured, the words mingling into the essence of the kiss as his lips covered hers, his hands sliding down to her waist. "To be sure, lass, I love everything unladylike about you."

The moment his lips touched hers, the quick flame of passion burned through their veins, setting their emotions on fire anew. Quickly they undressed, both quivering with anticipation. And through the morning, from dark to the breaking of day, Sheridan tutored Marguerite in the fine art of love. Again and again he carried her to the dizzy heights of ecstasy. Although he never declared love, he loved her. Both joyously laughed at their newly found emotion; both shared the warmth, the tenderness, the oneness. At break of day, they fell into a sated, peaceful sleep in each other's arms.

Chapter 15

Marguerite and Sheridan treasured their day, holding onto each minute as long as they could. Dressed and outside, holding hands, they savored the beauty of the sunrise with awed whispers and sighs. Like children, they noisily clamored over the rocks and through the woods, playing hide-and-seek. At noon they ate buttered bread and drank their wine. Afterward they lay and talked, finally dozing in the sunshine.

Sheridan awoke first. He turned his head and looked at the sleeping woman beside him. A slow smile crept across his face, and he flipped over. Propped on his elbow, Sheridan traced the blade of grass along Marguerite's upper lip. Grining, he stopped when she twitched her nose. After, when she breathed deeply and rolled her head to the side, he again tickled her. This time she lifted her hand and rubbed it across her mouth. The third time her lids lazily lifted, and she opened her mouth.

Before a word of protest could escape, Sheridan dropped the grass, leaned over, their eyes momentarily locking together in a timeless gaze. Their questions, their problems were left far behind as they communicated in that unspoken language of love and togetherness. Gradually he leaned closer, his face coming nearer and nearer, blocking out everything but his image. Again Marguerite breathed deeply, her nostrils filled with the scent of him.

His hands slid up her throat to cup her face; a deep groan vibrated from his throat, a soft whimper from Marguerite's. His lips parted slightly, his head slanted, and he softly laid his mouth over hers.

"You taste so good," he murmured, letting the words lengthen into the kiss. When he broke the caress, he raised his head and looked into her eyes, pushing curling wisps of hair from her face. "Have you always had curly hair?" he asked curiously.

Marguerite laughed. "Always. As a child I hated it. I wished I could be a porcelain beauty like Susanna and Mother. Small and petite with straight hair. I wanted so to be the grand lady, beautiful, sophisticated, and poised, but I wasn't." Again she laughed. "Alas! I was the hoyden."

Stretching out, Sheridan chuckled. "Somehow, love, I'm glad you are the hoyden. I can't conceive anything more boring than a grand lady." Locking his hands together behind his head, he said, "Besides I can't imagine you like that at all."

"Good," Marguerite declared, suddenly sitting up, "because I never got my wish. I'm tall, skinny, with curly brown hair. And when it gets wet, it's even curlier."

Sheridan turned his head and looked at the cold water that rushed in the river. "Can you swim, lass?"

"Um-hum," Marguerite answered, drawing her knees to her chest. "In a fit of rage Susanna informed me that I'm quite proficient at most anything that's unladylike."

This time Sheridan was the one to exclaim. "Good." Jumping to his feet, grabbing Marguerite's hands, he pulled her up. "Let's swim."

Marguerite's eyes darted from Sheridan to the river and back to Sheridan. "Here? Now?"

"Here. Now."

Giving her no time to protest, he lifted his hands, unbuttoned her shirt and quickly divested her of the rest of her clothing. Then he undressed. When both were naked, he caught her hand and ran to the water's edge, tugging her behind. Into the cold water he splashed, laughing at Marguerite's deep intake of breath.

"This is good for you, love."

Her teeth chattering, she stuttered, "Either make—a woman out—out of me—or kill—me."

Sheridan whooped with laughter. "Nay, lass, I made the woman out of you, and this won't kill you."

With abandonment they played in the river, laughing and talking. Finally when the sun began sinking in the western sky, Sheridan and Marguerite waded out of the river and stood on the shore, arm in arm, for the last time, watching the glorious sunset. As though in a trance, Marguerite viewed the orange, gold, and purple hues which were the backdrop for the burning red orb that was majestically setting in the western sky. Her heart fluttered, and her breath caught at the rich extravaganza of nature.

She lifted her face, turned in Sheridan's arms, and their eyes met. His lips touched hers, again lighting the flame of passion that surged through Marguerite's veins, setting her desires on fire anew. His lips moved on hers, the pressure firm but gentle. Wanting more, she moaned, winding her arms tightly around him, her hands savoring the feel of the hard, bulging muscles of his back.

"It's time to go, darlin'," he breathed, a certain sadness underlying his words.

"I know."

"I wish we could stay longer, but we can't."

"Sheridan, don't go. Stay with me."

"I have to go, love."

Of one accord both turned, walking out of the river, dressing on the bank. By dusk they had packed and were ready to leave. In a beautiful silence which both shared, they mounted their horses and began their return journey, saying little, riding side by side, holding hands. When they stopped in front of the church, Marguerite looked at Sheridan. He dismounted, hitched his horse, and turned to her. His hands clasped her waist, and he easily swung her out of the saddle.

Bemused, unable to say a word, Marguerite looked up at him, the moon illuminating her face. Pushing the hood off, Sheridan gazed for the longest time into her eyes.

"This—this is a church," Marguerite whispered inanely.

Sheridan's reply was tolerant. "Aye, lass, it's a church, all right."

"Sheridan . . ."

"Aye."

Because he cared and because he desired her more than anything in the world at the moment and he had to have her at any cost, he was going to marry her. Marguerite saw his lips curl into a gentle, beautiful smile. Her heart sang with joy.

"Oh, Sheridan."

Sheridan caught her to him, crushing her in his arms. He buried his head in the curve of neck and shoulder. "Yes," he whispered, "we're going to be married, Daisy Belle. We deserve a chance at happiness."

When they reached the covey of trees close to the manor house, they stopped and dismounted, Sheridan hitching the horses. Quietly they slipped through the fence into the garden. Quickly he unlocked the library doors and guided her into the moonlit room. Moving to the desk, he lit the lamp.

"It'll be best if you don't know where I'm going," he told her, picking up a pencil.

"You're—you're not staying here with me?" She couldn't conceal her disappointment.

"Not tonight, lass. I have one last chore to perform."

Although Marguerite knew none of the details of Sheridan's mission, fear clutched her heart. "Don't go," she begged, litsening to the warnings of her inner self. "Please don't go."

"I must," he replied with a finality that brooked no further arguments. He shuffled through the loose paper on top of Earl's desk. Writing as he talked, he said, "Pack your things and get out of here as quickly as possible. I don't want you here when Earl returns. Go to this address and wait for me." He handed Marguerite the scrap of paper. "The Shamrock Pub, owned by Timothy O'Gill, one of my closest friends. He'll take care of you, lass, in case—" Silence completed the sentence. "Don't tell anyone where you're going. *No one*. Do you understand?"

Marguerite nodded, crumpling the note in her fist. "Take me with you," she pleaded. "I don't want to be away from you."

Sheridan chuckled. "You'd make a fine soldier, Marguerite LeFleur, but I can't take that risk." He moved around the desk, taking her into his arms. "You see, I've grown quite fond of you, and I don't dare risk losing you now that I've found you, Mrs. O'Roarke." He kissed her, long and leisurely. Then he held her. Finally he eased her out of his arms. "As soon as I leave, Marguerite, go upstairs and take off those clothes. Pack and get out of this house tomorrow. Take no one with you but your two black servants."

Excited and happy at her newfound love but at the same time apprehensive about Sheridan's safety, Marguerite nodded her head.

"And, lass," he admonished, "don't tell anyone about our marriage." When Marguerite blinked surprised eyes at him, he said, "For your own safety." He clamped his hands on her shoulders and drew her closer. "I couldn't stand it, lass, if anyone hurt you because of me, and I have too many enemies who would. I don't want to get you involved in my fight."

"But I am," she whispered, lifting her face to his for a swift good-bye kiss.

Tears burning her eyes, she watched O'Roarke disappear through the doors, his cloak whipping about his tall body. Soon he was a part of the darkness.

Racing across the room, Marguerite bounded up the stairs into her bedroom. Quickly she undressed, returning her pants and shirt to the armoire. After she donned her dressing gown, she picked up her brush and walked to the window.

"Miz Marguerite." The soft knock and whisper interrupted Marguerite's solitude.

Marguerite flew across the room and unlocked the door. Jewel's black face relaxed into a smile of relief. "I'se so glad to see you, honey chile. I've never been so worried in all my born days. You traipsing all over this countryside in the black of night with dat man."

Marguerite chuckled. "That man happens to be my husband, and as you can see, I'm fine. No worse for the wear."

"Maybe. Maybe not," Jewel said, her eyes narrowing as she assimilated the full weight of Marguerite's confession. "You done married Mr. Sheridan?"

"I have, but we can't tell anyone yet," Marguerite explained. "Not until he gets everything straightened out. Now," she said, dismissing the subject, "we need to get all our things packed, Jewel. We're leaving in the morning."

"Thanks be to God!" Jewel murmured her relief. "I'm ready to go home, chile."

Marguerite returned to the dresser, laying her brush down. "I—I don't know if we're going back to America or not, Jewel. I hope so, but I don't know what Sheridan wants to do."

With fluid smoothness Jewel turned around. Her disapproving eyes locked on Marguerite's face. "Lawdy! Lawdy!" Jewel moaned, her voice vibrating her anxiety. "What has possessed you, chile?" She crossed her hands over her bosom and paced around the room. "I guess Mr. Sheridan is better than Mr. Taylor, but, honey chile—" She flung her arms open.

Walking into them, Marguerite laid her head on the black woman's breast. Jewel ran her hand down the back of Marguerite's head. "You love him."

"Yes."

"Does he love you?"

Marguerite knew. Deep down in her heart she knew Sheridan didn't love her as she loved him. But she couldn't speak the words into existence.

"I—I think so. He cares for me."

Jewel also knew. As if Marguerite were a small child, Jewel drew the young woman into her arms and held her, comforting her, reassuring her. Eventually Marguerite pulled away and smiled sheepishly at the older woman. Jewel walked to the armoire and opened the door, draping several dresses over her arm.

"We can be thankful, Miz Marguerite, that we wuz going to Dublin anyway. Least ways we got all our trunks out, so we don't have that to fuss with."

Deep in thought, Marguerite nodded. "We must get yours and Annie's things packed, too." Marguerite moved to the armoire and took the gowns from Jewel. Laying them on the bed, she said, "Let's go tell Annie that we're leaving in the morning. Then you can pack yours and Annie's clothes, and I'll pack mine."

Without disturbing the staff who remained in the house, Marguerite and Jewel packed their trunks. By midnight the last light had been extinguished, and everyone was in bed. But Marguerite wasn't asleep. A smile on her face, she curled into a ball and thought about Sheridan.

His black cloak swirling around him and his satin mask dangling from one hand, Sheridan pushed his hood from his head and stood in the midst of the cottage ruins, staring at the moon-glazed countryside. The breeze gently touched his face and played through his hair, blowing russet tendrils across his cheeks.

His gaze was set in the direction of the manor house, his thoughts centered on Marguerite. At least the marriage would be more than a convenience, he kept telling himself. To be sure, he had married her because of the fortune, but he had not married her for the fortune. He cared. Damn! He really cared for her. One night and day of making love to her wasn't enough. She was in his blood. He still wanted her. And like her, he had a foreboding about tonight.

247

Even with the confirmation—more especially with the confirmation he had found when he'd searched Earl's desk earlier—Sheridan didn't feel good about the raid; deep down he knew something was wrong, but he couldn't put his finger on it. Still the final decision belonged to the boys.

A noise jarred Sheridan from his thoughts. He didn't move, but he heard the footsteps, so soft and muted that to one untrained they couldn't be heard. He tensed, and his hand slipped to the hilt of his knife. He listened.

"Sheridan."

"Gavin?" Sheridan spun around. "Thank God, you're back. I've been worried about you. No word all this time."

Gavin Kenyon lithely jumped over the crumbling wall of the Sullivan cottage and walked to Sheridan. Like Sheridan, he was wearing a hooded cloak. He laughed softly.

"Now, Danny Boy, you know better than to worry about me, to be sure. Nothing is going to happen to Gavin Kenyon." Beside Sheridan now, Gavin laid a hand on his friend's shoulder and squeezed. "I wasn't going to let you do this one without me. I don't want you getting all the glory."

Sheridan lifted his hand, laid it over Gavin's and pressed, once again reminding himself of the bond of friendship that existed among the three of them: him, Gavin, and Shane. Without saying another word, Sheridan and Gavin turned, both lapsing into a pensive silence as they gazed into the distance.

One by one the men, all disguised with flowing robes, hoods, and masks, began arriving. Although they talked quietly and laughed, each felt the urgency of their mission. After the last man arrived, Sheridan moved to the table in the middle of what had one time been the Sullivan's kitchen, and the men circled around him. He began to talk in a low voice, outlining his plan.

Suddenly the watchman hissed through the ruins, "Someone's coming."

Quickly, quietly the men scattered, melting into the

shadows. On bated breath they listened to the muted hooves of the horse; they waited; then they heard booted feet as they moved over the rocky terrain. When the figure loomed over the crumbled wall, Sheridan and Gavin simultaneously lurched forward.

The three fell to the ground, one crying out, "Don't kill me, you clouts."

"Shane," Sheridan exclaimed, sitting back, peering through the darkness. "What are you doing here?"

"Aye," Gavin said, clearly intonating his disapproval.

Slowly Shane pushed to sitting position. Wiping the dust from his clothes, he chuckled softly. "To be sure, lads, you didn't think I'd let you do it alone, now did you? I want a chance to share in some of the glory."

Sheridan bounced to his feet and held his hand down for Shane. "What about your wound?"

Shane reached up with one hand and gingerly touched his shoulder. "A mite sore it be," he admitted, "but it's well enough."

"What about Stanton?" one of the group snarled. "You didn't lead him to us, did you?"

Shane spun around to his questioner. "O'Grady, to be sure, you know me better than that."

"You were staying in one of his cottages," O'Grady muttered.

"Without Stanton's knowledge," Shane returned. "Sheridan and Gavin hid me there, so Mary could nurse me." His chest shook as laughter rumbled out. "The good man would have been shaking in his shoes to know that an Irish outlaw lay in his backyard. He's not afraid of Taylor himself, but he's afraid of the authority which the man has; he's afraid of the evil which compels Taylor to use his authority."

Sheridan turned, moving to the far wall. Now he was more confused than before. To be sure, all were laughing and making jokes about the raid, but all knew the seriousness of the business. Without any of them saying a word, each knew Taylor and Clayborne were getting closer to apprehending them.

"Danny," Shane called, "what's bothering you, boy?"

Shane watched Sheridan slowly spin around, the cloak curling around his body like a funeral shroud. Shane closed his eyes and swallowed the knot in his throat. *Dear mother of God,* he thought, *is this a premonition of what's to come? It can't be!* He—they—the three of them—had never really considered death. They had played with it, toyed with it, but never had they considered it doing the same with them. They had considered capture, imprisonment, yes—but not death.

Sheridan spoke, his voice riding the wind. "Boys, I have a feeling about the coming raid." He turned, and the rocks crunched under his boots as he walked to the center of the human circle. "Everything has fallen into place too easily. We haven't felt the usual intervention by Taylor and the yeomanry."

"Now, maybe you haven't, Sheridan O'Roarke," one of the men declared, standing, "but I don't think you could quite convince Shane Dempsey of that point." His hand went to his mouth. "And to be sure, you can't convince me. Remember, I was on the other end of your fists, me darling, and 'twas no pleasure being beaten up and down the street."

Sheridan joined in the laughter. "Ahh, Mickey Flynn, you don't have a way with your fists, but you do have a way with your words. Taylor's paid well to hear what you have to say about Sheridan O'Roarke and the Wexford boys."

"Aye," Mickey droned lowly, "to be sure, Danny Boy, I have a way with words. And Taylor is willing to pay any price to get you. Your capture has become an obsession with him."

"Nay," Shane quietly negated. "Sheridan's death has become an obsession with him."

"We all know that," Gavin said, breaking the heavy silence that loomed over the small group. "To be sure, boys, we need to move to weightier subjects. Night is fast moving on, and—"

"That be true," Mickey said. "I suggest that you begin telling what you learned when you were in Dublin, Gavin, me boy."

"Aye," the others quietly chorused.

"Like Sheridan suspected, the letter in Taylor's office was part of an elaborate plan. Everything at the port in Dublin is too obvious. Secrecy is the word, yet the word is out that a big shipment is due. Red Coats are everywhere."

"Aye," Sheridan concurred. "And Taylor's making sure that the whole countryside knew he was traveling to Dublin." He paused, then said, "He's laying a trap, boys, and I'm not sure where it is. Dublin or Wexford or elsewhere. I have a feeling that no matter where we go, we're going to be caught."

"And you're talking like an old woman," Mickey cried contemptuously. "Running scared on us, are you?"

"Perhaps," Sheridan softly answered. "I don't like it, lads. I say we should pass this one up. Taylor isn't foolish enough to have the weapons sent to Dublin. Too much overland travel is necessary." He balled his hand into a fist and hit the table. "And he knows we're smart enough to guess that." Again he said, "It's a trap, lads. To be sure, it's a trap."

Shane moved, sitting on one of the larger rocks. The jar hurt his shoulder. Wincing and lifting a hand to the healing wound, he said, "Whatever you say, Danny. I'm with you."

"Aye, and me," Gavin added.

"As for me," Mickey spat, rising to his feet, "I say we have a show of hands. I'd say Sheridan is turning coward, lads." He moved around the circle, looking into the upturned faces. "In order to whip the British we need those weapons. They're the newest and the best from the Continent. We've got to get them, and this is our chance. Besides we know that Taylor is in Dublin."

"Aye," one of the men substantiated, "I'm the one who followed his coach."

"So what do you say, boys?" Mickey called.

After the chorus of "ayes," Sheridan nodded, but he was

still filled with misgivings. "I heard ye, lads, but I want to see a show of hands. Are *we* riding to Wexford Harbor?"

Silently the hands rose, not one exception. Sheridan pivoted the full circle. "So be it." Reaching inside his shirt, he pulled out a folded sheet of paper and moved to the table. "Get the candle and tin of matches, Mickey. We're going to need some light."

Mickey leaned backward and ran his hand across the tumbling wall, feeling for the hole where they hid the candle and matches. After Mickey set the candle on the table and lit it, Sheridan unfolded the map.

"They won't be expecting us at Wexford," Mickey said, leaning forward, his index finger traveling the map, "so why not send the larger group to Dublin, Danny, as a diversion. Four or five of us can handle Wexford."

"Nay, we'll send the smaller force to Dublin, the larger one to Wexford." The candlelight played across Sheridan's face as he looked at the group that crowded around the table. "Mickey, O'Grady, Shaunnesey, and Callaghan will hit the port at Dublin. The rest of us will go to Wexford. Agreed?" The gaze slowly passed from one man to the other. All but Mickey nodded.

"To Wexford Harbor I'd like to be going with you," Mickey said.

Sheridan smiled and shook his head. "I need you at Dublin, Mickey."

"Aye."

Sheridan lowered his head. "Listen to me, boys, as I tell you what we're going to do."

The small group crowded closer, each man listening intently to Sheridan's orders, every eye on the markings of the pencil. Each knew the penalty for one mistake.

When the candle had burned low, Sheridan dropped the pencil and straightened. "Be ready at the word, lads, and tell no one our plans," Sheridan said. "No one. Not your wives, your mothers, your sisters, or your lovers." O'Roarke caught one of the men by the arm and pulled him aside. "Kennie, I have special need of you tomorrow." The young boy lifted his head and nodded excitedly. "I want you to drive Mistress Marguerite and her servants to the Shamrock Pub in Dublin."

"Drive Mistress Marguerite . . . to . . . Dublin." All the excitement drained out of Kennie's voice.

"To be sure, Kennie. You're the only one with whom I would entrust Marguerite. Her life is in danger."

"You think I'm too young to go with the men," Kennie spat bitterly.

Sheridan laid his hand on the youth's shoulder. "I think you're a man, Kennie, a man whom I can trust. That's why I'm entrusting you with the most important thing—"

Sheridan stopped himself in time. Not knowing whom he could trust, he wasn't going to reveal his personal involvement with Marguerite. Nor was he going to let anyone know they were married. He wasn't going to let anyone use the knowledge to hurt her.

Sheridan smiled, his hand squeezing gently on Kennie's shoulder. "I'm entrusting you with the most important thing to our cause."

Kennie thought for a while; then he said, "What do you want me to do?"

Sheridan drew Kennie aside, and in low tones he gave him instructions. "Go the back roads, and make sure that you're not followed. Under no circumstances let anyone know where you're going with her." As he had instructed Marguerite, Sheridan said, "Absolutely no one. Not even one of us."

"And after we arrive at Tim's?"

"Wait for me there."

"I'd like to join the boys at the harbor."

"Don't leave Marguerite until I arrive. She's in danger and needs protection."

Clearly disappointed, Kennie pulled his hood over his head and stamped away.

"To be sure, this assignment doesn't seem glorious to you,

lad, but believe me, Marguerite LeFleur is vitally important to the cause."

Kennie pulled up short and jerked his head toward Sheridan. "To be sure, sir? You're not—"

Sheridan shook his head. "Nay, lad, I wouldn't be teasing you like that."

A grin split Kennie's face. "To be sure, Sheridan, I'll take care of Mistress Marguerite and see that she arrives at Tim's place safely. Mr. Taylor won't know where she is."

"I'm counting on you, lad."

One by one the men disappeared into the night until only the three friends were left. Gavin picked up the tin of matches from the table and returned them to their hiding place. Because his shoulder was aching, Shane remained where he was sitting. Preoccupied, Sheridan walked to the wall, again gazing at the manor house.

"What's wrong?" Shane asked, able to read Sheridan's moods.

"Nothing really," Sheridan returned. "Just a feeling that I have."

"Anything to do with Marguerite LeFleur?" When Sheridan didn't answer, Shane added, "Bridget said you were with her last night."

"Aye."

Gavin chuckled. "Danny Boy! Danny Boy! When will you learn to leave Earl Taylor's women alone? First Eliza. Now Marguerite."

"No price is too great for the cause," Shane mused aloud, looking across the moonlight clearing at his old friend. When Sheridan made no response, Shane said, "I understand that Marguerite and Earl are meeting in Dublin."

His eyes to the east, Sheridan said, "We'd best make haste, lads, and get out of here. Day is breaking, and we have work to do."

Chapter 16

The women reached the inn safely; however, because it was crowded, Marguerite was separated from Jewel and Annie. The two of them were together in servants' quarters on the bottom floor, she on the second story. Anxiously Marguerite paced back and forth between the bed and the night table. The longer she waited in the room, the smaller it seemed to get. Several days and nights of not knowing Sheridan's whereabouts was more than she could take. The suspense was making her jittery; the walls were closing in on her. *When was he going to come? Was he going to come?* She walked to the window and threw open the shutters, gazing up the road first, then around the courtyard.

From his perch on the bench by the water trough, Kennie called, "He'll be coming, ma'am. Don't you be worrying none."

A knock on the door and a soft voice drew Marguerite's attention. "I brought you some dinner, ma'am."

Marguerite moved across the room, opened the door, and took the tray. Peering around Marguerite, the girl saw the untouched food from lunch.

"The tea's hot, ma'am. At least drink that. You need something in your stomach. You haven't eaten anything all day."

"I will," Marguerite promised, smiling as she closed the door.

Returning to the table, she picked up the teapot and was about to fill her cup when she heard the thundering hooves. With no thought but Sheridan, she set the pot down with a thud and ran across the room. When she reached the window, she heard Nelson Clayborne shout, "Capture that boy. He's one of the O'Roarke's."

Then the door to her room burst open, and Earl sauntered into the room. "Good afternoon, my dear. How fortunate that I found you. This isn't where we had planned to meet." Although softly spoken, the words meted out punishment.

"Hello, Earl."

Drawing to her full height, Marguerite turned from the window, making her way to the table. With a steady hand, she lifted the teapot the second time and filled her cup with the steaming liquid. Marshaling all her control, she lifted the cup to her lips and sipped the tea.

"I'm disappointed to find you here," Earl said smoothly, lightly slapping his quirt against his thigh. "I had expected you to meet me in Dublin, but surely not in this hovel."

"A last minute change of plans," Marguerite replied. "Why are you here?"

"The same reason as you," he answered. He moved to the dresser and laid his quirt down. Then he removed his gloves and hat, laying them down also. "Sheridan."

Holding the saucer under her cup, Marguerite took another swallow of her tea.

"May I have a cup?" Earl requested, sighing deeply as he lowered himself into a chair. Watching Marguerite serve the tea, he propped his elbows on the armrests of the chair and bridged his hands in front of his mouth. "I've done so much to hurt you already," he said pensively. "I hate to bring you more heartache."

Marguerite's hand shook, and tea splashed into the saucer. Before Earl told her, she knew.

256

"O'Roarke and his men rode into a trap. He escaped, but according to reports I've received he's badly wounded."

"No," she whispered.

"I'm afraid that it's true," he confirmed, lapsing into thought.

With Hibernia's help he had set the trap, and he'd caught Shane Dempsey. But damn! Sheridan and Gavin were still at large—Sheridan badly wounded, one soldier had reported. He balled his hand into a fist. Would he ever taste the victory of capturing Sheridan?

Now he found added complications which worried and irritated him. He hadn't contemplated Marguerite's being so enamored with O'Roarke. But he should have known! Now he was playing the last hand in the final game between him and Sheridan. Everything rested on his winning the stake: Marguerite and her fortune.

Eventually he said, "One of Sheridan's men betrayed him." As he spoke, he stood and moved to his coat, rummaging through the pockets.

"No!" Marguerite gasped.

"You're such an innocent," Earl murmured, slowly crossing the room. "Such an idealist. I know it's hard for you to believe, but everybody can be bought, my dear. It's all a matter of finding out their cost. His was ten thousand pounds."

Her back to Earl, Marguerite's face turned ashen and the cup jiggled against the saucer. She almost passed out, but she refused to give Earl the pleasure of manipulating her emotions. She stepped closer to the window and leaned against the casement. Earl stood immediately behind her, and she felt the weight of something as it hit her on the shoulder. Turning her head, dropping her face, she saw her pearl necklace. She couldn't stifle her gasp.

"As a token of his good faith to me, the traitor returned your pearls to me."

Marguerite's fingers curled around the necklace, the

diamond cutting into her palm. She was nearer to fainting than she had ever been in her life. But still she refused to be used. And at all costs she must be careful not to say too much, not to reveal her marriage to Sheridan.

"What if this is an elaborate trap to ensnare you?"

"No, my dear." Earl's voice had never been so soft and tender, so full of understanding. "For your sake I wish I didn't have to tell you this, but my apprehending O'Roarke is the result of a carefully set trap. It's taken me a year, but this time I've got him right where I want him. If he's not killed when he's apprehended, I will have enough evidence to have him hanged as a traitor." His hands clamped on Marguerite's shoulders, and he whispered, "I'm sorry, Marguerite. Truly I am."

Jerking away from him, Marguerite said, "Don't lie to me. I know how badly you've wanted O'Roarke, and I know to what measures you've been willing to go."

Earl strode to the table, picked up his cup and drank the tepid liquid. "I'm not apologizing for having captured O'Roarke, Marguerite. I'm sorry because in capturing him I am breaking your heart." Earl set the cup on the table. "What are your plans now, my dear?"

She shrugged, setting the cup and saucer on the table. Absently she ran the pearls through her hands. She had always been apprehensive of Earl, but today she was frightened. His words and his actions were all to the extreme. His tone too controlled; his emotion too sorrowful; his grief too tangible. And Marguerite was too distressed to think straight.

"Will you come to Dublin with me?" he asked.

"No." Earl could barely hear the word.

"Will you return to the manor house until you've decided what you wish to do?"

"No."

Earl reached up to pick an imaginary piece of lint from his jacket. "I'll be most disappointed," he said quietly. "I promised your mother that I would look after you."

"Thank you," Marguerite returned stiffly, "but . . . I . . ."

"I'm not trying to force you into any long lasting decision, my dear," he said. "I think it would be better for you to stay here for awhile. Until you get over your grief and have time to think about what you wish to do."

Thinking of Mary O'Roarke, Marguerite said, "I—I would like to visit with someone." Her eyes fastened on the gold band on her hand. She looked at him pleadingly. "Please."

"All right," Earl replied. His voice was soft and warm, deceptively so. "You've fallen in love with O'Roarke, haven't you, Marguerite?" Marguerite admitted nothing. "That's not unusual," he confessed. "Sheridan has a way about him that attracts women, that makes them fall in love with him. I tried to warn you, my dear, but I guess experience is the best teacher, although I've been told that she's the harshest."

Marguerite closed her eyes. Her head was reeling, and she was nauseous. If Earl said, "my dear," one more time, she thought she would vomit. She just wanted him to be quiet, but his soft voice droned on and on. Then his hand clasped her arm.

"I'm going to leave Paddy and the carriage here with you. Both are at your disposal. Go wherever you must. Do whatever you must." He smiled. "Just remember: You always have a home at the manor house."

Repelled by his touch but astonished and perplexed by his kindness, Marguerite's eyes opened wider. Unconsciously she drew the pearls through her hands, clasping the diamond tightly in her palm. Her thoughts spinning, and wanting to put distance between herself and Earl, Marguerite moved to the window, gazing at the courtyard.

Earl walked to the door. With the same deliberated ritual that he had used when he removed his clothing, he now put on his hat, his jacket, and his gloves. When he held his riding quirt in hand, he said, "I'm leaving now, my dear."

Marguerite turned. "Earl . . ." Her stepfather stopped in the door frame. "Thank you for everything."

259

Knowing she couldn't see the gesture, Earl smiled. Perhaps all wasn't lost, after all. "Don't thank me, darling girl." He paused, then turned. "You see, I love you, too."

Without another word, Earl spun around and hastened down the stairs into the courtyard. He walked directly to Paddy. Talking loudly enough that Marguerite could hear but not so loud that she would be suspicious of his purpose, Earl said, "I'm leaving you here with Marguerite, Paddy. You are to follow her instructions implicitly. Take her wherever she wishes to go."

Paddy's eyes narrowed. He looked from Earl to the opened window on the second floor. "Are ye sure that's the way ye want it, sir?"

Moving so that his back was to Marguerite, Earl nodded his head, whispering at the same time, "Keep me informed of her every movement. O'Roarke will surely be joining her. By no means let her leave the country."

Rubbing his hand over his chin, Paddy nodded his head. "The lad, sir," he said, pointing to Kennie. "What are ye going to be a'doin' with him?"

Earl looked at the unconscious youth who was tied to the hitching rail. "Lieutenant Clayborne, did the boy talk?"

"No, sir. He doesn't know anything."

Earl nodded. "He's of no use to us. I'm going to turn him loose." Then he said, "Lieutenant, please rent me a mount from the proprietor. I shall be returning to the manor house alone."

Clutching the pearls, Marguerite stood in the window. She wanted to cry, but she had no tears left. Her eyes felt as if they were filled with sand. She watched Earl and the soldiers gallop away. Only when she saw Paddy cut Kennie loose did she stir from her bemusement. Looping the pearls around her neck, she raced out of the room, down the stairs, into the courtyard. Kneeling beside Kennie who now lay on the grass, she ripped off the bottom of a petticoat.

Handing it to Paddy, she said, "Get it wet for me, please."

When Paddy returned from the well, Marguerite gently washed the dried blood from Kennie's face.

"Paddy," he whispered through bruised and swollen lips. "Have . . . have . . . they got Sheridan yet?"

"I don't know, lad," Paddy said, "but not to worry."

"The weapons?" Kennie asked.

"An' to be sure, Kennie, me darlin', the Wexford boys got the weapons, and Sheridan hid them hisself, he did." Paddy chuckled. "No one be a'knowin' where they are, but O'Roarke hisself." Kennie chuckled softly. "Now, lad, we need to be a'movin'."

Moaning his agony, Kennie sat up. "Where are we going?"

Paddy looked at Marguerite. "Where do you want to be a'goin', ma'am?"

Marguerite looked at the ring on her hand. "I want to stay here. This is where Sheridan promised to meet me. I feel closer to him somehow."

"I can be understandin' that, ma'am. But O'Roarke won't be a'comin' now, ma'am. Earl's going to have men all around the place."

Wanting to tell Mary about her marriage to Sheridan, she said, "I—I would like to go see Mary."

"Nay, lass, that would put her into danger."

"What shall I do then?" Marguerite asked, a hint of despair in her voice. "Where shall I go?"

"Sheridan left me instructions to go to Seamus McNeil's cottage if anything went wrong with the plans. We'll wait for word there." Hopping to his feet, Paddy said, "Now let's get the baggage loaded onto the carriage. We've got a long way to go before dark."

The miles were long for Marguerite, and the time passed slowly. She twisted Sheridan's ring around and around on her finger, but instead of thinking about the joy of her marriage, she worried about Sheridan's safety. Having had time to gather her wits, she completely understood Earl's strategy. He was using her for bait. Somehow she had to get a message to

Sheridan, warning him not to join her.

When the carriage lumbered to a rocking halt, Paddy called, "Seamus McNeil's cottage. Now the three of ye get into the cottage. I'll take care of the horses and buggy." Climbing down, he said to Kennie, "Saddle a horse as quickly as you can, lad, and be on your way. Make sure you head in the direction I told ye."

Kennie's eyes darkened. "Are you sure this is what Sheridan wants, Paddy?"

Paddy nodded his head. "I'm sure, lad. Now on with it if ye want tonight to be worth it."

With a minimum of conversation, Paddy unhitched the horses, and Marguerite and Jewel disembarked. Supporting the exhausted Annie between them, they walked into the shadowed cottage as Kennie quickly saddled a horse and galloped away. Jewel led the old woman to a bed on the far side of the room while Marguerite moved to the fireplace, quickly building a peat fire. She filled the kettle with water and set it on the flame.

"Annie's not doing so well, Miz Marguerite," Jewel murmured in an undertone, coming to crouch in front of the fire beside Marguerite. "All this gadding about's been too much for her."

Marguerite nodded. "She's tired, but she'll be all right after she rests some." Picking up the candle that lay on the hearth, she tipped the wick to the fire.

"No, ma'am," Jewel said, "it's more than tiredness. She's acting like she's giving up on living. Right now, she's frightfully cold. Shaking all over."

"See if you can find some quilts in one of the other rooms," Marguerite instructed. Straightening, she carried the candle to the table and set it in the holder. "I'll fix us something to eat."

As Jewel disappeared into the bedroom, Marguerite walked around the kitchen, opening doors and looking in the cupboards. Finally she located a crock of butter and a loaf of soda bread. She was setting them on the table when Jewel returned to the room with a quilt draped over her arm.

"Looks like we ain't gonna starve." The black woman grinned. "Hot tea, bread, and butter don't sound none too bad to me, Miz Marguerite."

"And more," Marguerite added, pulling up the bench seat. She waved her hand. "Potatoes."

Jewel laid the quilt on the table. "As soon as I give Annie a cup of tea, Miz Marguerite, I'll be over here to help you fix some supper."

Picking up the quilt, Marguerite walked to the bed. Carefully she situated the cover over the old woman. Sitting on the side of the bed, she asked, "How are you feeling, Annie?"

Slowly Annie's lids lifted, but her eyes were fevered and lackluster. "I don't feel good, chile." She tried to smile. "I—I'm just tired."

"Rest then," Marguerite murmured.

"Here's you a cup of hot tea, Annie," Jewel said, coming to stand beside Marguerite.

Knowing Annie was too weak to sit up by herself, Marguerite fluffed two pillows and stuffed them behind the old servant. "Now," she said, leaning Annie back against them, "drink your tea. We'll have supper in a little while."

Returning to the fireplace, Marguerite and Jewel peeled and diced the potatoes. While Jewel washed them and put them on to cook, Marguerite rummaged through the larder. Grinning, she ran over to Jewel, her hands full of herbs.

"Not so bad." Jewel chuckled as she seasoned the potatoes. Laying her stirring spoon down, she picked up the kettle of hot water and walked to the table. "How about a cup of tea while we're waiting for supper to git done?"

"To be sure," Paddy exclaimed, pushing open the door and walking into the room. "An' what are we having for supper?"

"Potato soup, bread, butter, and tea," Marguerite announced.

Paddy smiled. "It sounds like a feast fit for the king hisself." Paddy looked at Annie who had lain back down, snuggling

263

under the covers. "How is she?"

"Not good," Marguerite murmured. "She's exhausted."

Paddy didn't hear Marguerite's last words. He rushed to the door, pressing his ear flat against the wood. "Get down. Somebody's coming," he hissed.

Marguerite blew out the candle; now the only light in the room was the fire. Dropping to her knees, she crawled into a darkened corner. Jewel crouched behind a chest, and Paddy behind the door. Breathlessly the three of them waited.

Marguerite could hear nothing. Then faintly she heard the whistling—the tune that Paddy always sang—the song about the wearing of the green. Still no one moved. The soft rap on the door—a code, Marguerite thought, peering through the flickering shadows at Paddy. Without revealing himself, Paddy turned the doorknob and let the door slowly creak open itself.

The wind blew into the house, wreaking havoc with the fire, sending spindly flames dancing all about, scattering ashes on the floor. Out of the dark, out of the night came a familiar voice.

"Paddy. It is I, Brice Stanton." Paddy's fingers curled around his cudgel. Brice heard movement and quickly said, "I mean you no harm, Paddy. Listen to me before you do anything." He waited. "Will you listen to me?"

"An' how did ye be a'knowin' about the knock and the whistling?"

"Sheridan."

"An' why would Sheridan be a'tellin' an Englishman our secrets? You aren't one of the Wexford boys."

"I am English, Paddy," Brice answered, his voice soft and patient, "and I am a Protestant, but I bought my property honestly and paid a fair market price for it. Most assuredly I am a Wexford boy. This is my land, and I'm fighting for our freedom as much as you or any other Irishman is. I don't like tyranny, no matter what name or flag she boasts."

264

After a long period of silence, Paddy said, "Speak, Mr. Stanton, I'm listening."

"I found Kennie on my property. He'd lost his horse and was badly wounded and delirious. He was raving about you and Mistress Marguerite being here, and—"

Paddy closed the door behind Brice. Suspiciously he asked, "Who hurt him?"

"I don't know." Brice looked at Paddy, the firelight casting flickering shadows over his face. Tucked under his arm was a bundle. "Whoever shot him, Paddy, was extremely close to the lad."

"What do ye be a'sayin', Mr. Stanton?"

As Paddy asked the question Jewel and Marguerite came out of hiding, and Brice walked to the table, laying the bundle down, pulling a handkerchief out of his coat pocket. Rubbing it over his face, he caught the back of a chair and dragged it from the table. Jewel stiffly pushed to her feet, stretched and moved to the table, picking up the candle. Moving to the fire, she lit it.

"I have the feeling that Kennie knew whoever shot him."

"Someone who Kennie trusted."

Brice nodded. "The Wexford boys walked into a trap today. Two were killed. Shane was captured, and Sheridan and Gavin escaped. Gavin is badly wounded, but he reached the old cottage on the back side of the house. I've hidden him, and the wife is tending his wounds."

Marguerite couldn't help the tears of relief that coursed down her cheek.

"Thank God for that," Paddy muttered. "Now we'll have to wait for Sheridan to send us word."

Brice looked at Paddy; he dropped his head and rubbed his hands together. "There's more, Paddy." Something in Brice's tone alerted Paddy to bad news. He moved back to the table. "Mary . . . Mary O'Roarke . . . she's . . . she's been killed, Paddy."

Jewel set the candle in the center of the table in time for

Marguerite to see Paddy's face drain of all color. His hands hit the table, supporting him for a moment. Then he crumpled over.

"Mary," he mumbled. "No, not Mary." He doubled his fist and hit the table. "Why Mary?" he demanded. "What did she ever do to anyone but good?"

"Earl was a madman, Paddy. Never have I seen him like he was today. He was consumed with purpose. The whole thing could have been a scene from a play, so well rehearsed was Earl. He demanded that I join in the search for Sheridan, and immediately we set out for Mary's cottage. So sure was he that Mary was hiding Sheridan and the weapons in the cottage that he ordered Clayborne and his soldiers to tear the house apart, stone by stone." Brice drew in a deep gulp of air. "They didn't find Sheridan, but they did find a box of the weapons, Paddy."

"But there's no way." Paddy exclaimed. "No one could have gotten the weapons, but—"

"No way," Brice said, "except—"

Neither man uttered the words, but both knew. Someone had planted the weapons, and whoever planted them was a traitor.

"Reckon you could do with a morsel to eat," Jewel said, heaving the black pot off the fire. "Got some bread and butter and a pot of potato soup."

Brice stuffed the handkerchief into his pocket and smiled gratefully. "I'm not so hungry, but—" He looked at the kettle on the fire. "I am thirsty."

"Then a drink you shall have," Paddy said, moving across the room to a chest. "Seamus McNeil is an obliging sort." Lifting the lid, he rummaged through the contents until he brandished a bottle in the air. When he was at the table again, he filled two cups with the whiskey. "Now tell me what happened to Mary."

"Mary ran into the cottage, trying to save some of her heirlooms. When Earl gave the order to burn the cottage, the lieutenant dragged her out, but Mary ran back. Earl ordered Clayborne to torch the cottage with Mary in it."

"I'll kill that—"

Brice laid his hand on Paddy's arm and squeezed. "Clayborne refused and Earl shot him in the stomach. Sweeping down, Earl then picked up the torch himself and threw it. Clayborne crawled into the fire and died trying to save Mary."

For long moments no sound but the sputtering of the fire could be heard. "I have her jewelry box, Paddy. That's all she got out before she ran back in." Reaching over, he opened the bundle.

Tears running down his grizzled face, Paddy lifted the lid, letting the plaintive notes flow through the room. "Her mother gave her this box," he said.

"It looks as if it were new," Marguerite murmured.

"Aye. When Earl had them evicted from the big house, he was so full of hatred that he destroyed nearly all their belongings. I found this." Paddy collapsed into a chair. "It was so badly damaged that I took it to Dublin and had it refinished and repaired. I had the music box put in for her."

Remembering the love in Mary's eyes when she had looked at the music box, Marguerite said, "She loved it."

"And I loved her." The old man laid his head on the table and began to sob his anguish.

Understanding Paddy's grief, Brice stood, moving to the other side of the room. Marguerite and Jewel also moved away from the table, letting Paddy grieve in privacy. Jewel replenished the fire and prepared dishwater. Marguerite poured Annie a cup of tea and filled a bowl with soup. Sitting on the edge of the bed, she fed the old woman. When Annie shook her head and slid back down, Marguerite pulled the quilt under her chin. Leaning, she placed a kiss on the wrinkled cheek.

"Sleep well, Annie."

Picking up the empty cup and the bowl, Marguerite moved nearer the fire where Paddy and Brice sat, drinking their whiskey.

"Give me dem dishes, Miz Marguerite," Jewel said, rolling up the sleeves of her dress. "I'll wash 'em while you talk with Mr. Stanton and Paddy.

Pouring herself a cup of tea, Marguerite sat down on the hearth. "Where's Shane?"

"At the manor house." Brice finally moved from the window.

"Is he all right? Have they harmed him?"

Brice shook his head. "No, that's not Earl's purpose yet. He's going to use Shane for bargaining power."

"Does Sheridan know?"

"I don't know," Brice replied. "Earl is having handbills printed and posted. He's promising amnesty for all the Wexford boys and freedom for Shane if Sheridan will give himself up, return the weapons, and sign a confession of guilt."

Paddy drained his cup in one long swallow. "The boys wouldn't let Sheridan give himself up, and Sheridan wouldn't be fool enough to trust Earl Taylor to keep his word."

"What are we going to do?" Marguerite asked.

"Nobody knows we're here, but Sher—" The words had no sooner passed Paddy's lips when he looked at Brice. "Do ye think Kennie may have told him that we're here?"

"It's quite possible, Paddy. Even now someone may be watching us."

"Aye," Paddy replied, standing, dropping his hands in his pockets, rounding his shoulders. "We'd best be thinking of getting out of here."

The knock on the door startled all of them. For a second they looked at each other. Paddy began to fan his hand through the air, motioning Brice into the bedroom.

"'Tis better that no one knows ye be working with us," he whispered. Brice nodded, slipping into the other room.

"Paddy," Bridget cried. "Please, Paddy, let me in."

"Bridget," Paddy whispered, rushing to the door. "What do ye be doing here?" he asked.

"Shane sent me," she sobbed, collapsing into a chair at the table. "They're going to kill him."

Jewel walked to the fireplace. Picking up the kettle, she prepared another pot of tea.

"Tell me about it," Paddy said, sitting down beside her.

"I was walking by the library when I heard the voices," Bridget said. "One man said, 'You've got to kill him. If you don't, the boys will find out that I'm the one who's been spying on them for you.' Mr. Taylor acted like he was frightened and didn't know what to do. He said the people wouldn't stand for it if he murdered Shane."

"You didn't recognize the other man's voice?" Paddy asked. "You've never heard him before?"

Bridget shook her head. "It sounded like his voice was muffled, like he had a handkefchief or something over his mouth." Bridget's hands balled into fists. "We've a traitor in our midst, Paddy. And none of us knows who he be. He's out there with the boys, helping them set up Shane's escape." Tears choked her. "But he's really setting Sheridan and Shane up. He's leading Sheridan into a trap. Once he's got Sheridan in the house, he's going to shoot him and Shane so Mr. Taylor can claim they were shot trying to escape." She looked from Marguerite to Paddy. "What are we going to do, mum?"

Tears sliding down her cheeks, Bridget continued, "You once asked me who I thought was the fairest in all Eire, Mistress Marguerite. Well, I'll tell you." She sobbed, "Shane Dempsey. I love Shane more than life itself, Mistress Marguerite. I don't want him to die. I'd do anything for him. I'd die myself if it would save him."

Marguerite reached across the table and took Bridget's hands in hers. Again they resealed the bond of friendship that had developed between them. "I know how you feel," she confided. "I love Sheridan the same way."

"Did anyone follow you?" Paddy asked.

"I—I don't think so," Bridget replied. Wiping the tears from her eyes, she said, "I'm sorry, Paddy. I was so worried about Shane that I forgot." She looked at the closed bedroom door. "Is—is someone in there?"

Paddy stared at the room for a long while before he said, "Nay, lass. We're all who be here." He smiled. "Now you make haste and get back to the house before Taylor misses you. Keep your ears and your eyes open. Let me know the minute you hear anything."

"Do you know where Sheridan is?" She looked from Marguerite to Paddy. "Please tell me if you do. I'll go get him. He won't let Mr. Taylor harm Shane."

Paddy wrapped his arm around Bridget and hugged her. "We'll take care of it, love. Ye jest ride on back to the big house and act as if nothing in the world had happened." He smiled. "To be sure, everythin' will be all right."

After Bridget was gone, Marguerite ran to the bedroom and opened the door. "Brice," she called softly, "you can come out now."

For a man as heavy as he was, Brice moved so swiftly and quietly that Marguerite started when he touched her shoulder. Returning to the kitchen, they clustered around the table.

"What are we going to do?" Marguerite asked.

"I dunno, lass. I dunno if he be wounded or not." He paced about the room.

All of them were aware of one another, but none of them were mindful of what the other was doing. Deep in thought, Brice drummed his thick fingers across the table, and Jewel refurbished the fire and put on another kettle of water. Marguerite ran her fingers through her hair, lifting it off the nape of her neck, and Paddy rubbed his hand over his chin.

"Where?" he muttered. "Where would Sheridan go?"

As Paddy spoke the words, Marguerite let her hair drop, and her face illuminated with sudden comprehension. She knew where Sheridan was. Softly she said, "I know where he is,

Paddy." She stood so quickly the chair fell to the floor. Spinning around, she ran into the bedroom. "I know where he is, and I'm going to him."

Brice looked at Paddy. At the same time both men said, "No, you're not."

"Tell us where he is, lass, and we'll go get him. It's too dangerous for you out there. Besides Earl is expecting you to lead him to O'Roarke."

Inside the bedroom, leaning against the door, Marguerite said, "I'm going. He needs me, Paddy."

"What if someone followed Bridget here?" Brice exclaimed. "Right now the cottage could be surrounded with Earl's men."

"To be sure," Paddy said, "but I doubt it." He angled his face in Brice's direction and smiled crookedly. "Whatever else he may be, Earl Taylor is intelligent and clever, Mr. Stanton. He knew that Marguerite would never lead him to Sheridan if she thought she be followed."

Brice nodded his head. "So Earl deliberately sent you off with her, and he's depending on you to report Marguerite's goings and comings to him."

"Aye."

Surprised by Paddy's admission, Marguerite cracked the door and listened. Brice's eyes narrowed, and he peered intently at the coachman. "Exactly whose side are you on, Paddy?"

Paddy yanked on his jacket, pulling the collar closer to his neck. He walked to the window, placing a hand on one side of the casement. "I be on the side of the Irish."

"Sheridan's?" Brice persisted.

"Nay, not necessarily Sheridan's," Paddy replied. "Until he purges his soul—and that he may never do—Sheridan Michael O'Roarke is fighting his own cause."

"What are you going to do?"

Paddy turned and looked at the white-faced girl in the door. "Will you tell me where Sheridan is, mistress, and let me go to him for you?"

271

Marguerite shook her head, her answer so low neither Brice nor Paddy could hear it.

"Do you trust me?" Paddy asked.

"Yes," Marguerite whispered, surprised at her admission, "I trust you."

"If you do, lass, you must tell me."

Marguerite opened her mouth to speak, but no words would come. Frantically she looked from Brice to Paddy. She didn't know what to do.

"If you want Sheridan to live, lass, tell me." Quietly Marguerite told Paddy about the cottage.

"To be sure," Paddy exclaimed delightedly. "Why didn't I think of that?" Paddy rubbed his hands together and moved back to the table. "Here's what we must do. I'll ride over to Mr. Taylor's and give him a report, so he won't be worried, and we won't be worried with people tailing us. Mr. Stanton, it be time for you to return to your house, and Mistress Marguerite, you and the two women will wait here for me to return." After Brice and Paddy left, Jewel said, "Why don't you lie down in the bedroom and get some rest, Miz Marguerite. I'll stay in here, so's I can tend the fire and Annie."

Exhausted and worried, Marguerite nodded. Stumbling through the door, she fell across the bed without undressing. In a matter of minutes she was in a fitful sleep. Several hours later she awakened. Flipping on her back, she lay still, listening to the sounds of the night. She heard the chimes on the old clock. Paddy had been gone so long. She turned her head toward the windows and saw the sun's golden rays slipping in through the cracks in the shutters.

Suddenly with purpose she moved, her feet hitting the floor. She pushed through the trunks until she found the one she sought. With hurried, clumsy movements, she unfastened the leather belt.

"Miz Marguerite." The door flew open, and Jewel filled the frame, her hands planted on her hips, her face screwed into a scowl. "What does you think you're doing?"

"It's been hours since they left," Marguerite grunted, lifting the lid. "Someone's got to reach Sheridan, and I'm the someone."

Jewel wrung her hands together. "I don't know why you didn't jest tell 'em where Mr. Sheridan was. Besides you promised them that you wouldn't leave here." Jewel saw Marguerite pull her shirt and trousers out of the trunk and shrieked. "Lawsy mercy, Miz Marguerite. You can't go gadding about de countryside in men's clothes." She shook her head. "Jest ain't ladylike, honey. Jest ain't. Yo grandpappy started this; he did! But he didn't live to see the day and rue it like me and your grandmammy did. Lawsy me, chile."

"I've got to wear these," Marguerite insisted. "I don't have time to be bothered with side saddles and skirts." Backing up to Jewel, she said, "Unhook my gown."

"Jewel." The low call from Annie sent Jewel scurrying into the kitchen. "I'd like a cup of tea, please."

Glad to hear strength in Annie's voice, Marguerite smiled. She moved to the single candle that sputtered on a table in the corner of the room and blew it out. In a matter of minutes her dress and undergarments lay in a heap on the floor. Quickly she redressed, walking out of the bedroom, draping a dark cloak over her shoulders.

"How are you feeling, Annie?" Marguerite asked, looking at the elderly woman who was propped up in bed with pillows.

Annie smiled. "Much better, Miz Marguerite." She cradled the cup in both hands. "I'm gettin' too old for these fast carriage rides all over the countryside. Plumb jarred my insides it did!" The three of them laughed. Annie's eyes raked over Marguerite's outfit. "And where do you think you're going in those clothes?"

"Yes'm," Jewel said, folding her arms across her breasts, "you tell her, Annie. I been trying, but she won't listen. Gadding around in men's clothes, trying to find Mr. Sheridan."

Marguerite moved to the bed and sat down beside Annie.

"I've got to go to him, Annie. He may be wounded, and his mother is dead. I'm all he's got left." Marguerite's eyes filled with tears. "I need to be with him. After all, I am his wife."

Annie laid her cup on the table next to the bed, and she took Marguerite into her arms. "I reckon you do, chile."

"You and Jewel will be safe here," Marguerite said. "I'll return as soon as I can."

Rising, she quietly moved across the room, opening the door, slipping into the cool gray mist of early morning. When she reached the horses, someone stepped out of the shadows.

"Earl! What—what are you doing here?"

Earl's smile was nasty. "After Paddy informed me of your whereabouts, and I—I learned about Sheridan's, I didn't want to leave you alone, so I came to get you, my dear." His eyes ran her height. "I don't suppose there's any need in my asking where you were heading in such a hurry." Lifting his hand, he beckoned the soldiers who surrounded the cottage. "Load the trunks on the carriage first. Then search the house, stone by stone. Leave *nothing* unturned."

Chapter 17

The next few hours were a nightmare for Marguerite. She tried first to reason with Earl, then just to talk, but he was preoccupied with other matters. He was a man possessed. His one thought was to locate Sheridan and the weapons and to seize both.

As the coach slowly lumbered away from the scene, Earl called, "I'll see you when I arrive at the house, my dear. Clean up and change your clothes by the time that I arrive. We'll have lunch together." He turned and moved toward the cottage.

The last words Marguerite heard were Earl's: "Search every inch. Tear it down stone by stone if you must. If anything's left, we'll burn it."

"How'd he know where we were?" Annie asked, peering out the window.

"Paddy." Marguerite sighed her disappointment. "Earl knows where Sheridan is."

Pushing her head back into the upholstery, she closed her eyes, squeezing back the recriminating tears. Why had she trusted Paddy? Why had she told him and Brice about Sheridan's hideaway?

When the coach stopped in front of the house, Jewel asked, "Do you want me to come up to your room with you?"

Marguerite shook her head. "No, I need some time to think."

"If you gonna change clothes like Mr. Taylor said, you're gonna need me."

"I'm not." Although she was exhausted and worried about Sheridan, Marguerite smiled. She patted the black hand that rested on her arm. Lowering her voice, she said, "Don't unpack, but rest as much as you can. I don't know what we're going to do, but we're going to do something."

The front door opened, and Elvira Simmons stood like a vulture in the aperture. "Good morning, Mistress Marguerite." A cynical smile tugged her lips. "How good it is to have you home again."

"Good morning, Mrs. Simmons."

"Would you care for breakfast, madam?"

"No," Marguerite said, shedding her cloak, slinging it across her arm. "I'm going to my room."

Looking at Marguerite's clothing disdainfully, Mrs. Simmons said, "I suppose you'll be wanting a bath and clean clothes."

Halfway up the stairs, Marguerite turned. "No, Mrs. Simmons, I do not want a bath nor do I want to change my clothes. I want to be alone. You may send me up a pot of tea."

"Humph!" Elvira snorted, following her up, the brass keys jangling at her waist.

As soon as Marguerite entered her room and closed the door, she heard the key grate in the lock. Her hand closed over the knob, and she turned it, pulling on the door. Locked in! Her first reaction was anger—explosive anger—but too much had happened recently for her to give anyone the pleasure of knowing they had elicited any emotional response from her, especially Earl and Mrs. Simmons. Smiling grimly, she walked to the dresser and brushed her hair, using a ribbon to tie it at the nape of her neck.

A soft tap at the door drew her attention. "Your tea, ma'am."

"You have the key."

After the maid left, Marguerite poured herself a cup of tea; then she paced around the room, wondering what had happened. Why had Earl come to get her, and where was Paddy? Stopping in front of the window, she opened the drapes, letting sunshine fill the room. She looked at her hand; she looked at the ring Sheridan had given her. Had they captured him? she asked herself the hundredth time, tears welling up in her eyes. Had he escaped?

Hours passed before she heard the key grate the lock again. The door opened again, and Earl walked in. Dwarfed in the large chair that she had dragged in front of the window, Marguerite was hidden from view.

"It's nearly lunchtime, my dear." He was closer, but she made no attempt to get up. "Why aren't you ready?"

"I'm not hungry."

Earl smiled. "You must eat to keep up your strength." In front of the chair, he saw her. The smile vanished as quickly as it came. "You haven't changed clothes, my dear."

"No."

He moved to the bed, reaching for the tasseled cord. "We can remedy that." He gave it several sharp jerks.

"I don't want to bathe or change clothes right now," Marguerite told him. "I don't intend to do either."

"You'll do both," Earl countered in that smooth voice Marguerite was coming to hate more. "I'll not have you playing the pouting child, nor will I have you running around like a . . . like a . . ."

"I'll dress as I please."

"No, my dear." The quiet tones were frightening. "You won't. As the mistress here, you'll dress exactly as it pleases me for you to dress. You'll do exactly what I tell you to do."

He walked closer to her. Frightened of the wild look in his eyes, Marguerite shook her head. Her voice was steady, but she pleaded with him. "I—I don't want to be the mistress, Earl. I'm not planning on staying here."

"We'll see."

"Where's Paddy?" Marguerite fought to keep the hysteria out of her voice.

Earl smiled. "After he reported your whereabouts and I found out where O'Roarke was, I sent Paddy on an important errand to Dublin," he replied. "I thought it safe to get him out of the way. He's proved to be a most valuable servant, worthy of his hire, and I wouldn't want anything to happen to him."

"As a traitor," Marguerite spat.

"Let's not call anyone names, my dear. I've learned to accept what help I can from whomever, and I've learned to forget names. It's a much safer way to live a long, prosperous life."

Striving for casualness, Marguerite said, "I'm not going to stay here."

"Yes, you are." Earl's tone was soft, but the command was brutal.

"You have no right to dictate to me like this. You're not my legal guardian."

"And I have no wish to become your legal guardian. I wish more than that, my dear. I wish to become your legal husband." The knock at the door demanded his attention. "Yes."

"Miz Marguerite rang?"

"Yes," Earl replied, irritated that Annie had answered the summons. "Please prepare her a bath."

"Is that all, sir?"

"That's all."

"Yes, sir." But still Annie didn't move; she wanted to be reassured that Marguerite was all right. "Miz Marguerite?"

"Yes," Marguerite answered.

"If you're going to change clothes, I need to come unpack your trunks so I can be ironing one."

"Get it later," Earl grated, clearly his patience at an end. "I'm talking with Marguerite at the moment."

"Yes, sir." Slowly Annie turned and moved down the hall.

Marguerite stood, the movement throwing her close to Earl. He reached out, clasping her hands in his.

"I want you to know that I've already made plans for our wedding."

"Our wedding!" she shrieked venomously, hatred vibrating in her voice. She tried to pull her hands from his.

Hearing the shout, Annie quickly spun about, retracing her steps.

"I have never felt about a woman as I feel about you," Earl confessed, his grip tightening. He pulled her closer. "I want you, Marguerite."

"I—I don't want you," she said, jerking herself loose and backing up.

"You will," he promised. "Give yourself time."

"No."

"Get used to the idea, Marguerite, because it will soon become a fact," Earl grated viciously.

Without thinking, Annie opened the door and quietly slid into the room, but neither occupant was aware of her entry. The maid saw Marguerite shrinking away from Earl; she saw Earl stalking closer and closer to her ward. Frantically Annie looked around. She had to do something! She couldn't let him hurt Marguerite.

"No, Earl," Marguerite answered, trying to reason with him. "I'll never feel that way about you. I—I love someone else. I meant what I said. I'm leaving here."

Earl's mask crumbled. His face contorted into ugly fury. His lips curled in a snarl; his eyes were metallic gray. "Don't lay any wagers about what you're going to be doing, Marguerite LeFleur, because you'd lose." His voice was venomous. "From now on, you'll do what I tell you to do without so much as an argument. When you've given me two things, you may do with yourself and your life what you please."

"I'll give you nothing!"

"First, you will give yourself to me in marriage so that I may have your fortune." He laughed softly. "Then you will give me your body so that I may have an heir."

"Never!" Marguerite was so shocked she couldn't talk above a whisper.

Earl emitted an animalistic snarl. "You'll marry me," he declared, "and you'll give me an heir. No bloody Irishman will ever get my property. I'll have a legitimate child who will inherit. A Taylor will always be at the manor house."

Marguerite tried to reason with Earl. "Please, listen to me," she begged. "You don't want to marry me. I don't love you."

"Love," Earl sneered. "Who's talking about love, my dear? Most assured not I. I'm talking about your fortune. I'm talking about using your body to produce me an heir. I don't need or want love." He laughed tauntingly. "That's all your mother offered me. The stupid woman thought I married her out of love." His hand clenched into a fist. "How do you think I felt when she told me that by the terms of your father's will at her remarriage, the fortune and the plantation reverted to you? I could have killed her."

Marguerite shrank away from Earl. He frightened her. He looked at her, his eyes wild and glazed. He was the personification of evil.

"Then I knew I must have you, my dear. You were young and healthy, just the woman I needed to give me a child." High menacing laughter filled the room. "And you were healthy and rich, just the woman I needed to refurbish my coffers, to give me the money to pay my creditors and save the house."

Earl slowly walked toward Marguerite. With each step that he took, she backed up one. Finally she was against the wall.

"But I had to get rid of your mother. She was a weak, sniveling woman who was in my way."

Standing by the table, Annie listened quietly to every word of Earl's confession. Her fingers curled into a fist. Marguerite's eyes widened in disbelief.

"That's right," he admitted proudly. "Poison. I killed her slowly. Put it in her food and her drinks. And I managed to get you over here." He squared his shoulders and smiled. "I'm quite proud of my machinations, my dear. I realized quite soon after meeting Susanna Reeves that she was a vain, jealous woman who could be manipulated. I'm the one who must take credit for having planted seeds of doubt in her mind; I'm the one who convinced her that you and Jordan had a budding relationship. And I'm the one who prodded your mother into insisting that you come stay with us."

"You're insane."

"No," Earl whispered, close enough that his breath blew across Marguerite's face, "I'm quite sane. Like the soldier I am, I knew what I must do and I did it. Now I have everything that I've ever wanted. The manor house is undisputably mine; O'Roarke is as good as dead; you and your fortune are mine." He laughed, the sound heinous. "I beat O'Roarke. He swore he would get you before I did."

Scared, unable to think straight, Marguerite forgot Sheridan's warnings. "No, you didn't beat O'Roarke," she cried. "He got to me first. We're . . . we're . . . already married." Marguerite drew to her full height, straightened her shoulders and lifted her head. She laid a hand over her stomach. "I—I could be with his child even now."

Moving as quickly as she could, Annie was almost behind Earl, but Marguerite's words drove him into a frenzy. "You bitch," he screamed, catching her by the shoulders and hurling her across the room. "You let that bastard make love to you. You married him." Marguerite fell, cutting her head when she hit the corner of the dresser. Stunned, staggering to retain her balance, she fell again when Earl threw his body against her.

"Leave that child alone," Annie screamed, shuffling across the room.

Swinging around, Earl slung his arm, knocking the old woman down. "Get out of the way." A wild stream of maniacal

281

laughter filled the room as he turned back to Marguerite. "But even your marriage to him won't stop me," he cried. "Once Sheridan O'Roarke's dead, you're a widow. I will have you, Marguerite LeFleur. I will!"

Wiping the stream of blood from her face, Marguerite panted, "But I'll be carrying O'Roarke's child, not yours." She looked over Earl's shoulders at Annie who slowly and painfully pushed herself up.

Earl grabbed Marguerite, his hand biting into her arms. He shoved her across the room and pushed her onto the bed, catching her decolletage in both hands. Marguerite cried out as he ripped her bodice open. Balling his hand into a fist, he hit first one cheek then the other. His eyes feasted greedily on the beauty of her breasts; his hands roughly cupped them as he kneaded them together.

"I have ways," he gritted. "I killed one of O'Roarke's bastards. I'll have no qualms killing another." He lowered his face, his mouth covering the tip of her breast.

"No," Marguerite screamed, horrified by his touch. She flailed and pushed against him, kicking her legs, all to no avail. She was no match for Earl.

Breathing deeply, clutching the night table for support, Annie crawled to her feet. Through hazy eyes, she saw Earl on top of Marguerite. Still hanging on to the table, the old woman looked around for a weapon. Her fingers touched something icy cold. She dropped her face and looked at the scissors. Her hand curling around the handle, she staggered across the room, her determination to save Marguerite giving her the will to walk.

When she was close enough, Annie yelled, "Get away from that child or I'll kill you."

Like a huge, ugly bear, Earl reared and spun around, turning his anger on the old woman. With fisted hand, he slapped her across the face. Annie reeled from the blow, blood running from her nose, pain shooting through her frail body. Crumpling to the floor, she dropped the scissors.

282

Marguerite screamed. Flying off the bed, she leaped on Earl's back. He tried to shake her loose, but Marguerite held on, clawing and kicking. Reaching behind, Earl grabbed a fistful of clothes, slinging her down, her head hitting the floor with such force that she was knocked unconscious. Winded and stunned, Earl stood for a moment looking down at her.

Thinking Marguerite to be dead, tears and pain blurring her vision, Annie reached for the scissors. Laboriously she crawled to her knees. Grabbing the bed covers in one hand, holding onto the scissors with the other, she hauled herself to her feet. Slowly she weaved across the room. When she was close enough to Earl, she drew back her arm. But she never struck him. Hearing her approach, Earl whirled around.

He grabbed Annie's wrist and twisted, trying to shake the scissors from her hands, but the old woman refused to drop them the second time. In the shuffle, Earl jerked her against his body, causing her frail wrist to turn, and Earl's weight forced the scissors into her chest. She cried aloud. Blood gushed from the wound, and she crumpled to the floor.

Drawing deep gulps of air and pushing his hair out of his face, Earl walked to the bed, jerking on the bell call. Then he walked to the night table and dipped a washcloth into the basin of water. Wringing the cloth out, he moved across the room, dropping to his knees beside Marguerite. His anger dissipated, he sponged her face. After awhile she opened her eyes and blinked at him, marshaling her thoughts as she pushed through the hazy corridor of consciousness.

"In the future this can be avoided," he said coldly. "You must learn to obey me."

"Annie," Marguerite whispered, memory rushing back. She rolled her head to the side, and she saw the inert form across the room, slumped against the bed, blood saturing the front of her dress. Marguerite sat up, the sudden movement leaving her dizzy. Disregarding her own pain, she rolled over, crawled across the floor and gathered Annie into her arms.

Annie lifted a weak hand and touched Marguerite's face.

"Get out of here, honey, and go home," she whispered, her voice so weak Marguerite could barely hear it. She coughed, spitting up blood. "I ain't gonna make it."

"No," Marguerite cried softly, "you can't die, Annie. You can't." Annie sighed, and Marguerite heard the hollow rattle in the old woman's chest. "Annie!"

Earl stood and returned to the night table, dropping the washcloth into the basin. Without any emotion to soften his voice, he said, "I'm sorry about your servant, Marguerite, but my killing her was in self-defense." As if nothing of consequence had happened, he continued, "Now I'm going to have your bath water sent up. I'd advise you to bathe and change clothes. I want you to meet me downstairs in an hour."

"What about Annie?" she sobbed.

"Someone's on their way up. I'll have them take care of the body," he replied callously, walking out of the room. At the door, he stopped and turned around, adding, "Although it's highly unusual, I'll allow her to be buried next to your mother."

Sitting in the wing chair in the library, Marguerite stared at the fire. She was beautifully dressed, and her hair was elegantly coiled on the top of her head, but her face was bruised and swollen, an ugly cut running across her forehead. Her smile was gone, and her eyes were dull and listless. She spoke seldom and then only in monosyllables. But Earl didn't seem to notice. He was so elated that he gushed conversation. He refilled his glass the third time.

"Now for some entertainment, my dear." He moved to the wall and yanked on the tasseled cord. When Mrs. Simmons opened the door, he said, "Has our guest arrived, Mrs. Simmons?"

"Not yet, sir."

He nodded, dismissing her. "Come, Marguerite. We'll go see how Mr. Dempsey is doing." Instead of moving toward

Marguerite, however, Earl walked across the room. He filled one glass with whiskey, another with sherry which he carried to Marguerite. "Here, my dear." Marguerite shook her head, but Earl pressed it in her hands. "I have a feeling that you're going to be needing this." Marguerite stood, and Earl cupped her elbow with his palm, guiding her through the house to one of the back rooms. Moving past two guards at the end of the corridor, he spoke to the one immediately outside the room. "How's our guest doing this evening?"

"Still hasn't talked, sir."

Earl shook his head. "Young idealists can be so stupid."

He unlocked the door and walked into the room. Marguerite followed. A lamp sitting on a table illuminated the room. Shane, tied to a straight chair, was sitting in a shadowed corner. His head was lowered, his chin resting on his chest.

"Good evening, Mr. Dempsey," Earl taunted, extending his hand, offering the glass. "I thought maybe you would like to have a drink."

Shane lifted his face and Marguerite gasped. It was so discolored and swollen that it looked like a grotesque mask. Through bruised lips, he mumbled, "Thank ye for yer hospitality, Mr. Taylor, but I don't think so tonight. Being beaten is one way to die; being poisoned is another."

Marguerite watched Earl's face contort. His fingers tightening on the glass, he threw the whiskey into Shane's face. The amber liquid, which mixed with dried blood, ran in rivulets down his cheeks and dropped off his chin.

"You'll talk," Earl promised with sinister laughter. "You can't hold out much longer. Besides, you'll soon have company. O'Roarke will be joining you."

Shane tried to laugh. "Nay, Earl Taylor, no matter who betrayed him, you'll not be a'catching, Sheridan O'Roarke. He's much faster and much more intelligent than ye be."

Earl drew his hand back and slapped Shane across the face, fresh blood dribbling from the corner of the prisoner's mouth. The door rattled as someone shook it.

"Mr. Taylor!" The cry was urgent. Both Earl and Marguerite looked in the direction from which the sound came. "I need to see you immediately."

"Lieutenant Smithson!" Earl hurried to the door, unlocked it and stepped aside.

Three men walked into the room. Sheridan, Paddy, and a uniformed officer whom Marguerite didn't recognize.

"Come on in, Mr. O'Roarke." Watching Marguerite's expression, Earl snickered. "I thought you might be needing the drink . . . my dear."

Sheridan's eyes moved from Earl to Marguerite. When he saw the cut on her forehead, the bruises, and the swelling, he felt the hot rush of fury; then his heart ached. But he kept his gaze impersonal; his face registered no emotion at all. He looked in the corner at Shane. Marguerite looked at Paddy who twitched nervously and dropped his head.

"Well, Paddy," Earl said, "you've done a good day's work." He laughed. "When you first suggested that you work with me, I couldn't believe it. I couldn't believe that you'd turn coat on one of your own."

"If you'll just be a'givin' me my money," Paddy said, bunching his cap in his fists, "I'll . . . I'll . . ."

"Take your Judas money, Paddy," Sheridan said, his voice icy cold and sharp, "and I hope to God that you have nothing but sorrow the rest of your life. Thank God, my mother didn't live to see you turn traitor to the cause."

Paddy laughed. "Not traitor to the cause, O'Roarke. Just traitor to you."

Inebriated, Earl laughed loud and hard. "Lieutenant Smithson, how appropriate that you brought Mr. O'Roarke here. I'm glad that he and Mr. Dempsey can see one another one more time before they die."

Marguerite pushed to the edge of her chair. "Die?" she whispered. "You haven't given him a trial?"

"He's a traitor, my dear," Earl said, never taking his eyes off Sheridan. "I don't need to go through the formality of a trial

286

and waste the taxpayers' money. We have all the proof we need of his dastardly deeds."

"And if ye don't have enough," Sheridan said, lapsing into thick brogue, "ye can easily make it up, can't ye, Earl? You're an expert at that."

"How does it feel being so close to the gallows, O'Roarke?"

O'Roarke laughed. "I'm not that close to the gallows to feel anything." Earl lifted a brow. "You aren't going to kill me until you find out where the weapons are hidden."

Earl's face reflected his surprise. He looked from Sheridan to Smithson to Paddy. Paddy and Smithson nodded their heads. Paddy replied, "That's right, sir. No one knows where the weapons be hidden but O'Roarke. Suspecting a trap, he laid a trap hisself."

"I might have known they wouldn't be in the cottage." Earl's hand curled into a fist. Suddenly a malicious smile curved his lips. "I can make you talk," he said. Moving across the room, his hand banded around Marguerite's arm, and he jerked her to her feet. "I have Marguerite."

Sheridan smiled. "Aye, Mr. Taylor, so I can see. Now that you have her, do you know what to do with her?"

"If you don't talk, I'll—"

Sheridan threw back his head and laughed. "You'll do nothing of the kind with her, Earl, because you need her right now. Until you get her legally tied to your side, you'll not be a'touchin' her or *her money*. As I see it, a fine mess ye be in, Earl Taylor." Sheridan's taunting smile widened. "And you'll not be getting her wed to you until her husband be dead, and you can't be getting her husband dead until you know where the weapons be hid." He taunted even more. "I had the marriage recorded in the church, Earl." He paused, then added, "I instructed the priest to mail documents and letters to support such a marriage to Marguerite's attorney."

Marguerite looked at Sheridan, her eyes opening in surprise. She remembered Sheridan's talking privately with the priest before the ceremony, and she remembered signing the papers, but she hadn't known what Sheridan intended to do with them.

"I could kill you right now," Earl gritted.

"Aye," Sheridan returned, "but you won't. You don't have any proof on me at all." He inclined his head toward Shane. "Him you do. But me, no. You must answer to the authorities about those guns, Earl. Already there are too many unanswered questions in your file."

"Mr. Taylor, sir," Paddy began, nervously shuffling from foot to foot, "I'd like to be a'leavin'. How about my money?"

Suddenly the window crashed, glass splintering all over the floor. A man in a black cloak, a hood, and a mask nimbly landed on his feet at the same time that the door opened. Earl shouted, "Get him." Smithson went for his gun, but Bridget rushed in from the hall, knocking the lieutenant to the floor, kicking his gun away.

"It's a trap," she yelled. "He's pretending to come rescue you and Shane, Sheridan, but he's working with Earl. He's the one they call Hibernia."

"Hibernia!" the man snorted through his mask.

"He's the one who betrayed you to Earl," Bridget cried out, running to Sheridan, clutching his shirt with both hands. "I overheard them talking, Sheridan. I rushed down here and told Shane about it, and he's the one who told me to go to McNeil's cottage."

Taking advantage of the disturbance, Smithson stretched his hand and picked up his gun. Easing to his feet, he lifted it and aimed. At the same time the hooded man looked at Bridget and raised his arm. Thinking he was moving toward him, Earl cringed and staggered back, stumbling against Smithson just as he pulled the trigger. Instead of hitting the masked intruder, Smithson shot Shane. Groaning, clutching his stomach, Shane fell, his chin bobbing against his chest. Spinning around, Sheridan pushed Bridget out of the way.

Sheridan's fingers banded Smithson's wrist, but the soldier was too strong for him to disarm. Jerking his arm loose, Smithson dropped the gun of his own volition. He drew his arm back, balled his hand into a fist and hit Sheridan on the chin. Sheridan stumbled back, reeling from the blow, but he didn't fall down. Using his body for leverage, his movement as force, Smithson rushed Sheridan, knocking him to the floor. Stronger and heavier than the soldier, Sheridan rolled Smithson under him.

In the next few minutes the room turned into bedlam. The two guards, stationed at the end of the corridor, hearing the ruckus, ran into the room, one of them drawing his sword, lunging toward the hooded man, the other going to Smithson's rescue. Bridget rushed to the chair where Shane slumped over the ropes that bound him. Her fingers clumsily worked with the knots in the rope.

"Shane!" She caught him in her arms as he fell to the floor; she rocked back and forth with him. "Don't die, my darling. Please don't die."

Grabbing Marguerite, Earl shot out of the room, racing down the hall, dragging her with him. Paddy, leaning down, picked up a knife that had dropped during the fracas and darted across the room, following behind them.

"Turn her loose, Earl Randolph Taylor," he called. "To be sure, she's not part of this fight ye have with O'Roarke."

Recognizing Paddy's voice, Earl felt no threat. "I need her," he yelled, yanking the protesting woman ahead, pushing her through a door. "And I'll see her dead before O'Roarke gets her."

"And I'll be a'seein' ye dead before ye take her with ye," Paddy shouted. "For the last time, turn her loose."

The door open, Earl turned, snarling with rage. "So you're one of them after all! Well, you won't get Marguerite LeFleur for your leader." One hand on the door frame, Earl shoved Marguerite through the opening.

Drawing his arm back, Paddy balanced the blade between his fingers. Taking aim, extending his arm in a flowing movement, he threw the knife, the metal unerringly making its way to the mark. Gasping his pain as the blade entered his inner shoulder,

Earl turned Marguerite loose so quickly she crumpled to the floor. He collapsed against the door, drawing in deep gulps of air. Summoning all his strength, he kicked her out of the way, stumbled through the opening and shut the door.

From where she lay, Marguerite heard the key grate in the lock. Paddy rushed up to her.

"Are ye all right, ma'am?"

Marguerite painfully pushed herself up, leaning against the wall. "I'm fine," she said. "Just winded." Helping her to her feet, Paddy led her down the hall as they retraced their steps. When they entered the room, they saw both Sheridan and Bridget leaning over Shane's prostrate form. Also on the floor were Smithson and the two guards, all three unconscious.

"Shane boy, can you hear me?" Sheridan asked.

Shane tried to smile. "I hear you, Danny." Blood ran out the corner of his mouth, and he coughed. "I—I never figured on death this soon. We always escaped, Danny."

"Aye."

"And I thought we would this time, too." He winced with pain; then he said, "Take care of Bridget for me." He turned his head and lifted a hand, running it down Bridget's cheek. "I love you, lass." He smiled a last time; his head dropped and life ebbed out of his body.

"Shane!" Both Bridget and Sheridan cried out at the same time.

Bridget looked at Shane's face, hers turning to stone. She looked at the hooded man, pure hatred in his eyes. Letting Sheridan take Shane's body, she stood. Tears running down his cheeks, Sheridan continued to hold Shane in his arms. Her head bowed, her body racked with tears, Bridget walked out of the room. In the hall she saw Smithson's gun lying on the floor. Stooping, she picked up the gun and returned to the room.

As she entered the room, she said, "I'll kill Earl Randolph Taylor if it's the last thing I ever do." She looked down at Smithson's unconscious body. "Earl beat him, and you shot him."

"Bridget, don't!" Sheridan shouted, galvanized into action, grabbing for her.

Before anyone in the room realized her intention, Bridget swung the gun and pulled the trigger. "But you're responsible for his death."

The huge man in the black cape fell to the floor.

"Now there is no more Hibernia." Bridget's words rang through the deathly quiet room.

"No," Sheridan softly repeated, looking from one dead man to the other, "Hibernia is no more."

Chapter 18

One leg stretched out, the other knee bent, his arm resting on it, Sheridan sat in a bed of sweet clover away from the river, staring at the waterfall. Errant shafts of golden sunshine dappled through the lush green canopy of tree branches. But at the moment Sheridan wasn't aware of the enchantment that surrounded him. He didn't hear the river's soft melody or the tinkle of the waterfall. He didn't smell the sweet clover. He didn't feel the warmth of the sunshine.

Scooting up behind him, Marguerite laid her cheek on his back. "I'm sorry, darling."

He picked a blade of grass and pulled it through his fingers. "This is the first time that the three of us have been separated in our lives."

"Is Gavin going to be all right?" she asked.

"Aye, but he must leave the country. He's been identified, so he won't be safe here anymore. Brice is taking him to Queenstown where Power is making arrangements for his departure to America."

"To Texas?"

"Probably not. Earl would suspect his going there." Sheridan put the blade of grass in the corner of his mouth. "More than likely New York, Boston, or Quebec. He'll change his name, so we'll never know." He lowered his head and closed his eyes. "He won't be coming back. He's the same as being dead."

"And Shane is dead."

Again he answered with a monosyllable. "Aye." After a poignant pause, he added, "But Shane was dead long before his body died. I don't know why, but his soul and his spirit died long ago, lass." Again he lapsed into silence; then he began to laugh softly, his voice suddenly animated. "When we were about ten, the three of us . . ."

Holding him closely, pressing her face into his back, Marguerite listened as Sheridan talked about his childhood: all the joys and the happiness. She listened as he shared his heartaches and griefs: the death of his father, the death of his friends' fathers and mothers. He talked about his mother. He talked about the lifelong pact of friendship between him, Shane, and Gavin.

"I—I would never have dreamed that one of them would betray us," he softly said.

"But Mickey Flynn hated you," Marguerite said, remembering the sadness on Sheridan's face when he pulled the mask from Mickey's face. "I heard him say so."

"Nay," Sheridan returned, his voice thick with tears, "Mickey didn't hate me." He paused. "Nor was he the one to betray me."

"But—"

Sheridan turned, pulling Marguerite into his arms. "Shane was the betrayer." Two tears rolled down his rugged face. "That's what hurts me so, love. Shane Dempsey was the one who betrayed me."

"No," Marguerite cried, the image of his swollen and bruised face still imprinted in her mind. "Earl beat him."

Sheridan shrugged, unable to answer that himself. "Maybe it was part of the plan," he suggested. "Or maybe Earl did it when he thought he no longer needed Shane."

"How do you know for sure that it was him?"

"Only he could have given Earl your pearl necklace."

"You're sure?"

"Aye."

Moments passed before Marguerite said, "You're—you're not going to tell Bridget!"

Sheridan shook his head. "Nay, she need never know. No need in her carrying the guilt of Mickey Flynn's death all her life, and no need in her knowing that Shane involved her with his betrayal. Her knowing won't make right the wrong."

Marguerite lifted her hands and cupped his face. Drawing it nearer, she gently kissed the teary trails on his cheeks. "Why?" she asked. "Did he hate you that much?"

"Nay, lass," Sheridan returned, burrowing his face in the sweet curve of her shoulder and neck. "He didn't hate me. He just found something he loved more. Ten thousand pounds."

"I thought Paddy was the one who had betrayed you," Marguerite murmured, her lips brushing against Sheridan's collarbone.

"That's the way it was supposed to have looked," Sheridan replied. "He and Brice were the only two whom I trusted. We knew that one of the lads was betraying us, but we didn't know which one. The night that Bridget came, Paddy took a big chance. He sent Brice to warn me, and Paddy went to the manor house. When he arrived by way of the garden, he heard voices in the library. Because the windows and doors were shut and drapes were drawn over the windows, he couldn't see, nor could he hear everything that was said. But he made out enough to know they were plotting my capture. Later that night when Paddy slipped in to see Shane, his suspicions were confirmed. Shane outlined the same plan to him."

"And you pretended to follow it, knowing it was a trap." He nodded. "What is Bridget going to do?"

"I don't know, lass. Paddy's taken her to her sister's place in County Cork." He smiled, moving so that both of them were lying down, Marguerite on her back, he on his side.

"What are we going to do?" she asked.

"I've been thinking—"

295

"So have I," she interrupted, an enigmatic smile hovering on her lips. Raising a hand, she ran her finger over Sheridan's chiseled lips, smiling when his mouth parted, and he caught it between his teeth. "I've been doing quite a bit of thinking."

"Aye, and so have I."

When he spoke, she removed her hand, and both of them moved at the same time. "About this," she whispered, her hand slipping behind his head, cupping the nape of his neck. She raised her head and pulled his closer to her. "So much about this, my darling." Then she repeated the words he had said to her in her moment of grief: "'Tis time you learned that in the midst of death is life—the life that I have to give you."

"And so you have, lass."

Sheridan closed his arms about her, gently crushing her pliant, unresisting body next to his. He held her, savoring the life she so willingly gave to him. Marguerite's hands moved up his back, her fingers tangling in the mop of thick, red hair. Each kiss grew deeper. Like a brushfire out of control, anticipation and excitement swept through both of them, setting every inch of their bodies on fire.

"I love you," she murmured over and over again.

Eventually the kisses were not enough; they pulled apart and undressed. Propped on his elbow, lying beside her, he ran his hand over her hip. He marveled at the silken texture of Marguerite's skin beneath his rough palm. As if he had never seen her naked before, he looked at her loveliness.

"You're mine," he whispered. "All mine. Earl Taylor will never have you. That I promise."

Marguerite heard him, but the words made little sense. She was aware only of the stirrings and demands of her body. Yielding to these primitive urgings, she gave herself up to him eagerly, holding nothing back. Her fingers furrowed in the crisp waves, and she guided his mouth back to hers, wanting to know again the sweet fierceness of his kiss, wanting every inch of her body possessed by the man she loved so much.

Sheridan's mouth devoured hers hungrily. His hand left her

breast to travel sensously down the flat stomach to the beckoning triangle between her thighs. His hand slid through the tuft of hair. With consummate skill and confidence tempered with love, his fingers entered and lovingly explored the most intimate part of her.

When Marguerite felt his hand between her legs, she felt as if she were scaling the highest mountain in the world. She felt the wind and the snow whirling about her, but she was too elated to feel more than her victory. At the same time she felt as if she were falling into the bottomless pit of a glowing, hot volcano, burning hotter and hotter. Her eyes closed, soft sighs whispered through her lips, and her head rolled from side to side in sheer pleasure.

Sheridan gasped as her fingers gently curled around his manhood. His ache turned from a dull throb of need to an acute wanting; he could restrain himself no longer. His body hurt with its need for release. Gracefully smooth, he moved so that she was beneath him. He eased his knee between her legs, opening them, spreading them apart.

One leg slid between hers, and his hands slipped under her hips to lift her to him. Marguerite sucked in her breath, welcoming his weight, welcoming his most penetrating touch, when she felt his masculinity gently probe.

Both sighed as the shaft of his desire slipped into the waiting sheath of velvety flesh. Their bodies were locked together. Their souls were bound together in love. Her fingers gripped into the flexed muscle of his buttocks. His hands pulled her hips up against him as he drove deeply into her silken softness. As he thrust deeply, more rapidly, more fiercely, Marguerite's body once more burst into an uncontrollable blaze of passion.

Filled with him, lying beneath him, Marguerite was unconscious of the gentle breeze that touched her body, lifting wisps of hair around her face; she wasn't aware of the sweet fragrance of the clover. But she was unbearably conscious of the heat of his chest as it pressed against her breasts, of his warm hands as they cupped her buttocks. She was aware of his masculine scent which filled her nostrils.

Conscious of the seductive movements of his body, of the strokes of his manhood within her, Marguerite slowly, rhythmically moved her hips. The deeper Sheridan thrust, the higher Marguerite soared. Then her breath caught in her throat, her heartbeat accelerated, and a knot of pleasure formed in her stomach. Suddenly she spiraled to that highest pinnacle of love, her body exploding into tiny particles.

When Marguerite gasped her pleasure, when her body convulsively quivered from the intensity of her feelings, Sheridan no longer held back. His hands tightened on her hips and he brought her against his thrust one last time. His movements verged on savagery and violence, but tempered with love, they merged into supreme ecstasy.

Their eyes closed, Marguerite and Sheridan drifted hazily in and out of sleep. Marguerite was vaguely aware of Sheridan next to her, of his hands still lightly caressing and touching her. She was acutely aware of the deep satisfaction of her body. She smiled and stretched, a sigh of contentment escaping her lips.

Pushing up on his elbow and leaning over her, Sheridan caught her hand in his and twined his fingers through hers. He chuckled softly. "You sound like a kitten purring her pleasure at being loved, my darling."

"I feel quite like that, love."

Opening her eyes, Marguerite stared into that face she loved so much. Although it was chiseled hard and sharp, it was tender with love. Her eyes lingered on the firm, sensual mouth that could smile so devastatingly. She lifted a hand and traced the strong jut of his chin and jaw. Her fingers moved over the prominent cheekbones to the beautiful nose. They traced the thick brows that shelved emerald green eyes.

As she stared into that dark, harshly handsome face, Marguerite remembered the first time that she had ever seen him. Arrogant, she had thought him to be. Ruthless. Powerful. Unscrupulous. All these he had proved to be. Yet she had found that small vein of goodness that ran through him, tempering all his harshness. As his lips nibbled at the sensitive skin of her palm, Marguerite trembled. Suddenly she felt extremely vulnerable. She was completely at this man's mercy. She loved him and was married to him, but he didn't love her.

Her thoughts in her eyes for him to read, Sheridan looked at her a little longer but said nothing. At the moment he was too unsure of himself to assure her. Finally he lay down again. In a semi-sleep they lay beside each other for a long time.

Much later Sheridan swooped her into his arms and carried her into the river. With a gentleness that was incongruous with his masculinity, he bathed her, his hands touching all those sensitive places, reminding both of them of the pleasure they had created together and shared. With the same tenderness he dried her off, scooped her into his arms and carried her into the cottage.

Loathe to break the magical spell they had weaved, neither talked. Unmindful of their nudity, Sheridan laid Marguerite on the bed in the corner of the room while he made a pallet on the floor. As soon as he had tossed the pillows on the quilt, he built a fire. Then he beckoned Marguerite to join him in front of the blazing flames. Uncorking a bottle of wine, he poured each of them a glass. Sipping their wine and propped on pillows, they lay side by side, gazing into the flames.

Holding her glass in her left hand, Marguerite twined her fingers through Sheridan's. "Where are we going from here?"

"Must we go somewhere else?" he parried, never taking his eyes off the dancing tongues of fire.

"You know we must," Marguerite replied, her voice barely above a whisper. "You're a criminal of the state, accused of treason, with a death sentence hanging over your head."

"I can't leave, Marguerite." Not Daisy. Not Daisy Belle but Marguerite!

Marguerite tensed. "Surely . . . surely you jest."

"Someone has to stay here and fight, Daisy. If I leave, our

group will fall apart. I must stay until I train a new leader." His voice vibrated with urgency.

"No."

"No." Sheridan looked at her and repeated incredulously, "You're telling me no."

"Your fight is over, Sheridan. Your mother, Shane, and Mickey Flynn are dead. Gavin has been banished, never to return to Ireland. For you only a death sentence remains. You don't have a chance," Marguerite pleaded with him.

"We can do it, Daisy Belle. We can defeat Taylor," Sheridan said. "You and I together. We can go underground."

Marguerite jumped to her feet, knocking the wine bottle over. Moving to the opened trunk on the far side of the room, she knelt, rummaging for her dressing gown.

"Hiding the rest of our lives. Never knowing from day to day if we'll be caught. Always living in dread of the day that someone will come tell me that you're dead. No," she cried, shaking her head, her hair swinging wildly around her face, "that's no life for me."

For long, heavy minutes her outburst hung suspended between them. "Then perhaps you must leave without me," he quietly offered, no emotion whatsoever in his voice.

Standing, her gown draped over her arm, Marguerite stared at him wide-eyed. She moistened her lips. "Do you mean that?"

Rather than answer the question, he said, "I still have a job to do, Daisy. I must stay until Taylor is defeated."

"Taylor's already defeated," she argued, putting on her robe. "With you alive he'll live in fear and torment the rest of his life. His only peace will come with your death, and if you stay in Ireland, his sole purpose will be to kill you."

"Marguerite," Sheridan said, rising, pacing back and forth on the flagstone floor, "stay with me a little longer. Fight with me." His eyes glowed with excitement and purpose. Marguerite could see plans and schemes already coming to head. "Without your money it's only a matter of time before Earl

300

must put the property up for sale." Suddenly he laughed, the sound airy and full of unmitigated pleasure. "With your money we can buy it. We—"

Marguerite stopped tying the laces down the front of her dress. She looked across the dimly lit room in astonishment. "With *my money* we can buy the manor house." She drawled the words, letting each one fall with a dead thud. "First, Earl. Now you."

"Nay, lass," Sheridan hastily explained, irritated with himself because of his inadvertent slip, "I didn't marry you for your money. I told you once and I'll tell you again. I'm not a fortune hunter, but since we have it we might as well put it to a good cause."

Marguerite didn't say a word; she just stared at him.

"Sweetheart, you don't understand what owning the *big house* means." He extended his hand and slowly balled it into a fist. "In the big house resides an awesome concentration of political and economic power. The landowner is the principal property owner and the major employer in his district. He can dictate the votes of his tenants and retainers. He is a magistrate, sitting with other justices of the peace of his own class, and he is in a position to harass those who resist his domination." His eyes blazing intently, he looked at Marguerite. "Can you understand what I'm telling you?"

"I understand," she admitted, two tears rolling down her cheeks. How well she remembered the southern mentality. "You're talking about power, Sheridan, absolute power."

"Aye, and I must be the man who has this power, lass. Only then can I free my people."

She lifted a hand to her throbbing temple. "I don't belittle your cause," she said, "but I don't think your entire purpose in fighting the English is to free your people. It's much too personal." She moved closer to Sheridan. "Why did you marry me, Sheridan? To keep Earl from getting my fortune?"

Sheridan hesitated a long time before he answered. Had he been a lesser man, he would have lied because the lie would have gotten him everything he wanted in the world at the moment: Marguerite and her loyalty; Marguerite and her fortune. But truth was an integral part of Sheridan.

"At first, I saw you as a means of bringing Earl to his knees."

Marguerite laughed bitterly. "I was nothing but a pawn, used by the both of you."

"It's different now," Sheridan told her, moving closer to her.

"How different?"

"I—I care about you, lass. I want us to have a life together. Perhaps in time . . . in time we . . . would come to love one another. We could have a good marriage."

"I don't need time to love you," she confessed softly. "I already love you, Sheridan. I would never have allowed you to make love to me if I didn't." He reached for her, but she backed away, shaking her head. "But you, Sheridan, I don't think you know how to love anymore." She paused, then added, "Or perhaps you don't want to love anymore."

"I know how to love," he said quietly, "and although loving is painful at times, lass, I want to love again."

"Then go to America with me, Sheridan. Build a new life with me over there. We'll have a family of our own."

"You're not asking for love, lass," he pointed out. "You're asking for a show of submission; you're wielding your authority and power. You're issuing an ultimatum, making me choose between the two things I want most in life. You and my country, and I cannot give up my country, lass."

"It's not your country," Marguerite stormed. "It's your personal feud against Earl." Tears sparkled in her eyes. "The two of you are just alike, Sheridan. This cause of yours is nothing but a horrible, bloody game between you and Earl. You use people. As if they were pawns, you manipulate them to your best interests. Then when they are no longer useful you easily discard them."

"Marguerite, just a little longer, and—"

"No, more time, Sheridan. Power has offered to sneak you

out of Ireland and give you a new identity, a new lease on life. If you don't do this, you'll be a hunted and haunted man. You'll never be effective against Earl now that you're wanted for treason. No matter how much money you have, you'll never be able to buy the manor house. At most you can kill Earl; then you'll have added murder to the charge." Her voice softened, and she pleaded, "Don't you understand, Sheridan. No longer is the local landlord the one hunting you, but the government."

Sheridan walked to the window and threw open the shutter. The evening breeze wafted through the room, blowing the soft curtains to the side. "Are you hungry, lass?" he asked, moving to the fire, stirring the simmering stew.

Marguerite looked at the cauldron. "Have you thought about our . . . about our having children, Sheridan?"

"Aye," he whispered, squatting in front of the fire, his back to Marguerite. "That's one of the reasons why I wanted us to be married, lass. I had no desire to father bastards." He turned. "Are you—"

"I don't think so." Walking to the night table on the far side of the room, she picked up a brush and gently pulled it through her hair. "But it will happen sooner or later."

"Let's eat now, love. We'll talk about our future later." He turned his attention to the stew.

"There's nothing more to discuss. Like you, I've already made my decision. I'm leaving with Mr. Power and his Colonists." Lowering her head, she played with the ties on the front of her gown. "I won't stay and take the chance that someday Earl will kill you and force me into marriage. I couldn't stand the thought that he would kill our child, and he would. He will transfer all his hatred of you to your children."

Sheridan recognized the truth in Marguerite's words. Without moving, he said, "I do care for you, and I don't want to lose you."

"Then you'll come to America with me?"

Part II

1840
Six Years Later in the Republic of Texas

Chapter 19

From the very beginning Texans were proud of their nation. The corn stalks grew twelve feet tall and miraculously renewed themselves each spring; the soil was so rich if you were to plant ten-penny nails, you would reap a crop of bolts.

Elegant Lady was one of the newest buildings in Houston, and it was one of the most beautiful. Her owner, Myra Goodwin, had seen to that; she believed in traveling in style, sparing no expense—to herself or to her customers. All the decorations had been specially ordered and shipped from New Orleans. An interior decorator, laden with the latest in materials and fashions and accompanied by several worthy assistants, had traveled all the way from Boston. Myra hired an accountant out of New York to handle the accounts and two ex-rangers, one to tend bar, the other to head her building security. Her women came from the most highly esteemed

307

brothels in the United States.

Very astute and intelligent, Myra stayed out of everyone's way and stepped on no one's toes unless she found it to be absolutely necessary. If she found it necessary, however, she could stamp quickly and hard. Not ashamed of being a prostitute and a madam but imbued with wisdom, Myra never flaunted her occupation into her guests' faces. Nor did she let the women who were a part of her staff.

Because the Elegant Lady offered the most luxurious accommodations in Houston, along with a multitude of services for diverse clientele, and because it was one of the safest places to stay when visiting the new frontier town, people were willing to pay Myra's exorbitant rates. They were willing to excuse the large gambling casino on the other side of the dining room and to accept Myra and the women on her staff as ladies—perhaps not ladies of quality but ladies, nevertheless.

In the casino, the bartender, a large, burly man, stood behind the bar. In the corner of the room, four men sat around a table. Three were nondescript workers, dressed in cambric shirts, trousers, worn boots, and sweat-stained hats; the other was a gambler, ruggedly handsome, poised and well dressed. Chuckling quietly, the gambler leaned across the table, raking in his winnings with both hands.

"Well, gentlemen," he drawled, his voice lilting and soft, "what do you say? Another game to see if you can even the score?"

The other three men who sat at the table with him laughed good-naturedly and shook their heads, all declining.

Rusty McDevin smiled. "Good. I do have another engagement, but I don't like to leave without giving you a fair chance of winning your money back."

"What kind of engagement do you have, Rusty?"

"That, Tom McGhee, is a personal question," Rusty said, stuffing the roll of bills into his pocket. Running his fingers down the gold chain, he extracted his watch from his waistcoat.

"Most questions do be personal," Tom drawled, totally

unrepentant for his curiosity, "when they pertain to people." Hitching his thumbs under his braces and shoving with his feet, he balanced the chair on the two back legs. He wiped the back of his hand across his mouth. "To be sure, Rusty Boy, I have a feeling that your being a bit evasive about the answer rightly gives us the answer."

"Yep," an older man concurred, bobbing his grizzled white head energetically, "reckon it do at that."

The old man's mouth puckered as he sucked his jaws in and out, and his larynx bobbed. Angling his head exactly right, he positioned his mouth and tongue with ultimate skill, spewing a stream of black tobacco across the room to land with a twang in the shiny, brass cuspidor at the end of the ornate bar. With equal skill and grace, he lifted a hand and wiped the corners of his mouth.

"He's gonna go to the little hat shop and pick up Miss Myra."

"To be sure," Tom said, waving his order to the bartender, "an' that's not all Rusty Boy be a'plannin' to do, lads."

Rusty laughed with the men, enjoying the lighthearted banter. "You're just jealous because you're too old to be doing it."

"Now, laddie," Tom huffed, the chair hitting the floor with a definite thump of indignation, "that goes to show how little ye be a'knowin'. Because I'm older than ye, I know how better than ye, and I don't need so much practice as ye do."

As the men guffawed with laughter, Rusty gracefully conceded this one to Tom McGhee. "While you gents sit around and talk about how much better you are with the women, I think I'll go do some practicing."

"To be sure," Tom said as the bartender set his glass of beer in front of him, "that's a good idea, Rusty. Then you can come sit with us and talk about how much better you are."

Shaking his head and laughing, Rusty turned and walked away, his shiny, black boots silently moving across the polished floor. He was tall and superbly built, broad of

309

shoulder but narrow through his stomach and hips. Because of his height, he ducked his head slightly as he pushed through the swinging doors.

Considering the way most frontiersmen dressed, Rusty was an oddity. Those who didn't know him smiled openly when they looked at his fashionable clothes. Silently they called him a greenhorn or tenderfoot. Those acquainted with the ex-ranger knew better. They respected him and his reputation. Nobody in the country could handle a knife as well as Rusty McDevin, except maybe James Bowie, and he died at the Alamo.

Rusty's bronze-green coat hugged his broad shoulders; his waistcoat accented his muscular chest and tapered to fit his flat stomach. His trousers molded his hips and thighs like a second skin. Reaching up, he pulled the brim of his hat lower over his face, shading his eyes from the glare.

Leaning against the railing, he folded his arms across his chest and contemplated the hustle and bustle of the new port city as it subtly changed from daytime to evening commerce. He smiled when he saw Myra Goodwin walk out of the millinery shop. He had liked Myra from their first introduction. Her being a prostitute and madam hadn't bothered him. She was an honest woman, one whom he trusted implicitly.

She was a daintly, lovely woman. Her eyes were a soft, gentle brown, her hair the color of honey. Although her dress was a bright yellow and black, the colors were subdued by elegant taste and design. One of the latest European fashions, it molded her shapely breasts and billowed softly from her tiny waist. Cocked at a saucy angle on her head was a new and silky creation. Holding a hatbox and reticule in one hand, she lifted the other hand in the air, waving her parasol. Raising his hand, Rusty returned the greeting, lazily shoving away from the rail.

Because the wagon ruts were so deep in the dry, dusty street, he moved cautiously to avoid stumbling. Looking both ways before he crossed, he saw an ox-drawn closed carriage slowly rumble toward him. The Mexican vaquero who was driving didn't catch Rusty's attention, but the bull-whacker on the horse beside him did. Riding sidesaddle, she was one of the most regal women Rusty had ever seen on a horse. Certainly one of the most beautiful bull-whackers, he thought, as he watched her freight caravan trundle by.

Her Mexican-styled riding habit, an irridescent midnight blue trimmed in silver lace and tassels, shimmered in the sun, giving the woman an erotic, sensual beauty. Because the sun was to her back, to Rusty's face, and because she wore a dust veil over her broad-brimmed hat, Rusty couldn't see her face. Her thick mane of hair, so brown it was almost black, was coiled into a thick chignon at the nape of her neck. He could imagine the sultry brown eyes and the thick dark lashes and brows that hid behind the gauzy veil. He could visualize the chin, held at an arrogant angle and the full lips, rose red.

Something about her arrested his attention. He liked the form-fitting bolero, its silver trim catching the sunlight. It accented her straight shoulders and erect back. He especially liked the way it hugged her firm, uplifted breasts and tapered to a small waist. The full skirt, devoid of numerous petticoats, flared out, smoothly covering the horse's flanks. In her right hand, the woman carried a whip. And from the confidence with which she rode, the skill with which she guided her horse, and the casual ease with which she held the whip, Rusty knew she was master of all three.

The woman, oblivious to the stares she was receiving from passersby, never looked to the right or to the left. She and the small train of wagons moved on down the street. So intent on watching the woman, Rusty bumped into someone.

"Sorry," he murmured, never taking his eyes off the receding figure.

"You'd better be more than sorry, greenhorn," the drunk growled. "You're the one what stole my partner's money at the poker table last night. You're a cheat and a thief. And we don't allow people like that in Houston."

Jerking his head around, Rusty stared disdainfully at the

man. His clothes were filthy, and he reeked of cheap whiskey and foul body odor. His long hair was unkempt; his face sported several days' beard growth; and dried tobacco stains colored the lines of his chin.

Guessing that the man was drunk, Rusty moved out of his way, hoping to avoid trouble in the form of a street brawl. "I play poker, stranger, but I don't cheat. I don't earn my living by stealing. You've got me mixed up with someone else."

"Are you Rusty McDevin?"

"I am."

"Then you're the one," the man raged, reaching for his knife. "And I'm gonna teach you a lesson you'll never forget."

Before Rusty could reciprocate the man's action, Myra reached their side, her beautiful smile flashing. She abhorred violence; it always drew unwanted attention—attention which she and her establishment definitely did not need.

Unobtrusively she pushed between them, saying, "Hello, Mr. Barnes, how nice to see you."

Henry Barnes's fingers slowly uncurled, and he released the hilt of the knife. His face wrinkled in irritation as he reached up, his hand fisting around his hat. Pulling it off and holding it in front of his chest with both hands, he said, "Howdy, ma'am. How are ya doing this afternoon?"

By the time Myra had guided Henry through the civility of commonplace greetings, her soft, husky voice, golden brown eyes, and sparkling smile had disarmed him. "Anything I can be doing for you?"

Embarrassed, Henry shuffled from one foot to the other. "Well, no, ma'am, I don't rightly reckon so. As I see it, this here is between the tenderfoot and me."

Myra's laughing eyes swept to Rusty. "Is it in regards to his gambling in my casino?" When Henry nodded, she said, "Then, Henry, it is my business. Shall we discuss this in my office later tonight?" Never giving him a chance to answer, she smiled, laying her hand on his lower arm. "I'm sure we'll be able to settle this peacefully."

"What time?"

Myra looked at Rusty. "What time?"

"It's your party. You set the time. If I can make it, I'll come. If not, go ahead and have a good time without me."

Myra's eyes flashed angrily as she looked at the closed, lionlike countenance. Maintaining her smile, she bit back her angry retort. Rusty McDevin was an enigma, one of the few men she had been unable to tame, one of the very few who was not enamored with her. While this irritated her, it also intrigued her.

She knew beneath the stately carriage and dignified demeanor was a man who possessed fierce passion, and she wanted to be possessed—totally consumed—by this passion. She wanted to be the woman to free him from his cage of discipline and to see all the savagery of his passion unleashed. She shivered with anticipation.

Pushing the erotic thoughts aside for the moment, she returned her attention to matters at hand. "Ten o'clock, Mr. Barnes. *And we'll all be there.*" Her last statement was an assurance she made to Barnes as she stared at Rusty.

"Okay," Henry grudgingly replied, irritated because his fun and games had been interrupted by Myra. But, he reconciled himself, there would always be another time. "I'll be there." His pale blue eyes finally settled on Rusty's face, but the gambler made no promise.

After Henry walked away, Myra looped her arm through Rusty's and guided him up the street toward the Elegant Lady. "Isn't Houston wonderful?" she asked, excitement animating her voice.

Preoccupied with the woman who had just ridden into town, Rusty absently glanced around as they crossed the street. Houston, Texas, was nothing more than shacks and log cabins built helter-skelter along unplanned streets. The populace consisted of opportunists of every stripe: lawless drifters, prostitutes, cardsharps, and belligerent former soldiers. They had arrived in droves and continued to arrive in droves, loitering around town, looking for easy money and fighting vicious brawls day after day.

Rusty shrugged, pushing open the doors and entering the lobby of the hotel. "I've seen better."

"What's wrong with you?" Myra cried, spinning around, finally giving vent to her irritation. "You're in an obnoxious mood today, and I'm tired of it."

Rusty smiled, the movement slow and easy, devastatingly erotic. Bending, his face lowered, his lips almost touched hers. Myra pouted for his kiss, but Rusty pulled away, laughing softly.

"I'm always in an obnoxious mood, Myra Goodwin, and you love it. You wouldn't have me any other way."

Unaware of the door that opened on the upstairs landing, unmindful of the woman who stood in the shadows on the second floor balcony, Myra licked her lips, spreading a sheen of erotic promise on her mouth.

"I'll take you any way I can get you, Rusty McDevin."

"Miss Goodwin," Harold Emerson called, walking out of the office, holding a stack of papers in his hand, "I need to talk with you immediately. We've got a problem. Carl's son was here last night. As a result we have all these signed markers."

Ignoring the well-dressed young man who bustled out of her office, Myra said dismissively, "Be right with you, Harold." Tiptoeing, she planted a quick kiss on Rusty's lips. "I usually get what I want." She smiled, calling over her shoulder as she moved to where Harold stood. "I'll see you later tonight in my suite."

Rusty grinned, never replying. The words were so provocative that anyone overhearing them would think he and Myra were having a clandestine meeting. Out the corner of his eyes, he saw the shadowed movement upstairs. With fluid motion, he turned around, his gaze unobtrusively sweeping the balcony. The woman stepped back, out of the line of vision, but Rusty saw the striking hat with the silver-lace trim. The mystery woman, and she was staying here at the Elegant Lady.

A pleased smile played on his firm, sensual lips. Her quick retreat to the shadows told him more. She was as interested in him as he was in her.

He walked to the desk. "Know who the woman is that just checked in?"

Looking up at Rusty, Joe Randolph, the desk manager, smiled, running his thin hands down the slicked, black hair that was parted in the middle and combed to both sides. Joe didn't have to be asked the second time. He knew immediately what woman Rusty meant. Ladies of quality in Houston were a rarity. Leaning over the desk, propped on his arms, he lowered his voice to a conspiratorial whisper.

"She's from out of San Antonio," he confided, always glad to share his wealth of knowledge. "Her gran vaquero said—"

"I'm not interested in the gossip you ferret out about people," Rusty dryly commented, not really listening to what Joe was saying. Jerking the ledger from the desk clerk's hands, he turned it around and said, "I want to know who she is."

"I wasn't going to give you the story of her life," Joe replied resentfully, still unaccustomed to the impatience of the Elegant Lady's security officer. "I was simply going to tell you that she didn't—"

Not really having heard what Joe said, Rusty looked up. "She didn't check in?"

"That's what I was going to tell you," Joe smugly droned, landing both elbows on the counter top, resting his hands between his fists. "Her gran vaquero signed in and paid for the rooms in advance. They're from a large ranch outta San Antone."

"Why didn't she give her name?" Rusty muttered, puzzled.

Joe shrugged. "The gran vaquero said the señora preferred not to give her name. Cash up front I didn't ask any questions. The lady's wish was mine." He paused for a moment, adding pensively, "This is the first time that I've seen 'em. Must be their first visit to Houston."

Disappointed, Rusty mused aloud, "Señora. That means

she's married."

"I would think so," Joe commiserated.

Looking into the balcony, he and Rusty watched the señora walk to the room adjacent to her suite. In fluent Spanish, in a voice so low Rusty could only hear the whispered tones, she spoke through the closed door as she knocked. The vaquero who had been driving the lead wagon opened the door, and the señora disappeared into the room.

"I'll bet she's beautiful," Joe said in a dreamy voice. "I can just imagine what her face looks like."

"Wonder if that vaquero is her husband?"

Joe chuckled. "If it is, they're sleeping in separate rooms. El gran vaquero, Juan Martinez del Santiago, and several other vaqueros who came in with them are sleeping in the adjacent rooms." Brushing a finger over the top of his left ear, then rubbing his hand over his chin and down his neck, he said, "I reckon she's rightly a lady, Mr. McDevin."

Rusty chuckled softly. "Remember this, Joe. All women may not be ladies, but all ladies are women."

"Mr. Randolph, I got 'em." A young boy, waving his hand in the air, shoved through the doors and rushed up to the desk. He slapped his hand on the countertop. "Here they are. Two theater tickets for the señora," he said almost out of breath.

"Thank you, Charlie Boy," Joe said, digging into his pocket. Handing the lad a coin, he said, "Here's your reward."

Reaching for the coin with one hand and brushing thick golden brown hair out of his eyes with the other, Charles grinned. "Thanks, Mr. Randolph. Anything else you'd like for me to do?"

Joe looked at Rusty and grinned. Lowering one lid over an eye, he said, "Well, I'm mighty busy right now. How about another coin if you run these tickets up to the señora's rooms, number twenty-four."

An enigmatic gleam in his eye, Rusty slid his hand across the counter, his fingers curling around the tickets. Picking them up, he looked at the performance date. Reaching into his

316

pocket, pulling out the roll of bills, he said, "Charlie, I'm on my way to my rooms. I'll be going by number twenty-four. I'll deliver these for you."

The grin vanished from Charlie's face, the sparkle from his eyes. His little face puckered in disappointment.

"But," Rusty said, "I'd like you to run an errand for me."

Charlie reached up, pushing the unruly swatch of hair out of his face.

"I'd like for you to go purchase me a ticket to the theater for tonight's performance. How much are the tickets?"

"Two dollars," Charlie mumbled, his eyes on the wad of bills.

Rusty thumbed off two. "Get me one of the best seats in the house." He thumbed off two more dollars. "As close to the señora as possible." He handed Charlie five dollars. "Whatever is left after you buy the ticket is yours." Charlie's eyes rounded like saucers and bugged out with surprise. "Yes, sir," he exclaimed happily. "Where do I bring them?"

Returning the remainder of the money to his pocket, Rusty picked up the pen and scribbled two notes. "Bring them up to number twenty-two." Nodding, Charlie turned, scampering out the door. Folding one of the notes, writing Myra's name across the outside, Rusty handed it to Joe. "See that Myra gets this immediately," he said. "I don't want her complaining when she finds that I'm not going to be here tonight." Addressing the second message, he said, "Get this to Stringbean even quicker. He's going to be more than irritated to find that he's on duty tonight." He took several steps, stopped and turned around. "I'd like to have a bath prepared, Joe."

"Yes, sir. Right away."

Theater tickets in hand, a rather smug smile on his face, Rusty moved away from the desk. Smiling and shaking his head in admiration, Joe spun his ledger around. Rusty McDevin was interested in meeting the señora. The desk clerk had no doubt that Rusty would accomplish his task. Once Rusty McDevin

317

set his mind to do something, he did it. And, Joe had to honestly admit, Rusty did have a way with women.

"Going to the theater, sir?" Joe called, amusement underlining his question.

At the landing of the stairs, Rusty's hands curled around the banister. He stopped, looked at Joe, and smiled. "Yes," he replied, his eyes twinkling, "I think I shall. A man can never get enough—culture." Chuckling at his own witticism, he turned. His hand brushing up the highly polished banister, he hurried up the stairs. When he reached the señora's suite, he knocked on the door.

"Yes?" The door muffled the woman's voice, but he knew it was the señora's.

"Hello, I'm Rusty McDevin from down the hall, number twenty-two. Since I was coming upstairs, Mr. Randolph asked me to deliver your theater tickets."

The silence was pregnant. Eventually the woman said, "Thank you, Señor McDevin. I would open the door and take them, but I'm dressing. Would you mind delivering them to Juan? His room is adjacent to mine."

His smile a grim one, his sigh one of disappointment, Rusty stood there for a moment, pondering his next move. "Since I'm responsible for their delivery, ma'am, I'd hate to slip them under the door. I'd never know if you—if the señora received them or not. Tell you what," he said, "I'll take them to my room. The señora can come get them later." He smiled. "Rusty McDevin. Number twenty-two."

"Señor," the woman cried out, but Rusty, a smug grin replacing the grim smile, was walking away, tucking the tickets into his pocket.

When he reached his rooms, he unlocked the door and walked into the spacious, ornate parlor, undressing with each step that he took. He slung his hat onto the sofa, absently pushing his fingers through his thick, russet waves. Without stopping, he headed for the small table on the opposite side of the room.

He shrugged out of his jacket, tossing it aside. He unbuttoned his waistcoat and slipped out of it. Shedding his cravats and collars, he tugged his shirt out of his trousers and opened it down the front. Stopping in front of a small table, he lifted the decanter and poured himself a glass of whiskey. Preoccupied with the mysterious woman, he pulled the lace curtains aside and looked out the window.

The knock at the door jarred him from his daydreams. "Your bath, sir."

"Be right with you," Rusty called, setting his empty glass down. In long, graceful strides he was across the room, flinging open the door. Instead of his bath, however, Henry Barnes rushed into the room, his fists flying in first, connecting with Rusty's chin, knocking the surprised gambler off his feet.

Barnes's eyes lowered to Rusty's prone body. "I know what you're doing," he shouted. "You and Miss Myra are playing games with me in front of my friends, making 'em laugh at me. Well, greenhorn, I don't like it." He pulled a long, ugly knife from his belt. "You're gonna pay fer it." His feet straddled, his shoulders rounded, his arms extended defensively. "We don't have room out here, mister, for the likes of you. Go back where you came from."

As the man talked, Rusty's eyes locked on the bloodshot ones, his gaze never wavering. Without moving he gently tugged his trouser leg up, his fingers sliding the knife out of his boot. Barnes breathed raggedly, his chest heaving with the exertion. Perspiration beaded on his forehead, running down his beard-stubbled face. His dirty shirt was wet across his shoulders and under his arms.

"I'd reconsider, Barnes," Rusty said. "You're drunk, and I'm not, so I have the advantage on you."

"Drunk or not," Barnes slurred, "I'm gonna take you on, tenderfoot."

"I don't want to fight you, but I will if you force me."

Swishing the knife through the air in menacing gesture, Barnes said, "Evidently you ain't been in Texas long, mister, but you're gonna stay here a mighty long time. When I get through with you, they're gonna bury you six feet under."

With feline grace, Rusty rose to his feet. "You'd best be findin' out if I be student or master, myself, stranger, before you take on the awesome responsibility of being the school master," he said, his pronunciation easing into Irish brogue. "You see, I've spent the better part of my life eluding death, and so far I've been the victor." His eyes contemptuously beheld the man who loomed over him. "I've had much better opponents than you, so I'm not about to let you take me down." His fingers curled around the hilt of a bowie knife, the sunlight reflecting on the shiny metal of his twelve-inch blade.

Henry's eyes ran the length of the deadly blade that tapered down to a double-edged point. His face lifted, and he stared into the cold, green eyes. Barnes laughed. "You ain't gonna frighten me off, waving that knife around."

"Too bad," Rusty quietly returned. "I had hoped it would sober you up. I was hoping to scare some sense into you rather than kill you."

As the gambler talked, Barnes began circling in the center of the room. Rusty's eyes never left Barnes. Suddenly the man lunged toward Rusty who danced out of the assailant's way.

"You think you're smart, don't ya?" the man sneered, lunging a second time, his blade catching in Rusty's shirt sleeve. "But ya ain't. You ain't gonna make no fool outta me. I'm gonna get ya."

His eyes never leaving Barnes's face, Rusty cautiously moved, brandishing the huge knife. His soft voice taunted Barnes. "Look at it, Barnes. It weighs nearly a pound. Bowie designed it to stab like a dagger, to slice like a razor, and chop like a cleaver, and I'm a master of all three techniques."

Barnes lifted one arm and wiped the sweat from his brow; the wet rings under his arms circled wider. He wanted to turn and run, but he couldn't. His friends were outside waiting for him; they laid wagers. If he turned tail and ran now, he'd be the laughing stock of Houston. Footsteps in the corridor; the squeaking wheels of the tea cart; the opening and shutting of a door. Every noise he heard gave him the jitters. Barnes's breathing grew heavier and more labored.

He could hardly keep his hand from trembling. He hadn't reckoned on this when he'd contemplated killing the gambler. Why he's nothing but a greenhorn, one of his drinking companions had said. Yeah, the other had chimed in, you can tell by looking that he's a tenderfoot. But Barnes knew this man was anything but a greenhorn or a tenderfoot. The man's confidence had stripped away what little courage Barnes had. Now he was stripping away his bravado, revealing Barnes for the coward he was.

Barnes nervously chewed on his bottom lip. He ran his tongue over his parched lips.

Long after the knocking stopped, Marguerite, clad in nothing but a thin dressing gown, leaned against the door, softly pounding her fists against the wood. Then she paced back and forth across the room, berating herself for being so stupid. In not playing into the man's hands, she had played into his rooms. She walked a little ways on the balcony, peering down at the throng of people who milled in the deeply rutted dirt streets. Her hand clenched around the banister. She couldn't get Rusty McDevin out of her mind. She could still hear the smug amusement in his voice when he told her he would keep the tickets until she came to get them.

When she had seen him in the lobby with Miss Goodwin, Marguerite had seen nothing but the broad scope of his back and shoulders and a glimpse of his side profile, but she had known that Rusty McDevin was a handsome man. From his blatant flirtation with the woman downstairs, Marguerite figured he was a womanizer. From the woman's reaction, Marguerite figured that most women would do anything to become his woman. Irritated with herself, Marguerite tried to push thoughts of Rusty McDevin from her mind. But the task was futile. Since Marguerite's shadowy encounter with the gambler, she was totally consumed with curiosity about Rusty McDevin.

"Your gown is ready, señora," the young maid called from the bedroom door.

"Thank you, Hortensia," Marguerite replied. She dropped the curtain and walked into the bedroom. With no conscious thought she dressed. The chemise. The petticoats. The pale-blue gown, trimmed in navy. Looking at her reflection, she reached up and smoothed the decolletage. She reached for the bertha, but Hortensia laid a detaining hand on her mistress.

Shaking her head, the maid said, "You don't need that, señora. You are a beautiful woman." She smiled, revealing lovely white teeth, and pointed at the lace cape. "You don't need this to hide you."

"*Gracias*, Hortensia," Marguerite murmured. "You are so sweet to me."

As Marguerite's fingers touched the lacy frills, she stared at the cape collar that would cover the greater part of her shoulders and all her breasts. She hadn't worn a low-cut gown in a long time, not since—not since— Smiling in the mirror at Hortensia, Marguerite stood.

"Perhaps I will leave it off," she announced. She opened her jewel box, the soft music tinkling through the room. "If I do, my necklace will show up."

Marguerite lifted the string of pearls up and looped them over her neck. But she didn't fasten them. She remembered what she must do and with whom. Slowly her hands dropped, and she replaced the necklace on its bed of black velvet. She reached for the bertha, draping it over her shoulders.

Smiling an apology at Hortensia, she said, "I'm going to get my tickets from *Señor* McDevin. He's quite a ladies' man, and I don't want him to think that I want to become one of his."

Hortensia giggled. "Perhaps that wouldn't be so bad, señora. He's quite a caballero. Umm, *muy magnífico!*"

"He's quite a man and very magnificent," Marguerite agreed, "but I have a feeling that he's quite conceited and used to having his own way." She grinned, excitement spiraling through her as it hadn't done in years, making her feel young again, taking the taint of widowhood away. "I think it's time, Hortensia, that *Señor* McDevin was taught a lesson."

Hortensia's black eyes gleamed, and her head bobbed in agreement.

"How do I look?" Marguerite asked, spinning around.

"*Muy bonita,*" Hortensia breathed in adoration. "*Muy bonita,* señora."

Taking a last look in the mirror, patting her hair, and picking up a lace handkerchief, Marguerite regally swept out of the bedroom through the parlor. Her hand closed over the doorknob, and she took a deep breath, sudden exhilaration surging through her. Anticipation heightened the rosy glow on her cheeks and reddened her lips. Excitement ringed her blue eyes in midnight, adding an erotic illusiveness to them.

She moved out of the room and down the corridor. She heard a scuffling noise and voices, but she didn't realize it was coming from number twenty-two until she stood in front of the opened door and saw the two men circling in the center of the room. Barnes, on the far side of the room, faced her. She saw only Rusty McDevin's back.

When she saw the knives flashing, her hand flew to her mouth, and her heart skipped several beats. She wasn't unaccustomed to frontier viciousness. She had been exposed to it ever since she'd come from Europe. But this, for some reason, was different. Her fingers slowly splayed, sliding down her cheeks and her chin, to curve lightly around her throat.

Barnes saw her standing in the door, and the expression on his face changed. When Marguerite saw the undisguised hatred gleaming in the man's eyes, when she saw the evil countenance, she gasped her fears. Reflexively Rusty's head turned, and out of the corner of his eyes he saw the señora. Taking advantage of Rusty's relaxed vigilance, Barnes suddenly hollered at the top of his voice. Knife extended, he plunged toward Rusty's stomach.

As the blade whipped through the air, grazing Rusty's stomach, Barnes lost his balance and stumbled. Twining his fingers together and centering the force of his entire body in his hands, Rusty hit the man across the upper shoulders, knocking him to the floor. Then he leaped so that he faced the door. His eyes on the stunned Barnes, he drew in a deep gulp of air. Lifting a hand, he raked an errant swath of hair out of his face, the thick russet waves shining copper red in the sunlight that streamed in through the window.

"No," Marguerite unconsciously cried aloud, catching hold of the casement to keep from collapsing on the floor. "No, it can't be. You're dead."

At the cry Rusty's face jerked up, and he glanced at the woman in the door. His adversary forgotten, Rusty stared at the woman who stood in the door. Blue eyes not brown! Her dark, shining hair that was brushed sleekly down from the center part plaited to cover the ears. She was older, but she was—

"Daisy Belle," he whispered as if he couldn't believe his eyes.

"Sheridan."

For just an instant, no longer than the blink of an eye, the sophisticated veneer called Señora Marguerite de la Flor del Sol no longer existed. In her place stood the young, vulnerable Marguerite LeFleur. But with the sweep of her lashes, Marguerite wiped all surprise, all emotion but one from her eyes. When Rusty looked into the beautiful blue spheres, all he saw was hatred.

Yet despite herself, Marguerite's blue eyes traveled over the rugged terrain of his face. The thick brows. The green eyes. The firm mouth. Her eyes lowered to the thick patch of russet hair that covered his chest. The flat stomach. She looked at the swirl of hair around his navel; she traced its growth until it disappeared into his trousers. When she lifted her face and looked into Sheridan's green eyes—when she saw the fiery passion reflected in his eyes, Marguerite's eyes flashed her contempt.

Barnes pushed up on his knees, then to his feet. Gripping the hilt of his knife in his hands, he swayed for a moment. He blinked his eyes, clearing his vision. When he saw Rusty, staring trancelike at the woman in the door, he smiled. Taking advantage of his opponent's distraction, Barnes drew back his hand. Emitting an animalistic snarl, he rushed across the room, knocked Rusty down and fell on top of him, the knife coming toward Rusty's heart.

Marguerite's scream was lost in the grunts of the fighting men. Reflexively quick, his attention once again centered on his assailant, Rusty caught the man's wrist with his left hand. Grunting, exerting all his strength, he pushed against the hand, but Barnes's weight was the momentum and force behind the weapon. Kicking his legs for leverage, Rusty tried to twist beneath the man. But he couldn't; Barnes was too heavy. Rusty dropped his knife and caught Barnes's wrist with both hands.

Incapable of uttering another sound, Marguerite stood, transfixed in the doorway, watching the struggle. She watched as Barnes made that last push. At the same time Rusty also made the last push, turning the knife blade, shoving a little harder. Barnes gasped, his eyes opened wide in fright and pain, and blood dribbled down the corner of his mouth. Impaled on his own knife, he collapsed on top of Rusty. For a moment the room was deathly quiet; the bodies stilled. Slowly Rusty pushed from beneath, heaving the dead body off. Breathing deeply and raggedly, he stumbled to the sofa and sat down.

As soon as he caught his breath, Rusty looked up, but Marguerite was gone. He staggered to the door down the corridor to her suite. Holding onto the casement, dragging in deep gulps of air, he banged on the door and shouted.

"Marguerite!"

But Marguerite didn't answer; Hortensia did. "I'm sorry,"

she said. "La señora is not here. She went to get her theater tickets from a Señor McDevin."

Sheridan glared around the maid, but he couldn't see Marguerite in the room. Yet he knew she was there. Gently pushing Hortensia aside, he moved as if to enter, but Charles, shouting from the landing, stopped him.

"Mr. McDevin! Your tickets."

Stepping back, Sheridan looked over his shoulder. As he watched the lad run toward him, Sheridan wiped the blood from his mouth with one hand, and using his shirttail, dabbed his stomach with the other. To Hortensia he said, "Tell Marguerite she can't hide forever. I'll be back." He turned, took several steps and stopped. "Tell her that's a promise." He walked back to his room, Charles following.

"Tarnation, Mr. McDevin!" Charles's eyes traveled from the bowie knife Sheridan stooped to pick up to the dead body. "What happened to you?"

"Practicing self-defense," Rusty dryly retorted.

"Looks like ya did pretty good."

"Depends on where you're looking from," Rusty said, pouring a glass of whiskey and quaffing it down, grimacing when the alcohol burned his cut. Pointing the empty glass at Barnes, he said, "From down there, lad, I don't think it looks so good." Sheridan laid the knife and the glass on the table.

"Oh," Charles softly exclaimed, suddenly remembering his errand, "here's your ticket to the theater, and Mr. Randolph asked me to deliver this letter to you."

Rusty laid the ticket aside and opened the letter.

McDevin,

I know my request won't come as a surprise, and I know your first inclination is going to be to crumple this letter up and throw it away. But, *please*, Rusty, read it. Be slow with your answer. Think first.

President Lamar needs you for a special assignment. We have intercepted a letter, indicating communication between the Mexicans and the Comanches. For what reason we don't know, but we're concerned about it.

Even if you don't return to the rangers and work with us on this assignment, please come to headquarters and take a look at the letter.

An old friend of yours and the Republic of Texas,
James Power

Sighing, Rusty lowered his head, crumpled the letter into a ball, and dropped it at his feet.

"Want me to take an answer?" Charles asked.

"No," Rusty replied. "I'll take the answer to this one in person, but you can run another errand for me."

"Sure," Charles cried. "Anything for you, Mr. McDevin."

"First, go by room ten and ask Stringbean to come up here immediately. Then on your way out, stop by the desk and ask Mr. Randolph to send someone up to clean the trash out of my room."

Charles's gaze automatically swept to the dead man. "Yes, sir."

Rusty walked to his jacket. Picking it up, he rummaged through the pocket for his money.

"You don't need to give me no more money," Charles said. He pulled the wadded bills out of his trouser pockets. "They didn't charge you extra for the seat, so I have this much left over. Maybe . . . maybe you'll be wanting some of it back?"

Rusty smiled. Reaching out, he curled Charles's hand around the money and pushed it toward the boy. "It's yours."

"Yes, sir," Charles snapped, a sunshine-bright smile lightening up his face.

Rusty smiled, watching the door close on the grinning child. Taking off his shirt and tossing it on a nearby table, he walked to the sofa, picking up his waistcoat. Gently he removed his watch and moved into the bedroom. At the dresser, he picked up a handsome jewelry box and wound the stem on the bottom. Setting it down, he lifted the lid, the notes tinkling through the otherwise silent room. Softly he whistled the familiar refrain, the plaintive tune stirring many memories for Rusty, some wonderful, some sad. During the years these memories had never been far away. They kept him company during the long hours of the night and never strayed far from him during the day.

Shutting the lid, he picked up the box, turned it over once again and unscrewed the winding stem. He removed the music board. Then he inserted the tiny key on the end of his watch chain into the stem hole and unlocked a hidden compartment. He extracted the papers.

Holding them in one hand, he absently slapped them against the palm of the other. He had to put them in a safe place—a place where no one would think about looking for them. What if a burglar stole his jewelry chest? What if he lost the papers? He didn't want to take that chance. Suddenly the papers were more important than they had ever been.

Smiling, he reinserted the letters, replaced and locked the hidden compartment, then attached the musical board. Last he inserted the winding stem. Taking his jewelry out and raking it into the drop drawer of the dresser, he gently shut the lid on the music box.

"Rusty!" Myra impatiently rapped on the door.

Quickly Rusty moved into the parlor, opening the door only wide enough for Myra to come in. Still wearing the same dress, she had thrown a black lace shawl around her shoulders.

"Charlie Boy told Joe that you—" Her eyes went from Rusty's disheveled appearance, to the cut across his stomach, to Barnes's prostrate form. "My God!" she shrieked, her hands flying to her face, her shawl slipping from her shoulders. "I know it's the style, but why did you kill the man in my place, Rusty? We could have settled this more peaceably, or you could have killed him out there on the street. Dear God, what are the ladies gonna think about the Elegant Lady now?" Her face white, she collapsed into the nearest chair. "This—this has upset me, Rusty. Pour me a glass of whiskey." Her voice was raspy like sandpaper. When she held the glass in her hands, she looked at his wound. As an afterthought, she asked, "Do you want me to bandage it?"

Grinning, Rusty looked at his stomach and ran his fingers along the slit. "No, it's just a scratch."

Myra's eyes moved to Barnes, and she grimaced. "What happened?"

Pouring himself a glass of whiskey and lighting a cheroot, Rusty sat on the sofa and quietly related the events leading up to Barnes's death.

"Why did he want to kill you?" Myra asked, color returning to her cheeks.

"A drunk out to prove himself," Rusty replied. Sloughing off the incident, he said, "People always seem to mistake me for a tenderfoot."

"I can understand," Myra said. "You're not at all what you appear to be." Standing, she paced agitatedly around the room. "Who are you Rusty? What are you?"

"I'm exactly what you see," he replied easily. "I'm a ranger-turned-gambler."

Myra sat on the sofa beside Rusty and leaned toward him. "Why did you leave the rangers? Why are you working for me?"

Rusty lifted a hand and lazily tweaked the end of her nose. "I'm working for you, lass, because I didn't earn all that much being a ranger, and I do enjoy the easy life. You pay me a salary to keep order in your saloon so that it will appear to be what it isn't." He grinned. "Decent. And while I'm working for you, I work for myself." He laid his head on the back of the sofa. "I've won quite a bit of money during the past two months that I've been employed at the Elegant Lady."

"You're not working tonight?" Myra asked, remembering Rusty's note.

He shook his head. "I'm going to the theater."

Myra hiked her brows. "The theater?"

Rusty grinned. "Thought I'd get me a little culture."

"I'll bet it's culture you're after," Myra snapped.

"Myra, Myra, quite contrary," Rusty chanted, a devilish grin moving from his eyes to his lips.

"Who are you going with?"

"Myself."

Again Myra slanted a skeptical glower at him.

"And, my darling, I have some more disconcerting news for you." He nodded his head toward the letter he had thrown on the floor. "I'm leaving for San Antonio in the morning."

Myra ran her finger around the rim of the glass. She had known that Rusty would be moving on sooner or later. He was the restless kind. But she had hoped that he would stay longer.

"The rangers?"

"Um-hum. Indian trouble."

"Will you be coming back?"

"Probably," he replied noncommittally. "This is the nearest place to home that I have."

Myra reached for the decanter and refilled her glass. "Tell me something about your past," she asked. Then she pleaded, "Anything."

Rusty stooped, picked up the letter and laid it on the table. Words from long ago came to haunt him. "I don't have a past, Myra. Nor do I have a future. Just a present. Just today." He strode into the bedroom, rummaging through the drawers for a clean shirt.

Myra followed. Seeing the jewelry box on the dresser, she curiously lifted the lid. "Is this the jewelry box you wanted me to keep if you ever left?"

Sheridan nodded.

"An heirloom?"

"You might say that," he sloughed.

Myra reached for the lacquered box, rubbing her hand over the highly polished finish. "Looks like it's very valuable."

"It is."

She turned it over, winding the stem. When she lifted the

330

lid, the soft music flowed through the room. She hummed the tune as she listened. "Irish?"

"Irish."

"What's the name?"

"'The Wearing of the Green.'"

The name meant nothing to her. "Why does a raw-boned, rawhide tough man like you have a music jewelry box?" She paused only fractionally before she asked, "Did it belong to an important woman in your life?"

"Two ladies actually," Rusty returned smoothly, skillfully eradicating any emotion from his voice, cleverly evading the truth. "I won her from Lady Luck to help Lady Liberty." When Myra pulled a face at him, Rusty grinned. "If I tell you more, Miss Myra, you will know as much as me."

"I wouldn't mind," Myra softly admitted.

"I would."

"Your bath, Mr. McDevin," a male voice called from the corridor.

He walked to the sofa, bent, and retrieved her shawl.

"Shall I take it with me now?"

Thinking about Marguerite, he hesitated, on the verge of saying no. But he had second thoughts. He would wait until he'd talked with Marguerite. He nodded. As Myra clutched it under her arm, he draped her shawl over her shoulders.

"It's time for you to be leaving, Missy. I need to get dressed."

Myra smiled. "Shall I stay and scrub your back, Rusty?"

"No."

More raps on the door: "Your bath, Mr. McDevin."

"Will there ever be a time for us, Rusty?" Myra whispered, totally oblivious to the man outside the door.

"Probably not." He again thought about Marguerite.

"There's someone else, isn't there?"

Rusty breathed deeply, her question like a knife piercing an inflamed, open wound. "There is."

331

The soft knock turned into a heavy pounding. "Mr. Mc-Devin."

Slowly Myra walked to the door. The music box tucked under her arm, her hand on the knob, her back to Rusty, she asked, "Who is she?"

"My . . ." He paused. "My . . . wife."

Chapter 20

The tall, wiry man, dressed in buckskins, opened the door and walked on to the balcony. Holding the banister, he leaned over and spit into the street, unmindful of the people who loitered beneath.

"To be honest, Rusty," he said, straighteing up, wiping the back of his hand over his mouth, "I'm glad you decided to go 'cause I'd hate to see us split up, but I'd be a'going to San Antone whuther you did or not. I'd much rather fight the Injuns and the Mexicans than be cooped up here in this saloon, fighting drunks and fools."

His hands dropped to the gun belt around his waist, gleaming with bullets. A bowie knife, inserted through the belt, slanted across his stomach, the hilt rubbing one side of his chest. A revolver was on the other side, a rifle in his hand.

Running his tongue between his cheek and lower gum, repositioning his tobacco, he muttered, "What time are you leaving?"

"Sunup."

"Where at?"

"From the livery stable."

"By ourself or riding with one of the trains out west?"

Sheridan shrugged. "We'll make better time by ourselves, but I hate to—"

333

"Me too," Stringbean said, divining his partner's thoughts. "Don't like to see them greenhorns at the mercy of the elements or the Injuns. Bad enough when they're left to the mercy of the trash that's filled this bayou."

Not one to mince words if necessary but also not one to waste them when unnecessary, Stringbean turned his back to Sheridan and moved across the room. The conversation over, his moccasined feet silently padded to the door. He opened it and walked out.

As soon as Sheridan had locked the door behind Stringbean, he moved into the bedroom and bathed in the cold water; however, he was oblivious to its temperature. All his thoughts centered on Marguerite. He quickly dried off. Taking only enough time to put on a clean shirt and trousers, he left his rooms, walking down the corridor to number twenty-four. He knocked on the door but received no answer. He knocked several times more with the same results.

Having seen Marguerite again disconcerted him, to say the least. Knowing she was in the room and not answering irritated him. Determined that she would answer, he pressed his lips together, braced his legs, and leaned his shoulder against the casement. The only direction he was moving was forward, through the door into Marguerite's suite.

"I know you're in there, Daisy," he called, "and I'm not leaving until you open the door." Impatiently he waited. When no answer was forthcoming, he called, louder this time, "Surely, lass, you know I mean what I'm a'sayin'. You know that I don't pretend to be a gentleman." He waited. "If this door isn't opened in about fifteen seconds, I'm going to knock it down or shoot off the lock. Whatever happens is up to you, madam. Me, I don't particularly care which you choose. I don't have a reputation to uphold."

Again Sheridan waited, and he listened. When he heard the click of the bolt, he smiled. The door opened, and a young Mexican girl stepped into the hall, a basket on her arm, a shawl wrapped around her head and shoulders. All Sheridan could see were the beautiful black eyes.

"Señora Marguerite will see you now," she said, as she walked down the corridor.

Grasping the knob, Sheridan shoved, the thick oak door silently gliding over the floor. As he stood in the aperture, his feet straddled, his hands on his hips, Sheridan's piercing gaze swept the room, stopping only when he saw Marguerite on the other side of the room.

"Please come in, Señor McDevin." The caustic command snapped through the air like the crack of the deadly whip she carried and wielded. "You've made a spectacle of yourself enough for one day. I don't intend that you should make one of me also."

When Sheridan didn't move out of the doorway, Marguerite said, "Come in and shut the door." Her voice was cold and aloof; her manner discouraging. "It's enough that passersby heard you yelling outside my door. I don't want people staring in as they pass by."

Without turning, Rusty reached behind and closed the door. "Hello, Daisy."

Marguerite trembled with remembrance when she heard him speak her nickname so softly. His resonant voice was husky and caressive. He spoke as if no other person existed in the world but her. She didn't answer, but Sheridan smiled tolerantly. He could understand Marguerite's reticence. She was as shocked to see him as he was to see her. She was overwhelmed with emotions, like him.

In the same soft, velvet tones, he said, "We have a lot of time to catch up on."

"We have nothing to catch up on," Marguerite corrected, her voice rapier sharp, icy cold, "but we do need to talk. That's why I sent Hortensia shopping."

The years of surviving alone in a man's world had strengthened Marguerite. Maturity and experience gave her a poise and aplomb that enabled her to project a facade of complete indifference. She veiled her expressions and eyes, allowing Sheridan to see none of her inner feelings.

Not liking this hardened veneer, Sheridan looked at her with narrowed eyes. "Thank you for the warm welcome."

"What did you expect?" she countered. "Open arms, tears, forgiveness, and confessions of undying love?"

"Maybe not that," he admitted, "but more than the north wind treatment."

Too nervous to sit down, he wandered around the room with maddening ease and deliberate slowness. He brushed his fingers over the tables, ran them over the backs of the sofa and chairs, pulled the curtain back and peeked out.

"You know when you left me in Ireland, you professed to love me."

"A child's delusion."

Sheridan's head snapped in her direction. "Hardly a child!"

Nervous herself, shaking like a leaf in a heavy wind and feeling as vulnerable, Marguerite sat down in a chair opposite the sofa. She watched Sheridan walk to the door and lock it. Taking the key out, he flung it on a nearby table and leaned back against the door.

"Locking me in?"

He shook his head. "No, locking others out. Looks like our conversation is going to be lengthy, and I don't want to be disturbed." He folded his arms over his chest and crossed his ankles. His smile was slow and devastating. "You're more beautiful than I remembered." His voice was soft and faraway. "You're more beautiful than my dreams."

Marguerite said nothing.

"I looked for you after I arrived in America. After I left New York, I headed for New Orleans." He paused, cautiously picking his way, hoping to elicit some kind of response from Marguerite. "I went to your plantation in Louisiana." Unable to penetrate her indifference, Sheridan lifted his hand and wiped a sheen of perspiration from his upper lip. "You sold it?"

She hadn't yet; she couldn't bring herself to part with it. She had allowed it to be put on a five-year lease, but Marguerite didn't tell Sheridan.

"I came here, but you weren't living in the Irish colonies, and port officials recorded the sinking of the schooner you set sail on from New Orleans to Aransas Pass."

That was true, Marguerite silently agreed. When she arrived in Liverpool from Ireland, she decided to journey to France to visit with her family. She, Paddy, and Jewel had given their passage to other immigrants without changing their booking. The schooner on which she had been booked for the last leg of the journey sank, and all passengers had drowned.

After another long period of silence, Sheridan snapped impatiently, "Dammit, Marguerite, say something. Don't sit there like a statue. I know seeing me again has resurrected a lot of painful feelings and memories, but surely it's also brought to mind some of the good ones. They can't all be bad, can they?"

Marguerite was too numb to think straight, too confused to speak. So she looked at him.

Exasperated, Sheridan lifted a hand in an old familiar gesture that tugged at Marguerite's heart; he raked his fingers through the thick auburn waves. Talking to a stone wall was one thing, he thought, but talking to a woman he'd turned into stone was damned near impossible.

"Marguerite, talk to me!" he thundered. "My, God! Tell me what you're feeling! What you're thinking!"

Sheridan's outburst shattered the shell of numbness that covered Marguerite. Suddenly, emotions flowed over and through her like a ravaging flood. She stood, a smile curling her lips. Victory wasn't quite as sweet as she had dreamed it would be all these years.

"You want to know what I'm thinking," she said, emotion thickening her voice so that it was almost a whisper. "I'm thinking how angry I am that Sheridan O'Roarke is resurrected. I was happy to have him dead and out of my life. I'm thinking how happy I've been for the past six years without him." She laughed, the sound bitter. "I've enjoyed being a widow for the past three years."

She reached up, pushing a wisping tendril of hair off her face. "You want to know what I'm feeling. I'm refeeling, Sheridan. I'm refeeling the agony of losing you, the agony of knowing you didn't love me, the humiliation of your using me—" Her voice throbbed with her emotions.

Unconsciously, Sheridan reached for her. But Marguerite jerked away.

"Most of all, Sheridan, I'm hating you. Hating you! *Hating you!*"

"Daisy—"

"Don't Daisy me," she shouted. "I don't ever want to hear you call me that again. I would prefer that you call me Señora Marguerite O'Roarke de la Flor del Sol."

"What you wish for me to do and what I do are two different things, señora," Sheridan gritted.

"If you stay in Texas long, Señor McDevin, you will learn that my wish is my command," Marguerite said. "At word my vaqueros will kill you."

"Perhaps at word your vaqueros would try to kill me, lass, but you don't need them to kill me. You're doing quite well with those dagger looks you've been sending me." He smiled sadly. "But you can't kill me, lass. Even death seems to spurn my company."

"I can understand. You're not the kind one chooses for a companion. Even death is discriminating."

Sheridan cast her a withering glance. "You may say you hate me, lass, and you may honestly think you do, but deep down you still care about me. I saw it on your face when you first recognized me. You cried it aloud when Barnes was about to stab me."

"I was surprised," Marguerite explained. "I had received word three years ago that you were dead. Seeing you alive was rather shocking. Furthermore," she added, her voice defensive, "I don't like to see anyone killed, whether he deserves it or not." Putting distance between them, she moved to the sofa and sat down.

"I was going to be hanged for a traitor," he confessed. "Faking my death was the only way I could escape alive. I was smuggled out on a ship bound for New York. From there I worked my way down here." He paused, then said, "But I promise you, lass, just as I promised Taylor. One day I'll return and take everything that belongs to me. Once again an O'Roarke will own the manor house."

Marguerite watched Sheridan as he talked; she studied every expression on his face. A few more lines, she thought. A little more weathered, but basically unchanged. His life still pivoted on revenge and repossession.

"You haven't changed, Sheridan. Not a whit." Laying her head against the back of the sofa, she smiled, warmth effusing her eyes. "Remember the first time that I saw you? In Ballygarrett. You were engaging in fisticuffs with Mickey Flynn in the middle of the street. A common brawl!" She chuckled. "And when I first lay eyes on you here in Texas, what are you doing?" She laughed again. "The same thing— brawling with the riffraff of the town."

Chaffing under her amused description, Sheridan said, "May I point out that he was brawling with me?"

Marguerite asked, "How are you earning your living?"

Pushing away from the door, Sheridan grinned. "For a while I was a ranger."

"What are you now?" Marguerite asked, her eyes running over the expensive shirt and trousers. "A ranger couldn't afford to be caught dead in those; besides he couldn't afford them, period."

"Chief security officer for the Elegant Lady," Sheridan returned.

Marguerite chuckled. "Chief security officer. The desk clerk told Juan that you were a gambler."

He shrugged. "Works better if people think I'm a gambler rather than a policeman." His eyes twinkled. "To keep up the guise, I gamble on the side."

Marguerite laughed, really laughed, the husky sound echoing through the room. "My, my! You're certainly a busy man. You earn your living by gambling; you entertain yourself with Texas's most illustrative madam, and in your spare time you kill off the riffraff of town."

"Do I detect a note of jealousy?" Sheridan asked.

Marguerite rolled her head across the back of the sofa. "Appalled but not jealous," she replied calmly. "In order to be jealous you must love or want to possess something. I neither love nor want to possess you. No matter what you think, you're nothing but a bad memory for me, Sheridan." She smiled. "For the record both Sheridan and Marguerite O'Roarke are dead. I'd like to keep it like that, if you don't mind?"

"I do mind," Sheridan snapped. "And it does matter to me what you think. I earn my living by policing the Elegant Lady; I add to my income by gambling. But I do not entertain myself with Houston's most illustrative madam. I like her, but I don't love her. I don't make love to her."

"No?" Marguerite dismissed with disinterest. "I saw you with her this afternoon. You almost seduced her in the lobby of the hotel."

Now Sheridan chuckled. "I did not. Myra and I are friends, nothing more. She and I do not have . . . have not had . . . a romantic relationship."

"I'm not interested in your relationship with the madam," Marguerite replied smoothly, rising and walking to the window, her back to Sheridan. "I was embarrassed by the spectacle the two of you made of yourselves."

"I can remember a day when you would have been interested, lass. A day when you would have made a spectacle of yourself with O'Roarke. I can remember more than a day, lass."

Marguerite started when she heard the words. Sheridan had moved so quietly that he was standing right behind her.

"Do you remember also?"

His hands settled on her shoulders. So great was the

340

sensation that surged through Marguerite that her hand shook. Summoning all her willpower, she moved away from Sheridan.

"I have forgotten nothing. Absolutely nothing!"

Staring into her eyes, getting no farther than the icy glaze, he said, "Believe me, Daisy Belle, I love you. I've always loved you."

He said the words that had been locked in the coffers of his heart for the past six years—the words he couldn't say when she went away—the words that may have kept her by his side in Ireland. Now they meant nothing to her.

"No, Sheridan," she softly contradicted, "you didn't love me. For a long time I thought you did. For the longest time I maintained my sanity hoping you did, but one day I realized that you and Earl Taylor were not so different. You, like him, simply wanted me and what I could give to you and your cause. You wanted me and what I had so that I couldn't give to Earl's cause."

She paused, thinking, carefully choosing her words. "I blamed you then, but later I understood, and actually every once in a while I was proud of you. I realized that you did love with a fiery passion. You loved Ireland; you loved your cause and the Wexford lads; and you loved revenge, but you didn't love me."

"Dear God, Daisy," Sheridan thundered, "what a cruel assessment! I did love you, but you gave me no alternative. You defined love, making it a box too small for me to fit into; when you enlarged it, you issued an ultimatum, leaving no room for me to move. 'Me or the cause,' you said. And at the time I felt an obligation to the cause, to the people whom I would have been deserting. If you had waited a little while longer before leaving, Daisy. Just a little while longer—" He sighed, pushing his fingers through his hair. "But going over the past and wishing it different isn't going to change it, Daisy. All we can do is work to change the future."

Marguerite lifted a hand and ran her fingers down her cheek. The glint of gold caught Sheridan's attention. Clasping her hand in his, he brought it down and looked at the gold ring.

Disappointed, he asked, "Where's the ring I gave you?"

"It's in a trunk at the hacienda," Marguerite replied. She sighed and closed her eyes. "I wore it for a long time, thinking you would come after me. Even after I'd heard that you were dead, I continued to wear it. But one morning I woke up, and I took it off. When I did, I somehow felt as if I'd finally gotten you out of my life. Now I could start living again."

Something inside Sheridan broke, and he wilted. He sat on the edge of the sofa, his elbows on his knees, his hands hanging limply between his legs. "I know I've hurt you, Marguerite, and I know that saying 'I'm sorry' isn't going to mean much. But I am sorry. Truly I am." Desperately he pleaded. "Give me a chance to begin all over again. We'll pretend that we're single again. I'll court you and show you how much I love you."

"It's not that simple," Marguerite replied, unaware that she was twining her fingers together. "You're no longer a part of my life. I've created a new one. One without you."

"Let's get reacquainted," he suggested. "Let me take you to the theater tonight and to dinner afterward."

Marguerite shook her head.

"You were planning on going, weren't you?"

Marguerite nodded.

Sheridan smiled his most persuasive, beguiling smile. "Then go with me. You'll enjoy your evening with me more than you will with your maid." When Marguerite made no reply, he added, "That girl who walked out of here is your maid?"

"That was Hortensia, my maid," Marguerite concurred. "But she's not my theater companion."

"Who?" Sheridan quizzed. "Juan?"

"As I said, Sheridan," Marguerite slowly, painfully began to explain, "you're no longer a part of my life. I—I—came here to meet a friend, Sheridan. We're going to the theater together."

"Who is *this* friend?" Sheridan's voice was hard and unyielding."

342

"Jordan."

"Jordan!" he thundered. "Jordan Reeves, the man who owns the plantation adjacent to yours! The man I've been competing with all these years!"

She nodded.

"What happened to his wife?"

"She died."

"How convenient! And he came running to get you and Blossom Hall?"

Anger, hot like molten lava, boiled inside Sheridan. Jealousy clutched his heart, constricting his breathing. He abruptly bolted up, his feet hitting the floor. Like a caged animal, he paced the floor.

"No, it wasn't like that at all. I went back home to check on Blossom Hall when Jordan's lease was up. As long as Susanna was alive, as long as you were alive, I'd refused to see him, dealing only through Sander. This time, when I learned about Susanna's death, I went to pay my respects to Jordan. And well . . ." Marguerite stammered, embarrassed to be confessing to Sheridan. "We—we discovered that we still— that—"

"Nay," Sheridan said, shaking his head, "don't be a'telling me that you love him, lass. I won't be believing that because I know you don't."

"Sheridan." Marguerite was finding the subject difficult to talk about. "Jordan and I . . . we're . . . well, we were thinking about marriage."

"That was before I came back, lass! Now ye can't be a'thinkin' that way." He smiled. "I know you, Marguerite LeFleur O'Roarke. Even if ye were free from me, even if I hadn't returned, ye wouldn't be a'marryin' Jordan Reeves."

The truth of Sheridan's comment irritated Marguerite. "I loved once. That was enough. Now I want to be loved."

"You need a strong man, lass, because you're a strong woman. Jordan Reeves is too weak for you."

"Please, Sheridan," she begged. "Get out of my life.

343

Officially Sheridan and Marguerite O'Roarke are dead. Let's leave it like that. I've built me a new life; build yourself one around your new identity." Her voice dropped to a whisper. "Please let me have a chance at happiness."

"With Jordan?" he sneered, the knife of jealousy and despair cutting him to the quick.

"He's the one I should have married."

"Maybe he's the man you should have married," Sheridan snarled, "but you didn't. You married me, and you're married to me. I want you. I want my wife."

"You want me now, but you didn't want me six years ago."

"Aye, lass, I wanted you six years ago, and I've wanted you every day since. Foolishness and pride stood in my way; they kept me from saying the words that would have kept you by my side." Deeply stirred, he lapsed into brogue. "After you left, I missed you so much that I thought I would go crazy." Sheridan closed his eyes, remembering the agony of those years, the loneliness he had felt. "I wrote you letter after letter."

"No," Marguerite exclaimed, shaking her head vigorously, "you didn't write me any letters! And you can't fault their not coming to me because of my purported death. You knew to write me in care of Sander Owen in New Orleans, and if you had, I would have received at least one of them. Not one letter did I receive in six years."

"No," he admitted, "you didn't receive a one. I said I wrote them; I didn't say I posted them."

"I wrote you," Marguerite quietly confessed, "and I posted them."

"I didn't get them."

"Not knowing how to reach you, Paddy suggested I write Bridget instead. In each letter I enclosed one for you which I asked her to deliver. I wrote you many letters through Bridget, but I never heard from you. So I drew my own conclusions."

"I never received the letters," Sheridan explained. "Chances are Bridget didn't either. Earl was after her, and she had to go into hiding."

"Where is she now?" Marguerite asked curiously.

Sheridan shrugged. "I don't know, lass. We're scattered all over the world by now."

A soft knock on the door interrupted them. "Señora, it will soon be time for us to meet Señor Jordan."

Marguerite walked to the table, picked up the key and unlocked the door. A vaquero stepped into the room. Despite his apparent middle-age, he held his back erect, walked lively, and his hair was jet black.

"Juan," Marguerite said, "this is an—an old friend of mine. Sheridan—" She looked at Sheridan, then said, "Sheridan McDevin. I knew him when I lived in Ireland." Sheridan's eyes narrowed, but he didn't correct her. "Señor McDevin, this is my gran vaquero, Juan."

"I am happy to make your acquaintance, Señor McDevin," Juan said, his handshake as firm as his voice was strong. After they had exchanged social amenities, Juan addressed Marguerite. "I have put Señor Reeves in a suite next to mine, señora. Shall I meet him at the dock by myself since you have company?"

Marguerite opened her mouth to speak, but Sheridan smoothly replied, "Please do. The señora and I haven't finished our visit."

Juan was surprised at Sheridan's impudence, but he said nothing. He could feel the undercurrent of tension. Saying his good-byes, he left.

"Don't you ever do that again," Marguerite barked as soon as the door closed.

Ignoring her, Sheridan grated, "Why Sheridan McDevin? Why not O'Roarke? Don't want them to know that I'm your husband?"

"You're the one who chose McDevin as your name," Marguerite parried. "Not me. And until I'm sure what role you're going to be playing in my life, you're Sheridan McDevin."

345

Shrugging, letting the subject drop for the time being, Sheridan asked, "What are we going to do about Jordan?"

"*We're* not going to do anything. Jordan is my concern."

"Wrong."

"Listen, Sheridan O'Roarke," Marguerite said. "You get out of here and leave me alone. I've been taking care of my life for the past six years, and I'll continue to do so. I don't need, nor do I want your interference."

"You don't need it; you don't want it, but you've got it, sweetheart." Sheridan grinned. "I'm back in your life, and there's not room enough for both me and Jordan. Now either you can tell Jordan about the returning husband, or I will."

"*You will not!*"

"I will."

Marguerite collapsed in the rocker, rubbing her hand over her brow. "Sheridan, you can't casually return to my life and pick up where you left off six years ago as if nothing has happened. Both of us have changed. Oh, Lord why don't you go away!"

"I can't, lass," he said, "no more than I can let you marry Jordan Reeves. I'm not dead, and I'm not planning on givin' ye a bill of divorcement. You belong to me, and I'll see to it that you'll not belong to another. Tell him tonight."

On those words Sheridan closed the door, turned and walked toward his rooms. He'd found Marguerite. This should be the happiest moment of his life, but it wasn't. She was in love with another man.

Marguerite pressed herself against the other side of the door, blinking her eyes, fighting the tears. "Damn you, Sheridan O'Roarke," she whispered, softly pounding her fists on the door. "Why did you have to come back into my life? Why?"

Chapter 21

Standing in the shadows in front of the theater, leaning against the railing, Sheridan watched Marguerite as she climbed out of the carriage. Like a callow youth, infatuated for the first time, his breath caught in his chest at her loveliness. Wearing a burnt orange and ecru dress, her only decoration a tortoiseshell comb in her hair, she was beautiful.

Sheridan's heart constricted when she looked at Jordan as if he were the only man in the world. She laid her hand in his, said something to him, and laughed, the soft tinkling sound reaching Sheridan's ears. He watched them walk into the building. Shoving away from the post, pulling his ticket from his waistcoat pocket, he looked at it for a long time.

Finally he wadded and dropped it into the street. He had contemplated attending the theater, but he decided against it. Knowing Marguerite was spending the evening with Jordan was one thing; watching them would be more than he could bear. Furthermore, he didn't want to push Marguerite too far. He would stand back and give her room. Turning, tilting the brim of his hat over his face, he returned to the Elegant Lady. Shoving through the thronging crowd in the saloon, he moved to a table in a secluded corner. He sat down beside his friend.

"Thought you had planned on an evening out," Stringbean commented dryly, never taking his eyes off the crowd that milled around.

"Changed my mind." Sheridan held his hand up. Seeing it, the bartender nodded his head. "Decided to see how I could do with the cards tonight." Sheridan watched Myra winding her way toward them.

Sitting down, she smiled her pleasure. "Either it didn't take you long to get culture tonight, or you didn't want culture tonight." When Sheridan didn't answer, she said, "Or maybe culture didn't want you."

"Myra, my love," Sheridan drawled, taking the whiskey that the bartender brought him, holding his glass up in front of him, "generally you know when to talk and when to be quiet. Tonight you seem to be transgressing your own rules. Will you kindly shut up and get off my toes?"

Myra laughed. "How about spending the evening with me, Rusty? I need someone to even the numbers and complete the couples."

"What kind of party?"

"The new commerce committee, husbands and wives. Dinner and speeches."

"Dull and boring," Sheridan quipped, finishing off his drink. The chair grated against the floor as he stood up. "No, thanks. I'd rather try my luck with the cards."

"You're in a nasty mood tonight, Rusty. Want to tell me about it?"

"No."

Rising with him, Myra laid her hand on his lower arm. "Rumor has it that some of the gentlemen won't be retiring with their wives, Rusty. Like you, they're looking for excitement with the cards. Hear tell they have a wad of money they just can't wait to lose."

"What time?"

"Eleven o'clock." Myra's eyes twinkled. "Escort me to dinner or no games."

Sheridan grinned. "Games, yes. Dinner and speeches, no. Absolutely not."

"I need you." She pouted cutely. "In more than one way."

"You don't need me." Sheridan tweaked the end of her nose. "You just need someone to even the numbers, sweet. Any man who's dressed halfway decently will do for the one way; any man who's halfway decent when he's undressed will do for the other."

"You're right," Myra conceded, totally unabashed by Sheridan's comment. "So I guess it'll be Mr. Emerson again." She chuckled softly. "I better go tell him. He'll be so happy to find out." Standing on tiptoe, she kissed Sheridan's cheek. "I do need you for later, darling. Meet me at ten-thirty in my suite."

Sheridan nodded.

"You don't know how much I appreciate this." Now she smiled coyly. "After the game, I'll be glad to show you how much."

"Got to get my sleep, love. We're leaving at sunup for San Antonio."

"I'm going to miss you."

"It's not like the end of the world, love," Sheridan gently reminded her. "I'll be coming back."

Myra smiled, pushing back her tears. Nodding her head, she said, "I know. Good-byes always make me cry."

As soon as Myra disappeared into the crowd, Stringbean said, "Carson at the livery stable said a train was advertising for scouts and riders. Moving out on Monday morning. Wanted to know if we wanted to wait and ride with them."

Sheridan shook his head. "Nope. We better get started in the morning. I'm curious about Power's letter." He looked at Stringbean. "What did you tell Carson?"

"Nothing yet. Told him I'd give him an answer in the morning. I weren't sure if'n you'd want to wait and ride with the woman," he quietly announced, his words holding no rancor.

He placed a hand over his mouth, veeing his second and third fingers over his lips. Sucking his jaws together, working them, he let go a stream of tobacco that sailed across the distance to land in the cuspidor.

"That feller over there," Stringbean said, nodding his head in the direction of the bar, "been scouting for some trading concern outta Matagorda. Got a mighty interesting yarn to spin." Sitting down again, Sheridan looked at the frontiersman Stringbean was talking about. "Saw signs of Injuns."

"Raiding party?"

"That's what's so interesting. He ain't sure," Stringbean replied. With a light springy movement he stood and silently moved to where the frontiersman stood. Tapping him on the shoulder, he said, "Come have a drink with us, friend, and parley a little bit."

Grabbing his mug of beer, the man smiled. "Thank ya kindly. Reckon I'd enjoy that." When he reached the table, he extended his hand to Sheridan. "Slim Smith."

While they exchanged introductions, Sheridan had their drinks refilled. Finally he said, "Stringbean says you saw Indians on your way here from Matagorda."

"Um-hum," Slim droned, swallowing his beer.

"Comanches, you think?"

"Comanches, I think. Cherokees, I think. Wacos, I think. Apaches, I think. Mexicans, I think. All of them I think maybe so," Slim answered, wiping his mouth on his sleeve. Stringbean and Sheridan looked at each, never uttering a word. "But it weren't no raiding party as fer as I could see. No black paint, and they wuz camped in a real secluded spot. Like they wuz hiding." His forehead wrinkled, and he squinted his eyes. "Looked like a parley to me." He flashed his toothless grin. "Of course, boys, I didn't git too near, so's I could be wrong." He lifted his mug, raised it to his mouth; then set it down again. "Funny thing, I'd swear I saw man in a Mexican general's uniform."

"Heat causes a man to see funny things," Stringbean drawled.

"Yep, reckon it do."

Sheridan ran his finger around the rim of his glass. "Where you headed from here?"

"I'm getting tired of traveling with these traders, so I'll reckon I'll be headin' on to San Antone," Slim replied, draining his mug.

"We're leaving in the morning," Sheridan replied. "You're welcome to travel with us."

"Mighty obliged," the man said. "Reckon I will." Rising he excused himself. "I thank you for the beer, gents, but I need to be hitting the hay. I'm pooped."

"Carson said a family struck out today for Victoria. Going alone. Hearing about the Injuns he tried to talk them into waiting until Monday so they could travel with a train, but they wouldn't hear tell."

Sheridan nodded. "I smell trouble, Stringbean, and big trouble."

"Yep," Stringbean returned. "Been brewing ever since them Comanches brought in that Lockhart girl last January."

"Seems like it's more than Comanches," Sheridan mused aloud.

"As I see it," Stringbean said, stretching his neck, cocking his head, and spewing tobacco juice into the cuspidor, "all the Injuns in Texas are joining together fer something big. Revenge probably." He lapsed into a pensive silence. Eventually he said, "I know who. I jest wonder where!"

"Maybe that's what the colonel wants to talk to us about. Maybe that's what Power is referring to."

"Could be," Stringbean muttered. "If ye'r gonna be here a spell, Rusty, I think I'll meander down the street ta see what's going on. Might stop by the stable and tell Carson that we're shoving out in the morning."

After Stringbean left, Sheridan tried to occupy himself with a game of cards, but he couldn't concentrate for thinking about Marguerite and her evening with Jordan. Finally he threw his cards in and quit. Shoving through the crowd, he walked out of the saloon, moving through the lobby to his room.

Without lighting a lamp or candle, he shucked his coat and threw it across the back of the sofa; he untied his cravat and dropped it on the reading table beside the French doors and then unbuttoned his waistcoat, tossing it into a nearby chair. He unlocked the doors and threw them open, walking out on the balcony. Because of the muggy heat, he tugged his shirt out of his trousers and unbuttoned it. In the dark he sat down in the cane-bottom straight chair, leaning back against the wall, and he thought about Marguerite.

His past rushed up to surround him, almost suffocating him with beautiful memories of Marguerite and her love. And today, when he'd seen her standing in the door, her face marked with fear, her hand over her mouth, he felt so foolish to think she still loved him, that they could begin all over again. Even later when he talked with her, he had labored under that same misconception. But now he wasn't so sure.

She was right. So much had happened, too much had happened, and both of them had changed. Changed too much for them to have a second chance. Yet Sheridan wanted her. His body ached with his need for her. His heart ached his loss of her with renewed pain. And Myra's promise of appreciation did nothing to alleviate that wanting and that hunger. A tear, hidden in the softness of night, escaped and trickled down his face. He loved Marguerite, and nothing mattered more to him than her happiness. *Was her happiness marriage to Jordan?*

He wasn't sure how long he'd been sitting here, when a soft light filtered onto the balcony and he heard muffled voices coming from Marguerite's room. Still he made no effort to go inside and get ready for the card game in Myra's apartment. When he heard the soft click of a lock, he turned his head in the direction of the sound.

He watched Marguerite walk out on the balcony and lean on the railing. The soft summer breeze caressed her cheeks and splayed through her hair, brushing wisps across her face. It whipped her dressing gown around her legs, outlining her slender figure.

"Did you tell him?"

Without turning, not surprised that he was there, Marguerite said, "Yes."

"And?"

"He suggested I get a bill of divorcement."

The legs of the chair thudded against the floor as Sheridan leaned forward. "The hell he did!" He moved toward her. "You're not getting a divorce!" He wasn't sure if he'd voiced a question or a statement, but either way he knew he'd voiced his fear.

"I'm thinking about it."

Sheridan's hands curled over the railing, tightly gripping into the wood. "I hate him," he seethed through clenched teeth. "I could wring his neck."

"Always the primitive, aren't you?"

"My God, Marguerite! I love you!"

"So does Jordan."

"But there's one major difference," Sheridan pointed out. "You don't love Jordan. You love me."

"You'd like to think so, wouldn't you?" She chuckled softly. "Your ego hasn't diminished one jot in the passing years."

Sheridan was irritated now; more, he was furious, but he held his emotions in check. "What's he going to do?"

"He's coming as far as San Antonio with me."

"I'll be damned!" Sheridan swore a second time.

"What are you going to do, Sheridan? Kill him?"

"If I have to," he grated. "He's not riding to San Antonio with you."

Exasperated, Marguerite explained, "It's as much to do with business as with me. He combined pleasure with business, Sheridan. He's going to San Antonio to look at cattle."

"That may be true," Sheridan conceded doubtfully, "but his main reason for traveling to San Antonio is to persuade you to get a divorce."

"I'd like to think so."

Sheridan made no further comment, and both lapsed into silence. Finally he asked, "What are you thinking about?"

"Nothing."

"Yes, you are. Like me, you've spent the entire evening remembering, Daisy. You've remembered the good times, the beautiful times, the loving times as well as the bad."

"Yes," she eventually whispered, "I have. I didn't see a thing; I didn't hear a thing that was going on around me. All I could think about was you."

"Doesn't that tell you something, lass?"

"Yes," she replied, looking down at the hubbub in the street. "This afternoon I was angry that you'd showed up at this point in my life, just when I was getting everything together again, but now . . ."

"But now . . ." Sheridan prodded when she didn't immediately explain.

"Now I realize that it's not as bad as I thought. Before I would have always wondered about you, about us, about my feelings for you. But now I know."

"And what do you know, lass?"

"I thought I didn't love you anymore, Sheridan." She swung her head, looking at him. In the dark she didn't see the expectant look on his face. "But now I know that I don't. I also learned that I don't hate you anymore." She smiled, turning toward him, straightening up. "Don't you see what this means, Sheridan?" When he shook his head, she said, "For all these years I've been emotionally bound to you, first in love, then in hatred. But now I'm free. I'm no longer emotionally bound. I don't love or hate you. I can divorce you without any doubts or recriminations. I'd be free to marry Jordan."

"But you're married to me," Sheridan reminded her, his heart almost bursting with hurt. "And I'll create such a scandal about a divorce that you'll never be respected again."

"I know. That's what I told Jordan." Her voice lowered. "I don't love you, but I'm married to you, legally bound to you."

Her words like a knife jabbed into Sheridan, not only cutting him, but twisting and gouging; the pain of losing her the second time obliterated reason.

"You do love me," he growled, resorting to primitive measures to prove the depth of their feeling for one another. He caught Marguerite in his arms, and he dragged her against his chest, binding her to him tightly. His mouth came down on hers in a desperate, urgent kiss, his lips grinding into hers.

Twisting in his arms, twisting her lips beneath his, Marguerite fought. In the struggle her comb fell out of her hair and slid across the floor. Her hands glided up his chest through the crisp, red hair, her fingers grazing his nipples, and she pushed. But with the touch of her flesh against his, dormant emotions awakened. She felt desire ignite in the core of her being, quickly blazing through every inch of her body. Momentarily her resistance flagged as she felt the betrayal of her body.

But she would not be betrayed a second time. Summoning all her strength, she pushed out of Sheridan's arms, lifted her hand and slapped him across the face, leaving the imprint of her hand on his cheek. Breathing deeply, she defiantly tossed her head, her hair tumbling around her shoulders.

"I told you not to touch me, Sheridan O'Roarke, and I meant it. You're not going to come sauntering into my life and pick up where you left off six years ago. I may be married to you, but I don't have to endure your advances and your pawing. We are through. What I felt for you is over. It's gone. If you take me, Sheridan O'Roarke, you'll take me by force."

Drawing in ragged gulps of air, he said, "I guess I had that coming." He gingerly rubbed his fingers over his bruised cheek. "I'm sorry. I didn't mean to hurt you." He waved toward her door. "Go on to bed," he breathed.

Slowly Marguerite moved toward the door. Before she stepped into the room, however, she turned and looked at Sheridan, but his expression was lost to the shadows. Pulling his shirt apart, he planted both hands on his hips, and he stared at her.

"You'll never convince me that you don't care for me." He heard the knock on his door. "And no matter how many times you tell yourself that you don't care about me, that you want a divorce to marry Jordan, no matter how loudly you may proclaim it, you'll never convince yourself."

Not wanting to hear his words because her heart was telling her the same thing, Marguerite said, "Someone's at your door."

"And mark my words, Marguerite LeFleur O'Roarke, I won't touch you again without your asking for it." He threw back his head and laughed. "And since you don't want anyone to know who I am or that we're married, I won't tell a soul. I'll let you be the one to decide when. But again, you can mark my words. It won't be long because you'll soon be begging me to make love to you."

The knocking was louder and more persistent.

"Rusty," Myra called.

"Rusty," Marguerite mimicked. "What an appropriate nickname."

"I called myself Dan McDevin, but Texans have a knack for placing a new name on a new face. My hair gave birth to this one." He grinned. "Believe me, Rusty was preferable to some of the others I heard."

"Rusty," Myra called again, "are you in there?"

"I'm out here on the balcony," Sheridan called. "I'll be there in a minute." But he didn't move.

"Come on," Myra called impatiently. "You promised to be in my room at ten-thirty. It's nearly eleven now." She laughed. "If you don't come on, your prize won't be waiting."

"You'd better go," Marguerite said, turning, walking into her suite. "You don't want to keep the lady waiting any longer. You don't want to lose your prize. And you'd better get it from her because you certainly won't get it from me."

"Marguerite," Sheridan called. She stopped, but she didn't look at him. "It's not what you think."

"I'm not thinking, Sheridan," she called over her shoulder. "Can't you get it through your head? I don't care what you do or whom you do it with." Her words mocked her as she shut the doors. She might convince Sheridan, but she knew she was lying. She was thinking; she did care.

Sheridan heard the grating of the key in the lock. Walking into his room, he moved directly to the lamp. Striking a match and holding it in one hand, he took off the globe and set it on the table. Then he lifted the chimney. He touched the wick, light flickering over the room. He walked to the door, unlocked and opened it.

"About time," Myra said, taking in Sheridan's disheveled appearance. "You're not even ready."

"I was tired," he replied absently. "I've been resting."

"Well, get dressed," Myra enjoined. "We don't have much time."

She ran to the sofa and picked up his coat and cravat. Looking around, she found his waistcoat where he had tossed it. When she grabbed it, a coin fell out of the pocket and rolled across the floor. Falling to her knees, she followed its flight with her eyes, reaching for it as it stopped its wobbly escape on the balcony. The palm of her hand landed on the coin, her fingertips on the tortoiseshell comb. Sheridan's coat, cravat, and vest in one fist, she picked the comb up with the other. Slowly she stood, holding it up for him to see.

"One of your friend's?" she said, her voice strange to her ears.

"No." Sheridan walked to where she stood. Taking his clothes and the comb from her, he said, "It belongs to the Señora Marguerite. She dropped it earlier."

Myra looked at the open doors. "She's—she's been here with . . ." Embarrassed because she thought she had interrupted something between Sheridan and Marguerite, hurt because it wasn't herself, Myra cried, "Rusty."

"Go on to your apartment, Myra," he ordered quietly. "I'll be along in a few minutes."

She nodded, slowly walking to the door. She didn't open it. She stood, her back to Sheridan. She whispered, "I'm sorry."

Because he liked Myra, he didn't want her to be hurt, but at the same time he intended to honor his promise. He would force Marguerite to acknowledge him and their marriage. He could be as stubborn as she.

So he said for the second time in the same evening, "It's not what you think. I was out on the balcony smoking a cheroot when the señora returned from the theater. Not knowing I was there, she came out for a breath of fresh air. Evidently the comb came out of her hair and slid across the floor."

After Myra left, Sheridan contemplated returning Marguerite's comb, but he thought better of it. Quickly he redressed, dropping the comb into his coat pocket. Blowing out the lamp and locking his room, he moved down the corridor to Myra's apartment.

Engrossed in his game, Sheridan had lost all count of time. His coat was hanging on the back of his chair. His waistcoat was unbuttoned, his sleeves cuffed several times. Leaning back in his chair, he looked at his cards and smiled at the man across the table.

"Your play."

Before the man could say a word, a sharp knock sounded at the door. Quietly so as not to disturb the men, Myra moved across the room, cracked the door, and peeped out.

"Need to speak with Rusty," Stringbean said.

"He's busy," Myra whispered. "Can't it wait?"

Stringbean shook his head, lifting his arm and shoving on the door at the same time. Silently he padded to the center of the room, to the table and the circle of light that illuminated four faces. He leaned over Sheridan and whispered in his ear. His gaze never straying from the men who huddled around the table, his expression never changing, Sheridan nodded.

When Stringbean withdrew as unobtrusively as he had

arrived, Sheridan said, "Gentlemen, I'll play out this hand. Then I must leave." Over the disappointed groans, he said, "But I'll leave you in the hands of Miss Myra. She deals and plays a pretty wicked game." He looked up at Myra and grinned. "I'm speaking about cards, gents."

After the hand, Sheridan pulled his coat on and walked out of the room and down the stairs. Moving to the back of the house, he entered the kitchen. Much to his surprise, he found Stringbean walking back and forth across the kitchen, bouncing a squirming, squalling baby in his arms.

"Is this our trouble?" Sheridan asked, a big grin creasing his face.

"The loudest part," Stringbean snapped, holding the dirty, bloodied baby out for Sheridan to see. "The Peterson baby. They wuz the hardheaded ones who wouldn't listen to Carson. Lit out by theirselves two days ago for San Antone. Attacked by Injuns, Myers says. Thought you'd be interested to hear what he's got to say."

The small man who noisily sopped bread in his beans vigorously nodded his head. He stopped eating long enough to say, "Riding through with the mail. Found the remains of the wagon and the family first. Little ways down I found Mrs. Peterson dead in a clump of trees in a ravine, the baby clutched to her chest. She wuz kinda on top of it. She musta laid that way intentionally, muffling its cries. Otherwise them devils woulda taken it."

"Which ones?" Sheridan asked.

"That's what's so peculiar," Myers said, cocking his elbow on the table, waving his bread through the air. "Seems to me like the Injuns are on the move. As I see it, different bands coming in. Appears to me, they're headed for the hills north of San Antone. I'd say about fifty miles north."

"Comanche stronghold. On the San Marcos River."

"Um-hum," Myers said, cramming the bread and a spoonful of beans into his mouth, chewing noisily.

"Where's Miss Myra?" Stringbean snorted, worried because the baby hadn't stopped crying since Myers arrived with it. "This baby needs some clean clothes and some food. Needs a woman's touch."

Sheridan grinned. "Myra's taking care of her guests." He moved to the cabinets, pulling open drawers. His hand full of rags, he walked to the fireplace, lifting a kettle of hot water which he poured in a dishpan. "Let's see what we can do to take care of it." Glancing at Myers, he asked, "How old do you think it is?"

Myers slurped his food from his spoon, and with his mouth full said, "About seven or eight months." He pointed his fork to the shoes. "Look at the toes. Scuffed up. I'd say it was old enough to be crawling about."

As Sheridan added the cold water to the pan, he said, "I think we're going to need a woman's touch, Stringbean. I can get the clothes off all right, but I'm not so sure about putting more on it."

While Sheridan talked, Stringbean nodded his head in agreement and walked to the door.

Unconsciously Sheridan said, "Will you go get Marguerite for me?"

Stringbean stopped dead in his tracks and looked at Sheridan, baffled. Not Miss Myra but Marguerite!

"Marguerite?" he questioned, breaking his cardinal rule of not repeating unnecessarily, but he didn't know a Marguerite.

"Yes, get the señora, the woman in number twenty-four. Myra has her hands full with her guests right now, and I don't want to create a stir."

"Lordy, boy, what do you think you're gonna create when I go pounding on the señora's door and tell her we have a squalling baby in the kitchen and Rusty McDevin wants her to come nurse it!"

"She'll come," Sheridan promised, keeping his eyes on the child, deliberately not looking at Stringbean. "Tell her that Sheridan sent you."

All Sheridan's actions since he'd entered the kitchen had

surprised Stringbean. Sheridan's asking him to go get the señora had baffled him. Sheridan's use of his Christian name dumbfounded the old man. But Stringbean never displayed his emotions, not by a flicker of the eyes or a twitch of a muscle.

With a curt bob of his head, Stringbean said, "I'll be right back with the señora."

"Well, Myers," Sheridan announced when he pulled the last, dirty piece of material from the baby's body, "the baby is no longer an it. It's a she."

"Good thing them devils didn't get her," Myers softly said. "Once they found her, they'd a'killed her along with the rest."

Sheridan's hands slipped over the child's chest, under her arms, and he picked her up, setting her in the pan of water. He sang to her softly, and as his big rough hands tenderly touched her, his voice did, too, both reassuring her. He bathed her, washing the grime away, singing and talking to her all the time. Her little body convulsively shuddered with deep sobs, but her screaming stopped. When Sheridan laid her on the towel on the counter to dry her, she balled a tiny fist and crammed it into her mouth and blinked the biggest, bluest eyes at Sheridan that he'd ever seen.

Sheridan laughed at her. He felt as if the baby were a part of him, his very own. "Hello, Daisy Belle," he crooned. "It's gonna be all right. Uncle Sheridan is going to take care of you." Looking at Myers, he asked, "Know anything about the family?"

"Can't say I do," Myers said, pushing his plate back. He wiped his mouth on his shirt sleeve, his hands on the legs of his trousers. Picking a splinter off the edge of the table, he poked between his teeth. "Purty big. Husband, wife, three boys, ranging from about twenty to six, two older girls, and the baby. All dead but that one. She be by herself now."

"No," Sheridan softly declared, "she's not by herself, Myers. If we can't find someone to take her, I'll keep her myself."

"Reckon you handle that mite purty good," Stringbean said,

returning to the kitchen as quietly as he had left. He walked directly to a window, poked his head out and spit. "But I don't see how no ranger without a wife can take care of a baby. Seems to me like you're lettin' your heart speak instead of your head."

"Probably," Sheridan answered, wrapping the towel around the baby. "But I know what it's like to have your family killed around you. I know what it's like to be all alone."

"Not many men alive who don't know all that," Stringbean dryly announced, refusing to let Sheridan become a victim of compassion and pity. "The señora said she'd be down as soon as she put on some clothes.

Picking Daisy Belle up, Sheridan laid her head on his shoulder and pressed her tiny body against his chest. Holding her against him tightly, he just swung from side to side, pressing his cheek against her head, softly singing to her. When Marguerite reached the kitchen, she stopped in the doorway, one hand on the casement, the other on her breast. For a second her heart lurched, and she thought she would pass out.

Would this giant of a man never cease to amaze her? she wondered. So much the fighter and the rebel rouser. The dissident. The insurrectionist. Big and brawny. But at the same time, she thought, her fingers gently curving around her neck, he was so tender and loving. She could hear the love and concern in his voice; she could see it every time his huge hand—the hand that had so skillfully wielded the bowie knife only hours before—engulfed the tiny piece of humanity in gentle love strokes. Marguerite could hear Sheridan's loneliness, his sadness. Her eyes filled with tears, and a knot formed in her throat, constricting her breathing. Her heart went out to the man.

"You—you sent for me."

Sheridan spun around and looked at her, the two of them transcending time and place. He saw the tears sparkling in her eyes, and he saw the love. Although it filled him with joy and gave him hope, he couldn't help but wonder if all the emotion was for the—for Daisy Belle.

"Thank God, you're here," Sheridan breathed. "We've got to do something for her. She's—"

"Yes, I know. Your friend told me." Marguerite took the baby from Sheridan and sat down at the table. As she cradled the infant in her arms, she rocked back and forth, listening as Sheridan told her what had happened.

"She's hungry," Marguerite said. "Put some corn and potatoes on a plate and mash them up. We've got to feed her." Bouncing the baby on her shoulders, she asked, "What's her name?"

"Daisy Belle," Sheridan replied thoughtlessly, using a fork to mash the food. When Marguerite turned to look at him, he said, "Her eyes reminded me of a woman I once knew."

Their eyes caught and locked. Marguerite smiled from the bottom of her soul, and she shook her head in amazement. At that moment Myra opened the door but was so surprised she didn't immediately move into the kitchen. The couple, lost in each other, drew her full attention.

From his perch on the windowsill where he viewed all that was happening, Stringbean laconically announced, "Ya got another guest, Miss Myra. She weren't here fer supper, but she's makin' up fer it now. Eatin' us outta house and home."

Breaking her gaze from Sheridan and Marguerite, Myra looked at the baby who cooed at her over Marguerite's shoulder. She smiled, her golden brown eyes filling with compassion.

"The Peterson baby," she murmured.

"You know her?" Stringbean asked.

"Not really. They needed some money to finish their trip to San Antonio, so I bought—" She shrugged, leaving the sentence hanging.

Stringbean didn't have to hear the rest of the sentence to know what Myra had done. She didn't believe in lending people money, but her carriage house was full of junk that she'd bought from them.

Sheridan shoved the plate of food across the table to Marguerite, and he watched as she dipped the spoon into the food and tipped it into the baby's mouth. Balling up her hands and throwing them in the air, kicking her legs, Daisy hushed her crying and grunted her approval.

"Do you want me to find her a home?" Myra asked, pulling another chair from the table and sitting down.

Sheridan wrapped one of Daisy's sable brown curls around his index finger. Curiously she lifted her face, smiled, and gurgled at Sheridan. She reached up, catching his fingers in her fist.

"I know a woman who just lost her baby," Myra continued, her eyes on Sheridan, an ache in her heart as she saw the expression in his eyes. She knew at that moment that he loved the señora, that he would never be hers. "She—she would be more than happy to take . . ."

Clean and full, Daisy leaned her head against Marguerite's breast and nuzzled her cheek. She was tired but fought sleep. When her little lids drooped, she suddenly jerked away, and she rubbed her eyes with the back of her hands. She squirmed. But Marguerite firmly pressed her head against her breast, holding her hand on Daisy's head and began to hum and rock.

Sheridan had always thought Marguerite was a beautiful woman, but tonight she was the loveliest he had ever seen her. He saw the beauty of her soul reflected in her face and eyes as she cradled the baby. This could have been their baby, he thought. His and Marguerite's. Unable to contain the sorrow that threatened to burst his heart, Sheridan abruptly moved.

"Mrs. Smith would love to have the baby, Rusty. She's a good woman—"

"May I take the baby back to the hacienda with me?" Marguerite asked, compelled to action by a driving force within her that she didn't completely understand. Her eyes were on Sheridan's back. "We have many niños who will be her brothers and sisters, and Jewel and I will take care of her as if she were our very own."

364

Sheridan spun around. "You don't have to."

Marguerite looked down at the sleeping infant. "I want to." Her eyes, as blue as the morning sky, sparkled. Spiritually she and Sheridan had been attuned; they had given birth to the child. "I feel as if Daisy were my own."

"That's settled then," Myra said, her voice unusually brisk. Spinning on her heels, she lifted her hand and wiped her eyes. She knew she had lost Rusty McDevin—lost him for good. He belonged to the Señora Marguerite O'Roarke de la Flor del Sol and to Daisy. Turning a smiling face to her guests, she said, "Good night, people. I'm calling it a night."

Her head held high, she walked out of the room toward her apartment. Stringbean and Myers mumbled their good nights and departed after Myra. Marguerite carefully wrapped the towel around Daisy and stood.

"Do you need me to help you?" Sheridan asked, reaching for Daisy, his hands grazing Marguerite's arms.

His touch was like a torch touching all her nerve endings, igniting a fire that trailed to the seat of her desire. She had to exert all the strength she possessed to smile at him as if nothing had happened. She laughed softly, the sound a mockery to her ears.

"I need to find some clothes for Daisy."

Unaware of the emotions blazing through Marguerite, Sheridan turned, once again rummaging through drawers until he found several cloths that would serve as diapers.

"This will do for tonight," Marguerite said. "Tomorrow I'll try to find something for her to wear on the trip home."

Holding the clothes in one hand, Sheridan picked up the lamp with the other and led the way out of the kitchen. When they reached her room, Marguerite said, "You'll have to help me. The key's in my pocket."

She moved Daisy and turned, thrusting her hip out. Tucking the cloths under her arm, holding the lamp in one hand, Sheridan reached into her pocket with the other, his fingers groping for the key. Taking advantage of the situation, he intentionally moved his hand as he chased the slippery metal. When his fingers touched her close to her most intimate place, Marguerite felt the fire shoot through her, and she drew in her breath.

Sheridan looked at her, devilish glints shining in the depth of his eyes. "Sorry," he apologized, totally unrepentant.

"I'm sure you are," Marguerite murmured, a slight shaking in her voice.

Sheridan chuckled as he swung the door open and led the way into the room. Setting the lamp on the nearest table, he reached for Daisy. Marguerite shook her head.

"Open the door to the bedroom and let me lay her down. The less we move her the better." The soft clothes tucked under her arm, Marguerite followed Sheridan to the bedroom. "I'll be back in just a minute to lock the door," she said.

While Sheridan waited, he eased his hand into his pocket, and he felt the comb. He pulled it out and looked at it. Then he dropped it on the nearest table.

Closing the bedroom door, Marguerite said, "Thank you for helping me."

Sheridan moved closer to her, so close his hands could touch her shoulders, so close she could feel the warmth of his breath. "I made a promise earlier today, Daisy Belle. One that's going to be sure hell to keep, but keep it I will."

Marguerite's body of its own volition swayed toward Sheridan. Their coming together was the most natural thing in the world. They melded together, their lips touching in a gentle beautiful kiss, the warmth of greeting soon turning into the burning heat of passion. Marguerite's arms circled his body, her hands climbing his back, her fingers finally clawing through the layers of material to reach the flesh beneath.

She moved her shoulders that imperceptible distance, her breasts grazing his chest. Sheridan's hands slipped down her spine and rested in the small of her back, his hands splaying across her buttocks. Gently he guided her to the thrust of his lower body. His mouth released her, and his lips feathered

366

across her cheeks and nibbled along her cheek and chin.

When his hand moved from her hip to her breast, Marguerite tensed. She realized who she was and where she was. Slowly she pushed out of his arms, pulling away from him. She knew that he had deliberately provoked the scene, but she couldn't blame him. She had been the one to initiate the intimacy.

"See, lass," he whispered, a tone of humble entreaty in his voice. "It's the same for both of us. You want me as much as I want you."

Holding her hands to her flaming face, she whispered, "I don't think it's wanting you in particular, Sheridan. Probably any man would do." She paused. "It's been six years since I've . . . since I've . . ."

Her words trailed into silence, but she didn't have to voice them for Sheridan to know what she'd been about to say. Anger whipped through his body as he recognized the truth of her statement, but he refused to accept it.

"No, lass," he whispered, "not just any man would do. If that were the case, you'd have been sleeping with one by now."

After Sheridan left, Marguerite didn't immediately return to the bedroom. She couldn't. Sleep was far from her. Battling her emotions, she paced back and forth in the parlor. Before Sheridan had returned to her life, she had been sure that she wanted marriage with Jordan. But now— She lifted her hand to her forehead. Sheridan was right; she wanted him—and only him!

Every emotion she had was keyed up to its highest pitch. Her needs which had lain dormant for so many years were surfacing. Yet she couldn't just wipe six years away as if they hadn't existed. She couldn't forget that Sheridan had made no attempt to reach her during that time. So many things which she couldn't forget.

Still Sheridan had been right about one thing this afternoon,

367

and she had been wrong. They did need to talk. Explanations were needed. Especially from her! She needed to talk to him. Marguerite walked to the table and picked up the lamp. Before she could take another step, she heard a soft rap on the door.

Sheridan, she thought, a smile trembling on her lips. Her heartbeat accelerating, she scurried to the door. She reached into her pocket, pulled out the key and inserted it in the lock. When she opened the door, she saw Myra Goodwin, standing in the corridor.

"May I come in?" she asked.

"It's quite late," Marguerite returned stiffly.

"I know it is," Myra replied, "but I want to talk with you. I have something for you."

Marguerite looked at the shawl which Myra carried in her hands. "Something . . . for . . . me?"

Myra nodded, brushing past Marguerite into the room. Walking to the sofa, she sat down, resting the object on her lap. Marguerite shut and locked the door and followed Myra to the sofa. She set the lamp on the nearest table, but she didn't sit down.

"Could I have a glass of whiskey?" Myra asked. "I'm a little nervous."

"Surely," Marguerite murmured, moving to the liquor table.

As she poured Myra's drink, the owner of the Elegant Lady said, "Rusty's leaving for ranger headquarters in San Antonio in the morning. I probably won't ever see him again." In front of Myra now, Marguerite handed her the glass. Taking it, Myra said, "I'm not being fatalistic, señora. I've always prided myself on being a realist."

She lifted the glass to her lips and drank greedily. She waved her hand to the chair across from the sofa.

"Sit down, please. What I've got to say will take some time." She watched as Marguerite complied with the request. "Even if Rusty comes back to Houston, he'll never come back to me." She smiled regretfully. "I had hoped that one day we . . ." She took another swallow of her liquor. Then she shook her head. "But that won't ever be, señora."

"Miss Goodwin," Marguerite began, "I don't know why you're confessing all this to me. You see—"

"Yeah," Myra said, "I see. That's why I came to you. I'm not a lady, señora; I'm called a woman of ill repute, but I have a brain, and I use it. I'm intelligent. I figured it out real quick. You and Rusty have something going."

Marguerite didn't attempt to deny it.

Myra set her empty glass on the sofa beside her, and she slipped forward. "Earlier Rusty gave me this to keep for him." She slipped the shawl off the music box. "He said it meant a lot to him and that no one was to ever know that it belonged to him."

She placed the jewelry box in Marguerite's lap. Marguerite ran her fingers over the polished finish. She wound it and lifted the lid, listening to the soft, plaintive melody that filled the room. She closed her eyes, going back in time and place, going back in years—to the day that Brice had brought the box to her and Paddy. She remembered giving it back to Sheridan when she left Ireland. Tears, unbidden, trickled down her cheeks.

"It belonged to his mother," Marguerite told her. "The only possession of hers that he has left."

"Would you keep it for him?" Myra asked, standing. "I have a feeling that he would want you to have it."

"But he gave it to you," Marguerite said, suddenly jarred from her reminiscences. A small ache inside her at the thought of Sheridan's giving the music box to Myra, she jumped to her feet. "What will he think about your giving it to me?"

Understanding Marguerite's feelings, Myra smiled and patted the other woman's lower arm. "This is what he would want. When he drops by my apartment in the morning on the pretense of telling me good-bye but really for the purpose of getting the box, I'll tell him that I gave it to you. He'll tell me that he wants to give it to Daisy, and I'll pretend that I believe him."

"You love him, don't you?"

"Very much," Myra said. "So much that I can't stand to see the haunted look in his eyes. So much that I'm stepping aside so he can find happiness."

"Have you . . . are you . . ." Marguerite stammered, then quickly apologized. "I'm sorry. I have no business to pry into your personal life."

"No, you don't," Myra replied, her smiling taking the sting out of her voice, "but I can understand why you'd want to know. You love him, too." Before Marguerite could protest, Myra said, "So I'll tell you. No, we haven't. Not because I didn't want to, but he wouldn't. Something always kept us apart, señora." She paused. "His wife."

Myra flipped the key in the lock, extracted it, and laid it on the washstand. Her hand closed over the doorknob. She twisted and pulled on the oak panel, walking into the corridor.

"He loves you."

Myra slammed the door, her words echoing through the room.

Chapter 22

Two riders on horseback topped the hill, stopping beneath the shade of a lone scrub oak; behind them trundled an ox-drawn wagon train, a billowing cloud of dust trailing it. Eight long, exhausting days out of Houston; one more to go, Sheridan thought. He lifted his hand to shield his eyes against the glare as he scanned the horizon for some sign of the returning scout. Seeing nothing but swirls of dust ahead and puffs of smoke, he turned in the saddle and held his hand up, stopping the train.

His white cambric shirt, partially unbuttoned, wet with perspiration, clung to his shoulders. His chin was shadowed with a day's beard growth. Sliding his hat back, he lifted his arm and wiped the perspiration from his forehead with his sleeve. Pushing forward in the saddle, squinting into the mid-afternoon sun, he once again peered into the distance, this time skyward.

"They speak mighty quiet, don't they?" Stringbean said, his alert eyes sweeping around in constant vigil.

Tilting the brim of his hat and readjusting it, Sheridan nodded his head. "Have you seen it?"

The other man spit. "Yep."

Both looked at the billows of smoke that dotted the sky.

"Thinking what I'm thinking?"

"Yep."

"I'll be glad when Juan gets back," Sheridan said. "I'm getting a little worried. I don't like it. I'll be glad when he can tell us something."

Stringbean wiped his arm across his face. "We don't have ta be a'knowin' how to read the smoke, Rusty, and we don't have ta have a scout a'tellin' us afore we know. Both of us sorta been feeling 'em all day."

The saddle creaked as Sheridan stretched and twisted, waving his hand and yelling to the wagon train, "Roll on!"

"Reckon we need to make as much time as we can." Stringbean said. "Get as far as we can. Need to reach the next water hole by dark so we can camp. I'll go alert the men."

Pulling the reins, Sheridan turned his horse and nodded. "While you're doing that, I better get back to the señora. She's going to be screaming about not stopping until we reach the river."

"Yep," Stringbean said, "she will, and you oughtta." Dryly he added, "I'm still trying to figure out who's wagonmaster on this here trip." When Sheridan glared at him, he chuckled softly, peering over his shoulder. "Her and that greenhorn are mighty thick."

"Yep," came the thick reply. Sheridan didn't like being reminded that Marguerite enjoyed Jordan's company.

"Can't figure you out though," the old scout said. "Saturday night she was Marguerite. Sunday morning she was the señora. Last night when ya'll was playing with Daisy, she was Marguerite again. How come she keeps hopping back and forth? Can't ya make up your mind which she is?"

"I can," Sheridan replied. "She can't."

"Want to tell me about it?" Stringbean asked. He grinned, displaying uneven, stained teeth. "I'd shore like to hear about it."

"It's a long story."

But Sheridan's curtness didn't deter Stringbean. "It's a long ride to San Antone," he returned philosophically, his eyes on

372

the coded smoke in the distance. "If'n we don't run into some Injuns, we'll have plenty of time for talk. And if'n we do run into some Injuns, we may never have no more time to talk. The way I see it, boy, it's time to talk."

Sheridan lifted his hand, gave his hat a final tug and looked over his shoulder at Marguerite and Jordan. He grinned when his eyes settled on Marguerite. She was wearing a shirt and trousers. Her hair was pulled into a knot on the top of her head, and she wore a broad-brimmed hat to shield her face from the sun. Like the men she carried a rifle and wore a gun belt around her waist; inserted in it were a knife and a pistol. Unlike the men, she carried a whip in her right hand.

Jordan, on the other hand, was fully and elegantly dressed in formal morning wear, clearly the greenhorn whom all the vaqueros and the wagoners enjoyed teasing. He wore his tall hat, white shirt, cravats, waistcoat, overcoat—but they were no longer crisp and clean; they were wilted and stained with dirt and perspiration. Sheridan shook his head as he watched Jordan mop his face and neck with the white handkerchief, trimmed in lace.

Reeling around, Sheridan galloped down the line of wagons until he was even with Marguerite and Jordan.

"This heat in unbearable," Jordan grumbled. "The sun is literally baking me alive. How long before we rest?"

"Texas summers are always hot," Sheridan returned curtly. People irritated him when they complained about conditions that were beyond their control. "Thought I'd tell you that we're not resting until we make camp for the night, and we're not making camp for the night until we reach the river."

"What do you mean?" Marguerite sputtered indignantly.

"Exactly what I said, lass. We're not resting until we make camp."

"We've been riding since before daylight. I'm tired, hot, and hungry."

"Good. You can be a'thankin' God that you're tired, hot, and hungry. When you feel, madam, it means you're alive, and

373

I'm doing my very best to see that you stay alive," Sheridan barked. "If you weren't tired, hot, and hungry, you'd be dead."

As soon as the words passed his lips, Sheridan regretted his tirade. It was a childish and jealous reaction. But he was tired, hot, and hungry, too. He was irritated because Jordan persisted in clinging to Marguerite. His nerves were on end. More he was concerned about getting all these people safely to San Antonio. With the frequent and recurring signs of Comanches whom they were encountering, his concern was growing.

"Looks like we'll be joining up with another wagon train fairly soon," Jordan surmised, taking his hat off and rubbing his handkerchief over his head. "Look at the smoke from their campfire."

"That's Comanche smoke signals, Mr. Reeves," Sheridan announced dryly, barely concealing his impatience with the planter. "That's why we're pushing these dumb animals as fast as we can. Probably every Indian for a hundred miles in any direction knows we're out here. Looks like we'll be running into a raiding party fairly soon."

"In that case, Mr. McDevin," Marguerite began, "don't you think it would be better if we—"

"No, ma'am, I don't!" he gritted angrily. "When I do, I'll let you know. Until then, *please*, carry out my orders."

"Look, Sheridan," Marguerite yelled, "you gave me no choice but come with you. But I don't have to take—"

"Marguerite, I have enough to worry about without your arguing over every order I issue. Will you please quit your griping and let me do my job."

Nudging his horse, he galloped away, showering Marguerite and Jordan with a cloud of dust. Eight days of Marguerite's continually questioning his orders and judgments. Eight days and seven nights of being in close proximity with her. So close to her but so far away. The wanting and needing hurting him so bad he could hardly stand it. But he was as stubborn as she. He was determined that she would make the first move. So far she hadn't, and that grated on him. She seemed to enjoy Jordan's company and sought it out more than his. All this, coupled with his concern about Indians, was too much. He'd be glad to get to San Antonio. There Jordan and Marguerite parted company. For good! He'd see to that!

"I don't know why he's so irritable," Marguerite muttered. "He's been like this ever since we left Houston."

Jordan understood. He knew exactly what Sheridan was feeling. "He loves you."

Staring after him, Marguerite mumbled, "So he says."

Jordan opened his mouth to say more, but his words were cut off by Marguerite's sudden jerk in the saddle and her craning head. He followed her gaze, and he saw the two men galloping their horses full speed toward the train.

Marguerite suddenly yelled, "Something's wrong." She sped to the front of the wagon train, leaving Jordan to follow.

"Indians," Juan shouted as he and Smith rode up. "Comanches. Not far behind."

He didn't have to shout the warning a second time. Nor did Sheridan have to give any orders. Stringbean had quietly alerted all the wagoners, who smoothly and immediately corralled the double-wing ox train. They maneuvered the tandem wagons, so that the two wings swung out simultaneously. As the arc formed, the wagon tongues faced inward. Wagon wheels jammed against each other, forming a solid phalanx, impenetrable except for one or two openings.

Fortification and defense began. The animals were unhitched and herded inside the corral. The men positioned themselves, loading their rifles and propping them against the wagon. Hortensia hid Daisy in a safe place and dropped to the ground, moving all the ammunition to a central location, so she could run unimpeded to reload rifles and deliver ammunition.

But the Indians took their time; they didn't attack immediately. Even though they gauged the passing hours by the movement of the sun, unlike the white man, they were not yet prisoners of time. Still they used it most effectively as a weapon against those who were.

The minutes dragged into hours. The travelers waited and nothing happened. Never relaxing their vigil, but giving no indication of their apprehension, the vaqueros and wagoners softly talked and jested with one another. Sheridan, Stringbean, Juan, and Smith, seasoned Indian fighters, stood equal distances apart inside the corral, their eyes straining in the distance. Although they were nervous and apprehensive— even scared—they were patient, ready to shout orders in an instant, determined not to start the battle prematurely.

"How long are we going to sit here?" Jordan called, crouching behind a wagon, his eyes scanning the horizon. "I don't see a damned thing except the heat waves, and I can't take much more of this waiting. We're wasting our time. We could be making time instead of cowering like cowards behind these wagons."

"Just 'cause you don't see nothing," Stringbean said, pulling a plug of chewing tobacco out of his pocket, "don't mean there ain't nothing to see." Holding the plug in his hand, he turned it over several times and blew on it before he took a bite. His mouth full, he mumbled as he chewed and stuffed it into the pocket of his jaw: "Seeing nothing generally means there's something out there—a Comanche. There ain't no swirl of dust in the air, and there ain't no more smoke talk, so they're out there, all right. Just gettin' us jittery. Playing a game of nerves with us. Getting the edge on us. Hoping we'll give up and move on out, spreading out so they can get the animals easier."

"If that's all they want, give 'em the animals then," Jordan grated.

"That isn't all they want, señor. The Comanches want our scalps to decorate their tepees and victory poles." Juan spoke softly. After a moment the vaquero turned to Sheridan. "They are coming, Señor McDevin."

Sheridan nodded. "Wait until we see the whites of their

eyes, boys. Don't shoot until I give the signal. We can't afford to waste any ammunition, and we don't know what tactic they will use to begin the battle."

Stringbean spit. The other three men moved to their positions. Between the two rangers, Jordan crouched behind a wagon. He heard the thudding hooves; then he saw the horses, wheezing as they raced into view. Jordan's eyes widened with incredulity. Dropping his gun and straightening up, he chuckled softly. He waved his hand in the direction of the herd.

"There's your Indians." Jordan's chuckle grew into mocking guffaws. "Nothing but a herd of wild horses."

"No, señor," Juan said, "that is no *caballada* of wild horses. Those are the Comanches. Only trained horses would circle the wagon train like these are doing." Juan continued. "The Comanches are excellent horsemen, Señor Jordan. They love their horses, and their horses love them. Even if the warrior is killed in battle, the horse will not willingly desert him. If you watch closely you will see a show of horsemanship like you've never seen before."

"Without seeing a rider, how can you say these are Comanche horses?"

"They brand 'em," Stringbean answered before Juan could reply. Without realizing it, the ranger released some of the tension that was building in him. "About two and a half inches from the point on one ear for the braves, on both ears for the chief."

Jordan squinted through the heated glaze of the summer afternoon, through the dust that swirled around the horses that raced around the corral. Perspiration broke out on his face and in his palms. Reaching up, he wiped his forehead with his sleeve, knocking his hat off. Around and around the riderless horses went.

"Why can't we see some sign of them?" Jordan hissed.

"Because they don't want us to. The Comanche can hang his

377

body under the horses's belly or neck when fighting. And he can shoot from any position on the horse—accurately—deadly."

"How do you know so much about the Comanches?"

Juan didn't immediately reply; he deliberated giving the question an answer. Eventually he said, "I am half Comanche, señor. My mother was a Comanche, captured by another tribe and traded to the whites when she was a young woman. Before she could be returned to her people, she fell in love with and married my father. But she never forgot her people, their history, or her language. She taught me all she knew about it."

Jordan's question answered, Juan lapsed into silence, his eyes never leaving the circling horses. Suddenly the red men, with spine-tingling shrieks, reared up and straddled their animals. Frightened, Jordan started, shrinking against the wagon box, cold sweat popping out all over his body.

"Do not be alarmed, señor," Juan consoled. "They will not fight for a while yet. At the moment they wish to taunt us."

"I hope they know that," Jordan sputtered, his voice a parody of its usual resonant timbre.

Understanding the tenderfoot's fear, the gran vaquero chuckled softly. "Sí, señor, it is true. Mira! They are being careful. They are not close enough for us to fire on them."

Peering around the wagon, Jordan watched the five warriors do feats of horsemanship that defied any he had ever seen before. They seemed to be an extension of the horse himself. Holding on to the horses' manes with one hand, they stood; then they jumped to the ground and ran, easily mounting and dismounting. Never turning loose of the mane, each warrior ran beside his horse, leaping gracefully from one side to the other. Finally when all of them were once again astride their horses, they rode away.

To the people huddled in the circle of wagons, the silence after the Indians left was heavier than it had been before they came. Anxiety ate on their nerves; every little noise caused them to jump. The heat of the sun unmercifully pelted down on them.

After what seemed like hours but was only about half an hour, Stringbean said, "About time."

"*Sí*," Juan murmured.

Jordan looked from Sheridan to Juan to Slim. All three nodded their heads in the affirmative. His grip on the gun tightened, and he braced himself for the worst. He heard the soft whinny of a horse long before he saw anyone; then he saw the lone rider slowly approach the wagon train. Jordan raised his gun.

"Don't shoot." Sheridan softly called the command but his words could be heard all around the corral. "He's here to parley. Let's hear him out."

When he was within shooting distance, the young brave stopped. Dangling from his saddle horn was a braided rawhide lariat. Over the Indian's shoulder hung a quiver, filled with arrows. In one hand he held his bow, and strapped on the same arm was a rawhide shield tanned so that it was flint hard, feathered, medicined, and painted to represent the sun. Inside the red circle and rays of the sun, the warrior had painted his tribal symbol.

Jordan inched up to Sheridan. "What's he wanting to talk about?"

"Valor and prowess as a warrior," Sheridan replied curtly.

"He will issue a challenge for single combat," Juan elucidated.

With a movement that was so swift and graceful that an untrained eye couldn't detect it, the warrior hurled a lance through the air, the point so sharp it sank easily into the hard, dry soil, the shaft whining as it vibrated. At the same time the brave's hands moved in the silent language.

"What's he saying?" Jordan asked.

"He's asking if anyone of us will answer his challenge, or like all white men are we cowards who will shoot him down

379

from behind the wagons with a long gun."

Juan, Stringbean, and Smith moved to where Sheridan stood.

"Whatcha gonna do?" Stringbean asked.

Sheridan shrugged. "I have no choice but to accept."

"Shouldn't be much of a contest," Jordan said, his narrowed eyes running over the youth. "He's not much more than eighteen or nineteen."

"With as many years' training to be a warrior," Stringbean announced, "these here devils have training camps all over where the young bucks are taught to be warriors." He lifted his arm, brushing it across his face, wiping the perspiration from his forehead. "If they survive that training camp, mister, ya can bet they're ready for war and battle, and ya kin know they're skilled in the art of killing their most deadly enemy—the white man."

Marguerite reached the men in time to hear the conversation. Then she heard the young brave taunt them in Comanche. She looked at him, sitting on his horse outside the corral, his face painted black for war. Slowly moving her head, she looked at Sheridan, wondering what he was going to do.

When the brave taunted a third time, a young vaquero pushed to the middle of the group that hovered around Sheridan. "Señor," he said, "I will answer the challenge."

"No, if anyone goes," Sheridan replied, "it'll be me."

When Marguerite heard Sheridan's reply, her heart sank to her feet.

"No," the vaquero said, shaking his head, giving voice to Marguerite's sentiments. "You are the wagon master. Your duty is to protect the people, and see that they arrive in San Antonio safely." He smiled, flashing even white teeth. "I will go."

When Sheridan shook his head, Juan said, "I do not say that Joaquin should be sent, Señor McDevin, but I must agree with him. You should not go."

"My God," Jordan grated. "Why shouldn't he go? A man

trained to be a Texas Ranger should be able to defeat that boy easily. I don't care how long or how well he's been trained."

Ignoring Jordan, Juan said, "I have seen this many times during my long life, señor. This is a raiding party of young men who are, so to speak, earning their spurs. The young warrior will call out and defeat as many in single combat as will come." The old man smiled gently. "We cannot afford to lose you in the beginning. Even if the Indians do not kill you they will fight us." The Mexican pointed to the hill. "See the great chief and his closest counselors are not taking part in the battle."

Sheridan glanced at the three mounted warriors on the hill; he looked at the one who waited immediately outside the corral, his position not having changed since he'd issued his challenge. The group inside the wagons could hear the jeers and taunts of the other warriors who remained out of sight.

Sheridan returned his gaze to Juan. "Ask him if the raid will end if I can defeat him."

Knowing the Indians would not kill him as long as they were parleying over the challenge, Juahn stepped over the wagon tongue, outside the protection of the corral. Speaking Comanche, he repeated Sheridan's question.

As if he were sculpted from stone, the brave stared at the vaquero, not so much as a muscle twitching. The only movement Juan could see was the blinking of those cold, black eyes. The Mexican was apprehensive, but he hid his emotions. He stared directly into the Comanche's face. Eventually the brave nudged his horse, rode to the lance and pulled it from the ground. Brandishing the spear in the air, he spit on the ground, openly showing his contempt for the white man's cowardice. Shouting something in Comanche, he rode away. Juan waited until the warrior was out of sight before he turned and moved into the confines of the wagon fort.

"What was he saying?" Jordan demanded.

"He calls all of us cowards."

"Then why in the hell wouldn't one of you stand up to him," Jordan scathed, stamping toward the wagon tongue. "That would have ended this whole thing. I'll go out there myself."

"No, señor," Juan said, his hand clamping around Jordan's upper arm. He pulled him around. "The challenge was merely a ploy to draw our men out and kill them one by one, and we cannot afford to lose one life unnecessarily." His fingers uncurled, and he loosened Jordan. "Bravery and foolishness are two different qualities, señor. Out here on the frontier we learn quickly to differentiate between them. Those who are foolish die early; those who are brave live to fight another day."

Sheridan nodded. "No matter how much the Indians may taunt us, we're staying right where we are."

Stringbean jerked his head and spit, a brown stain circling the dry, cracked soil.

Turning to Juan, Sheridan spoke. "Take care of the señora, Hortensia, and the baby, Juan. Your first duty is to see that they get out of this safely."

Blood-curdling yells pierced the quiet—war whoops that were unequaled by any other tribe of Indians. Hardly had the men inside the corral moved into their positions when they heard the thudding hooves. Indians, their faces painted black, rushed out of no where from all directions, making assault after assault. They sent volleys of arrows flying into the compound which the vaqueros answered with volleys of bullets.

An arrow pierced Sheridan's hat, knocking it off his head. Too busy shooting, he didn't take time to retrieve it or to cover his head with anything else, and in the afternoon sun, his auburn hair glistened copper, a temptation for any Indian. Even at a distance he could be distinguished from the rest of the frontiersmen. He yelled orders and kept his eyes peeled for holes in their wagon defense. Hortensia scurried around the compound, loading rifles and tending the men's wounds.

Then, as suddenly as they came, the Indians were gone, and the day was uncannily quiet. Speaking words of encouragement, checking on the ammunition, the supplies, and the wounded, Sheridan moved about. Satisfied that all was well, he returned to his post.

Dazed, never having been in an Indian fight in his life, Jordan slumped to the ground behind the wagon. He didn't move. He had learned during the past hour that if he wanted to stay alive he had to listen to and obey orders. He admired and respected Sheridan; albeit, he gave his admiration grudgingly.

Jordan pulled the dirty handkerchief out of his pocket and wiped his face and neck. Breathing heavily, he held the piece of cloth by two opposite corners and twirled it into a band which he tied around his forehead. He was perspiring so heavily, the moisture ran into his eyes, burning and blurring his vision.

Juan walked by. "Are you all right, señor?"

Jordan nodded at the gran vaquero. "I think so. I haven't had time to think about it yet."

Walking to the back of the wagon, Juan looked around.

"Is it over?" Jordan asked.

"No, señor," Juan returned softly. "The Comanches enjoy playing games with human lives. They are regrouping. Making us wait and wonder."

Stringbean ran his tongue between his lip and bottom gum and dislodged his cud. Spitting the soggy wad of tobacco on the ground, he walked to the water barrel and filled the dipper. He took a swallow of water and sloshed it around, rinsing his mouth out. Then he took a long drink. Returning to his position, slumping a shoulder against the wagon box, he pulled the plug out of his shirt pocket a second time. Ramming it into the corner of his mouth with precision, clamping down with his teeth, he gnawed off another bite. He chewed it, getting it thoroughly wet before he dropped it into his jaw. He spit the shredded bits and pieces out of his mouth and replaced the slowly diminishing plug to his shirt.

"Care for a chaw?" he asked Jordan.

Jordan shook his head.

"You fight purty good, mister."

"Thanks," Jordan replied, warmed by the praise. He stood

up, propping his gun against the wagon. Shrugging out of his coat, he threw it to the ground. He shed his waistcoat and his cravats, running his hand around his collar. "Feels good to get out of this," he said. He walked to where Sheridan stood. "When will they stop?"

"Indians have three times to stop fighting," the wagon master explained. "When we're all done in, when they have no more braves left to fight, or when they lose their chief."

"Which do you think will be the answer?"

"Never can tell," Sheridan answered noncommittally, his eyes grazing the hill where the three warriors remained. "I figure we got a fighting chance. Can't ask for too much more than that."

"Do you hate them?"

"The Comanches?" Sheridan asked. Jordan nodded. "No, I don't hate them. They're vicious and cruel, but I can understand them somehow. Strangers come in, take over your land, change your way of living, your religion. Drive you out so they can have what you've got. Not unlike what I experienced in Ireland, Mr. Reeves."

"Who's the Comanche chief?" Jordan asked curiously.

"They have many," Sheridan explained. "Each band is autonomous. I think Swift Horse is the chief of this particular group."

"You've seen him?"

"No, I saw his son." Again his gaze went to the hill, and he pointed. "If I'm not badly mistaken, that's Swift Horse sitting on the hill watching."

Jordan turned and looked at the three riders. "Afraid of fighting?"

"No, he's letting his boy spread his wings. This is the young one's battle. If he wins, it's feathers for him and a victory. It's scalps for his tepee." Changing the subject, Sheridan asked, "So far, Mr. Reeves, how do you like it out West?"

Rubbing his hand over his chin, still looking at the statue-still figures, Jordan said, "I don't. If you don't die from the elements, you'll die from the Indians. Marguerite must be convinced to get out of this savage wilderness and return to civilization. This is no life for a woman."

Sheridan's eyes narrowed, but otherwise his expression never changed. "Be some who say it isn't."

"If you love her, you'll persuade her to go."

"I love her too much to persuade her one way or the other," Sheridan replied.

"Here the devils come." The cry sounded throughout the compound.

Conversation stopped; men hunkered down. Jordan ran back to his position, dropped to his knees, grabbed his gun and waited. The charges began again; the yelling, the flights of arrows, the grotesque riders with painted features circling the train. Jordan pulled back behind the wagon to reload his rifle. He heard a groan and saw a young vaquero, an arrow in his chest, fall across the wagon tongue.

"Pedro!" Hortensia screamed.

Throwing his gun aside, Jordan leaped outside the safety of the ringed wagons and grabbed the wounded man. Oblivious to the frenzied cries, the arrows whizzing by, and the thudding hooves, he caught the vaquero by the feet and dragged him back to safety.

Jordan had pushed the wounded man under the wagon out of danger, but he was still exposed when he looked up. An Indian—an extremely young Indian, his face smeared with black paint, his features grotesque, his eyes flashing with contempt and hatred—looked into Jordan's eyes. Jordan froze. He'd never seen such intense hatred in all his life.

Taking advantage of the white man's transfixion, the Comanche drew back his arm and hurled his spear, sending it through Jordan's chest. With a muffled groan, Jordan stumbled and fell to his knees, finally crumpling into an unconscious heap. The Indian, pulling his knife from his waist, leaped off his horse and ran to Jordan to finish his task. He grabbed the white man by the hair, jerking his head up.

About to reload, Marguerite hastily scanned the circle. Seeing what was happening to Jordan, she raced across the compound. Throwing down her empty gun, she relied on her whip. With dexterity and skill that came from years of practice, she fanned her hand, the whip singing through the air, her fingers curling tightly around the handle. Suddenly a crack louder than a bullet sounded, and the rawhide snaked the Indian's upper body, biting into his flesh, clamping his arms to his side. Startled, he turned an angry visage on the woman.

His immobile countenance never changed, but inside he smiled. His obsidian eyes ran the length of her slender frame, clearly defined by her shirt and trousers. What a prize he'd found. He would be the envy of the tribe if he returned with a slave like her. Forgetting Jordan, forgetting the battle that raged around them, the brave spread his arms out, easily unwinding the whip, and slowly walked toward the woman. Marguerite faced her foe with calm and confidence. Slowly she walked toward him. Not in the least intimidated by his cold stare, she returned his gaze unflinchingly.

With a graceful movement, she drew back her arm a second time, the leather thong gracefully sailing through the air. She flicked her wrist, directing all her energy into the weapon she wielded. The whip cracked, the rawhide wrapping around the Indian's hand. She stiffened her arm, yanked, and pulled the Indian off balance.

Stronger than Marguerite, the Indian braced himself, his toes digging into the ground. He flipped his wrist several times, threading the leather around it. Falling to his knees, he jerked, pulling the whip out of her hand, causing her to fall. Quickly he leaped to his feet, grabbed his knife and ran toward her. When he fell on her, the gleaming blade was aimed directly at her heart. Screaming, Marguerite rolled out of the way, but the blade never touched her. When she opened her eyes, Sheridan straddled her body, his bowie knife in hand.

"Come on, ye filthy bastard," he softly swore, emotion spawning his thick brogue. "Fight a woman ye can! Well, now, let's be seeing how well ye can fight a man."

The young brave slowly pushed to his feet, glaring at the white man, hissing his hatred. Using a battle tactic for which the Indians were famed, he tried to instill fear through an unwavering stare. He never took his black eyes off Sheridan; he never moved. But the young brave saw no fear in the white man's eyes, no trembling in the hands. Suddenly the youth realized that Sheridan had outmaneuvered him. Rather than taking Sheridan prisoner visually, the youth had become the white man's prisoner.

Holding his hands out, the warrior began to circle. Anticipating the Indian's movement, Sheridan swung at the same time that the brave did. The Comanche danced out of the way of the first swing, but the second one hit its mark. Sheridan gave the brave a chopping blow to his right hand a little above the knuckles, cleaning all the flesh off of four fingers down to the bone, the knife lodging against his knuckles.

Grimacing his hatred, never showing his pain, the Indian lunged toward Sheridan, his knife jabbing into Sheridan's shoulder, his blood mixing with that of the white man. Sheridan felt the searing pain and the intense burning; his arm went numb. Closing his eyes, breathing deeply, he used all his strength to push the youth away. He brandished the knife through the air, one slice quickly and efficiently disemboweling his assailant.

Blood gushed out of Sheridan's wound, staining his shirt bright red, but it didn't deter him. Picking up the body of the young chief in both arms, he held it up and walked across the compound.

"No," Marguerite cried, leaping to her feet, racing after him. She reached out, clasping Sheridan's arms. "You can't go, Sheridan." Her voice died to an agonized whisper. "You can't."

Time hung suspended as Marguerite and Sheridan stared at each other. Only they existed. The blue eyes reflected a mixture of anguish and pleading; the green eyes, though cloudy with pain, apologized tenderly.

"Aye, lass, I must. I have no other choice."

"I—I have so much to tell you—so much that I must tell you. I don't want you to die."

"Remember, lass, I'm the lad that even death doesn't want." Strong white teeth flashed as Sheridan smiled. "We'll have plenty of time to talk later. I promise, Daisy Belle."

Sheridan turned, strode across the compound, and stepped over the wagon tongue. Standing outside the corral, the young chief's body in his arms, he yelled, "Here's Swift Horse's son. You may have his body only if you let us leave unharmed. If you don't, I'll cut his limbs off one by one and string 'em all over Texas. You'll never find them." Wanting to make sure they understood him, Sheridan ordered Juan to repeat his words in Comanche.

The whooping stopped as quickly as it had begun. The braves looked at their chief's favorite son, his oldest son. They looked at one another; then over their shoulders. All of them rode off. Nauseous and weak, Sheridan wanted to lay the body down, but he didn't move. Time stood still for the people inside the ring of wagons. Finally the Indians returned, a warrior no older than Sheridan in the lead. He rode up to the trail driver, dismounted, and walked to the body.

"Are you Swift Horse?" Sheridan asked in English.

The chief never replied. Speaking Spanish, Sheridan repeated his question. Still the chief refused to answer.

"Do you speak English?" Sheridan asked, his vision blurring, his head spinning.

Again the chief refused to respond. Turning slowly because of his dizziness, Sheridan motioned for Juan. When the vaquero joined them, Sheridan said, "He doesn't speak English or Spanish."

"*Sí*, señor," Juan concurred. "He doesn't speak either, but he understands Spanish, at least." Sheridan lifted his brows in question. "Swift Horse was sent to mission school as a child,

388

and he was taught Spanish."

Sheridan returned his gaze to the Comanche chief. "Why won't he speak it?"

"The Comanches hate the white men," Juan replied. "They refuse to be contaminated by them. They wish to remain a pure race; therefore, many of them are adamantly opposed to speaking the language and to intermarriage. They do not wish to have their culture mixed with the white man's."

Sheridan nodded, his eyes sparkling with admiration for the Comanche chief. Speaking in Spanish so Swift Horse would understand him, he said, "I understand, Chief Swift Horse. My people from over the water are much like yours, and we feel the same way about speaking the language of the invader. We have a saying that goes like this: As long as there be Irishmen who speak Irish the atrocities of the English will never be forgotten."

Swift Horse never acknowledged by word or movement. Instead he said in Comanche, "You killed my son, red-haired man."

As soon as Juan's interpretation ceased, Sheridan nodded, his green eyes centering on Swift Horse's black ones. "Aye, I killed your son, Swift Horse. If I had not, he would have killed me."

"You know who I am?"

Wishing they didn't have to speak through an interpreter, the boy's body growing heavier by the minute, Sheridan answered as soon as Juan ceased speaking. "All white warriors have heard of the brave chief."

"Humm," the chief droned. "I have heard of you, red-haired man." He looked at Sheridan with a mixture of hatred and respect. "Did my son die honorably?"

"Like a warrior, he died fighting a warrior."

"Good." With covetous eyes the chief looked at the oxen, the horses, and the weapons. The people he dismissed with a contemptuous casualness. "We want your horses and weapons."

"You can't have them."

Swift Horse's black eyes lingered on Marguerite. "What makes you think I will let you go once I've taken the body of my son? I have enough men to kill all of you. Then I can take the horses and the weapons."

"If you take the body of your son, you will give me your word that we can pass," Sheridan answered. "Once you've given me your word you will honor it." As soon as Juan had interpreted, Sheridan continued. "I am a man of my word also, Swift Horse. If you continue to fight us, I promise that I will leave nothing for you. Before I let you have them, I will shoot the horses and burn the weapons."

"You would destroy your horses and your weapons to keep me from getting them?"

"I will."

Swift Horse stood silently, contemplating Sheridan. "You believe my word, red-haired man?" Sheridan nodded.

Long, tense minutes passed. Sheridan stared at the chief; the people, hovering behind the circled wagons, stared. Finally Swift Horse spoke.

Looking at Sheridan, he said in broken English, "You, your people go, red-haired man. We meet another day when sun out or when moon belongs to Comanche. We fight—you, me. I win. You lose." He pointed to Marguerite. "I take squaw. She brave. Make good babies. Me want. She give me son for one you take."

"You'll have to kill me to take her," Sheridan said, the green eyes never flickering from the black ones.

"I do that. She your woman?"

"She's my woman."

"I like you, red-haired man. You brave warrior. I no speak English to coward."

"I like you, Swift Horse. You are a brave, honorable warrior."

"You go in peace this time, red-haired man. Maybe next time Swift Horse not able let you go."

Seeing the ever growing blood stain on the front of Sheridan's shirt, hearing the weakness in his voice, Juan was concerned about the wagon master. He didn't want him to pass out in front of Swift Horse. If he did, their chance of survival was slim. Ever alert, the vaquero stood immediately behind Sheridan.

Surprising all of them, Swift Horse included, Sheridan walked to the chief. "I will not put your son's body on the ground. Do you want to carry him, or do you want me to put him on his horse?"

"I take." Swift Horse took his son's body in his arms, and he turned without another word and walked away.

Sheridan also turned, and Juan followed close behind in case Sheridan should collapse before he reached safety. Juan knew that Swift Horse was letting them go only because of his regard for Sheridan's bravery. The vaquero wanted nothing to happen to jeopardize the truce.

Sheridan, holding his head high, his shoulders erect, moved back to the circle. Before he stepped over the wagon tongue, he heard Swift Horse's voice.

"Mah-rib-ba hite, red-haired man."

Sheridan looked at Juan who interpreted. "He has said, 'Good-bye, friend.'"

Stopping but not turning around, Sheridan called over his shoulder, loudly enough that the retreating chief could hear him, *"Mah-rib-ba hite,* Swift Horse."

With Juan's assistance he stepped over the wagon tongue and entered the compound. Marguerite rushed to him, and Sheridan draped an arm over her shoulder.

"How's Jordan?" he asked weakly.

"He'll live," Stringbean announced before Marguerite had a chance to reply. "Clean through the shoulder. Nasty hole but nothing vital damaged. We done cut the lance out and poured some whiskey in it. Got 'im in a wagon."

"Pedro?"

"Arrow wound. Not bad. He fell and hit his head, knocking

him out. That's why he fell outside the wagons." Stringbean chuckled. "He's feeling might fine right now. Little señorita is taking care of him and Daisy."

"Good," Sheridan murmured.

"Let me tend to your shoulder," Marguerite said.

"I'm all right," Sheridan said. "Just weak. I've lost a lot of blood." As he said the words, he slowly crumpled to the ground.

"Get these wagons hitched and rolling," Stringbean yelled. "We better be gitting outta here while the gittin's good." To Juan he said, "You git the train started. I'll help the senory take care of Rusty."

Chapter 23

His shoulder throbbing, Sheridan opened his eyes and blinked at the star-studded sky until his vision cleared. His gaze focused on the large full moon spreading its shiny beams over the rolling prairie. It was a bad omen. Not only was it beautiful, Sheridan thought, remembering Swift Horse's promise, but its silvery web was deadly. On the night of the full moon, Comanches attacked. But Swift Horse had given his word. Sheridan knew he could believe the chief—this time.

Wondering where he was, Sheridan listened for a moment to the nocturnal sounds around him: the night creatures, the warm breeze that soughed through the trees, the gentle lapping of the river. Squirming, trying to find a more comfortable position, he moved his hand, feeling the hardness of the wagon beneath him. He rolled his eyes to the right and saw Marguerite, hunched against the side of the wagon, her legs drawn up, her chin resting on her knees.

"Good evening," he whispered, the sound soft in case she was asleep. He didn't want to awaken her.

Immediately Marguerite scrambled to him.

"Why aren't you asleep?" he whispered, moving, wincing from the pain.

She scooted closer to him and leaned down. "I was worried about you. We couldn't get the bleeding to stop."

"Aye, I do feel a mite wet, and—" He sniffed. "To be sure, lass, I hope you didn't pour all that alcohol on me. I hope you saved a little to pour in me."

Tears of relief running down her cheeks, Marguerite nodded her head and laughed softly with him. "To be sure, Danny Boy. To be sure, I saved you some."

She scooted to the other end of the wagon and rummaged through some boxes. Finally she found a partially filled bottle of whiskey. When she crawled back, she said, "I couldn't find a glass."

"Don't need one," Sheridan muttered as he tried to sit up; however, the pain was so bad he fell back down, grimacing, holding his arm against his body. "Me father always said a man could drink better from a bottle."

Setting the whiskey down, Marguerite said, "Here. Let me help you."

Kneeling beside him, she eased him up, propping several quilts behind him. Uncorking the bottle, she tilted it to his lips.

"Ahh, lass," he said, swallowing the burning liquor, "that eases several kinds of pain at one time." Taking the bottle from her, he lifted it to his lips, taking the second swallow. "Me ole father always told me the value of a pint of stout."

Laughing, she asked, "Am I going to get a proper thanks for hiding that for you?"

"Aye, lass," Sheridan said softly, setting the bottle aside, "I'm going to give you a thanks, and a proper thanks, to be sure. For hiding me a bottle of whiskey, for tending to my wounds, and for being here when I woke up."

Although it hurt, he leaned forward and placed his hand on her shoulder, slowly pulling her to him. His face lifted, hers lowered, her tremulous lips pouting softly for his kiss.

Gently, ever so gently, his lips whispered over hers, lightly moving back and forth, teasing and tormenting her, doing the same to himself. With a groan, he pulled her even closer, disregarding the pain in his shoulder. His arm circled her body, banding her to him.

The kiss that had begun so tenderly, so tentatively, now deepened until both were drinking of the other's soul. The kiss was open mouthed and hot; a kiss that lovers share, an intimate kiss, the welcome mat of passion. Both knew they had charted a course from which there was no turning back. But neither was willing to admit it—yet.

Marguerite pulled away from him, drew her legs up, and laid her chin on her knees. Sheridan, squirming into the quilts, reached for the whiskey.

"Where's the little one?"

Marguerite smiled. "Daisy? She's sleeping with Hortensia."

"How's Jordan?"

"He's in a lot of pain. Fevered and fitful. He was thrashing about so, Stringbean said it would be better for him to sit with Jordan, me with you."

"Is that the only reason you're with me, lass?"

Marguerite waited for one breathless minute before she shook her head, whispering, "No, I'm here because I wanted to be with you."

Chuckling his happiness, Sheridan held the bottle by the neck with his right hand and raised it to his mouth, taking another swallow. Just the effort of holding it up tired him. Weaker than he thought, he lowered the bottle, setting it on the wagon bed with a thud. He breathed deeply.

"Are you all right?" Marguerite asked, scooting closer.

With pain-glazed eyes, he stared at her. "Nay, lass, to be sure I'm not." His brogue was thick. He laughed. "I don't mind drinking the whiskey, but I don't like smelling of whiskey." He took another swallow. "A bath I'd like to be taking. That I surely would." Another long drink. "Are we at the river?"

"Yes."

Suddenly Sheridan chuckled. "Here I am, lass, forgetting my manners." He held the bottle out to her. "Have a drink."

She shook her head. "We don't have much left."

"Then all the more reason for sharing, lass," he said. "You fought bravely today. Better than many a man I've seen." He smiled. "Here take a swig. Let's celebrate our victory and your bravery."

She smiled, still declining. "Ladies don't drink," she coyly replied.

Sheridan chuckled. "To be sure, lass, ladies don't drink, but then I remember your telling me one time that you were surely no lady. So . . ."

Placing the mouth of the bottle on her lips, he tilted it a little too high, whiskey running down the sides of her mouth. Marguerite swallowed, gasped, and coughed, the liquid pure fire down her throat.

"Ah, lass." Sheridan chuckled. "If you're going to be an Indian fighter, you must learn to handle your liquor." He took another swallow and held the bottle to her lips again. "Let me teach you how." He smiled. "I won't be a'spilling it on you this time."

Laughing and talking, the two of them lay together, propped on the blankets for a long time, drinking their whiskey. When they had finished off the bottle, Sheridan dropped it over the side of the wagon. Having consumed more than Marguerite, he was slightly inebriated.

"I'm going to the river and wash off," he announced.

"You can't," Marguerite argued. "You're too weak for one thing, and you'll drown yourself sure for another."

Sheridan chuckled. "Come with me and hold my hand."

"You know I can't."

"I know you shouldn't," Sheridan breathed, "but I know you will." He smiled. "Why don't you admit it, lass? It's in the cards."

His eyes drifted to the blaze in the center of the wagons, to Stringbean who lay on a blanket close to Jordan. Reflected in the firelight, the old man's gaunt, grizzled features were softened in sleep. Sheridan moved, grunting his discomfort.

"Lie down and try to rest tonight," Marguerite pleaded. "You'll be stronger in the morning. Then you can bathe."

His face winced in pain as he slid down the wagon bed. "I'm

going to take a bath tonight, lass. I don't like the stench of whiskey mixed with dried blood and perspiration. You can stay or come with me, whichever you prefer."

Marguerite looked at Stringbean, and she sighed. He and Juan were going to need all the rest they could get. The train's safe arrival in San Antonio tomorrow depended on them.

"Just a minute," she said grudgingly, squirming to the front of the wagon. "Let me get you some clean clothes."

Glad for the cover of night, Sheridan grinned. He hadn't doubted for a moment—well, he conceded truthfully, maybe he had doubted for just a moment that she would come with him. His eyes appreciatively ran over the curve of her buttocks as she bent over, rummaging through his valise. When she was through, she closed the satchel and draped Sheridan's shirt, trousers, and socks over her shoulder. She searched through more boxes and satchels, throwing more clothes over her shoulder.

Balanced on her knees, she turned, and Sheridan said, "Lass, you might see if you can find a little more whiskey." He gingerly touched his shoulder. "The throbbing's so bad I might be in need of more medicine, to be sure."

Marguerite couldn't glare at him long. Laughter bubbled up in her soul, demanding release. "To be sure!" she said on a trill of laughter. Returning to the boxes, she once again searched. Finally she waved a bottle through the air. "Do you think this will be enough to keep the pain down?" Hopping out of the wagon, she walked down the side and lowered the back gate.

Sheridan took the bottle from her and held it up, letting the moonlight reflect through it. He nodded. "This will kill quite a bit of pain, lassie." Tucking the whiskey under his arm, he said, "I'll carry the heavy stuff, my darling." With his uninjured arm, he reached up to pat the pile of clothes on her shoulder. "You carry the lighter load."

Holding the bottle to his mouth, he gripped the cork with his teeth and pulled. Dropping the cork in his hand, he lifted the other, taking a big gulp and swallowing. Handing the bottle to

Marguerite, he said, "I think it's time we went to bathe, Daisy, me darlin'."

Marguerite took the bottle, raised it to her lips, and took a swallow. She croaked, "Aye, I be agreeing with you, Danny Boy, me darlin'. It's time we bathed." Her voice vibrated a happiness and freedom she hadn't known in a long time.

Sheridan was thoroughly exhausted by the time they reached the moon-dappled trees that profusely lined the riverbank. Dropping the corked bottle, he pressed his palm on a large boulder and slowly slid to the ground, breathing deeply, nursing his wounded shoulder and arm.

"I told you not to come," Marguerite whispered, kneeling beside him, laying the clothes down. "You're too weak. As soon as you rest, we're going back to the wagon."

"Aye, I'm weak," he agreed, "and nay, I'm not going back so soon. It's much cooler out here, Daisy Belle. The breeze blowing over the water. Listen at all the night creatures." He paused a moment, then pointed to the river and said, "Look! In the moonlight you can see the ripples as they fan out in circles finally disappearing." He looked at her, her face gilded silver by the moonbeams that managed to twist through holes and loops in the canopy of leaves. "In the moonlight I can see you, Daisy."

He lifted a hand, touching her chin and the smooth curve of her cheek. He outlined the arched brows, the delicate nose. He traced her mouth, brushing in the fullness. He felt her lips tremble beneath his callused finger; he felt them part. He felt desire burn in the center of his being. He dropped his hand, pressing it flatly against her breast. He felt the cadence of her heart, drumming fast and irregular.

Marguerite looked into the face, gaunt with his hours of suffering. She reached up and gently raked her hands through the thick russet waves, dropping her hands, lightly scratching her nails over his beard. She smiled.

"I must look a sight," he muttered, lifting a hand to touch his bristly beard.

She shook her head, looking down at her dirty shirt and trousers. "What about me? I do look a sight!"

"Aye. The best sight I've seen in years, lass. You're beautiful."

"Beautiful!" she murmured the protest. "The way I look now!"

"You'll always be beautiful, Daisy Belle, because your beauty comes from within. Age will only enhance it." He lifted his hand from her breast and reached up, tucking errant strands of hair behind her ear. "When you're riding and fighting, it serves your purpose to have your hair pulled out of your way in this ball on the top of your head, but I like it better, lass, when it curls around your face."

The hand moved to the chignon, and the fingers deftly sought for and found the binding pins. He plucked each one out, tossing it on the ground, not caring where it landed. When her hair tumbled down, he splayed his fingers through it, softening it around her face.

"Thank you for taking care of me," he murmured, his hand sliding down her throat, splaying across her shoulder, the fingers gently closing over the soft flesh. "Thank you for being with me when I awoke. I needed you, lass."

Marguerite couldn't see his eyes, but she could feel the flame of his touch; she could hear the throbbing intensity of his voice.

"Sheridan." Marguerite's voice was soft. "I've been doing some thinking. When you were lying there unconscious, I thought about the possibility of your dying."

"No need to worry about me dying, lass. I told you that even death doesn't want me for a—"

Tears in her voice, Marguerite cried, "Stop it, Sheridan. Don't jest about something this important. I don't want your blarney." Her lips trembled; her eyes sparkled with liquid love. "For once, I want us to be completely honest with each other."

"To be sure," he sighed resignedly. "And what is complete honesty compelling you to confess, lass?"

"Sheridan, I never thought one time about Jordan today when you fought for me, when you were standing out there talking with Swift Horse. All I could think about was you, sacrificing your life for me. I was worried sick."

Tears streamed down her cheeks. Using the hand that clasped her shoulder, Sheridan tenderly pressured her closer to him, pressing her face into his uninjured shoulder.

"I can't stand to lose you again. I can't. I don't know if I love you." She wept, giving vent to all her pent-up emotions. "But I don't want to go through the agony of giving you up again."

"I love you, Daisy."

She lifted her face and, lifting a hand, rubbed it through the bristly beard. Her lips parted, and she guided his mouth to hers. Gently they touched one another, almost a virgin touch, as if they were discovering the taste and feel of each other for the first time. As he tasted the salt of her tears, a tremor rippled his body, and the bands of control broke.

Sheridan's lips slanted, his mouth opened, and he slowly led Marguerite into the deepness of passion. Desperation spurred her into urgency. Forced by years of waiting, compelled by the throbbing needs of her body, Marguerite had to touch him; she had to hold on to him. She cupped his head in her hands, moving her face and lips to his every command.

Caught up in the passion of the kiss, Sheridan moved his injured shoulder. His body convulsed with pain, and he softly groaned. Immediately Marguerite drew back.

"I'm sorry," she whispered. "I didn't mean to hurt you."

Breathing deeply, Sheridan slowly blew the air out, threading his fingers through his hair. "To be sure, lass, I'm the one who's sorry." He forced himself to grin. "Right woman but wrong time, wrong place." He took in several more deep gulps of air, laying his head against the rock.

"Are you all right?" Marguerite asked.

"No, I'm damned well not all right," he softly replied. "I hurt like hell."

Marguerite crawled closer to him and picked up the whiskey.

"Take another swallow or two," she suggested, "and let's get back to the wagon. You've exerted yourself too much."

"I haven't exerted myself enough," he grated, pushing the bottle away, "but if this continues I will, and you'll regret it tomorrow." He reached up, gently cupping his wounded shoulder. "My shoulder aches a little bit, lass, but I'm hurting inside, and no amount of liquor is going to assuage that pain." Dropping his good hand, he levered himself up, pushing to his feet. "Go back to the wagon, Marguerite," he grunted. "I'm going to take a bath; I'll be back as soon as I finish."

"I'm not going to leave you."

His back to her, he said in low controlled tones, "I'm doing this for you, Marguerite. I'm giving you the time you asked for. You know what's going to happen if you stay out here with me?"

Marguerite trembled, but she answered in a calm voice, "You're injured, Sheridan."

He spun around, facing her. "But I'm not dead, Marguerite, nor am I daft. Don't treat me like a little boy. I'm a man, with a man's wants and desires." He walked to where she stood. "Are you playing games with me, lass?"

Marguerite shook her head. She licked her dry lips; she swallowed the knot in her throat. "You . . . you asked me if it were possible for us to have . . . to have a second . . . chance."

Sheridan said nothing; he wasn't going to make her confession easy. Whatever she had to say had to be said without any coaxing from him.

"Is it possible, Sheridan?" she cried. "After all that's happened between us, is it possible?"

Without touching Marguerite—one of the hardest things Sheridan had ever done—he said, "Only if both of us want it badly enough that we're willing to make it work."

"Now . . . now that you're no longer consumed with the past, with retribution and revenge," Marguerite tentatively said, asking more than asserting, "maybe we have a chance for a future."

"No more talk of divorce, love?"

"No more," she promised.

Sheridan lifted his hands, again brushing recalcitrant wisps of hair from her face. Perhaps the wind of fate was blowing kindly for them. Perhaps they would have a second chance for love. Nodding, Sheridan chuckled, drinking from the same cup of happiness. His hand dropped to the neckline of her shirt.

"I think you could do with a bath, Mrs. O'Roarke."

"Aye, to be sure an' I could," Marguerite replied.

"If only you had some clean clothes with you."

Time stood still as Marguerite stared into his moonlit face. "I do," she whispered, the sound so soft Sheridan could hardly hear it.

"Then there's nothing to keep us from bathing."

Although working with one hand, he deftly flipped the buttons of her shirt through the openings down to where the material was tucked into her trousers.

"Nothing," Marguerite returned.

She stepped closer to him, gently easing the torn shirt from his shoulder, letting it fall at their feet. She looked at the buttons on his trousers, but she made no effort to touch them.

"I can't bathe with my trousers or my boots on, lass."

Marguerite swallowed convulsively. She couldn't believe how nervous she was. More than six years since she'd touched Sheridan so intimately, since she'd touched any man so intimately. Her hands shook so much she knew she couldn't unfasten the buttons.

"It'll . . . it'll be easier if I take your boots off first," she said.

Sheridan chuckled. Cautiously he sat down on the boulder, bracing himself with one hand as Marguerite sat down at his feet and pulled his boots and socks off. When he was barefooted, he patted his thigh.

"Put your foot up here, lass, and I'll tug with my good hand while you pull."

Laughing, Marguerite lay on her back and laid her foot on

Sheridan's leg. Clasping her hands just below her knees, she pulled while he anchored her foot between his legs. When the second boot came off, Sheridan motioned to the whiskey bottle.

"I think I'd like to have a swallow, lass."

Concern clouded her eyes as Marguerite scampered on her knees for the bottle. "Are you hurting?" As she reached for the bottle, her blouse fell apart, revealing the gentle swell of her breasts, painted silver by the moon.

"Aye," he answered, his eyes moving down the line of creamy flesh.

Her fingers closing around the neck of the bottle, Marguerite quickly jumped to her feet and uncorked the whiskey. "Here," she said, tipping the bottle to his lips.

Sheridan took a small swallow; then he closed his hands over hers, guiding the bottle to her lips. After she had taken several swallows, he recorked the bottle and set it on the boulder.

"Now, love," he whispered, pulling her closer to him, "I'd like to have my bath, but I don't think I can manage these buttons with one hand."

Slightly inebriated, Marguerite giggled. "Now I know why the whiskey," she whispered, her hands moving to the buttons on his trousers.

She pushed the buttons through the openings. Even through the fabric Sheridan could feel the warmth of her touch, each movement stoking the passion that blazed in him. When the flap was unbuttoned on both sides, it fell down, his trousers slipping a little way down his hips.

Marguerite moved closer to him, circling her arms around him, pushing her hand beneath the material of his trousers. Sheridan gasped as her warm, moist palms grazed his skin when she peeled his trousers below his buttocks, letting them slide down his legs.

Stepping back, her eyes moving from Sheridan's bandaged shoulder to his waist—to his burgeoning manhood, she pushed the buttons through the difficult openings in her trousers.

403

Bending, she stripped them off, dropping them and stepping out of them. Proudly she stood, burning under his gaze that slowly slid from her face to her feet.

At twenty-two she had been lovely; six years later she was even more beautiful than he had remembered. He didn't touch her; he simply looked, unable to get his feel of her beauty. He reached out, his fingers grazing her cheek. His eyes misted with tears. He'd never wanted a woman more in all his life. He wrapped his hand around the nape of her neck and gently tugged her to him.

"This is where you belong, Daisy Belle," he whispered, his head lowering, his lips touching hers.

His lips closed over hers in a warm, sweet hello kiss. Starved for his touch, starved for his love, Marguerite's body responded to him. Careful not to touch his wounded shoulder, she snuggled closer to his hard frame, her breasts pressing into his chest. She slanted her mouth and slowly parted her lips, guiding his into a warm, open kiss. She felt a deep ache start in the center of her being and diffuse through every inch of her body.

Following her lead, Sheridan's tongue gently entered her mouth, the kiss changing from greeting to blatant need. Sheridan altered his position, the thrust of his lower body pressing against Marguerite. His hand moved up her back, pulling her nearer at the same time. Marguerite could feel the heat and probing of his fingers; she could feel the heat of his thrusting manhood.

She lifted her arms, her fingers gripping into his back. She sighed her pleasure, loving the feel of his muscles beneath her hands. She wilted against him as his questing tongue touched all those sensitive places in her mouth. Twisting his mouth from hers, tasting her face, nibbling her ears, he whispered, "You don't know how long I've waited for this, Daisy."

"How long?" she asked with a lover's curiosity.

"For an eternity."

"Are you telling me that you've had no woman since me?"

His fingers kneaded into the soft curve of her shoulders. "I wish I could say that, lass, but I can't." Seeing the pain of disappointment on her face, he said, "I can't remember their names or their faces, lass. I was searching for one name and one face. I tried to find it in each of them."

He pulled her face to his, capturing her lips again. His hand and his lips continued their sensual assault, soft and gentle at first, then more urgently and roughly as both gave in to raw need. Sheridan pulled his lips from hers, spreading quicksilver kisses over her face—her nose, her eyes, her cheeks, the curve of her chin.

"I never forgot what you were like, love," he whispered. "Your passion. Your fire." His lips grazed her collarbone and the upper swell of her breasts.

Marguerite closed her eyes and sucked in her breath. "I never forgot you either," she whispered, her eyes luminous, glazed with desire.

As Marguerite and Sheridan stared into each other's eyes, everything outside each other disappeared for both of them. With the same magic they had years ago, they created a world for themselves. Sheridan wrapped his arm around Marguerite's shoulders and lovingly steered her toward the river. They waded into ankle-deep water. Sheridan went deeper, but Marguerite stopped, returning to the darkness of the shore for the soap and washcloths. Sheridan followed her a step or two.

Then he waited. When he saw her, he held his hand out and beckoned her to come. Smiling, she moved toward him, but she stubbed her toe on a root and dropped a rag. Bending, she splashed the water, reaching for it. In the moonlight that filtered through the lacy canopy of tree branches, Sheridan saw her stand up. He caught his breath, his eyes feasting on her exquisite beauty that was streaked silver by the moon.

Naked, her back to him, she stood regal and proud, her brown hair waving down her back. Mesmerized, Sheridan's gaze lowered from her face to her shoulders, down the smooth line of her back to the curve of rounded buttocks, the beautiful thighs, calves that tapered into shapely ankles.

"Marguerite," he muttered thickly. "Dear God, Marguerite!"

He gazed at the vision of loveliness that had haunted him day and night for the past six years. Yet she was more lovely than his dreams, than his memories. He didn't even have to touch her to love her. Just looking at her, he tasted the sweetness of her pert breasts. He felt the softness of her belly against his stomach; he felt the throbbing of her femininity beneath his hand. Raw hunger gnawed at him as he felt his manhood throb with desire.

"I love you, Daisy Belle LeFleur O'Roarke."

Mesmerized, her eyes never leaving him, Marguerite tossed the clothes and the soap onto the shore. She ran through the water. "I love you, darling." In front of him, she whispered, "Love me, Sheridan. I need you."

The words that he longed to hear, day and night, for six years.

"Are you sure?" he asked, his voice thick and husky.

"I'm sure." She smiled up at him. "Before I was afraid of being hurt again."

"Now you aren't?"

"I am," she confessed, "terribly afraid, but I've got to take the chance." She repeated. "I've got to take the chance." Slowly she held her arms out. "I've waited a long time for this, my darling."

"So have I."

They locked their arms around each other, their embrace a bridge, linking the past to the present and promising a future. Tightly they held on until assurance inevitably gave place to need and desire. Pulling back slightly, never leaving the warmth of his arms, Marguerite lifted her face; Sheridan lowered his. Their lips met, the mere touch igniting a passion that blazed through both of them, burning but never consuming them.

Sheridan's hand smoothed down Marguerite's back, his

palm cupping her buttocks, kneading them, pressing them closer to his burgeoning hardness. Palms against his stomach, she slid her hands up his chest, her fingers weaving through the thick mat of hair.

Together they slid into the water, Marguerite murmuring, "I want to see and touch what I've remembered all these years, what I've dreamed about. I want to replace the ghost with the real thing."

Unashamed, Marguerite ran her hands over his body, over every inch of masculine terrain. Gently her hands and her lips loved around his wound; then they moved to the broad shoulders, the chest, the flat stomach. Finally her fingers slipped through the thick tuft of russet hair, and her hand curled around his manhood. Lying back, pillowed on the water that softly lapped below his ears, Sheridan gasped his pleasure.

Marguerite knelt over him, careful to keep her weight off him. She spread kisses all over his face, his neck, his upper torso, before she laid her cheek on his chest. His hands touched the burning flesh of her back, his callused palm moving up and down, sending shimmers of delight through her. He made love to her, not leaving one inch of her body untouched. His hand, his mouth, his tongue, his endearments, all joined in the loving assault. Marguerite writhed to his caresses, and she gave him pleasure in equal measure.

"Now, Sheridan," she finally gasped. Sheridan caught her as if to move her beneath him, but Marguerite shook her head and whispered, "No, darling, I don't want you to hurt your shoulder. Let me make love to you."

"Ahh, lass," he murmured, "take me quick. I can't wait much longer."

Lifting herself above Sheridan, Marguerite laid her lips over his, guided them open with hers, and slipped her tongue into his mouth as she eased herself down on his masculinity. Sheridan's hand clamped over her buttocks, pressing her closer to his lower body, thrusting inward as she thrust downward.

Marguerite's tongue passionately assaulted Sheridan's, filling him with her love strokes as he slowly, carefully filled her with himself. Slipping her hands beneath him, she raked her fingers down his back to the flexed muscles of his buttocks, and she gently kneaded them, pulling them up against her body, pushing her hips in time to his thrusts of love, moving with him, loving—with him.

Unashamed, the lone rider, hidden in the trees on the far shore of the river, watched the two of them make love. Never stirring from his hideaway, he saw them frolic in the water afterward. He watched them walk out later. He never took his obsidian eyes off the woman until she was fully dressed. Waiting until the two of them returned to the wagon train, he moved to his horse, which he had tethered at a distance.

Riding off, his long black hair streaming behind, his shadow long in the moonlight, he smiled to himself. The whip woman and the red-haired man were good for each other. They were people to be trusted; they were friends.

Both dressed in clean shirts and trousers, Marguerite and Sheridan lay in the front of the wagon, blankets stuffed behind them. Sheridan's arm, draped over Marguerite's shoulder, pulled his unbuttoned shirt open. Her head on his chest, she ran her hands down Sheridan's chest across his stomach, her fingers splaying beneath the waistband of his trousers. She chuckled when she heard Sheridan's quick intake of breath.

Marguerite stretched sinuously, her unbuttoned shirt falling open, revealing her breasts. Sheridan's head moved, his mouth closing over the nipple. Marguerite breathed deeply as delight winged through her body. His gentle tug on her breast seemed to have its origin in the seat of her femininity. His hands slid beneath her body to close about her buttocks, squeezing them together.

"Are you coming to the hacienda with me?" Marguerite asked, rubbing her hands up and down his back.

"Later," he replied. "I've got to stop by ranger headquarters first. I may take another assignment, and I want to report this incident with Swift Horse. I was surprised to see him this far in."

"It's been a long, dry summer," Marguerite remarked. "Perhaps they are looking for food and water."

"Perhaps," Sheridan answered absently, his eyes on the figure who threw more wood on the fire. "Hortensia," he said softly, nudging Marguerite.

Marguerite quickly pulled her shirt and slid down in the wagon, not wanting her maid to see her. "Hortensia would never get over this," she said. "It was shock enough for her to see you in my room speaking to me as you were. She would die if she knew that you and I had . . . that we were . . ."

"Aye," Sheridan teased, his hand moving over her body, "and that we are going to do it again."

Marguerite chuckled. "No telling what she'll tell Jewel when we get home."

Sheridan laughed with her. "Are you still answering to your black angel?"

"More now than ever before," Marguerite replied. "Since we left Ireland she's become my keeper." Marguerite chuckled. "Will she and Paddy ever be shocked to see you!"

"Good or bad shocked?" Marguerite asked.

"Good for Jewel," Marguerite twinkled. "Beneath that dragon exterior, she has a heart of gold, and she loves you. I'm not so sure about Paddy. He's never forgiven you for what you did to me. It'll take him some time to get used to your being back in our lives." Looking at the stars, she said, "Just as it will me." In a small voice she said, "After what happened before I didn't think I'd ever be able to love again."

"I'm sorry, darling," he whispered. "I truly didn't mean to hurt you so badly."

"I know that now," she murmured. "I'm so glad we're over here, Sheridan, away from your past, away from all your bad memories. We can be happy here." Lost in thought, she

409

paused, then said, "We'll be so happy, Sheridan. I know you'll love the hacienda. Juan is teaching me so much. Mustangs roam freely, Sheridan. All we have to do is round them up and break them. Juan will teach you to be a vaquero."

Softly Marguerite continued to verbalize her dreams as Sheridan listened. The enormity of what he'd done began to hit him. What a fool he was! The place and time had changed but the circumstances were the same. He had had nothing to offer Marguerite six years ago and had even less today. And he was still caught up in his past. He had promised himself that he would one day return to Ireland to take what was rightfully his.

"Sheridan!"

Jarred out of his ruminations, Sheridan looked at Marguerite blankly.

She laughed. "Were you sleeping, darling?"

"Dozing," he fabricated, loathe to confess his thoughts and thus break the magic spell they had created. "Why?"

"I asked you two times when you thought you'd be coming."

"I wish I could say, darling, but I can't. I don't really know what my assignment is."

"Sheridan," Marguerite asked, uncertainty in her voice, "it's very important to me that you come to the hacienda immediately. Don't take this assignment. Let someone else do it."

Hearing the urgency in her voice, Sheridan said, "I'll have to think about it, love. Power sounded urgent in his letter."

Still not convinced, Marguerite murmured, "It's . . . it's going to be all right, isn't it, Sheridan?"

Sheridan closed his eyes, as he whispered, "Aye, lass, I promise it's going to be all right. Now that I've found you, I'm not going to turn you loose."

He reached for Marguerite, pulling her into his arms. He laid his chin on the top of her head. Sheridan simply held her, giving of his love and strength, marveling in the awesome power of her love. He reassured her with his presence; he promised her with his silence; he promised her by making no idle promises.

Always conscious of his wound, Marguerite moved gingerly. "I know I'm acting childishly," she confessed, "but having lost you once, darling, I'm afraid of losing you again. I'm jealous of anything or anyone that comes between us. Myra Goodwin. Your assignment." She brushed her fingers over one of his buttons. "I have a fear that something's going to happen to take you away from me."

"You're not going to lose me," he told her. "I meant what I said, lass. I'm back in your life, and I mean to stay." Sheridan moved slightly. Lifting a hand, he brushed her hair out of her face.

"I wish you could come to the hacienda now," she murmured. "I have so much that I want to show you. So much I want to say to you." Her voice lowered. "So much that needs to be said."

"Perhaps I can," he murmured, pushing thoughts of the assignment from mind. "I don't think I can stay away from you, love."

"I'm going to do everything in my power to see that you can't," she murmured, lifting her hands, her fingers splaying through the thick, rusty locks, the tips massaging the scalp.

"Sounds good to me," he murmured, unable to stifle a yawn. Drowsily he added, "Someone else can take the assignment. Someone who doesn't have the responsibility of a family."

"Thank you, darling," Marguerite whispered. "Now it's time for you to sleep."

"Aye," he murmured, yawning again, sliding down as she pulled the quilts from behind him. "Are you going to stay with me?"

"Yes."

Snuggling on her side, she felt Sheridan curl up, spooning his body to hers.

Chapter 24

Sitting in a circle around the large campfire, the blaze
casting a golden red glow on their faces in direct contrast to the
night that enveloped them, the Indians watched three riders as
they slid out of their saddles and hitched their horses to a low
branch on the nearby tree. Two wore capes and hoods; the one
was tall and broad shouldered; the other was smaller. The third
was an Indian interpreter. The Comanches assessed the group
of heavily armed vaqueros who had accompanied the three
riders. Though none showed it, all were alert and apprehensive; Indian and Mexican were distrustful of the other.

The two figures, draped in their swirling green capes and
hoods, moved out of the darkness, close enough to the flames
of the fire that the Indians could see the form but not close
enough that features were illuminated in the blaze. They faced
the flame, the muted glow casting eerie shadows on the triangle
that hid facial features in the folds of the hood. Greetings and
introductions were exchanged between the Mexicans and the
Indians with a minimum of talking, and the three visitors were
seated. Rituals were adhered to, the peace pipe smoked by
everyone participating in the parley.

Speaking first was one of the older tribal chiefs, giving long
orations of the past glories of their people; he lamented the
coming of the white man and his civilization; he pondered their

future as a free nomadic people. A younger tribal chief spoke next, vehemently repudiating the white man and his government, openly displaying the Indian's hatred for the white man's intrusion into Comanche land. All called for the white man's removal.

After this the chief of the war council for all Comanches spoke. "Listen to me, oh great Te-ich-as. I am Co-cho Nau-qua-hip, One-who-rides-the-buffalo. The white men have come to the land of the *Caum-onses*. They have taken our land; they have killed our buffalo; they steal our horses. But we cannot fight them, my brothers. We do not have enough young warriors to fight them. They are too many. Each new sun sees more wagons moving across *Caum-onses* Land."

Finally Pah Yoko, the great war chief who ruled over all the Comanche tribes in matters of life and death, stood. "Co-cho Nau-qua-hip has spoken the truth. Only one is our friend—called by the Cherokee Raven; called by the white men Houston. But one friend among so many enemies is not enough." The old chief lapsed into a silence that stretched into minutes. Sitting down, he reached for the sacred pipe, taking several puffs before he again spoke. "Always People Padivo Pah Yoko does what he thinks is best for his people." He stood, spreading his arms to encompass all the warriors who had assembled for the meeting. "That is why I have called all my people together—and all my brothers who live in Comanche land but who do not belong to the *Caum-onses*. This man . . ." He pointed to the biggest white man. "Man-who-wears-green wants to help us drive the white man from *Caum-onses* land." Again he sat, picking up the pipe, handing it to a chief who sat next to him. "I will let Toniets Tuh-huh-yet speak to the white man for us. He hears their language; he knows if they speak with a forked tongue."

The elected spokesman for the Indians, a tall, bronzed warrior rose, his black hair hanging straight and loose, a headband on his forehead. His black eyes contemptuously swept over the Mexican visitors. Speaking Comanche, he said,

"I am Toniets Tuh-huh-yet, called Swift Horse by the white people. You call yourself a chief of the Mexicans, but I do not see the clothes of a chief. You hide your face in darkness, and you wear the clothes of the white man who take our land."

Following the precedent set by the Indians, the caped figure rose, speaking in a deep, resonant voice. He motioned his Indian interpreter to his feet, speaking through him. "I am Trébol, spokesman for the Mexican government, and I am all that I say I am. I am Mexican, but I dress as one of the enemy so that I may slip through them without their knowing what I am doing." Pointing, he added, "This is General Hibernia."

Swift Horse listened, but the answer did not alleviate his doubts. "Why do you wish to meet with us?"

The Mexican's eyes moved around the circle of faces, shadowed in the firelight, faces that represented more than one tribe of Indians: Comanches, Apaches, Wacos, Cherokees. "We have heard about the courthouse massacre in San Antonio and the death of thirty-two Comanche women and children, excluding brave warriors and chiefs," he said. "I heard that you were seeking revenge. I heard that you plan to drive the white man out of Comanche land." He paused long after the interpreter's words ceased. "I am here to give you an opportunity to do just that." He watched the faces of the chiefs as his companion interpreted. "We want to see the white man driven out of Texas as much as you do."

A Cherokee chief stood. "My brothers, I am chief of the Cherokee, but I speak for all of us." He paused. When he received the nods and grunts of approval from the other chiefs, he continued. "All of us have felt the heavy and brutal hand of the white man. We know the one called Lamar, who is chief now, hates all Indians. He is the one who drove the Cherokee out of Texas and who killed our great chief The Bowl. Lamar is not like the Raven; he wants to drive all of us off our land." He pointed to the Mexican officer. "But I do not trust this man. He claims to speak with the authority of the Mexican government, but he dresses like the Texans. He speaks the

415

language of the Texans. I do not trust him. He is wanting to use us for his own gain. Do not include him in our revenge."

Another chorus of grunts could be heard around the fire. Swift Horse spoke again. "What the Eagle has said is true, Mexican. What are you wanting from us?"

The Mexican replied, "It's true. I'm asking you to do something for me. In return I'm offering you a chance to destroy all the white people in Texas."

"Tell us how."

"I'm inviting all of you to Matamoros for a conference with chiefs of the Mexican soldiers."

After the Indian translated the agent's words, the chiefs looked at one another, their expressions immobile. They whispered one to the other; finally one by one they nodded.

Swift Horse said, "We're interested in what you say, but we want to know more about this conference."

"We can guarantee you a successful raid down the Colorado River to the Gulf of Mexico," the agent explained, waiting for the interpretation. "Because I come from the same country as the people who live in San Patricio and Refugio, I can move freely among the settlers. I will know which areas are protected with soldiers and which ones are not. I can tell you where to find the best horses, cattle, and weapons. Because the white people trust me, I can tell you where to strike and give out false information to the Texans."

"Why are you willing to guarantee the success of a raid for us?" Swift Horse asked, wishing he could penetrate the disguise which the white man wore. "Why are you willing to turn against the Texans?"

"If you had the equipment and supplies, how many men could you muster?" the Mexican countered smoothly, never replying to the question.

The translation hardly ceased before Swift Horse asked skeptically, "You are going to give us this?"

"How many?" the general repeated, his voice lower, firmer. The interpreter's voice never changed, but Swift Horse could

416

hear the change in the Mexican's.

"You're wanting to know how many warriors all of us can gather?" Swift Horse asked, his hand sweeping the Indians who circled the fire.

"All of you."

Swift Horse walked the circle, speaking with the chiefs. Finally he returned to where the agent stood. "For the first raid we can have as many as five hundred warriors. If we are successful on the raid and capture many horses, mules, and weapons, we can have as many as a thousand."

"Good," the general replied. Stooping, he picked up a stick and started drawing in the dirt. "Here is what we propose. Unknown to the Texans, you," he said, pointing at Swift Horse, "and the Comanches are to sweep from your mountain stronghold above the San Marcos River, surprising the settlers a second time, as you move down the Colorado to the gulf, the same as before. The Cherokees are to move down and destroy the eastern portion of Texas; the Wacos, Apaches, and other allied tribes will raid down the Brazos and central Texas."

Swift Horse folded his arms over his chest and looked at the drawing. The other chiefs quietly talked one with the other. Eventually Swift Horse asked, "And what will the Mexicans be doing while we're fighting the Texans?"

"Each general, Canalizo, Woll, and Hibernia will sweep up from the south with a thousand men under each command." His stick moved swiftly across the dirt, drawing as the words flowed from his mouth. "Hibernia's troops will move up the Colorado; General Woll up the Brazos, and General Canalizo through the eastern part of the state."

"And what will you Mexicans expect from this?"

"The Mexican government wants to recapture San Antonio and the new capital, Austin."

"And what will the Mexicans do to the Comanche once we have driven the white men out?"

"I cannot say," the agent replied, again deferring to the truth. He paused for a long time before he asked, "Are you interested in meeting with us?"

"We must think, and we must talk among ourselves before we give an answer," Swift Horse replied. "The decision belongs to People Padivo Pah Yoko."

People Padivo Pah Yoko stood and addressed the council, his resonant voice clearly sounding. "I do not like this. The man, who speaks the language of the Texans, comes to us under the cover of night with a plan to kill and destroy the people who are his neighbors. All the Mexicans want are the two white settlements: San Antonio and Austin. This man cannot tell us what the Mexicans plan to do once the white men are gone." Pah Yoko shook his head. "I will not agree to let my people be used by this man."

Several of the older chiefs, Buffalo Hump and Swift Horse included, nodded their heads and voiced their agreement. The younger chiefs dissented. Pah Yoko turned to the Mexican officer.

"We don't know who you are; we don't know where you live. Yet you claim to speak for the Mexican government." The old man walked to where the Mexican man stood. He stared into the folds of the hood. "You told us what the Mexicans expected to gain by our war with the Texans. What are you getting out of it?"

The Mexican never flinched under the piercing gaze. A wise man, he knew that truth was his only answer. "I am getting paid by the Mexican government to enlist your help." He paused, then added, "But I also want to help you because I understand how you feel."

"How do we know that you speak the truth?" Swift Horse asked, moving so that he stood beside Pah Yoko.

"I live on a large hacienda in Coahuila, Mexico," the Mexican said. "I don't speak Spanish because I've recently come to this country from Ireland. I understand why you hate the white men because the same thing happened in my country. The enemy invaded, driving us out of our homes. They took our land, and if we let them they would have taken our identity." He paused. "Because the Mexicans do not want the Texans to learn of their part in this invasion, my mission is secret as is my identity."

"How do we contact you, man-who-wears-green, if we wish to join your parley in Matamoras?" Pah Yoko asked.

"Send a messenger to the trading post in Freedom Point." Reaching into his shirt pocket, the man withdrew a small sheet of paper. "Give this to the Mexican man who works behind the counter. He will set up a meeting time and and will see that I get the message."

Swift Horse looked at the sheet of paper. "What does the writing and the picture mean?"

A gloved finger touched the letters. Through the Indian interpreter, the agent said, "This is a shamrock—my token, my sign."

"What are the markings?"

The Mexican spelled the name, his translator speaking letter for letter. "General H-i-b-e-r-n-i-a." Then he explained. "Hibernia. The name of my nation. Ireland as she is pronounced in the language of the Mexicans."

Motioning to the two who had accompanied him, Trébol headed toward his horse. As he walked, he whistled a plaintive tune. Without a backward glance, he, General Hibernia, and the interpreter mounted and rode away.

The adobe building had been standing in San Antonio for a long time. Once it housed royal officers of the Spanish court; now it was rangers' headquarters. Built by the Spaniards when they first settled the area, it boasted beautiful workmanship, architecture, and functional innovations. The room, however, was sparsely furnished. A desk in the center of the room; an assortment of cabinets for storage of documents; racks on the walls for guns; several chairs and beds.

It boasted a huge fireplace built along one wall. A large open flue above it directed heat out of the building while a hidden chimney conducted the smoke out. Waist high, the top of the fireplace was a large, flat rock table with six holes. Over the holes were wrought-iron grills on which the cooking utensils sat. A second flat table of rock formed a shelf underneath for the fire.

Because it was hot, all the windows in the building were raised. Still in the heat of the scorching afternoon sun no breeze stirred. An annoying fly buzzed around the room. In the far corner, leaning on the back legs of the chair, Stringbean whittled, stopping every once in a while to spit and to swipe his hand back and forth in front of his face, warding the fly away.

Jack Mason, acting commander while Col. Mark Hamilton was out of town on ranger business, lounged against a windowsill. He had a thick bushy moustache which covered most of his mouth; the rest of his face was covered with several days' beard growth. His shirt was partially unbuttoned, and his sleeves were cuffed, his faded red underwear showing. Perspiration stained his underarms and shoulders.

Cleanly shaved, wearing only a shirt and trousers, Sheridan sat behind the desk, staring at a torn piece of paper.

Dear General,

I have met with the Indians, outlining your trade proposal. They have agreed to think about it and will let us know. As was agreed they will contact me if they wish to parley.

They are quite interested in the products which we wish to trade, believing they can muster 500 for the first trading—if they get what they need—and 1,000 for the next. They are quite interested in trading with the Mexicans; they have found the Texans slothful to keep their promises.

Remember not to make any promises you cannot keep. The Comanches will never forgive you, nor will they forget. Above all—

"No more?" Sheridan asked.

"All we got," the ranger replied, combing his moustache with the tips of his fingers. "Rest of it and the signature got tore off. Only thing we got to go on is that picture of a shamrock."

"Where did you intercept it?" Sheridan asked.

"On a Mexican outta Matamoras."

"When?"

"Several weeks ago."

"Did you get a chance to question him?"

"Yeah." The ranger walked across the room, lifting the coffeepot off the wrought-iron grill. "Want a cup?" When Sheridan and Stringbean nodded, he reached for the cups on the shelf above the stove. "Couldn't get nothing outta him. We decided to hold him until President Lamar had a chance to look at the note. You know how he is about them Injuns." The ranger grinned. "And more so now than before."

"Why now?" Sheridan asked.

"Jesus Canales, acting president of the Republic of the Rio Grande, has been here recruiting men so he can go into Mexico and fight the Centralist troops, leaving us high and dry."

"Did he get any?"

Mason nodded. "Col. Sam Jordan with over one hundred men; William S. Fisher with two hundred men; Juan N. Seguin with a hundred men; and approximately three hundred Mexican rancheros. Nearly five hundred men in the general vicinity of San Antonio, Gonzales, and Victoria."

"Leaving that entire vicinity vulnerable to Indian attack."

"Yep." Without a pause, Mason asked, "Whatcha want in your coffee?"

"Take it black like nature made it." Stringbean spat.

"Me, too," Sheridan replied.

Two cups full, Jack Mason carried them to Sheridan and Stringbean.

"What did Mirabeau have to say about this?" Sheridan asked, thumping his finger on the note that lay on the desk.

"He's worried. The Comanches are great ones for revenge, and they're still rankling about the council house affair last

March. He's worried about them and the Mexicans joining together for some kind of invasion." Leaning against the stone shelf that supported the wrought-iron grill work over the stove fire, the ranger took several swallows of coffee. "He's mighty puzzled, too. He's sure the feller what wrote this is a Mexican agent, but he can't figure out who."

"Messenger didn't give you any information on him?"

"Naaa. Says he never saw the agent during the daytime. Always at night, and the guy wore a cape and hood. His voice was muffled. Evidently he wore a mask."

"Didn't have no name?" Stringbean blew on the piece of wood that he was working with.

"Didn't give one that we could find out." The ranger turned around and refilled his cup. Watching the fly settle on the top of the stove, he picked up a paper and rolled it up. Holding his breath, slowly drawing his arm back, he kept his eyes on the pesky intruder. "Somebody killed the Mexican right after we brought him in."

"Someone who didn't want his name known," Sheridan mused aloud, his eyes still on the shamrock. "Yet someone who was willing to identify himself as Irish."

"Or maybe—" Stringbean craned his neck and spit out the window. "Someone who wanted us to think he was Irish."

Sheridan nodded. "Why does Power think I'd be interested in this?"

Swat! The paper landed against the fireplace table with such force the cup rattled. "Got 'em," Mason declared victoriously, brushing the fly away with the end of the paper. "I hate flies." He laid the paper down, removed the coffeepot off the fire, and picked up his cup. "Now what was you asking?"

"Why does Power think I'm the man for this assignment?"

"Well," the ranger drawled, "it's a long story. Kinda like this. We got to the Mexican right after he was shot. He kept mumbling something in Spanish. Nobody was here who could understand him, but we listened best we could." Walking to the desk, he pushed Sheridan's feet aside. Pulling open the drawer, he pulled out a sheet of paper and handed it to Sheridan. "Colonel Hamilton got one of the boys who speaks and writes Spanish to write down the sounds which we remembered."

Slowly Sheridan read the list.

"We couldn't make heads or tails about any of that," Colonel Hamilton said. "Just the San Patricio part. Since Power is the impresario for Refugio and spokesman for the Irish colonies, Mirabeau sent for him. He let him read the message and the list; Power was mighty interested in both."

Mason said, "One of them names close to the bottom of the page really got Power's interest. That's what caused him to write you that letter." Leaning over, the ranger ran his finger down the page, finally thumping it on a circled word. "This one. This be the one that got Power's interest."

Sheridan couldn't believe his eyes. He listened as Mason slowly read the letters. "H-i-b-e-r-n-i-a. Odd name fer a man, ain't it?"

"What's that saying?" Stringbean wanted to know, his sentence ending with a splat of tobacco juice out the window.

Standing, Sheridan moved to the door. "Hibernia," he replied. "Latin and Spanish for Ireland. Could simply be San Patricio de Hibernia—Saint Patrick of Ireland—or it could be . . ." His words thrummed into silence before he completed his statement. Unconsciously he reached up and rubbed his healing shoulder.

"Or it could be what?"

Perplexed, Sheridan shrugged, mumbling, "I don't know." He continued to speak. "So many Irishmen have come to Texas and Mexico in the last six or seven years. Two colonies in Texas alone: Refugio and San Patricio de Hibernia."

"So the name means something to you, too?"

Again Sheridan shrugged. "Not really. It could just be coincidental."

"Power didn't seem to think so. You were the first one he wanted to contact when he read this here list."

"I'm not right sure what all this here's about, Rusty," Stringbean said, "but what if'n the feller using that name ain't jest a coincidence?"

"Then . . . I . . . I have great reason to believe that Hibernia did not die seven years ago," Sheridan stated, his voice deathly quiet. "He's here in Texas somewhere."

After a long, unbearable silence, Mason ventured, "Well, Rusty, are you going to rejoin us long enough to find out about Hibernia?"

"I don't know," Sheridan replied, thinking about his promise to Marguerite. "I've got to think about it." He reached for his hat that hung on the rack immediately inside the door. Putting it on, he walked out of the building, across the busy plaza. He walked down the river, finally stopping, leaning against the trunk of a squat, gnarled tree.

So many years had passed. A lifetime! he thought. And he was so far away from Ireland. Everything he thought he had left behind suddenly loomed like a monster in front of him. Just when he and Marguerite had a chance of getting together again. Hibernia! Earl Randolph Taylor! What did it mean? Did it mean anything? No matter what the consequences, Sheridan knew he had to find the answers to both questions—for his peace of mind—for his safety.

"Want to talk about it?" Stringbean's voice softly jarred Sheridan from his ruminations. "Might help you make up your mind." He paused only long enough to spit. "If you're not going, I need to know 'cause I am. I didn't fight for the freedom of this nation for nothing."

"I don't want to go," Sheridan replied, "but I probably will, so I'll tell you about it." Without a change of expression, he said, "I figure you ought to know since you'll be going either way, with or without me."

As they walked down the river, Sheridan told Stringbean about his past, the Wexford lads, Hibernia, Earl Randolph Taylor, Marguerite LeFleur. By the time he had finished the story they were standing in front of a lovely Spanish house, owned by Annabella Antonia Silva Montalvo, an elderly woman who had befriended Marguerite when she first arrived in Texas.

Stopping beneath the shade of the sprawling trees that shaded the house, Stringbean asked, "Does this Hibernia feller know that you're over here?"

"No, he shouldn't," Sheridan replied. "People in Ireland think I'm dead. That's why I took on a new identity when I came over here."

"Do you know who this feller is?"

"I think so." Sheridan hesitated before he replied. Just the thought of who it might be hurt him. "Gavin Kenyon, one of my childhood friends."

Saying the name agonized Sheridan. Remembering the deaths of Shane Dempsey and Mickey Flynn opened the old wound, anguish and pain seeping out once again. Sheridan had known that one innocent man had died unnecessarily. Now perhaps two!

Nodding toward the building, Stringbean asked, "Gonna see the little lady?" Sheridan nodded. "Gonna tell her about this?"

"I don't know," Sheridan replied. "I want to, but I'm afraid, Stringbean. I lost her once because of my past. I don't want to lose her again." He paused, then added, "Most of all, I don't want to involve her in it. I don't want her life endangered."

"And you promised her that you wouldn't join the rangers, didn't you? Promised her that you'd go to the hacienda and stay with her?"

"Aye."

Hearing the drone of voices, Marguerite peered through one of the upstairs windows. When she saw Sheridan, her eyes lit up and her lips curled into a smile. She raced down the stairs through the house onto the veranda. Framed in the door, she waited for Sheridan to see her. As if he knew that she were standing there, he lifted his face, raised his hand and pushed his hat off his forehead. His face wreathed in a devastating

425

smile that never ceased to set her heart aflutter.

Holding her hands out, she raced across the tiled porch toward Sheridan. "You're back."

"I'm back."

"Did you get your business taken care of?"

"Mostly."

"Two whole days without seeing you," she cried, their hands clasping. "I thought you'd never get here." Close to him, she saw the shadow of worry in his eyes. She knew without his telling her that the news was bad. Looking beyond Sheridan, she smiled at Stringbean. "Won't you come in for a cup of coffee?" she asked.

"Thank you kindly, ma'am," Stringbean said. "Reckon I'd better head on back to the headquarters. I need to be talkin' to Mason. Gotta be gettin' ready to pull out." Lifting his hand in a salute, he said, "Be seein' you later, Rusty."

As Sheridan and Marguerite walked up the pathway to the house, she said, "It's bad news, isn't it?"

Loathe to talk about it, Sheridan shrugged. "Indian trouble at the Irish colonies, at a trading settlement called Freedom Point. Maybe Mexican interference from Matamoras. Lamar wants someone to check it out."

Marguerite shrieked. "That's wonderful!"

Sheridan turned surprised eyes on her. "Wonderful!"

In between gales of laughter, she explained, "I don't mean the message is wonderful. I'm happy that it's no worse than it is. You didn't feel so guilty about turning them down, did you?"

He grinned, shrugging her question aside rather than answering it.

"Now I can breathe easier." She laughed her confession. "I've been so worried that you wouldn't be able to go to the hacienda with me."

"No matter what I decided to do about the assignment, sweetheart, I would go to the hacienda with you. I'm not about to let you and Daisy Belle make the trip without your trusty wagon master."

He put an arm around her shoulder and squeezed tightly. Saying nothing for the moment, he let her think what she would. He owed himself this much, he thought. Not knowing the outcome of the investigation, he was going to make sure he left nothing undone. He would see that Marguerite reached her ranch safely. He would tell her then.

Laughing, joy radiating her face, Marguerite said, "Come on in." She clapped her hands for the servant. When the small Mexican boy appeared, she said, "Bring some coffee for Mr. O'Roarke."

"No," Sheridan called, "no coffee. I don't have time."

"No coffee?" Marguerite repeated.

"I can't stay long," he told her, and Marguerite's face fell. "I've got some business that I must take care of before we leave."

"When are we leaving?"

"Day after tomorrow. Before sunup." Glancing around to see if they were alone, Sheridan grinned. Taking her into his arms, he said, "I'd like to have a proper greeting."

Before his lips could touch hers, however, Hortensia came bounding into the room, Daisy in her arms, a woman in tow. "Señora, this is Valenzuela. She has agreed to travel to the hacienda with us as a wet nurse for the baby." Fully in the room now, Hortensia saw Marguerite and Sheridan quickly pull apart. Her face flamed red, and she stammered, "I'm sorry, señora, I didn't know Señor Sheridan was here."

Sheridan laughed, moving toward Hortensia. "No cause to be embarrassed," he said, making light of the girl's discomfort. "Here." He reached for the baby. "Let me see Daisy Belle."

Taking the baby in his arms, Sheridan held her for the longest time, looking at her beautiful blue eyes, listening to her happy gurgles. While Marguerite talked with Valenzuela and Hortensia, Sheridan played with Daisy Belle. When Marguerite dismissed the two girls, she sat on the sofa beside Sheridan. Daisy, however, was through playing. She screwed up her little face and puckered her lips, emitting a hungry howl. A frown on his face, not understanding the mercurial change in the tot, Sheridan looked at Marguerite.

Taking Daisy from the distraught man, Marguerite explained, "She's hungry, and she's tired. It's time for her feeding and her nap." She walked into one of the bedrooms, calling over her shoulder, "I'll be right back, darling." When she returned, Marguerite said, "Valenzuela and her baby will be going back with us. In order to get her to wet nurse the baby until we reached the hacienda, Juan promised to take her on to Matagorda to her family. Her husband has joined Canales's army." She paused, saying, "She's so young, Sheridan."

Sheridan moved across the room and took Marguerite in his arms. He knew what she was thinking.

"He may not come back, Sheridan, leaving Valenzuela alone to rear her baby." Marguerite couldn't keep the tears back. "I know what she must be feeling."

Sheridan held her. As much as he didn't want to tell her about his assignment, he knew he must. She had to know. He pulled her into his arms, lowering his face toward her uplifted one. Before their lips touched, Hortensia called out.

"Señora."

"Hell!" Sheridan muttered when Marguerite jumped out of his embrace.

"Come see what Señor Stringbean made for Daisy."

Chuckling softly, Marguerite said, "I'll be right back, darling. Let me go see." She took several steps, looked over her shoulder and asked, "Would you like to come?"

"No," he gritted, brushing his hand through his hair. "I know what it is. I watched him whittle it."

When Marguerite returned, Sheridan grabbed her hand in his at the same time he grabbed his hat. He pulled her out of the house. "Let's go somewhere. I need to talk with you without Hortensia bobbing in and out of the room."

He clamped the hat on his head, and he strode down the path, Marguerite running to keep up with him. "Where are we

428

going?" she huffed.

"To the river," he replied.

When they reached a quiet, secluded place, Sheridan stopped walking. Turning Marguerite's hand loose, he moved to the river's edge. Hitching his hands into his belt, he stared at ripples in the surface of the placid body of water. Marguerite sat on the grass in the shade beneath a towering tree.

Not knowing an easy way to tell her, Sheridan suddenly blurted, "I can't turn Lamar down, Daisy. I've got to go on this last assignment."

Marguerite was quiet for a few seconds. Plucking a blade of grass, she pulled it between her fingers. "Can't someone else do it?"

"Yes."

"Then why you?"

"He suspects the Mexicans of collaborating with the Indians for a repossession invasion." He lapsed into silence, but Marguerite didn't say a word. She waited for him to explain. "They have evidence which leads them to believe that an Irishman, living in San Patricio or Refugio, is the traitor who's working with the Mexicans."

Marguerite pulled the blade of grass so hard that it snapped. Tossing the two pieces down, she said, "And because you're Irish they want you to go after the agent?"

"Yes."

Leaping to her feet, Marguerite ran to where Sheridan stood. "Don't go, Sheridan. We've lost the last six years of our life together. Now we have a chance—a chance for happiness, for a marriage, for love—and a family."

Turning, Sheridan caught her in his arms. Holding her tightly, he laid his face on the top of her head, his cheek rubbing against the silky strands of hair. "No one else can go, sweetheart. Only I."

"Other Irishmen are in the rangers."

Sheridan drew a deep breath. "I'm the only one who can possibly recognize the agent."

"Recognize the agent," she repeated, tensing. "Who is it?" Her question was muffled against his chest.

"Hibernia."

He said the name so softly, Marguerite wasn't sure she heard it. She leaned against Sheridan for the longest time before she allowed the words to penetrate her consciousness. When they did, she pulled away from him, dry eyed and calm. She felt as if she were in a trance—as if she were outside her body, watching everything that was going on around her.

"Hibernia," she repeated in a deathly quiet tone.

"Aye, lass." Sheridan sighed.

"Our Hibernia?"

"I'm not sure," Sheridan replied. "However, it's ironic that this Mexican agent should be using the same name that the traitor used in Ireland."

"I thought Shane was Hibernia," she mused aloud. She felt the tentacles of fear as they banded her heart, constricting her breathing.

"So did I, lass, but now I'm not so sure."

"If it weren't Shane or Mickey, who was it?" Marguerite asked. Before Sheridan could answer, she whispered, "Gavin?" When she saw the anguish in Sheridan's eyes, she had her answer. "You've got to find out for sure, don't you?" Resolved to the inevitable, Marguerite's statement was dull and heavy. "You'll never be happy until you do."

"We'll never be safe if it is," Sheridan told her. He reached for her, his hands touching her shoulders, but she shrugged his hands off. "Marguerite, I love you."

Marguerite spun around, her eyes sparkling with tears. "I thought the past was behind us," she cried. "Dead, buried. Done with. Why, Sheridan? Why does he have to show up here? Now. Just when you and I are together again? When we could make a new life for ourselves?" The tears ran down her cheeks. "Why must you feel like you must find him?"

"I've already answered that," he softly replied. "And because I love you so much, my darling, I told you what I must do, even if it means losing you." He moved closer to Marguerite, his eyes gazing directly into hers. But he didn't touch her. "It's not a matter of my loving or not loving you, my darling. It's a matter of what I must do in order to retain my integrity as a man, in order to protect you and Daisy Belle."

"Will you always be a prisoner of your past, Sheridan?"

Sheridan had no answer; he could only look at her.

"It's a thief, Sheridan," she sobbed. "It's not only robbing you of a present and denying you a future, it's doing the same thing to me."

"I left the past behind, lass. It found me and has become a part of my present. Without my discovering who Hibernia is neither of us has a present together, much less a future." He stepped back. "Whether you want to admit it or not, if we don't find out who Hibernia is, he will be hanging over our heads the rest of our lives. We will live each day in fear."

"What about—about going to the hacienda with me now?"

Sheridan said, "I'll be going as far as the hacienda with you. Mason said Canales has recruited some five hundred men from the area, and I don't want you out there unprotected." He walked back to where she stood. Taking both shoulders in hand, he said, "Remember this Marguerite Belle LeFleur. I love you. I love you with all my heart."

Before Marguerite divined his purpose, he pulled her against his chest, his lips coming down on hers in the warm, soft kiss— one devoid of passion, full of promise and reassurance.

Chapter 25

Side by side, Marguerite and Sheridan stopped their horses
on the rise of the gentle hill and looked at the two-story adobe
ranch house that rested in the middle of the peaceful grassland.
Surrounded by colorful gardens and shaded by squat oak trees,
the hacienda had a stately if somewhat primitive beauty.
Haloed golden by the brilliance of the afternoon sun, it was
warm and friendly, a welcoming beacon to weary travelers. In
the tiled courtyard several women milled around the well and
pool, doing their chores; children ran to and fro, playing.

"Well? What do you think of the hacienda de la Flor del
Sol?"

Dressed in her Spanish riding habit, Marguerite tilted her
head inquisitively toward Sheridan, lifting the dust veil and
draping it behind the crown of her hat. She waited breathlessly
for his reaction.

Pushing his hat back, Sheridan looked at her, green eyes
sparkling with admiration. "It's beautiful, Daisy Belle. Truly
in keeping with your name." His lips twitched into a most
beguiling smile. "I do suppose that's the reason for all those
daisies." Reaching out to grab his hand, Marguerite laughed
with him and nodded her head. "I love you, Daisy Belle," he
murmured, his clasp tightening, his eyes telling of the depth of
his love.

As they sat there, enveloped by the serenity and beauty of the landscape, lost in their love, Juan smiled. He understood their preoccupation with one another, but he was weary, saddle sore, and ready to be home. Heaving forward, stretching, he waved and yelled, motioning the wagons forward. Moving down the hill, toward the huge barns to the rear of the hacienda, they slowly trundled by the two riders. Waiting until the cloud of dust settled, Marguerite and Sheridan nudged their horses, riding through the arch into the courtyard.

"Are they expecting me?" Sheridan asked, his eyes searching for signs of Paddy or Jewel.

"Yes. I sent a messenger ahead of us. I didn't think it would be fair for them to be unprepared."

"That bad," Sheridan muttered.

Marguerite nodded. "Give them time, Sheridan. Don't—don't be expecting too much too soon." Her voice lowered, and her smile softened her words. "Remember, you hurt us."

"Señora," a twelve-year-old cried aloud as he came running to greet Marguerite. "Welcome home."

"Thank you, Paco," Marguerite said, sliding out of the saddle, handing the child her reins. "Paco, this is Señor O'Roarke. Will you take care of his horse also?"

"Sí, señora." Paco reached for the reins to the other horse, leading both of them to the stables.

"When you've done that, you may check with Juan to see the surprise that we brought each of you."

Paco's black eyes glimmered with excitement. "A surprise, señora?"

Marguerite nodded her head and smiled. "One for today and another that's not to be opened until the fiesta."

"Well, child." Jewel emerged from the shaded veranda that ran the length of the house. Wiping her hands on the large apron that covered the front of her dress, she burst out of the vined arbor that shaded the porch. Arms outstretched, she hurried toward Marguerite. "It's about time you got home. I

434

was gettin' ready to send somebody out to git you."

"Oh, Jewel!" Marguerite rushed into the welcoming hug. "I'm so glad to be home."

"Not as much as I'se glad to have you home," Jewel stoutly maintained.

"How are the children?" Marguerite asked, pushing out of Jewel's arms.

"They'se jest fine." She picked up her apron and wiped the tears of happiness from her eyes. "Paddy's got 'em over at the corral, letting them watch the vaqueros break the new mustangs," she said.

Marguerite's eyes narrowed disapprovingly. "What about their lessons?"

Jewel chuckled. "Been doing their lessons jest fine." She glanced around the courtyard as if she were searching for someone. "Where's Mr.—" When her gaze landed on Sheridan, her voice lost its animation. "Where's Mr. Jordan?"

"He didn't come."

"Jest him?" Jewel said, her eyes never leaving Sheridan's face.

"Just me," Sheridan said softly, moving closer to Marguerite. He smiled, but not a muscle in Jewel's face moved. Dropping his head, Sheridan sighed. He understood the old woman's feelings, but her obvious disapproval of his coming bothered him.

"We'll talk about it later," Marguerite said to Jewel in an attempt to break the tension.

Marguerite was too tired to get into a heated discussion with Jewel at the moment. Because of her love for Sheridan she knew that she and Jordan had no future together—even if she were divorced. But she wasn't sure that she and Sheridan had a future. She was beginning to believe that Irishmen had only a past. At the moment she was too weary to think about it, certainly to discuss it.

Brushing by the woman, Marguerite moved into the cool salon, her boots tapping on the tiled floor. She shrugged out of her bolero, dust flying through the air, and she stripped the sombrero from her head.

"Right now I'd like to freshen up a bit." She laid her whip and hat on the entry table. Pulling off her gloves, she added, "I want to wash my hair, take a bath, and put on clean clothes." She turned to Sheridan. "What would you like to do?"

"Watch you." He grinned, pegging his hat on the wall.

"Then follow me, Mr. O'Roarke." Anticipation softly colored Marguerite's cheeks, and she smiled.

"Where do you want me to put Señor O'Roarke's trunk, señora?" a vaquero called from the entry.

"In my bedroom," Marguerite replied, moving in that direction, never slackening her pace.

Following Marguerite, Sheridan looked around, admiring the house. Although the summer heat was sweltering outside, the thick walls kept the house cool and pleasant, and the sweet, clean fragrance of flowers wafted through the rooms.

Marguerite opened the door and waved Sheridan in. "The master's bedroom."

Sheridan was impressed. The room was large and sunny, a window overlooking the corrals in the back of the house. The shutters were open, a breeze gently billowing the lace curtains. Against the far wall was an elegant four-poster bed, night tables on both sides. Next to the bed was a rocker. Two matching armoires of different sizes were on opposite walls. In front of the window was a large reading table and two chairs. Immediately inside the door was a large marble-topped washstand with a mirror above it, a bowl and pitcher sitting on top of it.

"Do you like it?"

Standing so close they almost touched, he said, "Where is the mistress's bedroom?"

Kissing the tip of Sheridan's nose, Marguerite grinned; then she walked to a closed door on the far side of the room. Opening it, she said, "In here, my lord."

"And what was the true purpose of these connecting

436

rooms?" Sheridan demanded.

Casting him a saucy smile, Marguerite teased, "Wouldn't you like to know!"

Sheridan was across the room in a rush, pulling her into his arms. "And you'll tell me," he growled playfully, "if you know what's good for you."

"What are you going to do if I don't?" Marguerite asked.

"You gonna take a bath and shave right now!" Jewel marched into the room, her eyes raking disdainfully over Sheridan's dust-ridden clothes and his beard-stubbled face. "And so is you, Miz Marguerite. Now git to your room right now."

Marguerite chuckled, slipping out of Sheridan's arms. "I'll see you in a little while, darling."

Pushing into the anteroom with her, Sheridan said, "But I wanted to watch you freshen up!"

"You jest git back in here, Sheridan Michael," Jewel called. "Both of you are too dirty to be bathing in one tub. 'Sides Miz Marguerite's got plenty to do with business about dis hacienda, so she don't need no distractions right now."

Grinning at Sheridan's grimace, Marguerite skirted into her bedroom, closing the door. Sheridan returned to his room.

"I don't like dat hair all over your face," Jewel said, throwing clean towels over the rack. "Be glad when you shave it off."

"I'm not," Sheridan replied, scratching his chin. "I'm growing a beard."

Shaking her head, the housekeeper said, "I'll send the tub and water in."

As she spoke, Paco lugged Sheridan's trunk in and set it at the foot of the four-poster bed.

"Anything else, *Tía* Jewel?" he grunted, looking at Jewel.

"Get the tub and two kittles of water from the fire," she instructed. When the boy darted out of the room, she returned her attention to Sheridan. She pointed to the washstand. "Clean water for shaving. Clean towels and washrags."

Looking at the pitcher on the night table, she said, "That's fresh drinking water." She turned, moving to the door. "If you need anything, jest pull the bell and somebody'll come running."

"Jewel."

Her hand on the knob, the buxom woman turned again and looked at Sheridan.

"I need your friendship." The green eyes pleaded with her; his smile tugged at her heart. "Aren't you the least bit glad to see me?"

Jewel's eyes softened, but her expression remained unchanged. "Yes, sir, Mr. Sheridan, I'm rightly glad to see you, but I ain't glad to see you back in my little girl's life. You hurt her. You hurt her bad, and she wuz jest gettin' over you. Now I'm jest wonderin' what your intentions are this time."

"I love her."

Jewel shook her head. "Sometimes love ain't enough, Mr. Sheridan. You need responsibility. You gotta be willing to make some sacrifices. And as I sees it, Mr. Sheridan, Miz Marguerite's done most of the sacrificing." She stared at him, waiting for a comment. When none was forthcoming, she asked, "Is you here to stay, Mr. Sheridan?"

"I'm here to stay," he announced, loving it when her white teeth flashed in a beautiful smile. "I have to complete one more assignment for the rangers."

Tears blurred Jewel's vision. "See, Mr. Sheridan, you come back in Miz Marguerite's life jest long enough to boot Mr. Jordan out. You create a hole, and you fill it for a little while, but when you're gone she's got nothing but heartache and grief." She lifted her apron and wiped the tears from her face. "Dat's why I ain't so glad to see you."

When the door closed, Sheridan paced around the room, thinking about Jewel's words. They hit him squarely between the eyes, scaring him. He walked to the connecting doors, but as his hands closed over the knob, he heard Jewel and Marguerite talking. He paused for only a moment before he retraced his steps. Leaning against the window casement, he looked at the corral. Deep in thought, he didn't really notice the old man who stood beneath the shade of the tree or the children who dangled on the fence, laughing and cheering the vaqueros. Sheridan didn't stir until he heard the knock on the door.

"Your bath, Señor O'Roarke."

When he opened the door, Paco walked into the room, carrying a large, elongated copper and brass bathtub. Setting it in the middle of the floor, he said, "*Tía* Jewel would like for me to bring your clothes that need to be washed, señor." Reaching up, he pushed an errant lock of shining black hair off his forehead. "Also she said send anything that needed to be ironed."

Sheridan walked to the trunk at the foot of the bed. Unfastening the leather straps, he opened the lid and pulled out a clean shirt and trousers. Throwing them over the boy's arm, he said, "I'd like to have these ironed for tonight." Holding the valise, he went on to say, "You can get my soiled clothes when you come back to empty the tub."

"*Sí*, señor."

Paco walked out of the room, returning a short time later with two kettles of hot water which he poured into the tub. As soon as he emptied the kettles, he raced out of the room again, calling over his shoulder, "I'll be back with the cold water."

By the time Sheridan had unbuttoned his shirt and dropped it in the valise, Paco returned with two more kettles of water. Once these were empty he looked at Sheridan.

"Is there anything else you'd like, señor?"

"All I want right now, lad, is to take a bath."

When Paco's eyes landed on Sheridan's dirty boots and lingered, Sheridan looked down, too. Both of them lifted their heads and grinned at the same time.

"I can polish them so they will look brand new, señor," the boy said.

"Anything will be better than this," Sheridan replied,

sitting down in the rocker. With Paco's help and with a great deal of grunting, he tugged both boots off and handed them to the servant. As he stripped his socks off, he said, "You'll get some extra coins for this."

"*Gracias*, señor," Paco called, running out of the room, boots under arm, kettles in hand.

When the door closed, Sheridan walked to the washstand, looking at his reflection in the shaving mirror. He scratched his cheeks and chin, and he grinned at the beard fuzz that covered his face. He wanted to shave, but he needed the anonymity a beard afforded. Moving toward the tub, he unbuttoned his trousers, but he hadn't stepped out of them when he heard another knock on the door. Sighing his exasperation, he yanked his pants up, holding them together with his hand, and walked to the door.

"Yes."

Standing there was a tot whom Sheridan judged to be no more than five or six. He was wearing a broad-brimmed hat that dwarfed him, the brim falling over his forehead and eyes. "Hi. Do you have another pair of boots?"

Sheridan's annoyance turned to puzzlement. "Another pair?"

The head bobbed up and down. "So I can work for you like Paco?"

Sheridan chuckled, immediately understanding. He shook his head. "Sorry, only one pair."

"Oh," came the frail reply.

"You want to earn some money?" The boy nodded. Turning his head, Sheridan glanced around the room, mulling an errand for the tot. This could quickly become an expensive habit, he thought. When he spied his valise, he said, "Wait here."

Closing the door, he stripped, dropping his trousers into the satchel. Yanking a towel from the washstand rack, he wrapped it around his middle. Then he walked to the dresser, picking up a coin. Valise and money in hand, he moved across the room,

440

cracking the door wide enough to pass the case through.

"Here," he said, handing the boy the satchel and coin, "take these to Jewel so they can be washed."

Sheridan saw the grin beneath the brim of the hat. *"Gracias,* señor," he called as he scurried toward the stairs, the valise weighing him down, impeding his progress.

Shutting the door once more, Sheridan leaned against it for a few seconds, waiting. When no more knocks came, he dropped the towel on the floor and eased into the tub, enjoying the luxury of soaking in the warm water. By the time he had washed his hair, bathed and dried off, he heard another knock at the door. Shaking his head, he grinned, wondering which one of the boys it was this time.

"Your clothes, señor." Paco's voice carried through the door. Again wrapping himself in a towel, Sheridan padded barefoot to the door, cracked it wide enough to reach for his clothes. By the time he was dressed, Paco called out, "Your boots, señor." When the door opened, a hand and two black boots, polished to a high sheen, materialized. Following them was a mop of black hair and a grin.

"How are these, señor?"

Taking them, Sheridan nodded his head and whistled his surprise and praise. "To be sure, lad, they do look like new. I do believe I can see my reflection in them." Setting them down in front of the rocker, Sheridan walked to the dresser, picking up several coins. "Here you go," he said, turning around, moving toward Paco.

"Gracias, señor." The boy dropped the coins into his pocket. "Michael and I will be back for the tub later. *Tía* Jewel said you could go into the salon if you wanted a drink."

Sheridan smiled, walking to the rocker. Sitting down, he put on his socks and boots. Once he was dressed, he returned to the dresser, opening a small metal case, extracting a cheroot. He held it between his fingers, rolling the tobacco between them, enjoying the feel. Lifting it, he placed it under his nose. Closing his eyes, he smelled it. Then he lit it.

A bath, he thought, and clean clothes. Now he wanted the pleasure of a leisurely smoke and a drink. His black boots clicked over the tile floor as he walked out of the room and downstairs into the salon. Moving to the assortment of whiskey decanters, he lifted one, filling his glass. He walked through the opened doors onto the tiled patio, sitting in one of the large chairs in the shade of the trees.

When he had finished his drink and his cheroot, he went to look for Marguerite in her apartment, but she was gone. Curious about the woman Marguerite had become during the past six years, he wandered around the room, looking at the European furnishings that should have seemed so incongruous with the Spanish architect of the house, but oddly they didn't.

He walked into the bedroom, standing in the door for the longest time, his eyes moving over the furnishings: another tester bed with a crocheted bedspread and rolled bolsters, marble-topped washstand and dresser, a matching armoire, a reading table, and chairs. He walked into the adjoining room— her personal room. Hanging on the wall by its handle was her bathtub. In the corner of the room was a fireplace. Sitting in front of its black, gaping mouth were two kettles; beside it was a pail of fresh water. Above the marble-topped washstand was a large mirror, and towels were folded across the brass rack. The chamber pot, framed with a wooden-holed seat, was inserted in a small cubicle. The curtain which afforded the user privacy was pulled to the side.

Returning to the bedroom, Sheridan brushed past the dresser, running his fingers over the finish. When he saw the jewelry box, he lifted the lid, letting the soft music flow through the room. He smiled when he saw the pearls. Picking them up, running them through his hands, he remembered that night so long ago when he had taken them from Marguerite—the night he had fallen under her spell—had fallen in love with her.

Suspending the neclace over the box, he started to return it to its black velvet bed, but the glimmer of gold caught his sight. Reaching into the box with his other hand, he picked up the ring—the ring he'd given to Marguerite so long ago.

"Don't you think you're being a little personal?"

Holding on to the ring, dropping the pearls into the box, Sheridan spun around. His back to the door, he hadn't seen or heard her enter.

"I thought you said this was packed away in a chest."

Marguerite smiled and walked into the room, her blue gown enhancing the color of her eyes. "That's a chest."

"You never forgot, did you?"

Her eyes shimmering, Marguerite shook her head, her whispered voice caressing his ears. "No, I never forgot." She held her hand out, and Sheridan slipped the ring over her fourth finger.

Clasping her hand in his, drawing her into his arms, he said, "I love you with all my heart, my soul, and my body, Marguerite LeFleur."

"I love you," she whispered, her face lifting for his kiss.

As the kiss deepened, Marguerite slipped her hands between their bodies, and she unbuttoned Sheridan's shirt. Needing to feel the heat of his flesh, wanting to touch him, she eased her hands beneath the soft white material, her palms caressing his warm skin. She felt Sheridan quiver.

Finally he lifted his mouth from hers, and he looked into her face as if he'd never seen her before. His eyes glazed with passion, he slowly pivoted her body, deftly unhooking the back of her gown. Pulling the bodice loose but not slipping the material from her breasts, he moved slightly, picked her up and carried her to the bed, laying her down.

He quickly divested himself of his clothes and sat down beside her, again looking, drinking his feel of her beauty. Admiration glistened in his eyes, and his finger traced the contours of her face, the eyebrows, the nose, her full lips, her throat. He untied the lace ruff around her neck. He leaned

443

over, his lips gently whispering down her neck and across her shoulders. Marguerite trembled from the onslaught of emotion.

"I envy your clothes," he said, his lilting voice beautifully soft. "They get to touch you all the time, and I so infrequently."

His hands caught the bodice of embroidered silk and gauze, and he slowly eased it down. His lips caressed the creamy white breasts that peeked above the thin chemise. His teeth gently nipped one of the straps, and he pulled it off one shoulder; then the other. His face burrowed into the scented cleavage, his chin pushing her undergarment down, exposing the breasts.

When Sheridan's mouth caught the tender peak, Marguerite gasped and clutched him closer. As he sucked, she felt desire burn through her body. She instinctively arched, pushing against him, wanting the completeness of his love. Reveling in the throes of passioned delight, Sheridan chuckled, his warm breath splaying against Marguerite's breast down her midriff. His lips moved lower, his face nuzzling beneath the layers of material.

She lifted her hands, trailing her fingers down his cheeks, tracing the sensual lines of his mouth. Quickly he opened his lips, gently capturing her fingers between his teeth. Marguerite laughed, then sighed as he brushed the tips with his tongue. He looked down and saw the small gold band. Opening his mouth, he released her fingers only to capture her hand in his. He turned it over, palm up, and he began to kiss the soft, pink flesh all over her hand up to the ring.

"My grandfather gave that to my grandmother," he murmured.

"I remember," Marguerite said, her voice breathy soft. "On their wedding."

"Aye, lassie, how'd you know that?"

"Your mother told me."

Sheridan laughed. "Women do be such gossips."

"And men such braggarts."

444

"Ah, to be sure, lass, but what lovers!"

The whispered words died into silence as he stared at Marguerite. Catching the material of her bodice and chemise in both hands, he pulled it lower. Slowly his gaze moved over her face, down her neck, to her breasts. Farther down he looked at the slim line of midriff and the tiny waist.

"So adorable," he murmured, his face lowering, his lips kissing the sensitive area around her navel, his warm breath splaying against her belly.

An afternoon breeze gently stirred through the room, blowing wisps of hair around Marguerite's face, cooly touching her fevered skin. She exhaled slowly, her stomach taut beneath Sheridan's lips, which moved in ever widening circles, the material of her dress slipping lower and lower.

"Don't," she gasped, her fingers tangling in his hair.

"Why?" he whispered, lifting his head, peering at her. "Aren't you enjoying it?"

"Yes."

Sheridan chuckled, the rich laughter billowing from the wellspring of his soul. "So I am," he said in the same caressive voice. "Here, let me show you."

Sheridan caught Marguerite's hand in his and pressed it against his hardness. Marguerite's hand instinctively curved, and she rubbed him. As she had done beneath his loving ministrations, Sheridan sucked in his breath, and he slid onto the bed, lying on his back, enjoying her touch. Marguerite leaned over him, her lips traveling his face as her hand gently touched his manhood. Her lips moved down the thick neck, across the collarbone.

When she stopped at the sensitive hollow at the base of his neck, Sheridan pleaded hoarsely, "Don't stop, Daisy. Love me." His green eyes were dark and vibrant, reflecting all his needs and desires.

Marguerite turned her head, her hair wisping across his chest that was covered with a thin film of perspiration. Mesmerized by his virile handsomeness, tormented by the

445

primitive surge of desire, Marguerite gazed at him in rapture. He reached up, cupping her face in his hands.

"Touch me, Daisy, my darling. Make love to me. Fill my wanting soul."

Her hair spilling around her face, the long curling strands brushing against Sheridan's chest, Marguerite lifted her hands, gently removing Sheridan's fingers from her cheeks. She lowered her face, her lips moving down his chest. Following the example of his love touches, her tongue swirled, and she gently sucked his nipple.

Sheridan's hands moved up and down the smooth line of her back as she spread kisses up his throat over his cheeks, her lips finally capturing his in a long, hungry kiss. She pressed against his chest, and her hand traveled down his body.

As she touched him, he sat up.

"Now, Marguerite. Now."

"Yes," she answered, sliding beneath him, welcoming the weight of his body over hers, welcoming his most complete touch.

"Don't you think we ought to be getting up?" Sheridan murmured, making no effort to move.

"Um-hum," she answered lazily. Reluctantly she rolled off the bed, dressing.

Sheridan, his lower body covered with the sheet, lay there watching her. After she pinned her hair into a coil on the top of her head, she sat on the edge of the bed.

"Hook me up, darling."

"Why?" he murmured, propping on an elbow, planting kisses over her shoulder and down her spine.

"Because I have someone who wants to see you," she said.

"Paddy?"

"Paddy."

Running across the room, she called over her shoulder. "I'll be right back, darling. Let me go get him."

Getting out of bed, Sheridan dressed and walked into the sitting room. Pouring himself a drink, he stood in front of the opened window. When he heard the door open, he didn't immediately turn. He couldn't. Too many emotions were assailing him. He set the half-filled glass on the windowsill.

"To be sure an' I recognize the hair."

Paddy's voice touched Sheridan's heart as well as his ears. He spun around. "Paddy," he whispered.

"Sheridan O'Roarke." Paddy's eyes roamed Sheridan's face. So like Mary's, he thought. The green eyes. The lips. Tears filled his eyes as memories filled his heart. "To be sure, lad," he said, his voice thick with emotion, "you're an O'Roarke, and ye'r not dead."

"Nay," Sheridan replied, his eyes watering, "'twas the only way I could escape the hangman's knot."

Sheridan was across the room before he knew it, his arms outstretched. He engulfed Paddy in a bear hug, swinging him around the room, both of them laughing. Wiping the moisture from her eyes, Marguerite slipped out of the room, leaving the two alone.

"And now, Sheridan," Paddy said when finally they quit jigging around the room, "tell me something about yourself since ye left Ballygarrett."

For several hours the men talked, not stopping until they heard the knock, and Marguerite poked her head through the door. Smiling, she asked, "May I come in?"

"To be sure," Paddy said.

Marguerite entered the room, a small boy in tow, his hat as big as he was. Standing in front of Sheridan, she said, "I'd like for you to meet Michael."

Leaning over, Sheridan extended his hand. Remembering the little fellow's visit earlier, Sheridan laughed. "I've already met Michael."

"You did?" Marguerite was surprised.

"He ran an errand for me."

Reaching into his pocket, Michael's fingers closed over the

447

coin. Pulling the grubby hand out, he opened his fist, showing off the money. Marguerite looked from Michael to Sheridan.

"I paid Paco to clean and polish my boots. This one came along later, wanting to run an errand."

"Mich—ael!" Marguerite quietly reprimanded, drawling both syllables of the child's name.

Totally unrepentant, the boy slipped the money back into his pocket and lifted his arms. He clutched the sides of his hat with both hands, pulling the brim down to his shoulders. His exprssion was solemn, and his eyes seriously studied the stranger, his gaze finally stopping on the red hair.

"Are you a ranger?"

Sheridan nodded.

Suddenly Michael's face exploded into a smile. He shucked the hat, a thatch of red hair falling into his freckled face. Pointing to his head, he said, "See. My hair is like yours."

Sheridan was like a man in a trance. Slowly he slid back into the upholstery of the chair. He felt as if every drop of blood had drained from his body. He could hardly breathe. Michael's eyes were the most beautiful shade of green that Sheridan had ever seen. He reached out, touching the mop of red hair; he ran his finger over the boy's nose, touching the spread of freckles.

"And your eyes are like mine," Sheridan finally said.

"Come, Michael," Paddy called from the door. "We must go take a bath and get ready for supper. Jewel will have our scalps if we don't."

Michael scampered across the room, retrieving his hat before he joined Paddy. "The Comanches would like to have my hair," he proudly announced. "Red is the color they use when they win, and my hair is red." Slipping his hand into Paddy's, he walked out of the room. But as quickly he darted back in. "Are you going to eat with us?" When Sheridan nodded, Michael grinned and raced toward the kitchen.

"My son?"

"Our son."

Sheridan strode to the window, picking up his glass from the sill. In one swallow he quaffed the remainder of his drink down. "Why?" he asked, his fingers tightening around the glass. Spinning around, he yelled, "Why the hell didn't you tell me before you left Ireland?"

"I didn't know until after I'd left," Marguerite calmly answered, her aplomb belying her emotions. She sat down in a chair, reaching into her sewing basket, picking up her embroidery. "After I found out, I wrote you letter after letter, but when I received no answer, I could only assume you didn't care." Dropping the thimble over the tip of her third finger, she pushed the needle through the linen, scarlet thread following. "I never heard from you."

"How old is he?"

"Five."

"What's—what's his full name?"

"He was christened Sheridan Michael O'Roarke." She whipped a row of dainty stitches atop the material.

Sheridan didn't know how to cope with his feelings. He was elated to learn that he had a son, but he was angry. He'd missed out on the first five years of his child's life.

"Why didn't you tell me before now?"

Marguerite paused in her embroidery. "I wasn't sure if you were going to become a permanent part of our life."

Sheridan slung the glass across the room, the crystal splintering as it hit the tiles. "Whether I become a permanent part of your life or not," he thundered, "I had a right to know about my son. You had no right to keep this from me." Fury raged through him. "If I hadn't come to the hacienda, would you have told me?"

Marguerite slipped the thimble from her finger, weaved the needle through the material, and lay the hoop in her lap. Meticulously folding the linen around the form, she said, "I don't know. I only know that I was selfish enough to want you to come because of me." She placed the embroidery in the sewing basket and lifted her head, looking directly into his face. "I didn't want you to come back to me because of

449

your responsibility to a child."

"But all this time," Sheridan muttered, "not to have told me, not to have hinted about it."

Marguerite stood, smiling. "I kept begging you to come to the hacienda, didn't I?" Sheridan nodded, but he didn't smile. Making no apology for her secrecy, Marguerite held her hand out for his. "Come. Let's go see Daisy before supper."

When they reached the nursery, Daisy was standing on the floor, pulling up on the rocker. Seeing Marguerite and Sheridan, she turned loose, falling on her little bottom. Gurgling her happiness, she scooted across the floor, using Sheridan's leg for a ladder on which to climb.

Laughing, he bent over and picked her up, tossing her in the air. Her screams and giggles of delight filled the hacienda. So occupied with her, neither Marguerite nor Sheridan saw Michael when he slipped through the door. Shrinking against the wall, he watched them with the baby. Eventually Marguerite saw him, and her heart was touched. Sitting in the rocker, she called him to her.

"What do you think about us keeping Daisy for your sister?"

Crawling into his mother's lap, Michael rammed a fist in his mouth. Shaking his head, he mumbled, "I don't want a sister."

Hearing Michael's cry, Sheridan handed Daisy to Hortensia and squatted beside Marguerite. "Daisy needs us to love her," he explained simply. "The Indians killed her mama and papa."

Michael only shook his head, his little eyes glittering with unshed tears.

"She needs a mama and a papa, but most of all she needs a big brother to take care of her."

Michael lay his head on Marguerite's breast. "She wants my mama?"

"No," Sheridan answered, "she's too little to know what she wants or needs. But your mama would like to be her mama, and I would like to be her papa."

Tears slid down Michael's cheek, and his chin wobbled. "I

don't have a papa."

With a wave of love unequaled to any force Sheridan had felt in his entire life, he reached for Michael, pulling the boy into his arms. "May I be your papa?" Unashamed of the tears that streaked his face, Sheridan crushed Michael in his arms, kissing the top of his head.

"Ouch," Michael complained childlike, pushing out of Sheridan's arms. "You're hurting me." Marguerite and Sheridan laughed through their tears. Suddenly Michael darted away from Sheridan, calling over his shoulder. "Bet you can't catch me."

Standing in the door, a twinkle in her eyes, Jewel said, "Well, I can, boy, and if'n I do, I'm gonna wallop your bottom. I sent you in here to tell your mama and papa that it's suppertime."

Running in front of her, Michael said, "We're playing, Jewel."

The black woman clamped her hands on her hips and declared, "Well, I ain't. Now all of you git to dat table before I spank you."

Michael stopped in his tracks. Clapping his hands and giggling, he squealed, "Papa, too?"

Jewel's gaze shifted from Michael to Sheridan. "Papa too," she drawled. Then she laughed. "I ain't afraid of none of you."

Picking Michael up, Sheridan threw him in the air, catching him. "Do it again, Papa," Michael screamed.

"Not right now," Sheridan said, hoisting Michael on his shoulder. "Let's go eat supper."

As Marguerite came abreast, Sheridan dropped his arm around her shoulder, and the three of them walked toward the dining room.

Chapter 26

Night settled its dark cloak over Freedom Point as two men rode in, leading a pack of mules. Stopping in front of the saloon, they dismounted and hitched their horses and mules to the post. The tall, slender one, dressed in buckskins, walked inside the noisy building; the bearded one stayed with the animals and goods. As the frontiersman pushed in the door, he reached up, pulling his coonskin cap lower on his forehead. Curling his hand into a fist, he hit the bar several times.

"Need a room."

"Sure thing." The bartender, a fat man whose shirt gaped open where it pulled across his stomach between the buttons, shuffled to where the frontiersman stood. "One dollar United States currency for each bed."

"What? That's robbery!"

"Take it or leave it, stranger," the bartender returned unperturbedly, picking up a rag and wiping the beads of moisture from his bald head before he rubbed the counter. "This is the onliest place in town where you'll be gitting a room and a bed. Two dollars if you want a private room."

"I'll take it," Stringbean grumbled, fishing in his pocket for money. "Two. One for me. One for the drummer."

The bartender held his hand out. When he closed his pudgy fist over the coins, he said, "Number two and three. Right

453

down that hall. Side by side." Reaching under the bar, he pulled out two keys and handed them to the stranger. "Privacy you want. Privacy you paid for."

Moving outside, the scout said, "Got two rooms. Two and three." He held the keys up.

"Good. Let's unpack these mules, get them to the livery stable and go to bed. I'm so tired I'm about to fall asleep on my feet."

"Me, too. But afore I go to bed, I'd jest like to have a good strong drink to wet my parched throat."

"That, too," Sheridan said.

For the next thirty minutes they unpacked the mules, carrying the goods into one of the rooms. When they were through, Sheridan headed for a table in the far corner of the saloon, and Stringbean stopped at the bar.

"Two whiskeys." He pointed. "Over at that table in the corner where me and my friend are gonna be sittin'."

Stringbean moved across the room to join his companion, escaping the smoke and din. Ducking so that he wouldn't hit the candle holder above his head, he pushed behind the table, pulling on a rickety chair.

The bartender brought two drinks to the table. "New around here, ain't ya?"

"Reckon ya might say that." The tall man ran his tongue around his mouth, dislodging his cud, spitting it into the rusty cuspidor nearby. The first swallow of liquor he swished around in his mouth before he spit in the receptacle; the second one he quaffed in one lusty gulp.

"What's your name?"

"Jest call me Stringbean. This here's my partner, Rusty. He's a drummer, and we're looking to do some trading."

"Reckon the trading post would be the best place for that," the bartender replied, easing away. His curiosity satisfied, he moved back to the bar. Calling over his shoulder, he asked, "Do you need a woman tonight?"

Both men shook their heads; Sheridan spoke. "Not tonight.

454

We've been in the saddle for days, so I just want to rest. We're going to be on the move again tomorrow."

The bartender wiped his hands over his big, moist lips, letting his fingers linger at the corners of his mouth. "Where ya'll headed?"

"Matamoras," Sheridan replied. "Thought we'd do some trading with the Mexicans down there." Emptying his glass, he asked, "Where's the livery? We been riding hard, and our horses need tending to."

"Down the street at Harry's. Blacksmith shop on the right. Ya can't miss it. He'll be in bed. Just knock on the door.

"You serve food in here?" Stringbean asked.

The bartender nodded his head. "Go on back to the kitchen. Rosie'll fix ya up with something." He grinned. "Just about anything you want, you kin git from Rosie. A Mexican vaquero traded some horses to a Injun fer her. When he got tired of her, he left her, and I took her in."

Getting up from the table, Sheridan and Stringbean pushed through the crowded room to the kitchen in the back. The room was hot, a large fire blazing in the fireplace. The windows were open, but no breeze cooled the summer night. Insects buzzed around the candles.

"Howdy, ma'am," Stringbean said, looking at the Mexican girl who squatted in front of the fire, stirring a pot of stew. "Bartender said we could get some food back here."

The girl stood, wiping perspiration from her face with the rag she held in her hands. Then she tucked black hair behind her ears. With lackluster eyes, she studied both men, giving the tall, older one a cursory glance, perusing the younger man. She liked his red hair and his thick beard. She especially liked those green eyes. Her lips smiled, but no expression touched the eyes.

"Sit down, señores, and Rosita will fix you a bowl of beef stew."

She reached on the shelf behind her for two pottery bowls which she filled with a savory stew, huge lumps of tender beef,

455

potatoes, and carrots. Setting them on the table, she said, "We have milk. Would you care for a glass. Fresh today."

"How about coffee?" Stringbean asked, tearing a piece of bread from the loaf that lay on a plate in the middle of the table. "Strong, hot, and black."

"Coffee for you, señor?" Rosita asked Sheridan. When he nodded, she filled two cups and set them on the table. Sitting down beside them, she asked, "What are you doing in Freedom Point?"

"Trading," Stringbean replied, his mouth full of food. "Traveled all the way from Houston to San Antone. We been to Victoria, Goliad, Linnville, and Refugio. Got a whole bunch of goods, don't we, Rusty?"

Too busy eating to talk, Sheridan simply nodded.

Rosita smiled at Sheridan. "Are you going to want a bath, señor?" Again he nodded. "I'll bring it up later."

Swallowing his food with a gulp of coffee, he said, "I don't know which room I'm going to sleep in yet."

Rosita laughed, the husky sound filling the room. Although it was beautiful, the sound did not come from Rosita's soul. "Do not worry, señor. I will find out."

After they finished eating, Sheridan left a coin on the table for Rosita. Then he and Stringbean walked out the back door, moving to the hitching post. Untying their horses and mules, they slowly walked down the street.

"Tell you, Rusty," Stringbean said, his words garbled as he refilled his mouth with tobacco, "I'm rightly tired of moving from town to town hunting this Hiberny feller. A ghost would be easier to find."

"Aye," Sheridan replied, lapsing into brogue. "To be sure, Stringbean, I think Hibernia is a ghost come to haunt me."

"We've been to every trading post between here and San Antone, and so far we've come up with nothing. Nobody's heard of this feller, and they ain't seen any unusual Mexican or Injun activity in the area. Fact of the matter, no Injun activity of any kind."

"Tomorrow is another day," Sheridan said. "We'll see what happens."

At the blacksmith's, conversation stopped. Stringbean knocked on the door. When there was no response, he knocked again. Finally they heard noise from the inside, and a voice called out.

"Yeah. What do you want?"

"Need to put our horses and mules up for the night."

By the time Sheridan returned to his room, he was almost asleep on his feet. Saying good night to Stringbean in the hallway, he unlocked the door and walked into room three. A lamp was lit, and soft light splayed across the crude floor and over the rustic furniture. A copper tub filled with water sat at the foot of the bed. Linen was draped over the rim, and a bar of soap lay on the floor.

Locking the door, Sheridan smiled. He was grateful to Rosita. Quickly he cleaned out his pockets, laying his personal belongings on the rickety dresser. Walking to the window, he raised and propped it with a stick, hoping that a breeze would come in the window, along with the insects. Returning to the center of the room, he stripped, letting his clothes lie where they fell. Climbing into the tub, sinking into the water, he soaked a long time before he liberally soaped his body, washing the grime away. Afterward he dried off and put on clean clothes. Placing his knife and pistol on the pillow beside him, standing his gun against the bed, he blew out the lamp and lay down.

Although he was tired, he didn't immediately go to sleep. He lay there thinking about Marguerite, wondering what she was doing now, wondering if she was missing him as much as he was missing her. Damn! He rolled over, spreading out, seeking a little coolness, this would be the last ranger excursion he went on. He wanted to be home with her and the children.

A smile played on Sheridan's lips as he thought about Michael, the splattering of freckles across his nose, the green eyes, the flashing smile. He could still see him now: fisted hands on both sides of his hat, putting it down around his head, his face solemn, almost cherubic, his eyes sparking mischief.

He thought about Daisy Belle, remembering his last promise to Marguerite. When he returned, they would formally adopt her and have her christened. He chuckled aloud, recalling Marguerite's heated outburst when they discussed the baptism.

"Sheridan, I don't want her named Daisy Belle. You can call her that, but I want her christened a good Christian name, like Mary Margaret or . . ."

Chuckling, Sheridan had taken Marguerite into his arms. "You have her christened any name you wish, love, but her name will be Daisy Belle O'Roarke, to be sure."

Marguerite had lifted her face to his, her hands climbing his chest, pushing beneath the material of his shirt. "I can't convince you to change your mind."

"Aye, you can," he whispered. "I'm a mighty weak man, lass, dreadfully sinful and easily led astray. I generally yield to temptation." His lips covered hers in a long, warm kiss that had deepened into a ravaging fire of passion.

Groaning, Sheridan tossed and turned. Muttering an expletive under his breath, he got up and walked to the dresser and lit a cheroot. He moved to the window and smoked before he tried to sleep again. When he returned to bed, however, he lay there for a long time. His getting up and smoking had been futile; his thoughts still centered on Marguerite and the children. Finally he dropped into a fitful sleep.

Hours passed before the scantily clad figure sneaked into town and climbed to the second story of the saloon. Crouching, the stealthy figure scooted across the balcony, moving to the opened window. As quietly, he raised up, threw his leg over the sill and entered the room where Sheridan was sleeping. His moccasined feet silently padded over the floor.

Sheridan awoke, not because he heard any noise but because he felt the presence. Without making a sound, without opening his eyes, his fingers curled around the hilt of his knife.

Forcing his breathing to remain even and shallow, he waited until he felt the intruder standing beside his bed. Then he leaped to his feet, his arms swinging, one grabbing the Indian by the hair of the head, the other lodging the point of the blade under his chin.

"Señor," the Indian softly cried, "it is I . . . Juan."

Sheridan dropped both arms. "Thank God," he breathed, reaching for the matches to light the lamp. "I was beginning to worry about you."

The acrid stench of sulphur filled the room as the match spit and sputtered to life. The flame illuminated the faces as it exploded into a huge burst of light. Sheridan lifted the sooty chimney and touched the flame to the wick. Returning his knife to the pillow, he sat on the bed.

"Did you find out anything?"

Looking around the room at the sparse furnishings, Juan shook his head. "I have seen no signs of Indians, and no one is willing to talk with me about anyone called Hibernia. Always I am referred to the settlement of San Patricio." Dragging the chair close to the bed, Juan sat down. "Have you learned anything?"

"Nothing."

"What are we going to do now?"

Pondering Juan's question, unconsciously running his hand over his beard, Sheridan didn't immediately answer. Eventually he said, "Stringbean and I are leaving for Matamoras in the morning. Why don't you leave ahead of us and see what you can find?"

The men talked a short while longer, setting up a meeting place and time. Then Juan slipped out of the room as silently as he had come. Sheridan walked to the dresser and picked up the metal case. Opening it and taking a cheroot out, he returned to the bed. Lifting the chimney off the lamp, he bent, touching the cigar tip to the wick. Pondering the situation, he lay down, bunching the pillows behind his back.

He was deep in thought and plans when he heard the noise.

459

Not sure what he'd heard, he quietly sat up, his eyes darting from the door to the window. He eased off the bed. He heard the sound again; this time he identified it. Someone was jiggling the doorknob. Capping the chimney, blowing into the funnel of his hand, he doused the light. Knife in hand, he tiptoed to the door, stretched flat against the wall so that he would be hidden when it opened. He heard the click of a key in the lock. The door opened, a wedge of light splaying across the darkened room.

"Señor." Rosita's whispered call echoed through the room.

Lowering his hand, Sheridan moved from behind the door. "Isn't it a little late to be calling?"

Holding the candle higher so she could see Sheridan's face, Rosita smiled and shrugged, her shawl falling from her shoulder to reveal smooth skin. "Not too late for what I have in mind, señor."

Sheridan liked the girl. She was clean and decent, untarnished by the kind of life she'd been forced to lead. And if his love for Marguerite hadn't been so strong, he would have been attracted to Rosita. Even now his body clamored for release.

"Sorry, Rosita, but I'm a married man."

Fully in the room, Rosita set the candle on the dresser. "I have entertained married men before, señor. If it doesn't bother you, it doesn't bother me." Her voice relayed no emotion; her proposition was strictly business.

"It would bother me, and it would bother my wife," Sheridan returned. Motioning toward the door, pointing with his knife, he said, "Now why don't you be a good little girl and leave."

Not understanding the man and wanting the money, Rosita was crestfallen. "You do not like Rosita?"

"I like you," Sheridan softly assured her. "But I don't want to sleep with you." Again he waved toward the door. "Now run along and let me sleep. I have a long journey ahead of me tomorrow, and I need my rest."

Rosita stared at him for a long time before she sighed and turned, picking up the candle. When she did, she saw the money. She reached out, running her fingers over it.

"I will make it worth your while and your time, señor. I am very good."

"Please, Rosita."

Her hand slid across the dresser, the tips of her fingers resting on the slip of paper—the message the rangers had intercepted. The drawing arrested her attention.

"*Es un Trébol,*" she murmured, leaning down for a closer look. "*Sí, es un Trébol!*" She ran her finger around the outline of the shamrock.

Sheridan closed and locked the door, moving to the dresser. "What are you saying?"

She drummed her finger on the sketch. "The clover, señor. Are you from the clover?"

"What clover?" Sheridan replied, trying to keep the excitement out of his voice.

"*Hacienda del Trébol Esmeraldo!*" she exclaimed, rushing on. "The Emerald Shamrock Rancho. The hacienda is beautiful, señor. I have seen it once when the Indians were bringing me from Mexico. They stopped there. I remember."

"They raided the ranch?" Sheridan quizzed.

Rosita shook her head, her hair flying around her face. "No, they met with two men, both of them wearing beautiful green cloaks. One man, called Trébol, was so big, señor." She lifted her hand in the air, measuring his height. "The other was not so big."

Sheridan's heartbeat accelerated. "Tell me about them, Rosita."

Closing her eyes, the girl said, "The day was cold, señor, I remember. The wind was blowing, and I was barefoot, wearing only rags. The cloaks looked so warm and so beautiful that I wished for one."

When she lapsed into silence, Sheridan said, "Can you tell me anything else?"

461

"I saw many soldiers, señor, but that is all. After the Méxicanos left, the Indians began moving northward again."

"What happened then?"

"One of the men from the hacienda rode with us. He took a liking to me, and he bought me." She leveled emotionless black eyes on Sheridan. "I was worth three horses, señor. Before we reached Freedom Point, the Mexicano left the Indians, taking me with him. When we reached Freedom Point, he left me, and Thomas—"

"Thomas?"

"The owner of the cantina. He gave me a job and a place to stay. I have been here ever since."

"I'm sorry," Sheridan murmured.

"Do not be sorry, señor," Rosita quietly replied. "I am grateful to be alive and to have been tortured no worse than I was."

"Would you tell me how to get there?"

Rosita set the candle down, and she stared into Sheridan's face for a long time, watching the light as it flicked over his expectant countenance.

"No," she finally said, shaking her head, "I will not tell you how to get there."

"It's most impor—"

"I will take you," she interjected smoothly, smiling—truly smiling when she saw Sheridan's start of surprise. "I would like to go home to my family, señor. If you will see that I get home safely and if you will give me some money, I will take you by the hacienda."

Sheridan nodded.

"Wish you'd let us go with ya," Stringbean said, squinting at the Mexican ranch in the distance.

Sheridan flexed his shoulders, loosening the wet material that clung to his back. He lifted an arm, wiping the sweat from his face; then he pulled his hat lower on his face. "I want Juan

462

to get back to the hacienda. I'm worried. And you," he said, his eyes on Stringbean, "I need you to get Rosita home." The girl sat astride her horse, a black shawl wrapped around her head and shoulders. "Besides, finding Hibernia is something I must do alone."

"Yep, reckon so," Stringbean said, spitting. "I'm kinda worried about ya, though. You're too personally involved in this Hiberny thing. Could mean the nailing of your hide to the wall."

"Señor Sheridan," Juan said, "I, too, have fears about your going into this alone. Perhaps if you don't want me to ride to the *Hacienda Del Trébol Esmeraldo* with you, you will let me wait out here."

Sheridan laughed, rubbing his hand over his cheeks down his beard, dropping it to the hilt of his knife. "Thank you, Juan, but no. I want you to go home to take care of our hacienda." Clapping the gran vaquero on the shoulder, he assured him, "I'll be home shortly after you."

Juan looked at Sheridan a long time; he smiled, lifting his hand to the brim of his hat in a waving salute. "Adiós, Señor, I will return home." The Mexican turned to Stringbean. "Adiós, Señor Stringbean." Then to both he said, *"Vaya con Dios. Hasta Luego."* Without a backward glance, Juan rode away.

Sheridan, nudging the horse with his knees, gently eased forward.

"Vaya con Dios, Señor Sheridan," Rosita softly called.

"Vaya con Dios, Rosita."

Sheridan slowly rode forward, looking back only one time. The two riders whom he left behind were mere dots against the golden fire of the setting sun. Turning, hunching his shoulders, Sheridan rode through the huge gate, not stopping his horse until several, heavily armed, vaqueros barred the way at gunpoint.

"Habla Español?" one asked. The other, an exceedingly tall, broad-shouldered man, remained silent.

"Muy poco." More than that, Sheridan thought, but no

463

reason to let them know. He might learn something if they thought he only knew a few phrases.

"*Inglés?*"

"*Sí.*"

At the order, issued in heavily accented English, Sheridan dismounted, holding his hands up as they pulled his weapons from his belt. He was relieved when they didn't check his boots for a concealed scabbard. The biggest vaquero, his face hidden by the huge sombrero, prodded Sheridan with a gun barrel in his back, guiding him through the courtyard to the main door of the salon. The other slipped into the library to announce the visitor.

Sheridan had walked to the opened doors and was looking at the garden when he heard the snap of boots on the tile. Glancing over his shoulder, he saw another tall, broad-shouldered man coming toward him. When the man drew nearer, Sheridan saw the crisp black hair and gray eyes.

The man spoke as he walked. "Sancho tells me that you speak English, señor?"

All Sheridan's worst fears came true. He recognized the voice; he recognized the face. Older maybe, a few more lines, but the man was Gavin Kenyon.

Extending his hand, Gavin said, "I am—"

"Hello, Gavin."

Gavin started, the color receding from his face. He knew the voice, but he couldn't see the face. It was covered by the hat and the beard. Reaching up, Sheridan caught the brim in his hand and whipped his hat off, his hair gleaming copper in the sunlight.

"Danny Boy!" Gavin whispered, his face lighting up, his eyes hungrily rushing over his old friend's face. Clapping his hands on Sheridan's shoulders, he laughed; he cried. "Danny Boy, you're not dead!"

"No, much to the contrary."

"We heard—"

"The only way I could escape," Sheridan explained, his

464

voice lacking the animation of Gavin's.

"How about a drink?" Gavin asked, clapping his hand for the servant. "A toast to old times, and a pint to loosen the tongue so we can talk about the new." Throwing his arm around Sheridan, Gavin led him into the library. "What brings you to Mexico?" Before Sheridan could answer, he said, "Thinking about settling down over here?"

"Yes," Sheridan replied, answering the second question first. He moved to the leather-upholstered chair, sitting down. Dropping his hat on the floor, he watched Gavin as he poured the drinks.

"Here in Mexico?" Gavin moved across the room, handing Sheridan his glass.

Taking a swallow, Sheridan shook his head. "Nay. Texas, I think."

Gavin opened his mouth as if he were about to say something, but he didn't. He walked to the chair near Sheridan. Hooking his hand under the frame, he dragged it even closer and sat down, leaning forward. His eyes glittered with happiness and excitement.

"How'd you get over here?"

Sheridan dropped his eyes from Gavin's face and looked into the glass. He idly ran a finger around the crystal rim. "You're not interested in what happened to the Wexford boys after you left?" Now he raised his face; he wanted to see Gavin's reaction.

Gavin looked at him rather oddly and squirmed uncomfortably in the chair. In a low voice, he said, "I know."

"How do you know?"

"We have many Irish immigrants here in Mexico. And I travel through San Patricio and Refugio quite frequently. I keep up with the news." Wanting to get away from such a painful topic, he said, "Now tell me about yourself."

Sheridan took a sip of the whiskey, savoring the taste and feel of it in his mouth before he swallowed. "After I left Ireland, I sailed for New York and from there to New Orleans in hopes that I would find Marguerite. When the port officials told me she had died on the trip over, I roamed around, finally ending up in Texas. How about you? How did you end up in Mexico? I thought you were in Canada."

Gavin chuckled and shook his head. "No, on board ship I met an Irishman who had relocated in Saltillo. He convinced me to come to Mexico. Said there was a fortune to be made." Gavin laughed, the resonant sound filling the room. "That caught me attention quickly, lad. So I've been here for the past six years."

"And from the looks of it, you've made your fortune."

With pride Gavin looked around the room, the walls lined with expensive books; he looked at the ornate furnishings, the paintings imported from Europe. He nodded his head. "Aye," he said, lapsing into brogue, "I've made a fortune."

"What kind of business are you in?" Sheridan asked.

"Merchandising."

Sheridan stood, moving across the room, setting his glass on a nearby table. Folding his arms across his chest, he stared at the courtyard. In the center of the patio was a huge well, circled with beautiful tile work. Lush gardens filled the area, making it an oasis in the desert. Tiled pathways crisscrossed the colorful beauty. In the shade of the vine-covered arbor, several women sat, embroidering and talking.

In the corner of the garden Sheridan saw the vaquero who had escorted him into the house. He was holding his sombrero in his hand, and he was earnestly talking to a woman whom Sheridan couldn't see because her back was turned to him.

Ever moving closer to his prey, seeking answers to his questions, Sheridan eventually asked, "What do you merchandise in, Gavin? Human life?"

Gavin stood also, setting his glass down. His eyes narrowed. "Ye've been acting strange ever since ye came into the house, Danny. Now what are you meanin'?"

Sheridan turned around, reached into his pocket and pulled out the note. Holding it up, he read it aloud. When he had finished, he said, "Nothing to point to you but this shamrock in the corner, Gavin. Nothing but the fevered rambling of a dying man," Sheridan charged, remembering the list of random words the rangers had compiled. "A man killed so he couldn't betray Hibernia's identity. Your messenger."

"Nay, I'm not masquerading as Hibernia, running all over the country as a Mexican agent."

"How about the Indians meeting you here, close to your hacienda?"

"Nay," Gavin said. "The Indians have never been close to the hacienda. My vaqueros would have informed me."

"A young girl, taken captive by the Comanches, said she was with them when they met here, close to the hacienda."

"That's preposterous," Gavin boomed, his exclamation giving way to amused laughter. "I'm too scared of those devils to meet with them."

"But you are a Mexican!"

"Aye," Gavin admitted with pride. "I'm a Mexican, and I believe that Texas still belongs to us. More, Danny, we will get her back, one way or the other."

"Even if it means killing all the white people in the nation?"

"No matter what it takes," Gavin said vehemently. "Join me, Danny Boy. Soon you can have hundreds of thousands of acres if you wish, a hacienda, servants." He shrugged. "Anything your heart desires."

Sheridan shook his head. "No, thanks, I don't deal in other peoples' lives. I try to save them. Right now I'm working with the rangers, and we're looking for Hibernia."

"Hibernia!" The hushed word hovered between them. In a daze Gavin moved behind his desk, but he didn't sit down. He stood, his fingers grazing the polished surface. When he overcame his surprise, he said, "I don't know anything about this, Danny Boy. I swear to ye, I don't."

"Like you don't know anything about Hibernia in Ireland," Sheridan said, moving to the other side of the desk, leaning over, staring into Gavin's face. "Selling me out for a paltry ten thousand pounds."

"Selling ye out!" Gavin thundered.

"Aye."

"I didn't betray you," he protested. "I was not, I am not Hibernia! How many times must I tell ye?"

"I always thought it odd that Shane was beaten so badly before he was killed," Sheridan murmured. "So many things that didn't fit into place. I never figured them out. But then I didn't try. Thinking was too painful at the time. But now I know. He wasn't Hibernia."

"No, he wasn't." The woman's voice came from the door. "To be sure, Mickey Flynn was."

Both men turned their heads toward the door.

"Bridget," Sheridan murmured.

"My wife," Gavin said, holding out his hand to her. He looked at her, love shining in his eyes.

"Your wife," Sheridan repeated incredulously.

"One can't live in the past, Sheridan," Bridget said, announcing her practical philosophy. "Aye, 'twas a fact I loved Shane, but he died. I didn't. Gavin gave me a reason for living; he became the purpose of my life." Bridget went into Gavin's arms, tilting her cheek against his cheek. Then she extended her hand to Sheridan. "How good to see ye after so many years."

Taking it, Sheridan asked, "How long have you been over here?"

She smiled. "I left with Gavin."

"But you—"

"I know. Everyone thought I was in County Clare with my sister. I had Paddy take me there, but I didn't stay. I was afraid. I'd killed Mickey, and Shane was dead." Moving out of Gavin's embrace, she shrugged. "I didn't know what Earl would do to me if he ever caught me, so I left. I didn't want anyone to know where I'd gone, not even Paddy. To be sure, Danny, ye must be a'knowin' how I felt." She spoke the words as if they excused her actions; then she smiled, the gesture softly pleading. "How did ye know that we were here?"

"He didn't," Gavin answered. "He's a Texas Ranger hunting a Mexican agent by the name of Hibernia."

"Hibernia?" Bridget murmured; then she laughed. "Don't ye think that's rather coincidental, Danny?"

Gavin picked up the slip of paper and handed it to her. As she read it, she lifted her brows in surprise. "What are you going to do with him if you find him?"

"I'm going to take him back to Texas."

"You don't have any jurisdiction in Mexico." Her voice was full of concern. "You could be arrested as a spy. Don't you think you ought to let the Mexican government take care of this?"

"Can't. We have reason to believe the Mexican government is behind it."

"Behind what?" Bridget asked.

"That's what I'm trying to find out," Sheridan replied. "It has something to do with the Mexicans and the Comanches, so we can only guess that it's a joint effort."

"I wish we knew something, Sheridan, so we could be a'helpin' ye, but we don't." As if that ended the subject, she asked, "Will ye be a'stayin' the night or must ye be a'goin' back to Texas?"

"I'll stay the night," Sheridan said.

Nodding and smiling her approval of his decision, Bridget stepped back and pulled on the tasseled cord. When the housekeeper opened the door, she said, "Tell Olivia that we will be having one more for dinner, and show Mr. O'Roarke to the guest bedroom, so he can clean up."

"May I have my weapons?" he asked.

"To be sure," Gavin answered. "I'm sorry about that, lad, but we have to be careful when strangers come. I'll have Sancho bring them up to your room."

Sheridan nodded his understanding. "You have your own soldiers?"

Gavin shrugged. "Not soldiers in the sense that you are

469

speaking about, Danny, but I have many vaqueros working for me. They provide many services, protection being one of them." Gavin's eyes narrowed, and his voice hardened. "But they are not employed to march into Texas with a band of Indians to wreak havoc and destruction on innocent people." Waving his hand toward the housekeeper, he said, "Now if you'll follow Ofelia, she'll show you to your room. You can clean up and rest before dinner."

Stooping to pick up his hat, Sheridan followed the woman out of the room and down a long corridor to the north wing of the house. He was puzzled; he'd been so sure that he was on the right trail. He had been so sure that Gavin was Hibernia, and everything seemed to fit—even Gavin. Still something bothered Sheridan. Something—but he couldn't put his finger on it.

After dinner Sheridan paced back and forth in his darkened room, unable to sleep, trying to fit all the pieces together. Finally in the wee hours of the morning, he walked on to the balcony to smoke. Standing here, the cool morning breeze playing against his face, Sheridan leaned against a post and thought about Marguerite.

Closing his eyes, he could see her on their last night together.

Having blown out the candles, he had lain in bed, naked, the sheet covering the lower part of his body. She was in her personal room, taking a bath.

"Sheridan!"

When he heard her voice, he had raised up on an elbow and peered through the darkness to the shaft of light coming from the doorway where she stood. Sheridan's breath caught in his throat; his blood felt as if it settled like heavy metal in his feet.

The muted light of candle fire had been the backdrop, its golden glow casting her silhouette through the sheer material of her sleeping gown. His eyes ran from the sweeping curves of her shoulder to her hips. What he couldn't see, he imagined, his body responding to her erotic entry.

Slowly she had moved toward him, his desire mounting, his blood rising and flowing through him so suddenly it caught his breath. His heart drummed erratically, his chest heaved as he tried to suck in air.

She still whispered in his ears: "I love you. I'll never love another man but you, Sheridan Michael O'Roarke. Please, please come back to me."

When he heard the soft thud of hooves, galloping in a hurry, and the anxious cry, Sheridan was jarred from his ruminations. He lifted a hand, wiping the moisture from his brow. Stubbing his cheroot on the railing, he slowly eased back into the cover of the vines. He didn't know why this rider, one out of so many, should attract his attention. Vaqueros had been riding in and out ever since he'd arrived at the hacienda. Still he peered over the banister at the two men who were in earnest conversation below.

One of them was Sancho. Sheridan could tell by the slant of the sombrero the man's body build and movement. From the disjointed words and phrases, which Sheridan was able to pick up, he recognized the sound of Sancho's voice. The other Sheridan didn't know. The stranger dismounted, hitched his horse, and the two of them ran into the house. Sheridan gripped the railing, leaning forward, straining to hear, but the man was speaking too low. All he could hear was the drone of language, not the enunciation of words.

Sheridan quietly rushed through his room, opening the door and slipping out. He walked to the landing. When he saw the two men standing in the salon, he shrank against the wall. Sancho was impassive; the stranger was impatiently slapping his gloves against his palm. In a few minutes Sheridan heard a door open and close. Footsteps and whispers. More footsteps. Another door opening and closing. Then silence. Slipping down the stairs, Sheridan saw the slit of light under the library door. He inched over and pressed his ear against the wood.

Sancho said, "We must do something. Things are getting out of control. First the ranger. Now this."

Someone answered, but the voice was too low for Sheridan to identify or to distinguish the words.

Sancho replied, "We sent word that we were ready to move, so the Comanches have left their stronghold. They are moving southward even now as we are talking."

Sheridan didn't hear more because a gun pressed his ribs. In deep resonant tones, slightly lilting with Irish brogue, an unfamiliar voice said, "Why don't you go inside, lad? You can hear much better in there." Reaching over Sheridan's shoulder, the man opened the door, nudging Sheridan into the room. "We have company, Hibernia."

Sheridan immediately saw Sancho and the stranger, but he saw no one else. For a long moment silence reigned in the room. Then Sheridan saw the hand on the armrests; he saw the dark hair as the figure rose.

"Tie him up," Hibernia said to the vaquero. "We'll decide what we're going to do with him later."

Sheridan couldn't take his eyes off Hibernia. "You," he charged.

"Me," Bridget confessed. Taking the gun, she held it while the man pushed Sheridan into a straight chair and tied him up. To Sancho she said, "All is going as we planned. In his bid for freedom from Mexico, Canales has depleted the entire area of available men; the Texans have no defense against them. I can't see why we have a problem."

"Bridget," Sheridan shouted, "you can't do this. You'll be responsible for killing innocent men and women."

Bridget pulled a handkerchief from her pocket. Tossing it across the desk, she said, "Put this in his mouth so he can't talk. I have enough to think about now without being disturbed by his prattle." In the same breath, she asked the stranger, "What about Woll and Canalizo? Have they begun to move

472

their troops northward?"

"No, señora." The stranger spoke for the first time. "And they're not going to."

"What do you mean they're not going to?" Bridget exclaimed. "I set this up and organized it for them."

The Mexican shrugged, nervously shifting from one foot to the other. "The Texans are suspicious; they suspect us of working with the Comanches. The generals don't think it is advisable for Mexico to become directly involved in the domestic affairs of Texas. As soon as the Comanches have destroyed the Texans, they will march in to offer aid." He grinned smugly. "Actually they will be marching in to repossess the province."

"But that's not according to our agreement with the Comanches," Bridget protested. "My God! Don't they know what those devils will do if they're crossed?" She paced around the room. "Send word to the Indians. Tell them not to attack until I send word. I must meet with Woll and Canalizo to convince them to keep their word."

The stranger shook his head. "Not me, señora."

Bridget looked at the man who had brought Sheridan into the room. "There's nothing for you to do but ride with him. You must talk those chiefs into waiting."

"No," the man adamantly said. "I went once for you, but not again. The Comanches would never let me leave."

Bridget's voice rose in near hysteria. "You must go, or all will be lost."

The door opened, and Gavin walked into the room. Having awakened and found Bridget gone, he'd been walking through the house searching for her. "What will be lost, lass?"

"This—this messenger," she said, waving her hand toward the stranger, "is from Freedom Point, Gavin. He said the Comanches are raiding through Texas." Bridget tried to keep the anxiety and fear out of her voice. "It's possible they'll come down this far."

"Doubtful," Gavin replied, slowly looking around the room.

473

"They've been raiding all around us for several months, and they've never touched the hacienda. Why should they now?" He looked into the corner behind his desk and saw Sheridan tied to the chair and gagged. "What the—" He spun around, glaring at Bridget. "Why's he bound?"

"He's—he's an enemy to our government." Bridget's excuse was flimsy.

Gavin moved close to Bridget, his hand banding her upper arm. "Tell me what's going on, lass."

Bridget jerked her arm from Gavin's clasp. "You want to know, Gavin! Then I'll tell you. I'm the person Sheridan is hunting. I'm Hibernia, Gavin, the agent Sheridan was sent to find."

Gavin's face blanched, and he stumbled back.

"And we're in a lot of trouble. Trébol and I promised the Comanches that we would supply them with three thousand soldiers if they would help us wipe all the Texans out. I sent them information, letting them know which areas were unprotected and when to raid. Now they're ready, but the Mexicans are getting scared and decided they would march into Texas after the Comanches had done the dirty work."

Gavin looked from one face to the other. "That's not your fault, lass. The Comanches won't do anything to you." Gavin moved to where Sheridan sat. Pushing the chair around, he untied the gag.

"She had a right to be afraid, Gavin," Sheridan said, flexing his mouth. "Bridget has met with them. Here at the hacienda. They know who you are and where you are."

Disconcerted, Gavin walked away without untying Sheridan. He didn't stop until he stood in front of Bridget. "Is he telling the truth, lass?"

Running her hands up and down her arm in agitation, Bridget nodded. "Trébol was my spokesman," she admitted. "I went along disguised as an officer, but I didn't speak. I just listened. In order to get their cooperation, we had to tell them who we were and where we came from."

"How could you have been so foolish!" Gavin gritted, clenching his fist, looking from Trébol to Sancho. "It looks like the two of you would have had enough sense to keep away from the Comanches."

"Well, we didn't," Bridget snapped. "Now what are we going to do?"

"As I see it," Gavin gritted, "we have only two alternatives. We can either stay here and fight, or we can start over in a place where they can't find us."

"The vaqueros will not stay and fight that many Comanches, señor," Sancho softly interjected. "They would not lay their lives down to those mudering devils for no amount of money."

"And I'm not leaving," Bridget maintained. "I've worked hard for this. I'll go talk with the Comanches myself."

"Bridie, ye cannot," Gavin said. "You've seen what those savages will do. They'll rape ye, lass; they'll torture you. You're talking nonsense."

"I didn't come this far to lose everything I own, Gavin. I've invested everything I have in this land and this ranch. I'm not going to let the Comanches take it away from me because the stupid Mexicans reneged on a promise."

Gavin reached for Bridget, pulling her into his arms. "Lass," he consoled softly, "don't get so upset. We have time to pack our things and move—move where they can't find us. We're young. We can start all over again." He smiled. "We have each other."

"Have each other!" Bridget spit disdainfully, pulling out of his arms. "That's not enough, Gavin. I want more than you."

Gavin cringed as if he'd been struck. "What do ye mean, Bridie?"

Her eyes shining with hysteria, she cried, "I want money, Gavin, and all the power and prestige that it brings. All my life I worked as a servant to other women. Yes, mum. No, mum. Curtsying to 'em; taking care of 'em. No more of that for me. Now that I've got wealth and prestige, no damned Comanche is going to take it away from me."

475

Gavin kept shaking his head in puzzlement. He had known that Bridget loved Shane when they first married, but through the years he had begun to think she cared about him; that one day she would come to love him as he loved her. He had been blinded to so many things.

"How do you think we got the money to buy this land, to build this house, and to furnish it? Let me tell you. I'm the intellect behind Hibernia—in Ireland—over here. I'm the one who goaded Shane into betraying Sheridan." Bridget looked at Sheridan, laughing her triumph. "He loved Eliza, you know. Went to Dublin to meet her so Earl wouldn't know. After she got tired of him and stopped seeing him, I kept reminding him that she loved Sheridan instead of him; I kept reminding him that Eliza and Sheridan killed his child . . . on purpose. I'm the one who fostered Shane's hatred of Sheridan, and I used him."

"No."

Gavin felt as if he'd been shot in the stomach; his insides burned; his heart felt as if it had swollen many times its normal size. His chest hurt so bad he thought it would burst.

"You killed Shane! You murdered Mickey Flynn."

"I killed Mickey, Gavin, but I didn't kill Shane." Seeing the contempt in his eyes, she said, "I had to, Gavin. 'Twas the only way."

"Nay. 'Twas the way you wanted it. You didn't love Shane, no more than you loved me, lass. You were greedy then as you are now. You used us. You used us to get what you wanted."

Bridget lifted a hand, pushing a strand of black hair behind her ear. She laughed softly. "Aye, Gavin, I used both of you. Stupid men the lot of ye were." The laughter grew louder. "Shane was gullible; he believed everything I told him. He believed me because I was Eliza's personal maid; I arranged all their meetings. I'm the one who planned Sheridan's betrayal, step by step. And I'm the one who ended up with the money."

Bridget moved slightly, her eyes darting from Gavin to Sheridan. "Why do you think I was so afraid of Earl? He found out that I was working with Shane; he alone knew why I killed

Mickey Flynn, and he wanted his money back because he didn't get Sheridan." She shook her head, the room filling with her maniacal laughter. "But I fooled Taylor, too, Gavin. Leaving with you, I escaped with the money, and I'm not about to lose it now. I've got too much blood on my hands. A little more isn't going to hurt."

Turning to the messenger, she said, "Return to the trading post. Send word to the Indians that I will bring my men and join them." Running out of the room, she said, "Come, Trébol, I'm going to talk to General Woll and Canalizo myself. Are you brave enough to accompany me to their headquarters?"

"No," Trébol cried, following her. "The vaqueros will not ride with you under these conditions. We do not know what the Comanches are going to do. We do not know what the generals are going to do."

Totally disillusioned with his wife, seeing her for what she was for the first time, Gavin caught her by the arm again. "Ye'r not going, Bridget."

"Who's going to stop me?" she cried, trying to yank her arm out of his clasp.

"I am."

"No, Gavin, you're not."

Falling against the desk, her fingers curled over the pistol. Picking it up, she pulled the trigger, shooting Gavin in the stomach. Groaning, doubling over, he fell to the floor. Throwing the gun down, Bridget raced out of the room. Trébol, Sancho, and the messenger fled with her, all going in different directions.

His hand over his wound, blood seeping through his fingers, Gavin grabbed on to the furniture and dragged himself to the chair where Sheridan was tied. "I didn't know, Danny Boy," he gasped, his voice weak. His hand slowly climbed the chair, and he tried to untie the ropes but he was in too much pain.

"In my boot," Sheridan said, "you'll find my knife."

Weak and dizzy, Gavin's hand circled the chair rung, and he held on. Breathing deeply, blinking to clear his vision, he fumbled until he found the knife. Slowly he withdrew it; weakly he cut the ropes. When Sheridan was free, he knelt down beside Gavin, looking at his wound. Standing, he pulled the cord forcibly.

When the housekeeper appeared, he said, "Take care of him. He's wounded badly."

Sheridan ran out of the library, searching through the house until he found the master apartment. It was empty and silent. Hearing the horse, Sheridan raced to the doors, stepping on to the patio in time to see a lone rider, silhouetted in the silver glow of the moon, disappear into the night, a cape flapping in the night.

Chapter 27

Sheridan and Stringbean reached Linville but not in time to warn the town. The Comanches had already been there and left. Every house and store had been sacked. The once thriving merchant village smoldered in ashes. Changing horses, riding as quickly as they could, Sheridan and Stringbean headed for the hacienda. All along the way they saw the same scene; they heard the same story. Death and destruction had visited nearly every home.

His heart heavy, Sheridan continued to follow the trail of destruction which the Comanches left behind. Though he hurt for those who survived the massacre, Sheridan's thoughts were consumed with worry for his family. Never again, he vowed, would he leave them alone and unprotected.

"Almost there," Stringbean announced as they reached the bottom of the rise. Holding his cap on his head to keep the wind from blowing it off, he pointed his finger. "Look, boy."

Sheridan followed the invisible line of Stringbean's hand. In the graying line of dawn's first breaking, against the black thunderheads amassing in the sky, he saw the ominous curl of smoke. Nudging his horse, fighting the gales of the coming storm, Sheridan galloped over the hill to the grassland below. Several of the buildings were still smoldering, and the gardens around the house were trampled. He saw no activity.

Sheridan's horse hadn't stopped when he jumped off its back and rushed across the patio into the salon.

"Marguerite!" he shouted.

Doors opened all through the house.

"Sheridan!" Marguerite rushed out of her apartment, her hair falling in soft waves around her face, her dressing gown whipping against her legs as she ran. "Thank God, you're home."

Thoughtless of his dirty clothes, Sheridan stripped his hat off his head, dropped it on the floor, and gathered Marguerite in his arms, holding her tightly. "Thank God, you're all right!" he murmured, blinking back his tears. "The children?"

"We're just fine," she sniffed, unable to hold him tightly enough. "Just a small band whom we were able to fight off. The main party skirted the area. We had nothing but minor casualties."

"Papa!" The yell filled the house. "You're home!"

By the time Marguerite had pulled out of Sheridan's arms, Michael landed in them. His grin stretched from ear to ear. "The Indians came, but we fighted them off, Papa." His eyes shining, he added, "One of them caught me and was going to scalp me." He reached up, splaying his fingers through his hair. "They was, Papa. Really they was! But Mama shot him dead." He turned to Marguerite. "Didn't you, Mama?"

"I did," Marguerite softly answered. "There's not much I wouldn't do for the ones I love."

"But Mama wouldn't let me keep the green cape he was wearing, Papa."

Sheridan looked at Marguerite inquisitively. She nodded. "It was a woman's cape, Sheridan. It must have belonged to one of his victims." She paused. "Thinking we could send word to the family, we looked for identification. Embroidered in the lining were the words *Trébol Emeraldo*."

Sheridan closed his eyes and nodded his head. He'd tell Marguerite about it later. Now was not the time.

"Well! Well! About time ya got home." Jewel joined them in

the salon. Standing in her familiar pose, hands on hips, she grinned, her beautiful white teeth flashing. "Ya waited till the Indians had come and gone, I see."

"Are you always complaining, woman?" Sheridan teased. "Will ye never have a good word for the man of the house?"

"When you become de man of de house, den I'll quit grumbling." Jewel laughed. Then she threw her arms out and cried, "It's sure good to have ya home, Mr. Sheridan. We rightly missed ya."

"It's good to be home, Jewel. I've rightly missed you." In two strides he was across the room, spinning Jewel around in a bear hug.

"Phew!" she sniffed. "I'll say you rightly missed me, Mr. Sheridan. Smells like you ain't bathed or changed clothes since ya left dis house." She wiggled out of his clutch and pointed to the bedroom. "Now you git in there and take yourself a bath right now, do you hear me?"

"Yes, ma'am."

Michael giggled as Sheridan meekly retrieved his hat and moved toward the master apartment.

Jewel turned to the child. "And you, Michael O'Roarke, you git in dat kitchen and hep me git some breakfast around here. Wif dat storm coming we can't clean up outside, but we sure can git de inside."

Sheridan grabbed Marguerite's hand and tugged her with him. "Come on," he whispered. "I don't want her giving you any orders. I have plans for us."

They lay together on the bed, Marguerite running her hands over his freshly shaven cheeks. She laughed. "Your face is so pale in comparison to the rest of you."

"Give me a day or two in the sun," he said, closing his hand over hers, stopping the straying of her fingers. "We're going to get out of this bed and clean up this hacienda. In a couple of weeks no one will know that the Indians were here."

"You—you won't be leaving again?" Marguerite asked.

Sheridan chuckled. "Only to file my report. Then I'm retired, my darling. From now on I shall devote all my attention to my wife, my family and my home." He flipped over, his feet hitting the floor. "Come on, lazy, let's get up before Jewel comes in here and gets us."

"And why are you so eager to be doing housework?"

"'Cause I'm going to have you outside helping me as soon as the sun pokes its head through these clouds."

Marguerite grinned, stretched sinuously. "I don't think so."

"And why not?" he asked, leaning back.

"I . . . I . . . haven't been feeling good lately."

"Oh? Pleading illness, huh, to keep from working with the rest of us?"

"How about pleading the belly."

"Pleading the belly!" Sheridan repeated the words with a reverential softness. When Marguerite nodded her head, Sheridan whooped and caught her in his arms. "We're going to have a baby!"

Thoughts of getting up quickly evaporated. They lay in bed discussing their growing family. Michael. Daisy Belle. The unborn baby. Girl or boy? Boy. Girl. No, a boy! No, definitely a girl!

"If it's a boy," Sheridan said, his eyes shining with excitement and anticipation, "I want to name it after Stringbean."

Marguerite went absolutely still. "Stringbean!" she exclaimed, bolting up, looking down at him, a horrified expression on her face. "You want to name our baby Stringbean!" Before Sheridan could answer, she cried, "I like Stringbean, Sheridan. I like him very much, but I don't want to name my baby after him."

Sheridan's soft chuckle burgeoned into gusty laughter. Tears sparkled in his eyes. When he finally caught his breath, he said, "Sweetheart, his name isn't Stringbean. It's Malcolm. Malcolm MacAdam."

Laughter quickly replaced the astonishment on Marguerite's face. "Malcolm," she repeated. "Malcolm Devin O'Roarke. Now that doesn't sound bad, to be sure."

"Perhaps," Sheridan whispered, sliding down on the bed, pulling her with him, "we could nickname him Stringbean."

"That will take a lot of persuasion, Mr. O'Roarke."

"I guess I should start now."

"No better time than the present," Marguerite whispered, her words lost in their kiss.

They were oblivious to the storm that raged outside the room. They didn't hear the rain pelting against the windowpanes nor the thunder that boomed through the air. They didn't see the jagged streaks of lightning that flashed in the sky. Harbored in love, they were safe from the wild, blowing wind.

Long, long ago, beyond the misty space
  Of twice a thousand years,
In Erin old there dwelt a mighty race,
  Taller than Roman spears.
Great were their deeds, their passions and their sports;
  With clay and stone
They piled on strath and shore those mystic forts,
  Not yet o'erthrown;
On cairn-crowned hills they held their
  council-courts.

Although this poem was written in the twentieth century,
the first recorded reference to Ireland was made in the sixth
century before Christ during the reign of Cyrus of Persia by
the poet Orpheus, who referred to the Emerald Isle as Ierne.
Aristotle cited Ireland in his *Book of the World*. To Plutarch
Ireland was Ogygia, the most ancient. To Tacitus, Caesar, and
Pliny she was Hibernia. To the Celts the isle was simply Eire.
The Viking invaders, who came in the ninth century and were
absorbed into the Irish, were the first to call their new island
home Eireland, Ir-land, or Irlanda, hence Ireland.

Unlike the Vikings, the next invaders were invited. In 1170,

Dermot, a deposed Irish king, sought help from Henry II of England. Pleased to have Ireland indebted to him, Henry gave Dermot permission to recruit Norman soldiers. With the help of the soldiers Dermot reconquered his kingdom, paying the Normans in land. When Dermot died a year later, Henry II was unsure of the barons' loyalty; therefore, he traveled to Ireland and forced them to recognize him as lord of Ireland.

The English didn't assert their influence again until 1534. In an effort to regain control of Ireland, Henry VIII took all power from the Norman noblemen who had controlled English interests in Ireland for many years and set up more direct English control. In 1541, Henry forced Ireland's Parliament to declare him king of Ireland and tried, with little success, to introduce Protestantism in the country.

Henry's children continued their father's policies throughout the 1500s. Mary tried to strengthen English rule by initiating the Plantation of Ireland. She seized land in central Ireland and gave it to English settlers. Using strong-arm tactics, Elizabeth attempted to establish Protestantism in Ireland. As a result, the Irish Catholics became more united and more bitterly anti-English than ever.

For one hundred years, a series of revolts against the English broke out in Ulster, a large province in northern Ireland. Elizabeth put down the last one in 1603, the year she died. James I, who followed as ruler of England, continued the plantations, this time concentrating his attention on Ulster.

The Irish, fearing both the extension of the plantation system and the fanaticism of the Puritans who were controlling the English government, rebelled again in 1641. Eight years later, Oliver Cromwell, the Puritan Protectorate of England, successfully ended the rebellion, giving more land to English Protestants and depriving the Catholics of more political rights.

James II became king of England in 1685. The first Roman Catholic to become monarch of England since Mary, he abolished many of the anti-Catholic laws. In 1688, the English people forced James to give up the throne and invited William of Orange, a Protestant, to become their king. Fleeing to Ireland, James organized an army, but William, supported by Ulster Protestants, defeated him in 1690.

Following William's victory, additional land was taken from Irish Catholics. Those of the dispossessed Irish who were not shipped to the Carolinas or West Indies were allowed to stay on their ancestral lands as menials, providing cheap labor. By 1704, Catholics held only about a seventh of the land in Ireland. Forbidden to purchase, inherit, or even to rent land, excluded from the Irish Parliament, and restricted in their rights to practice Catholicism, more than two hundred and fifty thousand Irishman immigrated to the American colonies between 1717 and the Revolutionary War.

In the late eighteenth century, Irish Catholics and Protestants joined together in a political movement known as The United Irishmen. In 1798 they staged another rebellion that the English brutally put down with the aid of Hessian mercenaries. Only in Wexford did rebels achieve any measure of success. During this uprising green was established as Ireland's national color. Many of the most memorable songs of Irish nationalism emerged, including "The Wearing of the Green." The brutal reprisals that followed the rebellion's end spurred another wave of Irish emigration.

Through legislation, England began to alter her policy toward Ireland. In 1801, Ireland officially became part of the United Kingdom of Great Britain and Ireland. The Irish Parliament was then ended, and Ireland sent representatives to the British Parliament. In 1829 the English Parliament passed the Catholic Emancipation Act which, after some one hundred and thirty-five years, raised most of the disabilities that had been legislated against the Catholic Irish.

The new legal provisions found little reflection in the practicalities of daily life. Irish tenants were still at the mercy of landlords, English mercantilist policy still bled Ireland economically, and the Catholic and Presbyterian Irish were still required by the tithing laws to give financial support to a church to which they did not belong.

In the spring of 1833 James Power, a Mexican impresario, after an absence of twenty-four years, returned to his hometown of Ballygarrett, County Wexford, Ireland, in order to recruit settlers for the Mexican province of Texas. Welcomed by the people, he passed out notices and handbills in surrounding villages and counties, announcing the purpose of his visit. The Irish crowded into the cottages where he spoke and listened to Power's description of grassy plains and rich farmlands, of thousands of acres to be had almost for the asking, and of a way of life free from the restrictions of their present condition.

On Power's return to Texas in December, more than two hundred and fifty families elected to accompany him. However, of the original group who set out for the New World, only eight lived to reach the Texas colony. Still the ranks filled as more flocked to the land of opportunity. A second group arrived at the port of New Orleans on April 21, 1834, and the third in June, 1834. Within a five month period, August through December, almost two hundred and twenty leagues of Mexican land had been deeded to two hundred and one grantees.

These emigrants, however, were not the first Irish to be associated with Texas and its history. The Irish have been a part of Texas from Spanish times to the present. They came as soldiers and statesmen in Spanish service; they came as colonials and priests under Mexican law. The two largest concentrations of Irish settlers in the nineteenth century, however, were at San Patricio de Hibernia (Saint Patrick of Ireland) and Refugio. Those Irish who came to San Patricio in 1829 were recruited from New York by two other impresarios McMullen and McGloin. These settlers had come from all over Ireland, joining McMullen and McGloin because they had been denied economic opportunity and social acceptance in the United States. Power's recruits, all gathered from south eastern Ireland, settled in Refugio.

Almost three years to the date after the arrival of Power's colonists, Texas was on the brink of revolution. James Power was elected delegate from Refugio to the convention of March 1, 1836. Through his influence Sam Houston was elected the second delegate. Thus, on March 2, 1836, Power was one of the signers of the Texas Declaration of Independence. On March 2, 1836, Texas declared her independence, and the Irish joined the Texans in their war.

The battle of independence was over, but the war was hardly over and independence hardly assured. Texans had to fight on several fronts, the two most important being the Centralist dictatorship of Mexico and the Comanches. In December 1839, on hearing rumors that Texas was combining forces with Mexican insurgents and planning to invade Mexico, the Centralist generals responded bombastically by proposing a campaign for the reconquest of Texas. Hastily the Texans assured Mexico that no such invasion was planned nor was it supported by the government.

Hardly had that problem been solved when another reared its ugly head. The next month, January, 1840, several Comanche chiefs, claiming to represent a general council of all the Comanche Indians, rode into San Antonio, demanding a peace treaty. Before the Texans would negotiate a treaty, they demanded that all white prisoners be released. The Indians agreed, and on March 19, 1840 the disastrous conference occurred. A group of sixty-five Comanches, led by Chief Muguara, rode into San Antonio. With them came their squaws and children, who played in the yard outside the council house, while old Muguara and a dozen younger chiefs went in to palaver with the commissioners.

The peace council was ill starred at the outset; neither the Texan agent who handled the conference nor the Indians were completely frank. The Texans were prepared to seize the Indians at the mere show of foul play, and the Indians, playing the Texans for fools, returned only one badly treated and deformed prisoner: thirteen-year-old Matilda Lockhart. After the child sobbed her piteous tale, the Texans demanded the release of all prisoners whom the Comanches held. The chiefs denied they had more; Matilda, however, insisted they did. She also informed the Texans of the Indians' plans to get as much ransom for the prisoners as possible.

During this talk the Indians acknowledged they had violated all previous treaties, including the agreement for the present meeting, but insolently demanded that they be given the opportunity to extract ransom for their prisoners. When the palaver reached an impasse, the Texans stationed their soldiers outside the council house and informed the chiefs that they were now prisoners, that they would be held as hostages, and that they must send for the other white captives to be brought in.

Nothing could be more terrifying than a dozen proud Comanche chiefs suddenly being told that they were to be locked in prison. Sheer bedlam broke loose. Screeching war cries, mingled with the roar of firearms, was made louder by the close quarters. The Indians fought like wild animals caught in a trap. But they were outnumbered and could not win against the rifles and pistols. In moments Muguara and his chiefs lay dead. All the tribesmen who had been waiting outside the house were killed, and twenty-seven wailing squaws and their children were taken prisoner.

A squaw was sent back to the Indian camp to demand that the white captives be brought in. She never returned nor, of course, did the Indians bring in their prisoners. According to later reports, the Comanches, enraged at the loss of their people, tortured more than a dozen white prisoners to agonized deaths. But their revenge was to be more fierce than this cruelty. They withdrew to the west, where they contacted other bands, and brooded and plotted during the spring and early summer. By July 1840, the most spectacular Indian raid of Texas was organized. Its execution indicates a more carefully planned raid than most.

Later evidence revealed that Mexican agents and Comanches had been communicating. Strangely coincidental, the Indians knew when and where to seek retaliation without fear of reprisal. In June, Antonio Canales, a Mexican insurgent, had recruited nearly five hundred Texans in the general vicinities of San Antonio, Gonzales, and Victoria. Ironically, in July, like wolves ravishing an unguarded lamb fold, combined bands of Comanches, estimated to total one thousand warriors, raced into southwest Texas. A Mexican letter, taken later from the body of a dead Indian, had suggested that such an attack in that area would be profitable. The Indians skirted the major settlements and struck in a great sweeping arc east of San Antonio south toward Victoria and Linnville, murdering only where they raided and plundered.

Other sources state that two Mexican generals, collaborating with and encouraging the Comanches on this raid, made promises of troop support. Allied tribes were to equip a formidable war party of one or two thousand Indians for a grand raid down the Colorado to the Gulf, plundering and devastating the most highly populated portion of Texas. The Cherokees were to destroy the eastern portion of the state; the Wacos, Apaches, and allied tribes were to raid down the Brazos and central Texas, utterly wiping out the Texans. Generals Canalizo and Woll of Matamoras, with some two thousand Mexican calvary, were to rush forward, capturing San Antonio and Austin.

On August 6, 1840, according to this source, the Comanches, having received word that the Mexican troops were ready to move from the south, suddenly swept from their mountain stronghold above the San Marcos River, surprising all settlers in the path of their destruction. By the time the Comanches had raided as far south as Victoria and Linnville, they realized they had been tricked. The Mexicans were not going to join them. Taking their plunder and captives, the Comanches headed for home. Before they reached the safety of the hills on the San Marcos, however, they met the Texas Rangers. After a bloody battle, the surviving Comanches managed to escape into the hills.

Whether the Mexicans had directly influenced the Comanches to raid and had reneged on a promise of support in the form of troops has never been proven. But subsequent events seem to indicate the Comanches thought so. Two months after the Victoria-Linnville raid, the Comanches regrouped and entered Mexico. They killed, scalped, burned, and destroyed everything in sight. Their track could be traced for miles by the burning ranches and villages. They carried off many female prisoners and thousands of horses and mules, escaping safely to their stronghold in the mountains with their plunder.